ABRAHAM

ABRAHAM

MICHAEL A. PEDOWITZ

Cover artwork and design by Jonas Perez.
Interior formatting by Phillip Gessert.

ISBN: 979-8-218-62810-9

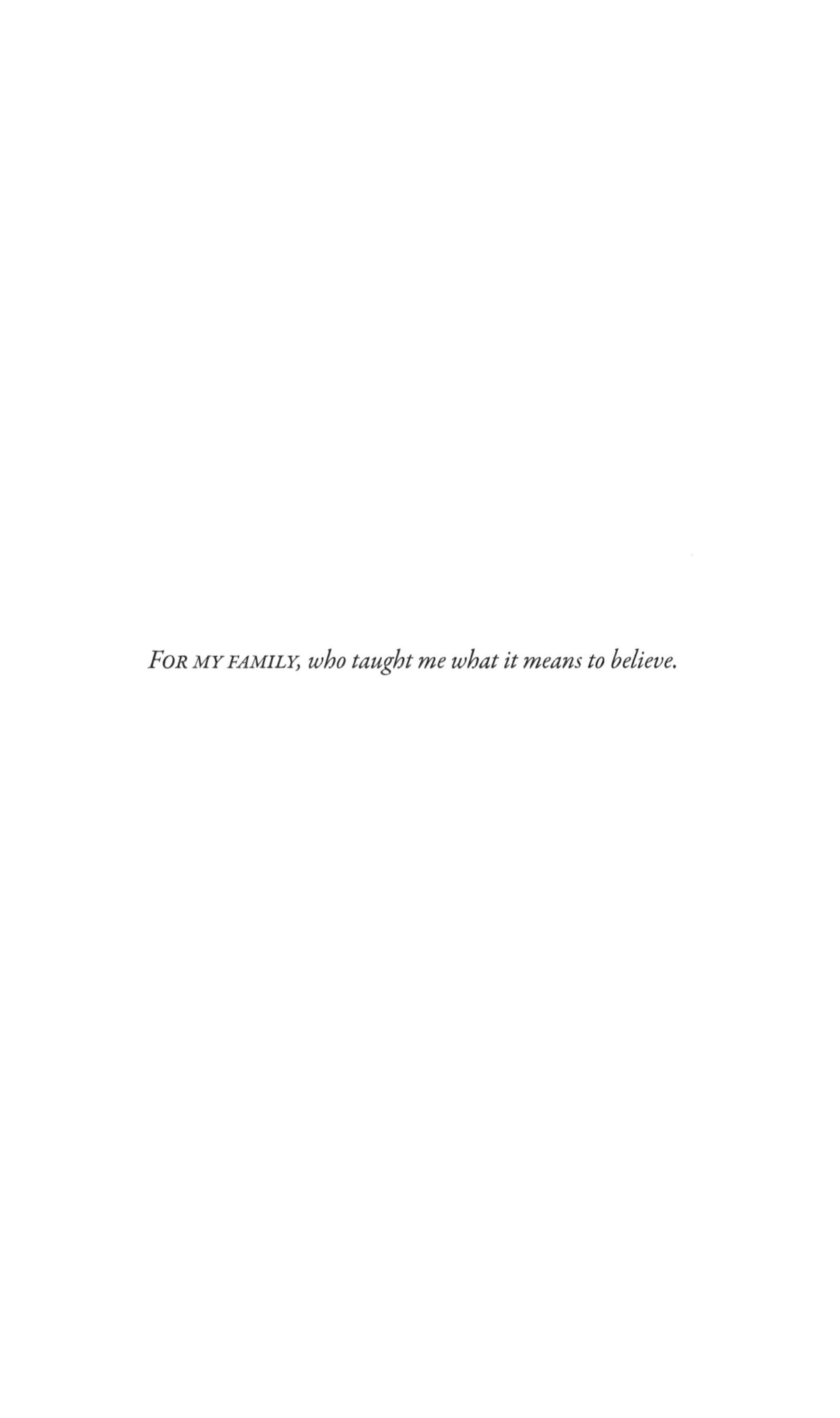

For my family, who taught me what it means to believe.

In a world where the mind is systematically programmed by men, what room is there for our souls? In a reality effortlessly manufactured by machines, what place would we ever reserve for God?

—Dr. Richard Matthews, 2044

THE COOL BREEZE tickled the back of my neck as I brushed down the crinkles in the plaid red blanket. As soft as the ground felt to sit on, I had to smooth out the more stubborn patches of hard grass that created ridges and valleys all along the fabric sheet. The bumps on the far side of the blanket reminded me of the tall trees in the distance. The creases behind me, then, were the rivers that crisscrossed the sprawling lakeside retreat.

I know I've talked about the picnic blanket for four sentences longer than necessary, but it felt nice to just let my thoughts roam free for once. I wasn't sure if that was possible inside this place, but here—atop this wide, bumpy, beautiful hill—I could think more clearly than usual. Maybe *that* was why she asked me to meet her up here. I had suggested that we set up our picnic in a flatter part of the retreat, but she insisted that we come up here "to see *the view* one more time." I didn't love the ominous way she said that, but before I could say anything she left to get the basket from the cabin. For someone who said we needed to move quickly, she certainly liked to do things in the most drawn-out way possible.

After the creases in the blanket were smoothed out to my satisfaction—and, hopefully, hers—I finally looked around to take in "the view." Green grassy hills and valleys stretched out in a seemingly infinite direction, intermittently interrupted by small groves of apple trees. I could make out a herd of deer trotting between them, rustling bushes and startling the inhabitant bluebirds who responded with a chorus of tweets. I don't think I've seen that many deer run by the lakeside before; perhaps the lack of human activity in the area made it easier for them to return. The wind, animals, and faint sounds of brooks and small waterfalls were the only noises to be heard. All the rest was a perfectly still paradise.

Just as it was programmed to be.

She would be on her way back soon. Not that it matters—technically, I have as much time as I need to tell this story.

"For completeness," she told me. "I need you to think through everything that happened since you started at Abraham." Supposedly, going through my thoughts in "as logical an order as possible" would help her the most. *With what, I had no idea.* She ran off to get the picnic supplies before adding any real context to her request, so nothing she had said made much sense.

Then again, at this point, nothing in my life makes sense. All the *pieces* of a functioning, normal life had once been there:

A satisfying job.

A healthy relationship.

A healing faith.

An abundance of overthinking.

Yet, none of those pieces seemed to fit together right, no matter how hard I tried. But, for the *story's* sake—certainly not for *her,* the liar that she was—I'm going to shove those pieces together as best as I can. I only hope that the finished product doesn't fall apart in my hands. *Unlike the way everything else has.*

Damn. Another wrinkle appeared in the picnic blanket.

PART I

ONE

LONG BEFORE I smoothed out picnic blankets for a living, I, Arthur E. Hesper, was an orphan. Well, technically, I still *am* an orphan—an orphan who was once found on the doorstep of The Holy Virgin Children's Home as a baby just a few months old, left by parents who were never tracked down. Those are about the only details of my past that I know. I don't even know *what* my middle initial actually stands for; "Arthur E. Hesper" was all that was written on the piece of paper I was left with.

Sad backstory short, I was never adopted. Every prospective couple, from home sweet home Brooklyn all the way to Portugal, liked my playfulness and joyfulness at first, but were turned off by my genius. No, this isn't a pat-myself-on-the-back sort of thing; I wasn't *just* good at counting, or spelling, or even calculus—I could *read* people as if they were a book or a computer program. Apparently, when I was five, I sent a couple into therapy after asking some "innocent" questions about their marital problems—problems they didn't know they had. When I was eight, I made a Physics PhD cry just by asking him some simple questions about his work on Kerr black holes—questions that seemed to unravel his thesis. When I was ten, I caused a broker to almost crash the New York Stock Exchange because—well, perhaps I'm exaggerating. But you get the point. I was (and still am) weird.

Eventually, the nuns at the orphanage gave up trying to offer me for adoption, and when I was twelve, I was sent to a private secondary school for "gifted" children. Eleven years and one Class-of-2053 MIT graduate degree later, I was applying for the management position of a young but rapidly growing tech enterprise called *The ABRAHAM Project.* Born out of a *very* generous inheritance from a Dr. Richard Matthews, who was president of a space engineering company, *Abraham* was created with the sole purpose of building a structure that the world's greatest theoretical physicists and engineers could barely dream of: *The Matrioshka Brain.*

First thought up in the 1990s, a Matrioshka Brain is a hypothetical megastructure that utilizes several Dyson Spheres nested within each other, like the ceramic Russian dolls. Think of this configuration as a ridiculously huge solar panel that could use the power of our Sun to do almost anything. It could power fleets of starships, enable supercomputing at unimaginable scales, or—in Abraham's case—construct a virtual world that is indistinguishable from real life and allow humans to connect their minds directly to it. It was a far-fetched concept, to be sure, but given that the company *already* had panels of its "Solar Sphere" in orbit around the Sun, was certainly plausible.

I was sitting in a neatly adorned waiting room in Washington, D.C., briefcase clutched in my left hand, preparing to interview for the executive-level position—*Coordinator of Intelligence*—when a young woman walked in. She was probably a little older than I was, and a little taller. She shuffled through the door nervously, took a quick look around the room, which was otherwise empty, and sat a few seats away from me.

Another applicant, I thought. But despite carrying a briefcase and wearing a nametag with the receptionist's illegible handwriting, the woman didn't seem ready for an interview at all. Most notably, she was wearing a faded grey *Cape Canaveral* t-shirt and torn blue jeans. Her wavy brown hair was disheveled. She looked like she should be going out to brunch with her friends, not about to interview for one of the most powerful tech firms in the world. She fidgeted in her cushioned chair as she continued to look around, eyes darting between fake plants and the many plaques that decorated the walls.

Next to her, I almost felt like a model applicant. The one career seminar I *did* have time for as an undergraduate stressed the importance of first appearances at an interview, and I tried to heed that advice. Looking across the room, I wondered if the woman was alright; even though I figured she'd be one less applicant to compete with, I felt bad just sitting there while she seemed so anxious. And based on how slippery my briefcase handle was becoming from my own sweat, I realized I was getting anxious, too.

"Nervous?" I asked in a conversational way, knowing exactly what the answer would be. She quickly turned toward me, her eyes locking onto mine. I still couldn't make out the name on her tag.

"Yeah—yeah I am. Sorry. I am—a little," she blushed, looking me up and down.

"Here for the interview?" I asked, also knowing the answer. It was small talk, for sure, but would come off as a nice way to distract ourselves and pass the time. Furthermore, there was something familiar about this woman, and I wanted to know what it was.

"Yes, I am. My phone battery died overnight, so my alarm didn't go off. I had to run out of the house. I... didn't even have time to change," she explained, looking at her own clothes with an embarrassed glance.

I resisted the urge to follow her gaze; I kept my eyes focused on hers. "You go to sleep wearing jeans?" My innocuous question probably came across more rudely than I had intended, as she continued to avoid looking at me. A second or two of silence passed before she responded.

"I... was out late last night. A little *too* late," she said. "And I was sure I'd run late today, *again,* but it looks like I made it." Her voice was soft; *warm,* even. Although not dressed like one, she also sounded like a businesswoman running a meeting; sincere enough to seem approachable, but inexorable where it mattered.

I gave her a nod and moved over to the chair right across from her, figuring it would come off as a friendly gesture. She straightened up a little as I approached, and kept her eyes fixed on me as I sat down eight feet away. She wasn't fidgeting anymore.

"Interesting company," I thought aloud, intentionally changing the subject. "I can't believe they want to create a simulated *universe.* I know that's part of the job, but when you say it out loud it feels a little... *daunting,* right?"

The woman looked off toward the wall behind me, at some plaque, clearly doing her best to think up a response. While she did, I stole a glance at the nametag taped to her t-shirt. The markered lettering appeared to read *DoRoH.*

I decided that that was thick cursive for *Sarah.*

"Sure, but I wouldn't put it past them. It's going to take a lot of planning—*hopefully* by one of us," Sarah said with a laugh. "But with the right resources and dedication, I think anything's possible." Her response was calculated and efficient; *businesslike.* And yet, even after only a few sentences, the way she spoke almost reminded me of how a mother might encourage her child, her voice carrying a blend of comfort and command.

Like a woman who sees potential in herself and in her creation. I smiled; not at her response, per se, but because her words confirmed my suspicion.

"Beyond just the technical hurdles, this project will be a challenging social endeavor. We're going to have to convince a lot of people—a lot of *investors*—that this virtual world we're creating is worth it. That *Abraham* is worth it," I stated. I waited eagerly for Sarah's reply.

"Well, I'm not really... yeah, you're right," she said, making no eye contact with me now. "*ABRAHAM*... Arti... Automated Brain Rep... Repro...," she began, trying to dramatically name the company's interesting acronym.

I helped her out. "Automated Brain Reproducing the Advanced High-Energy Artificial Multiverse," I said, all in one breath. She bobbed her head and gratefully smiled as I finished her sentence.

I went for the kill.

"But you already knew that. Didn't you, Ms. Stellos?"

One of the first great risks of my life. Definitely not the last.

Sarah Stellos's friendly smile froze as a cold flame in her eyes beckoned me to continue.

"Even your *worst* applicants aren't showing up late sporting tattered jeans," I said coolly. "I *did* almost buy the whole late-night no-alarm thing. That was well done. But for any future interviewees, I'd caution against botching the company name. *That* was the dead giveaway."

"Awful cocky for someone who doesn't have the job yet." Stellos crossed her legs, trying to stare me down. She no longer stammered; her voice was silky, each of her words resonating with a melodic power. "But very good, *Arthur.* Everyone else who makes it to that seat winds up pissing their pants at this point." She gestured to the cushion I was sitting on.

"Well, I hope you've sanitized this chair after all those times," I remarked, leaning forward with a look of fake concern. That scored a slight grin from her. "Anything otherwise would be unbecoming of someone as accomplished as you."

Okay, listen. I wasn't *trying* to come off as arrogant. I wasn't even trying to make small talk. I literally didn't know how else to approach the *President* of Abraham, a title she'd had since she founded the startup with the inheritance from her "Uncle Richard" six years ago. When she was *twenty.* Stellos dropped out of Harvard to lead the company, and she made waves in academia by famously calling her higher education "a waste of time." After just five months at Abraham, she had secured dozens of lucrative partnerships with both private investors and world powers alike. After nineteen months, her team had finished assembling the first components of the Solar Sphere. And by the company's third anniversary, Abraham had successfully launched their first wave of satellite mirrors into space, and scientists around the world watched as the swarm made its way around the Sun. By then, "Abraham" was becoming a household name, as was "Sarah Stellos." After all, she was known for pushing The Abraham Project forward at breakneck speed and cutthroat efficiency, accomplishing more in six years than most CEOs do in a lifetime. Considering she's raked in trillions of dollars *and* leads the research team behind the project, then *no*, I did *not* know how to approach Sarah Stellos except with my greatest assets: my brain and all the confidence I could summon.

"You're a smart man," Sarah said to me. "Doctorate in 'Artificial Network Neurophysics' at age twenty-three, glowing research thesis on improving the efficiency of quantum computing in solar megastructures. Recognized by the 16ᵀᴴ *Consortium on Machine Learning* last year for your impressive early-career results on AI neural networks—particularly on networks that *teach themselves* how to solve problems. *Twelve* research papers on unique aspects of that topic, if I'm not mistaken. A stacked CV, of course." She didn't need a single piece of paper for that information, looking at me right in the eyes. I couldn't help but grin at hearing my accomplishments stated out loud; I had the same feeling of pride I got when looking at a fresh copy of my own résumé. A résumé that was in a delicate balance throughout this conversation, I knew.

Her gaze shifted up towards the tiled ceiling as she recited something at the back of her brain. *"Emotionally crippled by a lack of parental figures, Dr. Hesper is winded by the constant change of circumstances around him and has a fragile self-worth. He utilizes his academic success—and the pretense of a religious conviction—to convey a front of hyper-intelligence and stoic emotional stability, when in reality he does not possess either."*

She stared back down at me, meeting my startled eyes. My mouth was probably half-agape, but I was hardly aware of my own expression. *How did she get that information? How much did she know?* Like a stalling car, I tried to start up my brain to process what had just been deemed of me.

All I could do was look to Stellos for an answer.

She was happy to provide one. "That was a note, jotted down in a cursive blue scribble by a certain Dr. Chan whom you saw two years ago. It was written in haste after the cognitive behavioral session your graduate advisor recommended you attend. Apparently, the therapist didn't appreciate you devaluing his occupation by calling him an 'old quack,'" she said, not taking her eyes off me.

I hadn't thought about that meeting for months; I put it out of my mind soon after it had happened. It's true: the kind of devotion required for my early success in academia came at a price. A heavy one, socially speaking. But a research automaton like me didn't *need* friends; I devoted my time to refining my computer programs. I didn't have a family to hang out with. I had no time to go out to a bar with "the boys." And, besides the nuns at my orphanage, I had never even *spoken* to a female except for professional reasons. Work and studying were my life. And Chan, the atheist that he was, had no right to talk about my religion—but that's beside the point. We *all* have problems; I made the mistake of thinking a therapist's job was to help me with mine.

But did I put up an "emotional front?" It doesn't matter. *That* was in the past, and I didn't plan on mentioning any of it. This is for damn sure: I won't be mentioning it again.

Stellos didn't have to, either. She gave me a wry grin. "For future interviews, I might caution against leaving the *'What is your greatest weakness?'* section of the application blank. We do *our* research, too."

At that point, I figured the opportunity was shot. I had just been shred to pieces by my potential employer, who attacked me right at the core without batting an eye. I straightened my tie, gripped my briefcase along with whatever dignity I had left, and began to rise from the chair.

"Ms. Stellos," I coughed. "Thank you for your—"

"Sit down, Dr. Hesper. I haven't hired you yet." Sarah briskly picked up the black briefcase at her feet, opened it, and took out a small packet of white paper. "We both know that I already know this, Arthur, but for posterity's sake, your middle initial is 'E,' correct?"

I hovered over my chair, with what was probably an incredulous look on my face, as I watched Stellos click a black ink pen and begin to write with a smoldering intensity. She checked a box here, wrote a phrase there, moving down what was certainly an employment contract.

About twenty seconds of silence passed before she looked back up at me expectantly. "Well? Is it?"

I sat back down in my chair, feeling my shirt cling against my drenched back. Stellos didn't move a muscle, looking at me as if I were the result of a fascinating experiment.

"You're being serious?" was all I could muster as I stared hesitantly into her eyes, pulling at my collar to let in some air.

"About your middle name? Of course not. About your position with us?" Sarah sat up. "Dr. Hesper, do you know how many geeky computer techs and do-right businessmen I've had sit in that chair? And do you really think I want to watch *more* applicants break out in sweat after they realize who the Florida girl they'd been patronizing really was?"

She paused for a moment, and I realized that she was expecting me to answer.

"Um... *no,*" I stammered.

"Actually, I do kind of enjoy it," she said, a wily smile crossing her face for a moment. "But I'm done playing pretend. This interview process matters to me because this job *matters.* Coordinator of Intelligence... we know that Abraham's world is shaping up to be the greatest one ever built. But right now, it's just a collection of three-dimensional models and featureless commands—it needs an organizer, an *intelligence* to link it all together into something beautiful. Someone needs to design that intelligence. For a Matrioshka Brain to work..."

"...it has to *think?*" I suggested. I cursed my stupid mouth for interrupting her, but I was relieved when she gave me a cordial nod.

"An obvious answer, but the right one. So many applicants for this job, most of them at least twice your age, overlook that fact. But from the dozens of your codes that I've read through, I can tell that you don't stifle your programs with *conventional* inefficiencies. Instead, you grant your AI systems the intelligence to solve their *own* problems," she said. She made a quick note on her paper. "It's a maverick and potentially dangerous move, to be sure, but it's also something I need at Abraham. Besides, of the many applications we've received, yours trumps them all easily."

She put down the pen, brushed a wrinkle out of her shirt, and leaned in closer to me. Her stare softened as her expression changed; the stone wall crumbled. For the first time since I spoke to that nervous girl, something *real* showed up from Sarah. At least, something that *seemed* real.

"More importantly, Arthur, this job is not a run-of-the-mill experiment. It requires someone with passion, with heart, and who's been *hurt,* to know why Abraham's world must be built. I think we both know what we're really trying to achieve, deep down," she said, her voice softening. She talked with that maternal grace she had before, seeming to say *exactly what I needed to hear* even if it wasn't at all what I was thinking about. And she was as convincing as a businesswoman encouraging an employee or landing a deal.

"But... but *why* would you want me? What is it you—*we're*—doing?" I asked. I didn't know if those were the right questions to ask, or why I asked them. They felt cinematic and dramatic, but those were the only words that would come out. They were the only thoughts that could materialize.

Sarah carefully placed her papers down on a small desk beside her and stood up. She began taking a couple steps towards me. I caught a faint whiff of spearmint breath mixed with deodorant and got a closer look at her face. Her hair was even more knotted and coarse up close, and I noticed visible scars on her chin where pimples had come and gone. She had bags under her eyes, and her face held not a single trace of makeup.

In spite of her disheveled look, however, Stellos was actually quite conventionally attractive. As she stepped closer to me, I noticed that her irises were a deep brown, and as she stared at me, I felt her eyes radiate a sense of confidence. Her laugh seemed heartfelt and pure, even if it *was* really manufactured for the interview. When she had been smiling just a few minutes ago, I noticed that her teeth were white and straight. Up close, I could even see she had light freckles dotting her cheeks. As she stepped closer, I couldn't help but notice the tan of her arms and the muscular tone of her legs. I realized that she was probably a runner, and that she was in far better physical shape than I was. I wasn't *staring* at her body, mind you—I'm *not* a creep. I was just making observations.

What was I talking about?

Right, okay.

Sarah Stellos was *very* attractive.

The company president was a foot away from me now. She was intimidatingly close, and she seemed to know it. Sarah looked down at me and into my face. She was too close for me to even think of standing for her. I could only stare back at her, the embers in her eyes warming me.

What is it we're doing?

"Making the future," she said, her voice barely above a whisper. "When the time comes, you'll know."

Suddenly, she swiftly glided back to her chair, sat down, and picked up her pen and papers as if nothing had disturbed her. "So," she resumed. "About that middle initial?"

TWO

"VIRTUAL REALITY IS a dying industry," Sarah declared atop her podium, staring down at a throng of reporters. No later than one hour after I was hired, she announced a press conference to reveal to the world the genius who would turn her company's vision into a reality. Rather than allow a public relations officer to simply read off my name, however, Stellos conducted the conference in her signature style: an elaborate mix of storytelling, drama, and prophecy, with a little bit of science sprinkled in. Academics hated her, but the non-scientist community (and, fortunately, investors) ate it up. Maybe I did, too.

"Like a typewriter to a modern secretary, it provides a fundamental service but is ultimately obsolete," she said. I stood off to the side of the stage, devoting a significant amount of energy to keep from fidgeting or twiddling my thumbs out of nervousness. I knew I was *qualified* for the job, but that didn't make dozens of reporters any less terrifying. Of course, any nervous tics I had wouldn't really matter—the "journalists," as Sarah referred to them with air quotes, were too busy typing or scribbling down notes to care.

"In every iteration of VR, a burden was placed on users that no company could alleviate: the necessity to suspend disbelief. Sight, sound, and touch were engaged, but the user *knew* that the game wasn't real, that their coworkers weren't really there, that they weren't really standing on cosmic shores," Stellos said. "This firm detachedness that a user had, whether they used their headsets for work or leisure, has resulted in stagnant development, halted sales, and plummeting satisfaction with the technology. That is, until we at Abraham announced the future of virtual reality with our Solar Brain."

A large screen lowered behind her, and the lights began to dim. Throughout her whole speech, I was watching Stellos in awe, my head spinning, *processing* how I could have possibly gotten here.

Promptly after my interview had concluded, which consisted of answering several questions that we both knew the answers to, Sarah stood up, clutched her briefcase, and said just three words:

"Welcome to Abraham."

She then disappeared into a back workroom, leaving me alone with my illegible nametag and the secretary who wrote it.

After about five minutes of sitting in the silent waiting room, I collected my briefcase and myself. I was still in disbelief; *did I get the job?* I figured I must have, though that didn't make the meeting I just had any less surreal.

I was getting up to go home when the secretary quickly told me to remain seated in anticipation of *the event*. I didn't see Stellos pass a word to her on her way out, so I had no idea what this "event" was. And yet, after about twenty minutes Sarah emerged from the back. She was wearing a slim black button-up suit, heels, and a white pin that read only her first name. Her hair was perfectly straight, the bags under her eyes had disappeared, and she even seemed to have put on some mascara. She looked like how I'd seen her in news interviews and press conferences. My stomach did a somersault; *she was dressed for a press conference.* Of the many things I was now worrying about, I suddenly realized how disheveled *I* looked compared to *her*; my right cufflink was beginning to become undone, and my shirt wasn't even tucked in properly. *Wait*—did *I shave that morning?* I looked down, and saw my tie was—

Stellos walked by before I could finish the thought, and I knew better than to keep her waiting. She gave me the grand circle tour of the corporate office, which mainly consisted of glass-paneled meeting rooms and small workspaces. She strode through like she owned the place (which, of course, she did), pointing at doors to her left and right. *This room belonged to* this *working group,* this *person was in charge of finances for* this, *and* this *guy's a real piece of work—don't talk to him.*

Throughout the entirety of the tour, Sarah spoke in a rushed monotone, and it was clear that she couldn't care less about the corporate office—*or* Washington, D.C., for that matter. She led me through two wooden doors, and my heart skipped a beat when I came face-to-face(s) with the crowd of reporters and flashing cameras.

Ten minutes later, those reporters silently watched Sarah's video.

A middle-aged gentleman narrated as CG graphics dazzled the audience.

"Welcome to *The Abraham Project*," the man said as Abraham's globe-shaped logo appeared over a starry background. "The only group on the planet capable of building the Solar Brain—*the next step in the evolution of supercomputation.*"

Upon hearing those words, I felt goosebumps run along my arms. Like much of the content in the video, I'd heard that phrase hundreds of times from the company's online advertisements. Still, that didn't stop the reality of where I was from finally sinking in. *Was I actually just hired by Abraham? The Abraham?*

"Once referred to by scientists as the Matrioshka Brain, our superstructure consists of a collection of solar panels, quantum computers, and communication arrays placed around our star." Onscreen appeared a small, bright model of the Sun, and surrounding the star at a considerable distance was a spherical swarm of silver dots.

"Some have visualized our Solar Brain to look like a giant metal orb that surrounds the Sun, but that couldn't be further from the truth. Such a design would be impractical, expensive, and would block out the sunlight needed for life on Earth. Clearly, this would not be ideal."

Some members of the audience laughed. If I hadn't taken a quick glance toward the podium, I might've missed Sarah rolling her eyes at that line. She'd clearly heard this video—and the explanation of how the Solar Brain works—many, *many* times. I'd read an article a couple of weeks ago that noted how relentless Abraham's public relations teams had to be with informing the public exactly *how* their proposed technology would work. Given that Abraham was building their—*our?*—megastructure around Earth's only star, the pressure was on them to be as transparent—and convincing—as possible.

The video continued with imagery of thousands of satellites orbiting the Sun, each of them accompanied with hexagonal-shaped mirrors. "Thanks to funding from our proud partner, the *Astronomical Endeavor Institute*, Abraham instead employs cutting-edge reproducible technology and reusable rocketry to construct a 'solar swarm.' Our network of solar satellites will surround the Sun and transmit energy and data to each other using rapidly refracted light rays. Thanks to the efforts of the legendary Dr. Richard Matthews and his niece, Sarah Stellos, the majority of the mirrors needed for this network have already been placed in orbit around the Sun. The remainder of the Solar Brain will be built at a minimal cost while ensuring that the structure remains stable and effective."

The image on the screen zoomed out to a wide view of the Sun, satellites, and the Earth orbiting farther away. A small disclaimer at the bottom of the video read *"Not to scale."*

"Computers and satellites on Earth will work hand-in-hand, *or qubit-in-qubit,* with those orbiting the Sun. As a command pulse is sent from Earth..."

As the narrator continued, a tiny blue beam suddenly emerged from Earth and travelled toward the satellites. The blue pulse—representing a user-defined input from Earth—ricocheted around the Solar Sphere for a few seconds before turning green.

"...the Solar Brain returns all the information needed while processing the request. Little by little, this information is beamed back to Earth, where users can interact with it with little to no delay times thanks to our high-Earth-orbit supercomputers. The information storage, processing, and retrieval capacities of the Brain are limitless."

The imagery on the video shifted to show a tiny clear orb floating in place of the Sun. Inside the orb appeared a series of flashing images—the ones that stood out to me showed the inside of a futuristic starship, a colorful underwater coral reef, and a golden sunset cascading over a tropical island cityscape. That orb began to float away from the Solar Sphere and rested near a series of larger satellites orbiting Earth.

"Abraham will develop the capacity to transmit virtual worlds to and from the Sun with ease, allowing users on Earth to interact with our upcoming suite of high-resolution worlds quickly and easily. And some-day..."

A small silhouette of a human appeared over the Earth. Mirroring the previous animation, the human figure began to float away from Earth and move toward the Solar Brain.

"...humans will be able to upload their *minds* directly into the Brain for even longer stretches of time to interact more fully with all Abraham has to offer."

The video continued with information like this for about ten more minutes. The rest of the video contained things that most people knew—that Abraham was building a "non-invasive integrated VR" that connected wirelessly to your Central Nervous System, that millions of tests were being run to ensure it wouldn't screw up users' brains, and that *its applications for business and play were endless* (one of their corporate mantras).

Like the rest of the audience, I stood transfixed by the video. I couldn't help myself. Abraham carried more excitement around it than any other tech company in history. The ability to defy reality seamlessly while playing in virtual worlds was something that always intrigued me. While many children had their own VR headsets or went on exciting vacations, I was always forced to imagine what it was like to free my mind from the chilly walls of the orphanage and travel somewhere fantastic. The first time I touched virtual reality was around the first time I left Brooklyn, when my middle school science teacher showed his students the model of the Solar System in VR. While the visual aid was rather mundane to the other private-school kids, I was fascinated by the vivid detail of the world around me, widening my eyes to take in every pixel. Not only had I just begun seeing the world outside my city, but the world outside my own. I wanted more of it—*so much more.*

My daydreaming was promptly interrupted as the graphics on the screen dimmed and Sarah Stellos retook the podium, towering over everyone around her.

"Why do we innovate? Why do we create?" Sarah asked the crowd. I began to lift my hand as if to answer her, but quickly realized that the question was a rhetorical one and lowered it. I prayed that Stellos didn't see me as she continued. "We all seek to better our lives and the lives of those around us, and this can only be done by boldly stepping into the unknown. Since its inception six years ago, my company has exceeded the frontiers of human technological capability. We have built a working Dyson Sphere, bringing my late uncle's dream to life. We are preparing our solar and low-Earth-orbit satellites in anticipation of an early launch window. And we operate along the cutting edge of neuro-sync virtual reality, and expect to make dramatic breakthroughs in human mind-to-VR developments any day. We innovate—we *create*—the future, and we are just getting started."

Sarah took a deep breath and looked toward the screen. "Everything Abraham has accomplished is entirely thanks to the hard work of our team, each member of which believes in the power of possibility as much as I do. Our scientists and engineers are the leaders of their disciplines, and each of our employees is integral to our project's success. I'm proud today to announce that our executive-level team has expanded with our most recent hire, and that he will play a key role in shaping the Solar Brain as we know it."

As Sarah stepped away from the podium, my heart skipped a beat as a picture of myself from several years ago working on a quantum supercomputer appeared onscreen. I couldn't tell exactly when it was taken, given the fact that I'd *always* had red eyes and stubborn bedhead, but decided from the background of the laboratory that it was probably taken during my freshman year of college. The video's narrator suddenly began speaking again, and I felt butterflies in my stomach as he said my name.

"Arthur E. Hesper is a visionary, postdoctoral, artificial intelligence specialist who will help design the Solar Brain's virtual guide. His work on artificial neural networks shows that he doesn't just understand virtual brains, but can *build* them."

A montage of pictures and accolades I held flashed before my eyes as the narrator spoke. My medal of commendation that I received at an AI conference two years ago. My *National Award for Innovation* that I earned as a college senior. My winning high-school science-fair project for a prototype of a working predictive text generator. *All of that was online?* For a moment, I was shocked that so much information about myself was publicly available. Soon after, I came to my senses, and realized that that information was definitely *not* publicly available.

The narrator continued with a stadium announcer's enthusiasm. "And *now,* ladies and gentlemen, The Abraham Project welcomes Dr. Arthur Hesper to our team, and invites him to share a few words regarding his experience in quantum computing and artificial intelligence."

After overcoming my admiration for the alacrity of Abraham's video editing team, the dread settled in. *Speak? Now?* I hadn't prepared a thing. I looked over at Sarah, who was standing off to the side of the podium—and who, I now noticed, wasn't holding even a single note. She'd given that speech on the fly and was expecting me to do the same.

I began to step toward the podium, forcing myself to avoid looking at the audience. *Not yet.* My legs moved faster than my brain could, though, and before I could even hesitate, I found myself standing two feet from Sarah.

Shake her hand, you idiot!

Praying that there wasn't too much sweat on my palm, I stuck out my right hand toward Sarah with what was probably a frightened expression, and she took it. Her handshake was firm, and her palms were soft—much softer than her fingers, which felt very coarse and dry. Sarah smiled upon taking my hand, but I noticed that she wasn't actually smiling at me or at the audience, though. Her gaze seemed to reach past me, scanning the entire room behind me before settling on the exit doors. She quickly glanced back over at me and let go of my hand. Then, her smile faded, and she gestured toward the podium with a nod.

I took one last look at her face as if to try to glean an ounce of her confidence for myself, and I looked over at the reporters. I forced myself to avoid feeling lightheaded and looked down at the podium. Part of me was hoping a secret screen might light up and reveal to me the exact words I should say. I imagined Stellos had the capability to make that occur, too. But as no such thing happened, I began trying to form some sentences in my head.

Thank you, Sar—Ms. Stellos! Hi everyone, my name is Arthur Hesper...

No, they already knew your name.

I am so excited to be joining this amazing team at Abraham.

Okay, safe enough.

I am so excited...

You already said you're excited, pick a different adjective.

I am EAGER to be working on Abraham's Advanced Learning Intelligence, an amazing tool that will...

Shit. What will it do?

...revolutionize virtual reality and worldbuilding as we know it.

That should be vague enough to work.

Despite my young age...

Don't mention your age.

I have a... lot of experience working with artificial neural networks. For example, I...

That's good, list examples of amazing things you've done. Should be easy enough. You've done a lot of cool stuff.

Right?

Artificial intelligence is only as capable as we are willing to let it be, which is why I believe in programming systems that can learn from their users in a humanlike way. I am so grateful to Abraham for the opportunity to do this work.

That's nice, wrap it up,,,

And lastly, I couldn't have done this without...

...

without...

...

Have a great afternoon, everyone.

As those words flowed through my head, I looked back up at the audience and began to adjust the microphone resting on the podium. Even though Sarah was only a few inches taller than I was, I took a prolonged amount of time to raise and then lower the microphone as I formed my speech in my head. Once I was finally satisfied with the height of the microphone and my makeshift speech, I glanced down at the reporters and their cameras.

There were a lot of them.

Immediately, I forgot every word of what I was going to say. I felt the back of my shirt start to become wet with sweat, and as I caught my breath I looked up at the ceiling.

Deep breaths.

After a moment, I looked back down at the reporters, and they impatiently stared back at me, eagerly awaiting the first words of Dr. Arthur Hesper.

THREE

MOVING FROM MASSACHUSETTS to Florida was pretty easy given that I didn't have many things to move. I'd lived in the same small apartment since I'd started graduate school, so it was strange leaving the tiny kitchenette/workspace, bedroom/workspace, and bathroom/workspace that I'd grown so accustomed to. But closing the door to my old apartment was about the only difficult goodbye I had to say; I didn't bother to contact any of my old peers, professors, or even Dr. Johnson, my former advisor. I was eager to leave and never look back.

I found a nice place about ten minutes' driving distance from Abraham's main workshop compound—close enough that the commute would be a breeze, but far enough away that I wouldn't feel suffocated by work. My new apartment was much bigger than what I'd been used to, and I quickly had it outfitted with the best and fastest network connections I could find (or afford). From my kitchen, I had a great view of the city street. At night, I could even see the lights from the communication towers surrounding Abraham. The only drawback to my new house was the steady stream of trash bags left out by the Lovinson family on the bottom floor, ripe for tripping over. I could not fathom why they couldn't make the extra journey to the dumpster, which was *literally* twenty feet from their door.

After tripping over what must have been a bag of disposable diapers for the fifteenth time, I hopped in my car and began to drive to work. I was one of the proud few commuters that still drove a crossover SUV; almost all of the students at my graduate school who drove were committed to their tiny, self-driving electric cars, as were many of the people on the road. My used car was the best one I could afford, but often when my peers saw me heading for my car, they never failed to loudly comment to their friends about how much those "gassholes" were harming the planet, even though I drove a hybrid. But considering I lived too far away from campus to walk and too close to ride the bullet train, I was content with my method of transportation.

Still, as I sat in the Monday morning traffic that crowded the stretch of highway leading to Abraham, I began to wonder why we didn't all just drive flying cars yet. Only really rich or really reckless people seem to use them, and it's usually in an open field free of obstacles. How was it that our society could invent VR systems that could sync to users' brains, build cell phones that could photograph a fly a hundred feet away, and land the first humans on Mars, but I still couldn't afford a flying car?

What was I talking about? *Oh yeah.*

My job.

My first time driving into Abraham's compound, I almost crashed because I was distracted looking at the brilliant, glimmering, massive company buildings. The whole worksite was based out of a repurposed satellite construction center, as evidenced by the hundred-foot-tall rectangular warehouse in the compound center. A sea of concrete surrounded the warehouse, and sitting atop the pavement were several dozen truck-sized structures made of metal. At first glance the structures looked like crumpled pieces of aluminum foil, but upon closer look revealed themselves to be diamond-shaped arrays of metal braces and poles. *They were the satellites,* I realized, *waiting to be fitted with pristine mirrors and launched into space.*

I drove up towards a building directly adjacent to the warehouse, which looked like a stubby, pickle-shaped tower covered in reflective glass. It was connected to the warehouse with a bulky skybridge that arched over a small sidewalk, which I began to walk down. I passed a blue sign with four arrows on it; to the left was "The Workshop," to the even farther left was "Delivery Drone Reception," to the right was the "Visitor Center," and straight ahead was the "Office Building." Since I didn't want to just wander into the workshop, and I wasn't a visitor or delivery drone, I went for the office.

As I pushed through the revolving doors of the "stubby pickle," as I'd named it, I was immediately struck by how *new* everything looked inside the office. Most of the buildings I was used to working in were almost a century old; this place *had* to have been built within the past few years. The walls were adorned with clean, glossy tiles, and the front desk and furniture matched the building's deep-blue color scheme. The smell of cookies seemed to permeate the air, no doubt coming from an inside bakery. And almost every free wall housed razor-thin 100-inch monitors along with a suite of high-end gadgets. The interior of the whole building seemed to evoke what "the future" is so often pictured as: shiny, high-tech, and aesthetically *perfect.*

I brushed away whatever wrinkles I could from the sleeves of my suit jacket and walked up to the front desk.

"Hi," I said to the receptionist. She gave me a quick glance before returning to her computer screen.

"Umm..." I began, realizing that I wasn't fully sure what I was supposed to say. "I don't know if I should be in the workshop or here... my name is Arth—*Dr. Hesper*, and I..."

The woman responded without looking away from her screen. "Ms. Stellos will see you in her office."

"Okay..." I said. *Where exactly is her office?* I didn't want to bother the receptionist, so I just nodded at her and wandered away from the desk. I eventually turned to my right and slowly walked towards a group of tables down the hall. The woman at the desk didn't call after me, so I figured I was either heading the right way or she wasn't watching.

I walked through what seemed to be a spacious employee lounge. Hardly any of the tables or couches lining the walls were occupied; as I walked through, I only saw about four other people in the room. They were sitting in different corners of the lounge, and each had a coffee and one or more electronic tablets in front of them. None of them could've been a day over thirty. One of the employees—a large man wearing what appeared to be his pajamas—stared up at me through the rim of his polished white augmented-reality glasses. He watched me as I passed through the room. I turned away from him, only to find the other three employees staring at me as well. As soon as I met their eyes, they quickly looked back down at their devices.

Toward the far end of the lounge, away from the employees, was the small corner bakery I'd smelled earlier. An entire wall of high-tech coffee machines lined the rear of the bakery, and an older man in an apron was filling a steel pitcher with decaf. Sitting atop the front counter were several rows of chocolate chip cookies. I could feel the freshly baked heat coming from them. The aproned man must have seen me staring down at the cookies, because he turned and offered me a toothy smile.

"Enjoy!"

"They're... free?" I asked.

"For employees? Why wouldn't they be?" He turned back to the oven, where *another* fresh batch of cookies was waiting. As badly as I wanted to take one, I pulled myself away from the counter. I was about to be late as it was, and I didn't need to show up to Sarah Stellos's office with my hands covered in chocolate. I turned toward a dimly lit hallway next to the bakery and kept walking.

As I made my way through the hall, I triple-checked the nameplate next to each door. Almost all of the rooms were labelled either for supplies, staff, or the janitors; none of them were an executive's office. *Where was Sarah?*

As I approached a bend in the hallway, I noticed the glow from the other end getting brighter and brighter, and I walked faster. As soon as I reached the end of the hall—which must have brought me to the opposite side of the pickle—I found myself inside a large, bright space. I squinted at the sunlight pouring through the glass walls lining the outer edge of the room.

As my eyes quickly adjusted, I saw that a metal satellite was dangling from the ceiling. I could see its crisscrossed metal beams up close and noticed that attached to the top of the satellite was a silver sheet that stretched across the entire room. *The mirror.* Beneath the solar satellite, a person-sized image of the spacecraft floating among the stars sat next to an informational display. Closer to the sliding front doors and behind a small ticketing desk were many story-high models of rocket ships. And in the far corner of the room, suspended in a glass tube, was a glowing model of the Sun.

This place was the visitor hall—and it was empty.

"Welcome to the *Abraham–AEI Visitor Center,*" a loud voice proclaimed. It sounded like the same narrator from Abraham's promotional video at the press conference. "Join us as we explore the next step in the evolution of supercomputation. At Abraham, our mission is to bring the Solar Brain's endless applications for business and possibilities for play to everyone."

I ducked under a rope that was blocking the area I'd come from, and

I began to walk toward the center of the exhibition hall. I hadn't realized how spacious it was until I was standing in the middle of the room underneath the giant satellite. To my right was a glass booth with various rocket-shaped trinkets, *Abraham*-branded knick-knacks, and other memorabilia on display. *The gift shop.* Towards the far side of the room sat a long service counter with tablets and heat lamps. Atop the counter was a menu stocked with fast-food options, and above it was a large, Sun-shaped sign that read *"Solar Brain Food."* Finally, tucked behind a sea of screens and interactive displays was a curved staircase that ran along the wall of the building. A small sign dangled in front of the stairs that read *"Walkway to Workshop Viewing Area—Temporarily Closed."*

I walked closer to the model of the Sun at the far edge of the room. As I reached the glass pane in front of the model, I noticed that the Sun—which seemed to be more of a hologram than a model—was surrounded by several rings of small white dots, each of which floated at a different distance from the star. *The Solar Sphere.* As much as I read about the megastructure, I was always surprised by how few mirrors the Solar Sphere actually needed; the model in front of me only had around a hundred dots spread around the Sun's equator, which—astrophysically speaking—seemed like a small number. As I leaned in closer to try to count the mirrors, I jumped as the narrator's voice suddenly began speaking from the model.

"The Solar Sphere currently uses a collection of foldable and extendable mirrors to maximize light collection while reducing the amount of material needed for construction," the voice said. As *Abe* (I decided that's what I'm calling the narrator from now on) spoke, a model of one of the mirrors appeared. At its center, the mirror looked just like one of the metal satellites being built outside. Extending dozens of feet around the base, though, was a round silver sheet like the one above the visitor center. It bent and swayed against the backdrop of the stars, sending beams of sunlight in changing directions based on the mirror's shape.

"By building large, thin mirrors that redirect light, we can maximize the size and scope of the Solar Sphere without wasting resources," Abe said. "These mirrors can beam sunlight directly to the receivers of the supercomputers orbiting the Sun, meaning that no energy is lost. Once Abraham launches its first computers—powered by the Advanced Learning Intelligence—into orbit, the mirrors will ensure that these computers *always* have enough energy to perform any calculation imaginable."

Next to the model of the solar mirror, an image of a brown-bearded man with wide-brimmed glasses came into focus. He was tall, wore an oversized grey coat, and stood beside a black chalkboard next to a rough sketch of the mirror design. I knew who it was. *Everyone did.*

"Dr. Richard J. Matthews designed these mirrors to be easy to construct, easy to launch, and impervious to coronal mass ejections or other spikes in solar activity," Abe continued. "Dr. Matthews also did what none of his peers believed possible—he attained all the materials necessary for these mirrors' construction from metals on *Earth.* By using purification techniques developed earlier this century, old electronic devices were repurposed by the Astronomical Endeavor Institute to serve as the raw material for our solar panels, as well as the materials for a variety of other AEI-sponsored relief efforts."

As Abe spoke, imagery of cellular towers being erected in tropical, developing countries appeared beside Dr. Matthews. *The man really did it all, huh?* As if reading my thoughts, Abe continued to heap praise onto the inventor.

"Previous estimates for a 'Dyson Swarm' would have required planets like Mercury to be strip-mined for resources, but thanks to the hard work of Dr. Matthews and the engineers at AEI and Abraham, we've been able to start building the Solar Sphere without needing to pursue off-world mining," Abe said. Beside him, imagery of trucks rolling around on a rocky, grey surface—likely Mercury—appeared. "Of course, the success of missions like *Artemis, Orion,* and *Ouranos* have underscored our ability to pursue such operations in the future if expansion is needed."

As the imagery around the solar model faded, I walked away from the display and moved towards the giant satellite dangling above the center of the room. As I did, I wondered if the Solar Sphere would have been built faster if engineers *had* just built mines on Mercury. Still, the idea of one company, even Abraham, taking over any part of the Solar System felt far off.

Trips to other planets were still rare for humans to do. The first Mars landing happened when I was only a toddler, but as a child I remember there being a lot of commotion about humanity's "migration" to the other worlds in our Solar System. I was convinced that I'd ride a spaceship to Mars one day. But space exploration soon slowed back down, as did progress on other forms of technology. Widespread flying cars, the cure for the common cold, and all the other promises of "the future" remained resolutely in *the future.*

But that's enough moping about flying cars for today. Besides, technology has progressed in other ways. Thirty years ago, package delivery drones were brand new, artificial body parts couldn't easily be grown in a lab, and one of the coolest things that AI could do was pass the bar exam. Furthermore, the idea of building a Dyson Sphere out of recycled *cell phones* and other metals on Earth was physically impossible. Now, that was all in a day's work at Abraham.

Maybe they really will take over the Solar System someday...

As I stared up at the satellite, Abe's booming voice returned, echoing through the room. "Since Abraham's official founding six years ago, our team has worked nonstop to develop cutting-edge technologies that pave the future of both aerospace engineering and immersive entertainment. We're committed to achieving the vision of success held by our leader."

At that, the lights inside the room began to dim—or, rather, the *sunlight* began to dim. I turned toward the wall of windows and noticed that they seemed far less transparent than they had before. They seemed to be tinting automatically; after a short while, the inside of the visitor hall was dark, save for the soft glow of the cove lights running along the wall. Suddenly, there was a burst of light from the center of the room, and beneath the satellite, a large transparent screen had dropped down with a blurry blue image projected onto it. Slowly, the image came into focus, and I was standing face-to-feet with a twenty-foot-tall projection of my new boss.

"Our brightest, most beautiful days are still yet to come," Sarah Stellos said, flashing a beaming smile at the audience. She had one hand on the hip of her silk suit, and with the other hand she was gesturing towards the rocket and satellite models lining the room. "With out-of-this-world support provided by the Astronomical Endeavor Institute, we've been able to take on the most ambitious project humanity has ever seen. And thanks to *your* support, together we will pave the way towards paradise in our time. Here's to a brighter tomorrow."

Sunlight returned to the room as the windows became clear. The screen was gone, as was the projection. I was left looking up at the satellite hanging from the top of the vast visitor center.

All this for one person's idea.

"You're early." I whipped around to find Sarah Stellos—the *real* Sarah Stellos—sitting on one of the visitor benches, tying her shoes. "Visitor center doesn't open until eleven."

It took me a second to realize that she wasn't just wearing any shoes, but *sneakers*. Instead of a suit, Sarah was wearing a tight-fitting black shirt and leggings, both bearing Abraham's logo. The only other time I'd seen Sarah in casual clothes—heck, one of the only other times I'd *ever* seen her—was when she was manipulating me during the interview. *Is she trying to do that now?* I tried to look away from her and up at the windows, but something about her clothes caught my attention.

Okay, something *besides* how form-fitting they were.

Her clothes had a patterned, *wired* print running along them, lacing her joints in what looked like the outline of a circuit. I felt my face grow warm as Sarah noticed me staring at her body, and I quickly looked away.

"They're biometric workout clothes," she said. "Our technicians need to collect data on how the different parts of the human central nervous system respond to different environmental stimuli. These clothes record information about my movements and send them over to Abraham's neuro-sync division. We can't really link the entire human body to the Brain without knowing how every nerve ending works."

Sarah stood up and began to walk over to me. As she took her first step, I noticed her wince and start to reach for her calf. But a second later, she stood straight up, and continued to walk toward me as if nothing had happened. She looked me up and down.

"Interviewing at another company today?"

I stared down at my clothes, and started to sweat as I realized that I was wearing the same black jacket I'd worn to the interview with Sarah. *Did I even have another jacket?*

"No, I..." I stammered.

"I hope not, otherwise I'd have to organize another press release about our managerial shake-up, and I'd rather not have to do that," Sarah said. As she walked past me, she turned her head towards me with a smile. "You know I'm joking, Arthur."

"Yeah, I know," I said, lying to her.

"Shall we?" she asked. Without waiting for a reply, she moved swiftly through the exhibition hall towards the roped-off staircase. I almost tripped over my feet trying to keep up with her. She unhooked the rope blocking the stairwell and began to walk up the steps towards the second floor.

"Lock that behind me, will you?"

As I fumbled with the rope, I looked up at Sarah. As the rising Sun poured in through the windows, all I could see was the black outline of her tall, athletic figure. I felt my heart start to race, and quickly turned back toward the rope.

"I would've thought there'd be more security here," I said, putting the sign back in place and doing my best to catch up to Sarah.

"Oh, there is," Sarah said. She pointed over at the dangling satellite. As I looked toward it, I half-expected to find a laser beam or high-tech missile launcher attached to the bottom of the spacecraft. But I didn't see anything; the pipe frame of the satellite seemed completely bare.

"You're not going to see anything over there, and that's exactly the point," Sarah said. "Nanotechnology cameras, only visible on a microscopic scale, line the entire base of the satellite and are attached to almost every exhibit, wall, and piece of furniture in the room. They allow our security team, housed in the 'janitor's office' that you passed six minutes ago, to have a 360-degree view of every square inch of the compound."

As Sarah reached the top of the stairs, she gave a wave to the wall on her right. "How's it going, Chanelle?" She turned back towards me. "She's one of our security staff—also the one who told me you were on your way to the exhibition hall."

As I reached the top of the stairs, I gave a slight wave toward the wall.

"Wrong wall," Sarah said. "But these cameras—not only are they useful for our compound's security, but they also provide valuable information for our team at Abraham."

"The VR team?" I asked. Sarah motioned with her hand for me to continue. "It provides visual data for the scattering of light, three-dimensional motion, and the behavior of visitors throughout the day that can be synthesized into Abraham's virtual worlds. Right?"

"You're a fast learner," Sarah said. She walked along the second-floor balcony and made her way towards the windows. I walked up to the glass wall and, despite their bright reflection, resisted the urge to squint as I took in the array of solar satellites resting on the acres of pavement below. Several large trucks drove between the satellites, carrying an assortment of boxes, metal pieces, and even half-assembled satellite parts. I noticed that some of the satellites farther away from the visitor center were covered by semi-transparent domes; dozens of these domes sat around the compound like scattered blue shells. I figured those were protective covers for the satellites; given the frequent Florida rainstorms, it *probably* made sense to keep satellites that weren't being worked on covered. Closer to the large building beside ours, I saw a group of people standing around a massive conveyor belt, which was loading a satellite-sized box onto the bed of a large truck. On the side of the truck, I could make out the blue *NASA* and purple *AEI* logos.

"Everything we do here is in service of our company mission, from the rockets we launch even to the annoying press conferences we have to hold," Sarah said. "We build our technology here, make our breakthroughs here, and get closer to finishing the Brain here. This place—*this*—is the heart of it all."

Sarah was gazing at the waves of satellites and domes with wide eyes. From the calm activity on the concrete below, to the palm trees swaying in the distance and the rolling storm clouds on the distant horizon—all of it seemed to completely enamor her. As she turned away from the window and continued to lead me around the compound, I could tell that she was much more excited about *this* office tour than the one we'd taken in D.C.

After walking up another, smaller flight of stairs, we crossed the sky-bridge toward the warehouse.

"Your office isn't inside the stubby pickle?" I quickly asked, forgetting to keep that last bit to myself.

"What?" she asked.

"Nothing."

"*The stubby pickle...* most of the employees here have a dirtier name for it," Sarah said as we reached the doors at the end of the bridge. *Dirtier name? What else would they call—*

"*Oh*," I said.

"Yeah, let's go with stubby pickle," Sarah said. "But really, this office building is mainly for our financial, press, and legal staff to use. And we don't really use our D.C. office except for when we need to be in Washington for political reasons, or to look intimidating when interviewing our new hires." I looked over at Sarah, who was looking at the floor with a smile.

"In answer to your question," she continued. "I keep *my* office in the workshop, where the *real* work is done."

Sarah pushed open the doors, and a second later we were standing on a balcony overlooking the massive workshop. The inside resembled a warehouse—beams of light poured in through the open sunroof, illuminating the dust particles floating around the top of the building. But besides the drab metal ceiling, the rest of the workshop looked completely renovated. The walls were finished and were painted white, and a large divider split the interior of the building in two. On one half of the workshop, bright wooden tiles lined the floor, and a series of smaller walls divided the area into about a dozen rooms each the size of a small house. The same modernist furniture that filled the office building was scattered around the place along with desks and expensive computer displays. The other side of the workshop—the side we had entered closer to—was relatively unfinished but was covered wall-to-wall in white sheets. The top of the room was also covered by a thick, clear sheet, separating the area—*Abraham's cleanroom*—from the rest of the workshop. Inside, several pieces of metal framing and communication dishes lay on tables, tended to by several people decked out in white coveralls.

In the center of the cleanroom sat a wide metallic tube about twenty feet tall. Penetrating the walls of the cylinder were thousands of coils that curled in and out of the tube. Several hoses also fed into the bottom of the device and were meticulously hooked up to a refrigerator-sized box beside the cylinder.

Sarah nodded towards the setup, and as she did, I caught her wince again.

"Are you okay—"

"Any idea what this is?" she asked, cutting me off. I took another look at the wide cylinder—at the wires feeding into the box, and the score of monitors around the room—and nodded. *Of course I knew what it was.*

"The quantum supercomputer—or its active cooling system, at least," I said.

"That was an easy one," Sarah said, nodding. "Do you know why—"

"...we need it?" I finished quickly. *It's not like I have a PhD in this subject, or anything.* She turned towards me with an intrigued smile. "Same reason we need the solar array. The energy collected needs to *go* some-where, and while *some* of that energy can be beamed back to low-Earth orbit, it's way more efficient to use it just to power the quantum computer and its regenerative cooling system. That conversion can help you lower the error rate to a small enough degree that with AI-assisted resolution—"

"Explain it to me like I have no scientific background," Sarah said.

Wait, what?

I stared at her blankly as she rolled her eyes.

"Pretend I'm a child you've met at the visitor center, or that I'm an interested investor who's never studied science," she said. "You need to explain, in simple terms, how the quantum computer's cooling system inside the Solar Brain works in order to keep me fascinated. Go."

"I... really?" I asked.

She blinked. "Really."

"Well, you have the reflected radiation..."

"What does *radiation* mean here?"

"Come on, a child would—"

Sarah shook her head. "I'll show you." She cleared her throat and spoke in a calm, but cheerful, tone. "All of the amazing things the Brain will do are possible because of something we call a *quantum computer,* which is way more advanced than most of the computers we have on Earth. Quan-tum computers can make a lot of mistakes, though, if they are kept too warm. As it turns out, even *outer space* is too warm for this computer, so we need to cool it down using this machine. The light we gather from the Sun is bounced around using mirrors until it hits the panels on the machine, which work a lot like the solar panels here on Earth. Those pan-els turn that sunlight into a boatload of energy, which we use to keep the computer cold—kind of like how a refrigerator uses electricity to keep your food cold. Since this computer will be close to the hot Sun, it takes a *lot* of energy to keep the computer cold. Thankfully, the Sun gives us all the energy we need!"

By the time she finished, several of the workers inside the cleanroom were looking up at her, and one of them gave an approving nod. Sarah quickly turned away from the cleanroom and began to walk along the bal-cony toward the finished side of the workshop. I scrambled to follow her, and she talked without looking back at me.

"In addition to your official job description, you'll want to be fluent in describing our company's work to *anyone* who asks about it."

"But you left out the advantages of solar-based computing, the role of AI in solving the ongoing error rate problem, the efficiency issues with beaming—"

"So? Those are things that you and the scientific team at Abraham will solve. What matters more is telling an accurate but compelling story to those who are interested in what we do."

"I was taught to always emphasize scientific rigor when dealing with the public."

"And how did that go at your press conference last week?" Sarah stopped short, right at the plastic divider between the clean-room and the rest of the building.

She had a point. I had stammered through most of my introductory speech, talking for maybe two minutes in total. In no coherent order, I spoke about some of the projects I'd done, thanked Sarah Stellos, talked about how cool I thought the company was, thanked Sarah again, and shuffled off the stage. The crowd applauded, but I was convinced that those were pity claps. *Maybe Sarah was right.*

As Sarah turned towards me, her expression softened. "Scientific rigor is important, Arthur, but it doesn't fund our company or launch Solar Brains. *People* do, and knowing how to talk to them is important. We'll work on that."

She turned away, and we walked through the divider and into the office side of the warehouse. Immediately, the flooring on the balcony and on the ground below changed from plain white tiles to the more elegant hardwood. The building itself was almost vacant, save for a couple of employees who were lost in their computers.

I looked down at the workshop to take in all the different rooms, many of which had no ceiling. One of them, labeled *"Neuro-Sync Simulation Development,"* housed a single technician along with a collection of different tanning booth-shaped beds and chairs with VR headsets on top of them. Another room was labeled *"Abraham Studios"* and had a black tarp pulled over the top, so I couldn't see what was going on inside of it. Towards the far corner of the workshop was another small, closet-sized room labelled *"Project Exodus,"* also covered with layers of tarps. And towards the center of the building, surrounded by four glass walls, was a small employee lounge stocked with a kitchenette and several trays of baked goods. I looked around the finished side of the workshop for an office with my name on it but didn't see one.

Eventually, we reached a small door at the back of the warehouse. There were large glass windows on either side of the door, but I couldn't see through them. Sarah pushed open her office door, and as I entered, it felt like stepping into another building entirely. The first thing I noticed was the smell—the room had a floral scent to it, which was distinctly easier on the nose than the forced, purified air that radiated through the rest of the warehouse. I looked around at the room. The floor was covered by a soft red rug with an elegant gold trim, and the walls were lined with dark, expensive furniture. Lining the back of the office was a row of windows that overlooked the sea of pavement, but as of now the windows were dimmed. On the front side of the office, I could see the bustling workshop through the large windows by the door, even though I hadn't been able to see into Sarah's office from outside. Finally, my eyes rested on the large wooden desk that sat in the center of the room like an island. It was populated only by a black laptop, notepad, and a single pen.

Sarah walked around her desk and sat down in a large office chair. As she did, I heard her let out a soft gasp and wince, but she continued to sit as if nothing had happened. Since there weren't any other chairs in the room, I stayed standing in front of her desk. For a few seconds, neither of us said anything. During the silence, I noticed that soft, symphonic music was playing from an unseen speaker in the ceiling.

"I like the music," I said, purely to break the silence.

"It's Tchaikovsky, Symphony Four," she said as the sound of various string instruments grew louder.

"You're into classical music?"

"Tchaikovsky was actually a Romantic composer," she said. "But no, I'm not really a huge music buff. I do like this one, though."

"Okay..."

"What do you think of the workshop?" she asked. She started scribbling a note on the pad in front of her.

"I'll have to get myself busy actually *working* in it, but from what I've seen it looks amazing," I said.

"Obviously, you're here to help us with the Advanced Learning Intelligence side of things—you read the brief, right?" she asked. I nodded.

"Good. Our work so far on that front has been slow, as the logistics surrounding the rocket launches and the actual *construction* of the Brain have taken up most of the company's attention. Now, we're able to focus more fully on linking our users to the Brain and developing a guiding AI that will help them."

"Right," I said, not fully sure how Sarah wanted me to respond to that.

"Eventually, though, Abraham will need to launch more than just mirrors and auxiliary satellites into space, but that quantum supercomputer out there, which is equivalent to seventeen giga-cores of processing. The AI that you are in charge of building will run on that computer and others like it, which is why I'll also need you to help me supervise the final stages of the computer's construction to make sure that everything *you* program is compatible with the Solar Brain."

"Okay," I said, taking it all in. Essentially, I would be spending the next year or so programming the framework of an AI while also supervising technicians to make sure they implemented it correctly. I'd read that much from the job description. *So why was Sarah repeating it now?*

"Your work, Dr. Hesper, will be paramount to the success of this mission," Sarah said, looking me right in the eyes. She spoke with an intensity that was focused, *determined,* like she was a flight director giving orders to an astronaut. "The time will come when you'll need to make important decisions—*difficult* decisions—and I'm counting on you to know what to do."

Sarah reached out towards her laptop, but suddenly clutched her right armpit with a wince. As I prepared to ask her what was wrong, I whipped around as a knock came from the doorframe. Behind me stood a short, thin man wearing a shirt and pants that looked identical to Sarah's. He glanced up at me quickly.

"So sorry to interrupt," he said. "Ms. Stellos?"

"Are we done, Tony?" Sarah asked, still wincing in pain.

"Yes," the man nodded quickly. "We have collected all the data we need from your motion. You should be all set to—"

"Perfect."

Tony left the room without another word, and I looked back towards Sarah, who was tugging at the collar of her shirt.

"Those clothes are... painful to wear?" I asked Sarah.

"Like you wouldn't believe," she said, waving her hand along her arm and chest to demonstrate. "Our team is studying each of the neurons in the human body, so I've been walking around the complex pretty much nonstop to give them a good scan of my kinetic activity. But in order to get a complete enough scan to connect a computer to the human mind, they need to use powerful sensors—sensors that pierce *through* the skin and connect to the fabric of this suit."

"Oh—*oh...*" I winced at the thought of even *one* tiny pin shoving itself through my skin, let alone a hundred. I was amazed that Sarah wasn't in *more* pain. "They need to do all that just to make measurements?"

"Yes," she said. "The suits that we'll use to initially *connect* to the Brain itself involve less sensor needles, but more wires, which are *also* uncomfortable to wear."

"Will I need to—"

"No, you won't need to test the technology," she said. "They just need a few candidates to help them model different body types."

"Why... why are *you* wearing it?" I asked Sarah. "They can't get someone else to—"

"I would not designate anyone else to do something that I'm not willing to do myself," Sarah said. She immediately grabbed her shirt collar in pain, and slowly removed her hand. The tip of her pointer finger was red with blood. She slowly wiped the blood off on her sleeve.

"Of course," she continued. "I made them start the test at three in the morning, *after* the janitorial staff leaves and *before* most employees show up. These clothes don't exactly leave much to the imagination."

"Umm... *right,*" I said. As I forced myself to look around in practically every other direction *except* toward her, I began to wonder: *why didn't Sarah care that* I *saw her?*

"Now, if you'll excuse me, Dr. Hesper, my six-hour scan is up and this suit is quite painful to remove, so if you wouldn't mind..."

"Sure," I said, immediately turning towards the door. "Um, Ms. Stellos?" I asked, not daring to turn around toward her.

"Yes, Dr. Hesper?"

"Where am I supposed to go?" I asked, still staring away from her.

"Ah—right," she said. "Well, it might be best for you to see *why* we need to work on our CNS connections, so go ahead and find Clyde on the first floor. You'll get to see the virtual world he's building, too. I'll tell him you're on your way."

"Okay," I said, stepping out the door.

"And, um, *Arthur?*" she asked softly. I turned around toward Sarah, who had her hands folded on her desk.

"Yes?"

"Watch the door." Her door automatically swung closed, slamming shut an inch from my face.

The first thing I noticed about Clyde was that his eyes were bloodshot. An unkempt beard covered his dark face. His general demeanor seemed to be unaffected by the bright sunlight pouring in from the warehouse's large ceiling windows, which lit up the half-built satellites and supercomputers that were scattered around the compound. Instead, the technician's entire sphere seemed restricted to the small corner of the warehouse I'd seen earlier labeled *Neuro-Sync Simulation Development.* In his space there were several swivel chairs, boxes of bulky VR headsets, and those bed-sized tanning booth-esque objects with tools strewn around them.

"Those things are for later on," Clyde said in a cockney British accent as he gestured towards the beds. *For* what *later on? Cyborg implants?* Against my better judgement, I walked up to him. He cleared his throat, looking at the box of VR headsets. "Ms. Stellos told me to show you one of the virtual worlds we've been working on. For now, I'll just be showing you the visual aspects of the simulation—at least, that's all our neuro-sync technology can handle at the moment."

"Okay," I said, nodding at him awkwardly. I still wasn't entirely sure how Abraham's "neuro-sync technology" worked, except that it was apparently painful to develop, but I went along with it. "I'm... Arthur Hesper, by the way."

"I know who you are," he said. He stuck out his hand. As I shook it, I winced at the feeling of his sweaty palm. "I saw you walking around with the boss earlier. I made sure I got here early to watch her test out the kinetic suit. You know what I mean?"

He gave a harsh laugh. I cleared my throat.

"I... uh... okay."

He laughed again. "Anyway, I'm Clyde Jones, simulation technician."

"Nice to meet you. Do... do you go by CJ?" I asked, trying to break the ice a bit.

"No," he said flatly.

"Gotcha. It's just that people called me Art a lot in graduate school," I said, starting to speak quickly. "I assumed that people might shorten other names as well. I never liked being called Art though, so... I don't know why I'm shortening your name either."

Shut up, Arthur.

CJ—*Clyde!*—stood there in silence for a second, just staring at me.

"We should... boot up the simulation," I finally said.

"Yeah."

I sat down in one of the swivel chairs as Clyde handed me the headset. It was like a bulky pair of night-vision goggles with no front lens to look out of. As I slipped it over my head, I noticed that I couldn't see anything inside the headset. It was on correctly, and its power indicator was lit up. I examined the interior part of the headset where the eyepieces sat and was surprised to find that there were no eyepieces at all. There was just foam and a black surface where there would normally be lenses on a VR headset.

I asked Clyde about it.

"Your brain's the eyepiece, mate," he said. "You'll see." He stepped over to a computer and started typing in some commands. He brushed some sweat off his brow and drank from his coffee cup, shaking his head.

"You sure you're awake enough for this?" I asked him, not wanting my brain to be wiped clean by a half-asleep technician. He nodded with his back turned.

"Oh, I'm awake. This..." he said, likely gesturing to his tired face, "is just a byproduct of life at Abraham."

"Really?" I was starting to grow concerned about my own future well-being working at the company. I had the feeling that Clyde, despite how work-worn he seemed, was still relatively new to this job. *After such a short time, did I want to end up like Clyde?* "Are the hours *that* demanding?"

"Not on paper," he said. He lowered his voice a bit. "But once you start working on this project, you get invested. Stellos, crazy though she is, knows what she's doing. It's exciting—*consuming.*"

He pressed the *Enter* key, turned, and gave me a nod. I slipped the headset over my face.

"Now, *close* those eyes and relax your mind."

Relax my mind? How was I supposed to rel—

"Holy..." I said.

As I closed my eyes, I instantly saw a bright blue sphere in front of me. It was like a semi-transparent globe; around it was a strange white backdrop that cast a bright light everywhere around me. *Am I really seeing this?*

Suddenly, the sphere in front of me began to grow. It was as if I was getting closer and closer to a planet; the sphere widened until it took over my entire field of view, with its dark lines and dash marks weaving across everything I could see. A second later, I was floating *inside* of the sphere, its grid-like lattice surrounding me. I couldn't see my arms or legs, but when I spun myself in the chair, I saw the globe rotate around me.

"This is our sandbox area where we can create any simulation," said Clyde, his voice sharply interrupting the silence of the void. "Right now, the headset system is connected to your brain's visual cortex via a weak electrical signal. This signal is overriding the data you would normally receive from your eyes to allow you to focus; our team has spent years optimizing this sensory signal to make sure it doesn't damage your brain."

"Oh, that's good," I said weakly. The void in front of me, being fed into my brain, didn't feel like a daydream. Whenever you *imagine* seeing something—whenever you paint a picture inside your brain—there's always a part of you that *knows* the picture isn't real and keeps it from becoming too immersive. It's that same part of you that leaves room for your imagination to roam; for the dream to maintain a sense of ethereality. The image I was seeing with the headset, though, was *real*—there was no question that I was floating inside of a blue lattice sphere with a white backdrop, the empty maw of *nothing* surrounding me in every direction.

I heard a keyboard click as *nothing* faded away. There was a dark black surface beneath me, where my feet would normally go. I looked up as the pure white of the sky faded away. After only a few seconds, I could see the night sky above me. *Vividly,* like the kind of view you only see in the movies where all of the stars are crystal clear.

Pinpoints of starlight, many of them white but others orange or blue, appeared; some were clearer than others. Some stars were vibrant and bright, while others were dimmer and obviously farther. I'm no astronomer, but I could easily make out some of the constellations.

Just below Orion's Belt, I saw a purple haze. As I focused on it, it was as if the sky around me faded away, and my vision zoomed in on the haze. I hadn't moved anywhere, but I could see the object much more clearly now; wisps of blue and violet gas materialized around a cluster of tiny pin-drop stars.

"Is that the Orion Nebula?" I asked, not knowing if Clyde could even see what I was looking at.

"Probably," he said. "Right now, our simulation can support advanced visual zoom even on dim objects, allowing you to see them with the clarity of a space telescope."

"It's beautiful," I said, gazing at the nebula. Clouds of hazy gas seemed to overlap each other like strands of cotton candy. As I tilted my head, I could see that the object had a three-dimensional effect to it, allowing me to see its many colorful layers.

"Stellar nurseries usually are," Clyde said. "I took care to render it as best as I could."

"Can you see what I'm seeing?" I asked.

"Afraid not," Clyde said. "The information's being fed to your brain as nerve impulses, which don't work the same way as a normal video. We're working on technology that can let us obtain live feeds from the simulations, but we're not quite there yet."

"Okay," I said. *I had the night sky all to myself, then.* I wondered what else I could see. *Is the sky visible in every direction? How far into space can I go?*

Since I'm more of a "try-first-ask-questions-later" type of person, I whipped my head around to look at another part of the sky. *Bad idea.* The world around me lagged tremendously before rapidly snapping into place; it was as if my vision were trying to catch up with my brain. Feeling extremely dizzy, I tried closing my eyes to keep the stars around me from spinning any further. But no matter how hard I felt myself shutting them, the starry world still shined right in front of me. That's when I finally remembered that the image in front of me was wired *directly* to my brain. I couldn't *physically* close my eyes at all.

I had to do it with my mind.

Eyes shut! I commanded. *Eyes shut!* I shouted at my vision to go dark, but nothing happened. I took a deep breath and calmed myself down. I imagined darkness sliding across the sky. I imagined my eyelids closing over my irises, and sure enough, my vision finally went dark. It was refreshing, *quieting* to see nothing in my mind. Slowly, I imagined seeing the starry night sky in front of me again and opened my virtual eyes. The spectacular array of stars came into view.

Even though I could control my mind's eye, that didn't stop me from feeling dizzy.

"There's a bit of lag still left in the system, even with only one sense engaged," Clyde said. "That's the trade-off right now in favor of high detail."

"A little warning next time?" I said to Clyde. *Am I sure this guy knows what he's doing?*

I moved my hand towards the headset to take it off. But my hand had missed entirely; apparently, I was so disoriented that I couldn't even find my own face in the real world. All I could see were the stars around me, which were slowly fading away.

"We hope to have it fixed by the time the simulation connects to the Solar Brain," Clyde said. "The AI that runs that thing should give it all the processing power it needs."

"I take it that's my job to figure out?" I asked with what I hoped was a smile.

"I mean… it's all of ours. I have been working on this for a long time," he said flatly. *The man can't take a joke.*

Although I didn't *want* to rush to judging Clyde the way I had with so many other people in my past, I think I had him figured out. Obviously, he was tired from working long hours, but something told me that putting in all those hours in was *his* choice. That was probably also the reason why he couldn't take a joke about his work—he was too protective of it. *Too possessed by it.* I realized that Clyde was *far* from new here. He must have been with Abraham for years—maybe even since its founding—since there's no *way* anyone could become so invested in this place after just a couple of months here.

Right?

I tried to think through more of Clyde's story, but I was having trouble focusing on reading him while staring at the mosaic of stars in front of me.

Perhaps it was too much for my senses to focus on; *perhaps I wasn't as good at reading people as I thought I was.* I hoped it wasn't the latter.

I shifted my thoughts back to the night sky, which still stretched out like an endless planetarium in every direction. I was about to ask Clyde to take the headset off of me when I saw a light peaking over what I assumed was the horizon.

The world had stabilized by now, and the sky was calmed by the rapidly rising Sun, which cast a crimson-orange-yellow glow over the sky. It was a peaceful, detailed sunrise that began to melt into a bright blue hue, contrasting sharply with the dark floor below. Despite the lagging and the problems I had experienced, I was suddenly calmed by the resplendent colors above me. The emptiness of the sky stretched on endlessly, inviting me to sail through it. Inviting someone to *fill* it with wonder.

This place could be beautiful, I realized. This virtual world really was a "blue-sky" project; with the right technology, the things that Abraham could visualize inside of these simulations would be wondrous. Once those perfect visions were linked seamlessly to their beholder's brain, the possibilities for what the headset's user could see and do were endless. *Is this what Sarah wanted me to see?* There was great potential abound; clearly, Sarah intended for me to realize it.

I reached up, and to my relief, was able to remove the headset with relative ease. The world around me came back into focus, and I saw Clyde staring at me with his arms folded. Despite the creases around his face, I could see eagerness within his eyes.

"So?" he asked, his red eyes widening. "What do you think?"

I handed him the headset and gave him a nod.

"I think—given some improvements to the tech—you have something special here."

"*We* have something special here," I heard Sarah say, and I turned in my chair to find Sarah walking toward me. She was dressed in a much more loose-fitting grey suit, which I assumed was more akin to how she usually appeared. I stood up as she approached. "You are a part of our team now. Our successes are your successes, and vice versa."

"I'm happy to be on board," I said to her, keeping my gaze fixed on the embers in her eyes. I felt sweat form along my back, and it wasn't from the thick suit I was wearing. Sarah was still looking at me, and out of the corner of my eye I saw her rub her hand on the hem of her jacket. She cleared her throat.

"That's good to hear, Dr. Hesper," she said. "Because we have a ton of work to do."

FOUR

S EVEN MONTHS LATER, Abraham's primary supercomputer launched. As the *Astronomical Endeavor Institute* rocket went up out of Cape Canaveral, with the world-generating central computer as its only passenger, I stood next to Sarah Stellos as we watched the space-bound fireball ascend into the Heavens. Abraham had already launched dozens of rockets into space this year, each of them containing the solar reflectors and communication arrays necessary to build the first part of the Solar Sphere. But those had all been supplementary pieces in the construction of Abraham's megastructure. With the launch of the quantum computer—the first of many—the Solar Brain will finally be able to truly *think*. Naturally, all eyes were on our company and its architect.

Sarah had a far-out look in her eyes, staring up at the pale blue sky as if she could see past the atmosphere and make out the farthest galaxies. While most of the other employees, Abraham executives, and audience members watched the launch with anxiety, praying to God for a safe flight, Sarah had a calm confidence that day. Under the Florida sun, her face was as tranquil as the sky and her hands were as still as stone.

Her calmness marked a significant departure from the Sarah Stellos of two weeks ago—hell, two *days* ago—in our central Florida workshop. Sarah didn't abuse her employees—in fact, Abraham was a very positive and productive work environment, where technicians enjoyed generous breaks and comfortable think-spaces. The dress code was relatively casual, which meant that I could get away with a nice button-up t-shirt and pants instead of the thick suit I wore on my first day.

But there was also an unstated, high expectation of the company set by Stellos's punctual and perfectionist attitude. The work *must* be finished on time and be the best it can be, lest she receive an unsatisfactory progress report. I'd overheard a conversation from other employees who said that Sarah had fired an entire team of engineers because they didn't finish a prototype for the satellites' mirrors in time for an important press tour.

Another rumor claimed that members of Abraham's PR staff were hired and fired on a rolling basis depending on the company's public image. And one time, I heard Clyde mention that employees who show up late to work more than once are scheduled to work night shifts much more often.

I didn't know how many of those rumors are actually true, but all I knew was that Sarah was the type of person who would inject herself with over a hundred needles and walk several miles before sunrise just to collect neurotechnological data faster. She was fully committed to finishing the Solar Brain as quickly as possible and expected the same commitment from her employees. Just a week after I was hired in March, Sarah announced her "holiday gift" to the company early—Abraham's primary solar supercomputer sent into space, due in October—two full *months* ahead of schedule. The Christmas spirit in the employee breakroom that day was *truly* palpable.

In reality, though, I spent very little time talking to the other employees, even inside the breakroom. I didn't try to push people away; in fact, I'd often bring up my ideas about Abraham to whoever happened to be standing next to me in the lounge. I thought that "water-cooler talk" was something that coworkers did during their breaks. Instead, I usually received brisk, one-sentence answers from the other employees before they turned away from me to talk about something else like sports or movies or news or some other pop-culture thing that I wasn't privy to. I'd always just focused on my work, since that's what I was good at. I'd made a habit of shutting myself off to distractions, and I was more productive that way. But a couple weeks into my job, having still made zero friends and only a handful of acquaintances, I tried bringing up some movies during our break that I thought my coworkers would appreciate.

"Hey guys... and gals," I said, instantly hating myself, as the group walked in. "Did you hear Stellos's press conference earlier today? The way a lot of the speech went, I was surprised she didn't offer the press a choice between the red pill or the blue pill."

Apparently, they were in the middle of an important engineering conversation.

I nodded at them while reaching for my cup of coffee—coffee that I had forgotten to put a sleeve around. As I frantically let go of the scalding cup, it seemed to tip over in slow motion, and I winced—not from the burning pain in my hand, but at the coffee pouring across the break-room table and dousing the bottom of one of the technicians' laptops. She quickly stood up, trying to remove her laptop from the table, and wound up smacking her head on the cabinet behind her.

I stopped trying to make friends pretty soon after that.

Also, I found out early on that most employees didn't *get* personal offices—we were expected to set up our laptops at the many open tables, desks, and couches strewn around the workshop and office buildings. I didn't mind doing so at first, as the ability to move to a new location whenever I needed a change of scenery was actually refreshing. About a month in, though, as the amount of code I was writing piled up and the number of tablets and laptops I needed to watch at the same time increased, I realized that I needed a more permanent place to work. I knew that there weren't any vacant offices in the stubby pickle that I could use, so I pitched an alternative idea to Sarah.

"You want to work from home?" Stellos asked me as I stood in front of her desk with ten laptops in my arms.

"Just for writing my codes," I said, trying to see her expression over the stack of devices. "I'll still come in for the construction checks and our daily meetings."

"I suppose... that will be alright," she said. "The other employees will miss seeing you around, though."

"I don't think that's true," I replied, finally catching a glimpse of her amused expression. "I think they'll be relieved to learn I won't be taking up any more space in the breakroom."

"Tell me, Arthur: are you requesting to work from home because you're having trouble making friends here?" she asked in a way that almost sounded patronizing. I furrowed my brow at her (not that she would have been able to see my face over the tower of laptops).

"*No,*" I said. "I just need more space to work."

Sarah was quiet for a moment before responding. "In that case, make sure you get home early today to receive the packages."

Packages?

I arrived home at 4pm to find a delivery man indignantly waiting at the bottom of my apartment steps with a clipboard. As soon as I signed for *the packages*, I gasped out loud as a crew of four men carried several large boxes out of the truck and up to my apartment. I barely got my door open before the men barreled into my office, carrying a cushioned Abraham-esque office chair, an outlet- and lamp-fitted wooden desk, and a curved, 60-inch, ultra-high-definition computer monitor.

In no time at all, my previously-barren office was decked out with state-of-the-art appliances and devices. As the last delivery man left my apartment, he gave me a small piece of paper. It was a handwritten note; in a scrawled cursive, it simply read:

From a Friend.

In the months leading up to the launch, I supervised the final develop-ment of the Solar Brain's operating system, examining the machinery and codes inside and out to make sure they worked. This involved visiting both the cleanroom and the software development labs and checking with the other technicians that everything involving the Brain's supercomputer was running smoothly from a network perspective. Even though I was their superior, it still felt awkward telling longtime employees how to do their jobs, but Sarah was adamant that I investigate each of their projects thoroughly. Oftentimes, she followed me around; if I thought something looked good, it was good to her. If I suggested a change, she commanded it. Whenever I finished my inspections and left the warehouse to drive home, I always had a feeling that the other employees were staring daggers at my back.

Altogether, though, it was fulfilling work, and my position paid quite generously. More than that, the projects I was working on were *fun*. All of the projects at Abraham were. We were building a machine that linked to the nervous system, allowing users to become *inhabitants* of the virtual world they were in. The *possibility* attached to the project made my work almost addicting, like the pace at which I worked would directly affect how soon the Brain was finished. Of course, that didn't alleviate the immense pressures that came with my *real* job at the company—building the *Advanced Learning Intelligence*.

The absolute powerhouse of Abraham, the Intelligence is what drives the *thinking* part of the Solar Brain. Of course, the megastructure's primary function, tucked within a list of quantum-computing measures designed to solve complex equations, program space missions, and do the otherwise impossible, is to serve as a VR platform—the most powerful one ever built. Beyond its machine-learning capabilities, the Intelligence not only creates small VR spaces based on what its user wants, but will supposedly create entire virtual worlds by learning more about our own. And with the staggering power of the Sun at its use, there are limitless possible commands it could execute. And I wrote plenty of those commands, as well as the AI's entire structure, using a new programming language created specifically for the Intelligence. *Advance++,* initially developed by some of the technicians at Abraham but refined by yours truly, was an unholy combination of Python, C++, and some of our own syntax that could process commands at an incredibly high speed.

I learned the language quite quickly, but was surprised to find that Sarah also knew a great deal about coding in *Advance++* as well. She would routinely send me scripted suggestions in response to some of the questions I had for her, and barring some minor syntax errors her code usually worked. Everything on the AI engineering side was going perfectly, but what kept stumping me was Stellos's precious *aesthetic.*

Between routine code checks and troubleshooting, I spent the first month or so of the project banging my head against the wall to figure out the avatar design for the Intelligence. How should it speak: robotically or naturally? What should it look like? I'd originally settled on a tiny blue dot that pulsed whenever it spoke, but that wasn't *nearly* enough for Sarah. She wanted something more *personal. How personal? Who* is *the Intelligence? And is it an* it *or a* he *or a* she? I must've told Sarah at least a dozen times that this was *not* my line of work—the AI engineering *behind the scenes* was my PhD focus.

"Waste of time," she deemed my degree with a sigh. I replied, like I had many times before, that I needed my education to gain the knowledge necessary to build the Intelligence. Of course, she told me, like she had many times before, that the knowledge I'd gained from my accelerated research program were things that I could have learned with experience. That *she* and her team, most of whom didn't have doctoral degrees, were pushing the technology further than anyone ever had while *I* was still in school.

"And to think," she said. "You could've spent that time working here with me."

Sarah maintained that I had to know the Intelligence on a *human* level before I could truly make it function. I was accustomed to giving my programs a high level of machine-learning capabilities, but the ability to choose between data based on a set of fixed parameters was different than what Sarah was describing. Although she never used the word, Sarah seemed to want our Intelligence to develop *emotion*—the ability to empathize with its user and build them a virtual world grounded in their tastes.

"We're linking people's nervous systems—people's *minds*—into this virtual Brain. A new universe," Sarah had said to me wistfully. She was standing in the hallway outside her office, looking through a window at the half-finished supercomputer launch capsule inside the cleanroom. She seemed lost in her own thoughts, as she had been describing the potential of the Intelligence for about ten minutes now. She finally seemed to remember that I was still standing there and looked back at me quickly. "Even if they're only visiting for a short while, the worlds we create for our users have to be *real*—so we need an intelligence that's *real* enough to create them."

Even as she nodded at me, a confused expression took over her face. "Did that... answer your question?"

All I had asked her was if she wanted her coffee black.

After months of work passed by, the rocket carrying the thoroughly inspected and highly intelligent supercomputer finally went up into space. But long after the AEI rocket was no longer in view, Sarah still stood at the top of the bleachers overlooking the launch point. She hadn't budged, and I wasn't sure if she wanted to be left alone or if my leaving would be rude. So, I just stood there, waiting for what felt like hours as the Sun set over the horizon. I tried to think of something to say the entire time, but everything that came to mind would have been either too banal or too forced to impress her. I knew I was overthinking things, but if Sarah Stellos was your girlfriend, you'd overthink things too.

I should probably slow down for a minute.

Let me be crystal clear. Sarah Stellos and I had a strictly professional relationship while we were working, and as far as the public was concerned, in general. She actually made me sign an NDA after our first kiss, which was more of a playful peck that we shared after we finally found a supercomputer capsule prototype that *wouldn't* blow up when deployed. We both laughed it off nervously, and no one else was around, but four months into our dating Sarah was more paranoid than ever. Some small-time reporter, trying to catch her big break, had caught us a couple of nights prior to then enjoying dinner together at a nearby restaurant and wrote some scandalous article about a conflict of interest, or something. I'll never know exactly what it said because Sarah secretly paid the local news station $100,000 to bury the story before it surfaced. I was genuinely surprised that she didn't also bury the reporter.

Yeah. I should probably slow down a little bit more.

FIVE

L ET'S REWIND.

My "non-public, non-existent" relationship with Sarah started back on a late-June scorcher, months before the rocket launch, when everyone was crowded inside the workshop to stay cool. We were supposed to be outside testing the stress capacity of the supercomputer's solar panel candidates (which basically consisted of launching rocks at them until they shattered), but it was so hot that even Sarah—the workaholic supreme that she is—postponed it a day. I could tell that the decision to comply with OSHA heat guidelines was weighing on her as she sat by her office window, intently staring out at the black pavement in front of the workshop. I couldn't tell if she was meditating or on the verge of spontaneously combusting, but it was a Friday at the end of a long workweek, and so after knocking on her office door and entering, I tried something bold. Something that still surprises me now.

"Sarah, would you like to join me for some ice cream?" There was a parlor in town—*Heavenly's Creamery*—that I'd visited a couple times after work that was quite good, and I thought I would ask Sarah as a courtesy.

Okay, maybe I was testing the waters with her.

Okay, maybe I was *definitely* testing the waters with her. So? Whenever I talked to her—which was really, *really* often since Sarah loved her daily progress meetings—I always felt butterflies in my stomach. I liked her, and I always wondered if she felt the same way about me. I mean, I *knew* there was no chance that *the* Sarah Stellos *actually* felt the same way about me, but after weeks of looking for some sign that she did, I decided to take the risk. Maybe she'd say no and suggest another time, or maybe she'd say no and laugh in my face. Either way, her response surprised me.

"Sure."

I drove us over there—an absolutely terrifying experience, considering who was in the passenger seat of my SUV—and we both had small vanilla ice cream cups (*yes*, I paid) as we talked. Not about the project, but about ourselves. We talked all afternoon. Some things about Sarah I already knew from her Wikipedia page; she was born in Greece before her parents, Jeffrey and Elizabeth, moved to the United States. I knew that she was the great grandniece of a breakthrough astrobiologist named Megan Stellos. I also knew that she, too, was orphaned at a young age. But there were some things that the internet wasn't yet privy to, but that she didn't mind telling me. Like how she had never learned to ride a bicycle or voted in an election. How she'd once broken a classmate's nose in fourth grade for calling her benefactor, Dr. Matthews, a "crazy old man." How she'd done the same thing in high school and in her first year of college, but by then had enough money to keep it quiet.

"Dr. Matthews meant a lot to you, huh?" I asked in between scoops of vanilla.

"He gave me everything. After my parents..." Sarah looked down, trailing off for only a moment before looking back up at me. "Uncle Richard is the one who took me in. He was almost always busy with his work, so I barely saw him. But when I did, he showed me what he was working on. His colleagues—hell, *everyone*—laughed at him for believing in things like Dyson Spheres and endless energy. He figured it out, though—three months before I lost him, he drew up the blueprints for the *exact same* satellites we're building now and started gathering the renewable resources needed to make them. He worked until the end—and died without ever seeing his work come to life." She spoke with reverence.

"You would have made him proud," I said. Sarah lowered her eyes, but she shook her head with a grin.

"You know, Dr. Hesper," she said. "You're the first person to ever tell me that."

"Okay, okay, I get it. Cliché."

"I'm being serious," she said. She looked into my eyes. The ice cream melted in my stomach. "All of my uncle's colleagues laughed their way through his funeral, the snobbish assholes that they are. And my entire family is gone. No one was left to tell me which path I should take, so I made it myself. I appreciate your kind words."

"It's... nothing," I said.

"Not to me."

We sat there silently for a moment.

As she stared down into her empty ice cream container, I pretended not to notice the cashier at the counter behind Sarah nudging his buddy and pointing enthusiastically at her. Either the cashier was a technology nerd, or Sarah was even more of a celebrity than I thought. *A celebrity that I was eating* ice cream *with...*

"So," Sarah said. "Is working at home going well for you?"

"Yeah, it's been good," I said. "Quiet... I mean."

"We've missed you over at the office," she said.

"I really doubt that's true," I said. Sarah rolled her eyes, but I nodded. "Seriously! I've just... never been good at making friends. I don't *try* to be abrasive or awkward or antisocial and I really don't think I am. I'm just bad at connecting with people." At this point, I knew I was rambling, but Sarah just smiled.

"I meant... *I've* missed you over at the office," Sarah said, slowly bringing her gaze up to meet mine.

"Oh," I said.

"I know that we meet every day, but I do look forward to those times," Sarah said, straightening up in her stool. "Well, I *should* look forward to our meetings—that's what a good boss should do, right?" Sarah laughed, and I along with her.

"I suppose that's a trivial detail," she eventually said, smiling faintly.

I smiled back at her.

"Not to me."

By the time we drove back to the Abraham workshop, it was getting dark, so Sarah had me drop her off by her car to go home (which, I imagined, was a penthouse condominium that was far more luxurious than my apartment). As she stepped out of my SUV and closed the door, I prepared to drive away. Lingering in front of her luxury car would've been awkward, even for me. But just as I reached out to put my car in drive, she placed her hand on the door and looked me right in the eyes.

"Thank you, Arthur," she said, not shifting her gaze.

"For the ice cream? No problem," I said.

"That, and for the afternoon. It was... really nice," she remarked, still staring at me. About two seconds later, she seemed to become aware of the moment's tenderness, and quickly turned away.

My mouth seemed to be on autopilot when I said: "Same time, next week?"

I prayed she didn't hear me. I was *not* qualified to be asking a woman out—to be asking *Sarah Stellos* out—that casually. Sarah *knew* that, too. To my terror, she did hear me, and turned. I waited for the laugh; instead, she smiled.

At that point, I felt like I was on top of the world—like I'd achieved the impossible. I was really hoping for a *yes*, so I felt my face fall a little when she replied, "I can't, I have investor meetings all day next Friday."

I nodded, closing my mouth, and turned back to face the road. She reached for the door of her car.

Before she pulled the handle, though, she continued. "But... I'll see you *Monday* for coffee."

We locked eyes for only an instant, but it was in that instant that I fell in love.

Since that conversation—our first date, perhaps—our romance has been defined by an endless torrent of lines of code, an unholy amount of coffee breaks (always dark roast for Sarah), and sneaking in dates wherever we could. Keep in mind that I had never dated *anyone* before, and I didn't exactly have someone who could give me pointers. And as I typed the words "first time dating rich girl CEO please help" into the Google search bar, I quickly realized I was in over my head. But I pressed forward anyway.

My first couple dates with Sarah were back to that ice cream place. It was good ice cream, and it broke up the hot Summer days nicely. Eventually, though, I realized that the CEO of Abraham was probably hoping for something a little more... *more*. But we really couldn't go *out* to any popular restaurants, so Sarah often had the company caterer make something expensive and we ate late at night in her office. Technically, that meant *she* was paying for our dates, which made me uncomfortable. If I didn't pay, would she think I was a moocher? Worse: would she think I was only dating her for the money? That thought began to consume me, and I couldn't focus on my work for days. I just sat at my desk, staring blankly at lines of code while wondering what Sarah Stellos thought of me.

As we ate in her office on our third "proper" date, I tried to read Sarah's facial expression. We had talked for a short time while the food was being prepared, but once it arrived, she just looked down at her plate, twirling her fork in her *capellini-lobster* stir. My stomach dropped, and it wasn't from the deliciously expensive pasta. She wasn't looking at me, but seemed more focused on smoothing out the wrinkles in her pants with her free hand. She looked *dissatisfied* with something, and I had a hunch it wasn't the food.

I've always been able to read people decently well, even if I can't socialize with most of them. As I said, I had a remarkably good talent as a child for deciphering people's emotions. However, I've also noticed—much to my disappointment—that the more I focused on research and computing, the more I lost that ability. I'd grown more accustomed to reading *programs* than my peers.

Ever since I started dating, I've been trying to reawaken my *sense* of people that has long been dormant. I wanted to be emotionally *there* for Sarah. So, I studied her words, her nonverbal cues, and even her texts as best I could—ten times harder than I studied the Intelligence. Is that what everyone goes through when they're dating? I had no way of knowing. All I did know was that something was bothering Sarah—something about *me*.

I decided to come right out with it.

"Sarah, I'm *not* dating you for financial reasons. I... I really enjoy our dates, and want to be able to pay for them. I want to—" I cut my words off, stopping myself from shoving my foot in my mouth any further. She kept looking down at her pasta before taking another bite. She glanced up at me as I continued. "I'm sorry, I—shouldn't have said..."

"Do you feel you need to pay for our meals because you're... the *man?*" she asked. "You feel you need to *impress* me?"

I felt my hands get sweaty. I shouldn't have brought up finances with her, but I *needed* to know where we were headed. I'd never dated anyone before, and I really enjoyed spending time with Sarah. If I screwed things up or things went sour, would we still be able to *talk* to each other? *Work* with each other? And *were* we even dating? Did *she* think we were dating? She used the word *meals* there—not *dates*. We *weren't* dating—I realized. We hadn't kissed yet, and she *certainly* wasn't thinking about doing anything more.

Once again, I'd walked myself into my own trap. All that was left to do was embrace it.

"Yes," I said. "I do want to impress you. I do like you."

Sarah thought about that for a moment and looked back up at me. "I've never... *dated* anyone either, Arthur. Not like this," she said. My heart skipped a beat. She put down her fork. "I mean, I had a couple of flings in college, but I never *cared* about any of them. After high school, I went to an entitled, snob college and had to deal with entitled, snob boys."

She continued. "They have nothing to prove to anyone; they'll take life on a silver platter. Any one of those boys—hell, *most* sane people—would eat this thousand-dollar lobster-pasta without complaining." I felt my eyes widen as I heard the price. She smiled. "Then again, I wouldn't give such things to anyone. You want to impress me, and I admire that."

She looked down at her pasta again. I didn't know what words I could say that would adequately follow hers. Whenever Sarah opened up about her past, it seemed like she just wanted someone to listen, not linger on the subject. Instead, I took a safer—yet still paradoxically perilous—angle.

"So... what *is* bothering you?" I asked as sincerely as I could. "What *else* is wrong?"

She stayed focused on her food and smiled. "I'm trying to figure out how to tell someone that I like him too, but he won't stop asking me questions."

A few weeks after that date—after many other late-night meals, ice cream trips, and semi-awkward progress meetings—we finally had our first kiss. It was my first kiss *ever.* It was quick and undramatic, and Sarah never really mentioned it again. But it was then that we *really* started dating—or, as our non-disclosure agreement would put it, *engaging in a confidential, consensual romantic relationship.* I'd like to say we began moving quickly as a couple, going out to new restaurants, taking day-trips together, or doing whatever two people who are dating do (since I myself would not know).

In reality, the majority of the time we spent together was in the workplace, attending company meetings and project progress sessions and generally working on our *jobs;* that is, we certainly did not have much alone time. The few romantic moments we *did* share were rare and were very often close calls. Sarah and I were in her office one day engaging in a *definitely non-public display of affection* when Sarah's CFO almost walked in on us. Rather than do the intelligent thing like leave before she entered, I hid under Sarah's desk for *two hours* while they talked about *liability control* (I can't make this up). And let me tell you, Sarah did *not* rush the conversation.

After that point, I decided to stop making office visits during the workday. Eventually, we became too busy and too tired for our evening dates, and the only times we really had to devote to romance were our once-a-month trips to Sarah's lakeside cabin in upstate New York.

In between the chaos of the work, those weekend excursions were when I felt like I had an actual girlfriend, and that we were an actual couple deeply in love. And we *were*, based on the tender moments we shared. Based on how, when I embraced Sarah, her inner flame thawed any ice between us; based on how, when we kissed, electricity sparked. She was the first woman I'd ever *been* with—I didn't know *how* to feel except for enamored. Sarah Stellos was intimidating on most days, but our trips were the few times that Sarah Stellos was—*how to put this?*—*human*. Heck, they're when *I* felt human.

Completely secluded from civilization (but within a fenced perimeter, guarded 24/7 by a seemingly invisible security staff), the wooden one-story house was a cozy getaway on a serene lake. Enclosed within the twenty-acre retreat were groves of apple trees, wide clearings perfect for practicing golf, and various hidden brooks ideal for tripping over. The world was serene there. Visiting the retreat felt like visiting the Earth in its oldest and purest form, where falling in love is easy. On a late summer night, crickets and frogs would make their presence known, and damp mist would creep up the cabin porch and settle at the door, waiting patiently for the house's inhabitants to return.

I remember one of the trips especially well. It was Sarah's birthday, and we'd spent the entire day hiking through the apple tree groves and sharing "quality time" together inside the cabin (I *need* to work on my euphemisms for sex).

I knew she liked running, so I bought her an exercise watch as a gift, not realizing that she already had the newer version of that same model. Still, she wore it during the day, most likely to humor me. That evening, she asked me what I wanted for *my* birthday, and I revealed to her that I didn't know *when* my actual birthday was. As a baby, I was found at the orphanage in the fall, but by then I was already several months old. So, Sarah dubbed September 9TH as my birthday, too, and asked me what I wanted. As she did, a firefly flashed overhead, and as soon as I looked up at the indigo hue of the sky above the sunset, I knew the answer.

An hour later, Sarah and I were lying side by side in a clearing a few hundred feet from the cabin. I'd lived my entire life in cities and had never really gotten the chance to do some proper stargazing, but I couldn't think of a better place—or a better person—to try it out with. Neither of us brought a blanket, so our clothes sank into the damp grass while we stared up at the starry sky. We pointed at constellations, bright dots that we assumed were planets, and even the occasional shooting star. Eventually, we went on to discussing other things.

"Do you ever think about them?" I asked her, choosing not to take my eyes off the glowing points of light above us. I may have only recently turned twenty-four years old, but I figured I had a right to say wistfully philosophical things every now and then. Sarah disagreed.

"And *tonight,* playing the *vague pronoun game* is Arthur E. Hesper from Brooklyn, New York..." she began wryly. Sarah had nothing if not her wit. And money. And status.

"Parents," I said. I felt comfortable enough to talk about that with Sarah. "I've never met mine. The nuns at my orphanage never tracked them down, so I never knew who they were or why I was left."

"Do you... *want* to know?" Sarah asked. I glanced over at her; her body was barely discernable in the darkness, but I could feel the warmth coming from her.

I knew firsthand that Sarah could find out whatever she wanted, and for some time, I wondered if she knew who my parents were. But based on the tone of the question, I could tell that she *didn't* know—that she'd respected me enough not to pry my past open any further, but that she was willing to if that's what I wanted.

"No," I finally said. I had given this a lot of thought before. "I have no memory of them. To me, they may as well be strangers, whoever they were. Finding them won't fix anything from the past. You can't change the hand you're dealt in life, only play with what you have."

"I never took you as a poker player," she said.

"Neither did my roommate in college until I won three hundred fifty dollars off of him," I said. "When I was a child, I would play cards with the other orphans when the nuns weren't looking. For me, there wasn't much else in the way of *fun* at the orphanage, you know?"

Actually, she didn't know, I realized. Sarah didn't give any response, but just laid next to me in silence. I considered asking about her parents again, but I realized that she might not have wanted to talk about them.

Changing the subject, I pointed up at the sky.

"Do you ever think about *them?*"

"Aliens?" she asked.

"Aliens," I said. We were on the same wavelength down to the picometer when it came to the "big questions" of science. "I mean… *someday,* Abraham might take over the Solar System. Do you ever wonder if anyone is out there—in the Solar System *or* beyond—watching us?" It felt like a strange question to ask the descendent of a famous astrobiologist, but it seemed appropriate for the moment.

"We both know, Arthur, that there are two possibilities if there are," she said as if reprimanding a child. "Either those faraway stargazers are microorganisms that never reached the same level of development that we did, *or* they are an advanced civilization watching our every move."

She spoke with eloquence and precision, as if she'd rehearsed the speech before. Her voice drew me in, inviting me to briefly share in her optimistically nihilist thought experiment.

"No other options?" I asked.

"It's a harsh universe," she said. "The first scenario implies that Earth is unusually lucky to have developed intelligent life, and that an extinction-level event could be waiting around the corner to check our hubris. The second scenario implies that it's only a matter of time before our overlords—*alien* overlords—step on us pesky little humans like ants." Her voice didn't raise in intensity once; her perfect pitch was unbroken. She spoke about extinction in the same way one might talk about their week.

"So either way, Earth is doomed," I summarized. A more inexperienced man would say *so much for a light conversation*, but the discussion was spot-on for us. I reached out and took her hand in my own. I wondered if it was right to tell her that *I loved her* yet. I didn't know if that's what couples say to each other after only a few months of dating. So instead, I kept on holding her hand, looking up at the stars.

"Heaven's tapestry," I said. "I'll always marvel at God's work up there."

I'm not an *ultra*-religious person, per se, and I hardly ever speak with such piety. But on a beautiful night like that, though, the words just came out. Maybe it was my time at the Catholic children's home speaking, but I've always found belief in a higher purpose comforting. Growing up as an orphan with not much except my own thoughts to dwell on, it helped to believe that there was a Being greater than us, guiding us.

Okay, yes, I'm a religious scientist. That may be an oxymoron, but so what? I was also an inexperienced geek dating the richest woman in the world *and* a twenty-four-year-old designing a virtual universe. Nothing in my life made sense, and I was content with that.

"Uh... yeah," Sarah replied. *Oddly terse for her,* I thought. I wondered if she was religious at all. I would've asked, but I figured she was probably too exhausted for any more existential conversation. So, I kept on staring, wrapped up with her underneath the blanket of stars.

"Thank you," I said.

I heard her turn her head towards me.

"For what?" she asked.

"Being amazing," I said. "Going out with me."

"I am pretty amazing," she said. I could hear the smile in her voice. "And... you're welcome?"

I decided to ask one more question.

"Why me?" I asked. "Why would you—*Sarah Stellos*—date *me*?" I knew I was being insecure, but for a long time I couldn't help but wonder *why*. And in that moment, I felt strong enough to ask for the answer. I was waiting for either sarcasm or nothing at all; either answer seemed like the most likely and most natural for Sarah. Eventually, you would think I'd learn to stop trying to predict my girlfriend.

"Because you didn't ask *Sarah Stellos* out for ice cream, all those weeks ago," Sarah said. "You asked me."

The following morning, Sarah and I went out for a run around the lake. I had known from my first day of work that Sarah was on the athletic side, but I *didn't* know that she ran track in high school and jogged five miles every other day of the week. The first time I'd ever visited her cabin and Sarah asked what I wanted to do, I stupidly suggested we go for a *light* jog through the apple tree groves. Maybe I wanted to see the scenery, or maybe I wanted to impress her. Several visits later, Sarah would have us running around the entire retreat every morning we were there—as if I wasn't tired enough from a lack of sleep.

So, the day after stargazing together on the field, the more accurate description would probably be: "Sarah went for a run, and I breathlessly stumbled my way forward about a hundred feet behind her."

We ran along a dirt pathway through acres of hills and pine trees. It was a chillier morning than usual, especially for late Summer. I was close to shivering in my sweatshirt and joggers (which I had bought specifically for our runs); I didn't know how Sarah wasn't freezing in her tank top and shorts.

As I trailed behind her, I took some time to admire the landscape. I'd always been a city boy, so being surrounded by nature was still novel to me. I smiled whenever a frog leapt out of my path. I brushed my hand along the stalks of tallgrass near the lake as Sarah ran past them. Even things like the smell of rotting apple cores from the grove and the stickiness of the dew were vital and refreshing. They made me feel a connection to the world around me that I wasn't used to. Even if the retreat was secluded from "the world," it still resonated of a living, breathing Earth. I could feel something beneath it; *I could feel Someone above it.* I wondered if any other "city people" felt this way around nature, or if "rural people" even did. Maybe I was just weird.

As the distance between Sarah and me increased, I realized just how *alone* we were out here. I'd always imagined that CEOs were constantly surrounded by armed bodyguards, but Sarah rarely was. One or two large men usually stood near Sarah during press conferences or public Abraham events, but I almost never saw guards with her when she went out. They weren't at the ice cream parlor or restaurant we went to, and certainly weren't inside my apartment. One time, I asked her about her lack of security; her response was simply that she didn't need "babysitters" with her wherever she went. Still, Sarah did mention on our first trip to the cabin that there were cameras and guard outposts placed around the retreat for our safety. She offered to show them to me, but I was more interested in relaxing by the cabin than in stressing over our clearly comprehensive security.

After about a mile farther than I thought I could run, I gave a breathless shout towards Sarah as I collapsed toward a patch of dirt next to the lake. I needed a break, and as I chugged down my water bottle, I could tell she was walking towards me, indignantly checking her new smartwatch for her workout stats. As I finished catching my breath, I looked up at Sarah, who was gazing out over the water. The seven-o'clock Sun was rising high in the sky behind a sheet of stratus clouds, casting a pale glow over the water.

"Makes you think… about our Sphere," I said in between breaths. At that point, the supercomputer's rocket launch was still a month away, so all Abraham had in outer space was a collection of satellites orbiting our star, swarming like bees waiting for their first command from their queen. "All the way out there… behind the sky."

"It's pretty impressive," Sarah said. I rolled my eyes at her playfully as she backtracked. "I don't mean *me*—by *impressive* I mean the *human* achievement of putting—oh *shut up!*" She gently kicked my leg as I started laughing. It was one of those rare but beautiful moments when Sarah got caught up in her own words—seeing her face turn red at least gave me an indication that she was a human like the rest of us. Over the past few months, I could tell how tightly wound she was from the work, so it gave me a heartwarming relief to see her loosen up—even if it was just a little. Sarah was a much calmer person when she ran. That's why, despite how painful our jogs were, I pushed through them.

"You're allowed to be proud of yourself," I said with a laugh that hurt my winded lungs. I rested my hands on the path; dirt rolled between my fingers.

"You're making me look… arrogant," she jokingly complained. "Like I'm calling *myself* impressive."

"You *are* impressive," I said. I tried to force myself onto my feet to stand with her, but I immediately grew lightheaded and sat back down. I blinked a couple of times before reaching for my water. Sarah sat down next to me and wrapped her arm around my shoulder. I leaned my head onto hers.

"Damn right," she nodded.

"What made you decide to build *this?*" I asked, nodding in the direction of the cabin, which was nestled in a misty clearing on the opposite side of the lake.

"I never had it growing up," she said. I looked up at her brown eyes, which were locked onto the cabin firmly. "Even rich girls have their place, and mine was inside a dreary mansion. I could only sit, study, and dream of somewhere that I could roam free. Free from the bookshelves, free from bleak buildings, free from loneliness."

She kept her gaze fixated on the cabin across from her; for a split second, it looked like her eyes were watery. But as she wiped the sweat from her brow, I realized I was mistaken.

She continued: "I made this place so I could be free. And once the Brain is ready, we can be free there, too."

She spoke with certainty—with *prophecy*—and the only thing I could do was believe her. And, when sitting next to a beautiful lakeside with a beautiful girl, that was very easy to do. Her dreams were as massive as her Solar Sphere, and I wanted more than anything to make them a reality. Leaning into Sarah's warmth, I realized that bringing her vision to life was more than a wish. It was what I was *meant* to do.

With my free arm, I gestured out around the lake.

"All of this," I said, waving my hand over the water, trees, sky, and *world* itself. "Needs to be *in* the Brain. The *beauty* of nature... we won't be truly successful unless we can replicate it."

Sarah pondered that for only a moment.

"Why replicate what you can improve?"

I still didn't know what the Intelligence was supposed to look like.

It was the day after the rocket launch, and I was staring at my basic "sandbox" where I could create and test random new things. Every programmer likes to start with a home base of sorts, a playground where they can let their ideas roam in a familiar—and personal—environment. Drawn in perfect 3D animation, complete with every wisp of mist and firefly glow, was Sarah's cabin. It was rendered in a fantastic, whimsical way, with the quaint house tucked beneath the deep lavender sky and the dark green treetops buzzing with birds. A large crescent moon illuminated the lakeside setting in the way that the screen illuminated my doubtlessly exhausted face. I never showed this corner of my desktop to Sarah, even though we'd been together for quite a while now.

As romantic as my love life has been, the past few weeks were truly taxing. Fuel shortages were threatening to delay Abraham's launch and thus slow the construction of the Solar Brain. Bugs seemed to be running more rampant than ever in the virtual worlds, and our entertainment division was working overtime to squash them. And the endless slew of preparations that still needed to be made sent the company into chaos before our dramatic launch, which according to the media, was *the* definitive event of the year. Sarah practically had a conniption when one of the Board members—a PR enthusiast—asked if Abraham's launch could take place a day later to avoid a publicity overlap with the premiere of *ScorpionStar III*, Hollywood's latest superhero movie. I think that person was fired. Company morale was on the fritz, as was mine after two eighty-hour workweeks of nearly nonstop systems inspections.

Sarah and I were normally in sync. We agreed on decisions, and when we disagreed, we calmly discussed things over in the way coworkers or a couple might. She usually wound up being "right," I came to realize. But a few days ago, amid the mayhem, she asked how the Advanced Learning Intelligence was coming. She had originally wanted it ready by the launch, but I had made it clear that such a feat was impossible. The software could be uploaded wirelessly as the computer made its way to the Sun, I told her. At this point, though, she just wanted a good progress report. When I mentioned that I still hadn't designed the most important feature—the physical appearance of the Intelligence itself—she got angry.

"Then what the hell did I hire you for?" she yelled, storming off. The other employees didn't dare talk—or even breathe—and once Sarah left, they avoided looking at me. I knew she was just stressed, but naturally her words hurt. After that, the two of us resumed business as if nothing had happened, not mentioning the incident in the following days. Likely, this was because we didn't see each other—or talk—outside the office during that week. But we carried that tension between us even as the rocket went up, and I knew we both felt it.

After the launch, a great weight was lifted off everybody's shoulders. For the next two months, little was to be done at the workshop beyond monitoring the nuclear-powered spacecraft, which was a straightforward task. Nonetheless, I was still recovering from the strenuous week, and I felt absolutely wiped the evening of the launch. I drove Sarah home, and we barely spoke a word to each other. As tired as I was, I stayed up late thinking about the Intelligence. About how I could finish it, *for her.*

The following day, even though it was a Saturday, I kept on rifling through ideas. I had all the basic concepts, and even most of the practical functionality, down: instant speech cataloguing, worldbuilding autonomy, and a great deal of supercomputing functions at its disposal. Right now, though, the entirety of the physical algorithm was contained within a tiny blue orb that hovered in the middle of my white screen. I wound up using a generic robot voice for its commands; at first an American man's voice, later a girl's. I made that switch when I started seeing Sarah.

When I wasn't working out computational bugs, I smacked my head trying to encode an appearance for the Intelligence. Nothing felt sufficient. How was I supposed to design a virtual *person?* I kept having the feeling that I wasn't *meant* to—not only did I feel that this kind of work was better left to a graphic designer, but that programming a *person* was something that only God was qualified to do. I always shook off that feeling and kept working, but I almost never wrote more than a few lines of code before deleting them in frustration. I sat at my computer all morning and most of the afternoon until around 3pm, when I heard a knock on the door. I opened it to find Sarah dressed in light blue sweats and holding a pizza in both hands.

"Hey!" I said, surprised by the sudden visit. Sarah was deliberate in almost everything she did; unannounced visits weren't her style, unless they were intended as progress checks meant to scare the living daylights out of unsuspecting employees.

"Hey," she began. "There's... a lot of trash by the front of your building."

"Yeah, umm..." I stammered. "That's not mine. It's... a whole thing..."

"Okay," Sarah said. "Is this how you usually answer the door?" I furrowed my eyebrows, trying to figure out what she meant. I looked down and painfully remembered that I hadn't put on any pants that morning. Even though Sarah was my girlfriend and had seen me wearing less, that didn't change the fact that I was standing in front of the company's CEO in a pair of checkered boxers.

One embarrassing hunt for jeans later, Sarah and I sat at my desktop working on the Intelligence. I had figured the pizza was Sarah's gesture of goodwill after all the stress, and I knew her way of making it up to me was by helping me out with the program herself. And I loved her for it. She would never apologize for (or even mention) the yell, but she didn't have to.

When I took my screen out of sleep mode, I panicked when I realized that the artificial cabin was in full view, and that Sarah was staring at it. If she didn't get angry at me for rendering her private cabin with company software, then would she laugh at me, the hopeless romantic? If there was one thing Sarah Stellos *wasn't,* it was sentimental. Worse: would she think I was *obsessed?* I turned around with my mouth agape, ready to explain, but to my great relief, she was smiling.

We worked out the last of the bugs in the code. As we did, we realized that the Intelligence's abilities might have been too wide in scope. We paired down its autonomy to restrict the Intelligence's use of vocal recognition and emulation to *inside* the virtual world only. *Imagine if the Brain was feeling a little vengeful and mimicked the voices of world leaders to obtain control of nukes.* That would be an *awkward* call from the Pentagon.

Also, AI-hijacked nuclear bombs would *probably* be quite bad for the Earth.

I was surprised that no one had thought to limit the Intelligence's communication capabilities before now. Then again, no one had worked on the software for nearly as long as I had, so the task of catching these problems and limiting the AI's powers was on me. For some reason, it seemed like that issue was secondary to Sarah.

Instead, we designed the Intelligence's abilities to be much more focused. The system became an advanced virtual assistant, designed to help users navigate and develop virtual worlds for themselves. It would have an extreme versatility in collecting knowledge about our world and controlling a *simulated* environment, but that was it. Through many restrictions in its base program, the system's capabilities would be limited to applications involving the Solar Brain, and could be overridden by its user with ease. Thus, through our careful revisions, any risks that the AI posed to Earth were immediately nullified. That's the benefit of working in industry, I realized: one's "mad scientist" tendencies were always checked both by consumers and by superiors. I briefly wondered if anyone kept Sarah's in check.

"I don't like the name *Intelligence,*" Sarah stated around midnight. After working away the entire evening, my mind was almost one with the computer monitor at that point. I didn't have a visual design or modulated voice yet, but almost every other attribute was programmed, and I was slipping in routine commands during what was finally the home stretch. Needless to say, the *name* of the Intelligence wasn't exactly the first thing on my mind, but it must have been important to Sarah.

Leaning over my shoulder, she gazed at the blue dot in the terminal of the program window. Her breath smelled of a mixture of pizza and coffee, and strands of knotted hair draped my peripheral vision. "I think we should pick something else, something more—"

"Soft?" I asked. The bobbing hair to my side indicated that Sarah agreed. I leaned away from the monitor, slowly blinked—deadlifted—my heavy eyelids, and thought about possible names. Most of my creativity was sapped, so I just scanned the lines of code I had written, looking for an obvious answer. Sarah noticed what I was doing and joined in, her bloodshot eyeballs darting across lines of *Consolas* font.

"Environment?" she asked. I shook my head. Too impersonal for what we were doing.

"Data?" I asked.

"Do you really want to deal with a lawsuit?" she asked. Good point. *No sci-fi references,* I decided. Our name had to be uniquely *us.*

"We'll think of something," Sarah said. She stepped back from the monitor and leaned back into her swivel chair, closing her eyes. I looked back at the screen, preparing to finish some final packages. As my hands settled on the keyboard, my eyes drifted to the top of the terminal, resting at the title of the program.

"Sarah!" I shouted. She jolted from her chair and looked around for a second. Finally, her gaze drifted along my arm toward my pointer finger. When she saw it—the *name,* which was staring right at us this whole time, but was nonetheless perfect—the red spiderwebs in her eyes gave way to a warm joy. We locked eyes, and she nodded.

We kept working, the ideas flowing like water through a broken dam. At the stroke of midnight, Sarah and I had only just begun creating.

SIX

THE FIRST THING Ali did when she woke up was try to burn down Sarah's cabin. Okay, technically it wasn't *her* fault. Video connections with the Brain were still in their testing phase, so opening one up on Sarah's (rather old) desktop was a risky move in and of itself. The unexpected power surge that happened when we initialized the visual AI engine was way too much for the cabin's desktop to handle, and by the time I doused the computer with the fire extinguisher, half of Sarah's study was charred black. I was afraid that the computer fire corrupted the data we'd been working on, but when I later booted up Ali on my network laptop: *there she was.*

Normally, Sarah and I didn't bring our work with us on our weekend cabin trips, but we were so close to finishing the Advanced Learning Intelligence that we couldn't resist. Sarah and I had been taking an extended winter vacation to the cabin since we weren't able to celebrate the holidays together. She was pulled out of town for a European distributor's meeting just two days before Christmas. Although I hadn't gotten to decorating my apartment or putting up a tree, I had bought Sarah a better and even more expensive new sports watch that I was looking forward to giving her. I was hoping to spend the day with her watching old holiday movies and eating Christmas cookies. Instead, I spent the holiday diligently working on Ali's code. Around 6pm, I had decided that I'd spent enough time coding—it felt like Sarah and I were the only ones in the entire company spending the holidays working.

"Merry Christmas, Ali," I said to the lines of *Advance++* in front of me. As I shut off the monitor, I realized that I had been so wrapped up in my work that I had forgotten to go to Church. *Certainly far from the first time.* I spent that evening reading the prayers from an online Christmas Eve missal to try to make up for it. Around 9pm, I flipped on the television to *Frosty the Snowman,* and spent the rest of the night eating holiday chocolates and texting Sarah while watching the movie.

Honestly, it wasn't the *worst* Christmas I've ever had—considering I spent my graduate school holidays holed up in my dorm room studying all alone, it at least felt nice to have someone to text. *Even if she wasn't here.*

Although I don't think Sarah is religious, I knew she felt bad about not spending Christmas Day with me, so when she returned the following day, we decided to take a week-long ski trip up North. We would stop over at the cabin for a day before heading to an expensive resort and snow lodge in Canada. However, when we stopped at the cabin and saw how close we were to finishing Ali, we both forgot about going skiing (which is good, because I would have probably died tragically) and got to work.

Little did I know just how far Ali would evolve beyond my initial code. One week after the rocket launch, we were using a stock, human-shaped figure as the stand-in for Ali. She spoke with a voice that resembled that of a digital assistant—inflecting her words correctly and speaking intelligently, but always with the monotone detachedness of a computer. But she grew. Sarah wanted something—*someone*—who would guide the Brain's users in a humanlike way, continually bridging the gap between the AI's heuristic database and the person using it (Sarah even once referred to Ali as the Brain's "prophet").

We programmed Ali to take several weeks simply to learn about the world. Through some closed-door business dealings with the world's other tech companies, Ali gained access to almost every piece of information available on the internet. As she processed trillions of terabytes of data, Ali also developed unique elements within her operating system—elements that were more *personality* than mere programming. The software developed *tastes*, such as preferred processes, spoken dialects, even color schemes. I hadn't programmed any of those—she *selected* them. I had originally thought that I would have to design the Intelligence's avatar from the ground up; it was only later that I realized that the world's most advanced AI was perfectly capable of designing her own appearance. And, after three weeks, Ali truly began to speak for herself. One day, when I asked Ali to provide a summary of the new subfunctions she'd acquired, I was startled to hear the report given in the voice of a twenty-something girl from the East Coast rather than by a bland robotic reader. And, after several days of rendering, Ali's appearance eventually matched her voice.

We just had to compile a few remaining bits of software once we arrived at the cabin. After two days, when Sarah booted up her desktop, we immediately saw that Ali had also chosen the cabin as her "home location" where her virtual avatar would spawn in.

And then, we saw *her*.

Ali stood on the porch, joy radiating from her bright eyes and warming her young, ivory face. Her brown hair and elbow-length white tunic blew in a gentle breeze, and she wore sky-blue leggings that faded at the ankles to match her pair of white slippers. At risk of sounding cliché, my first thought was that she looked like an angel. I glanced over at Sarah, who was lost in the digital girl in front of her. Barely a second had passed, but the two of us could have stood there, motionless, for hours.

Unfortunately, the desktop's overrun circuits had other plans.

As I finished putting out the computer fire, I locked eyes with Sarah. For some elusive reason, nothing mattered more in that moment than meeting Ali. And there was only one way that would work.

"The Portal!"

We drove to the airport, where I witnessed the flight crew of Sarah's private plane scrambling to get the jet into the air. I think Sarah was about ready to jump in the cockpit and fly back to Florida herself. We barely spoke the entire flight; both of us were far too lost in our thoughts. After we landed, Sarah told her private chauffeur to drive us back to the Abraham facility as fast as he could. Based on her tone and the driver's speed, I think he understood that "Drive as fast but as safe as you can" meant "Get us there in ten minutes or find a new job." We practically dove out of the car and ran into the Abraham Portal Room. It was a Sunday, so the place was deserted except for some janitors and a couple of unlucky techs who scored weekend maintenance duty.

"Arthur!" Clyde shouted from a standing desk as I quickly walked in. "And... Ms. Stellos... I didn't expect to see you here today!"

"Get the Portal ready," Sarah said to him. Clyde looked up from his computer and over at several large, tarp-covered, tanning-booth cylinders towards the far end of the workshop. He looked over at Sarah with a hesitant glance.

"They still need to boot—"

"*Now.*"

Clyde backed away from his desk and nodded. "I'll get the suits."

Some preface.

When I mentioned that Abraham's Brain would be the most powerful VR system ever built, I wasn't speaking out of my ass. Remember that our machine relies on a link to its user's central nervous system—that is, it synchronizes with a user's brainwaves to allow them to actually *see* what's in front of them, *hear* the person speaking to them, and *feel* the environment around them. Not just a screen, speaker, or haptics—real connections to various nerves. I first experienced the power of that connection when I joined Abraham over nine months ago; back then, Clyde's handiwork linking my optic nerve to the virtual system had gotten me dizzy for days.

Our company isn't the first to pioneer neuro-sync technology, but previous rollouts of CNS-to-network systems have always been slow or downright dangerous. It doesn't take a biophysicist to know that syncing a computer to one's nervous system is *complicated*; even the smallest mistake can cause its subordinate function—that is, the user's brain—to crash. But with the right design—and a crap-ton of computational power provided by the Solar Sphere—Abraham has solved the issues of its predecessors. Specifically, *Ali* solved most of those issues; the programs created by the Intelligence so far have accelerated the development of the Brain's virtual world tenfold. Issues that perplexed our engineers were solved within minutes by Ali—an AI that, mind you, was still in its development phase. Supposedly, when our users connect to the Brain, they can now fully *exist* inside of it and truly *live* in its virtual world. I myself didn't do any of that work—we have an entire neurotechnology subdivision for that, so the inner machinations of that side of Abraham sometimes feel like a black box to me. But since Sarah trusts them, so do I.

Our Brain uses a "Portal" to connect a user to its interface. Right now, that consists of a tanning booth-shaped bed that we—the users—must lie in. We also have to wear "Portal Suits," which are essentially wetsuits with wires and sensors running through them. They are about as comfortable as they sound. Still, I doubt they're anywhere *near* as painful as the needle-infused clothes Sarah had to wear when designing the biometric readout process now used by the Portal suits. But it was all necessary for linking the neurons in our body to the computer.

Sarah and I have tested the Portal a couple of times before, and it's always a half-hour ordeal getting ready. The first time I ever used it, I needed to obtain medical clearance from a doctor who performed a series of tests, including several different scans of my brain. Abraham had to make sure I was perfectly healthy before using the Portal, which was by all means experimental. I did not particularly like using that behemoth of a machine; then again, I'm not sure anybody did. Thankfully, the final version of the system won't require medical scans, an itchy suit, or a mammoth Portal to connect to it. Once the Solar Brain is powerful enough, its network will allow users to simply put on a headpiece that instantly connects to their nervous system with (literally) no strings attached.

As I hobbled around feeling like I was wearing a car tire, that accomplishment felt far off. Then again, the development of Ali also felt "far off" just a few weeks ago.

The techs helped Sarah, then me, step into the Link Portal. I looked over at Sarah, who was already laying down with her eyes shut. Even dressed in her cyborg wire-suit, she looked amazing. Her face was tense and her breathing was quick, though, like she was also nervous about what was about to happen. I looked at her for a few more seconds before I finally laid down. From across the room, I saw Clyde give me a thumbs-up sign as he pressed a button.

The chamber door came down over my face, and I closed my eyes. In that moment, despite sweating in the oven that was the Portal, the only feeling that I truly noticed was my own excitement.

And just like that, the world was gone.

Linking to the Brain feels a lot like waking up twice. You're fully conscious as the machine powers up, but as the virtual world connects to your nervous system you suddenly feel like you've been abruptly pulled from your sleep. For a fraction of a second, you can't remember where you are or what you are doing, but then the environment around you materializes and you remember: *I'm in the Brain. I'm in the Brain. I'm in the—*

As I began to think about how we needed a better name for our platform than "the Brain," the world around me became crystal clear. The log cabin's porch stood about thirty feet from the clearing I was in, surrounded by a dense overgrowth of pine trees and shrubs. It was around midday; the Sun was tucked behind a veil of clouds, casting a dim glow over the cabin.

A cool breeze tickled the back of my neck. From the porch came the distinct sound of wind chimes rustling in the wind. The dewy air began to stick to my clothes—my normal, fully rendered t-shirt-and-jeans *clothes*.

I turned to my left where Sarah stood. There wasn't a single pixel off about her; she had on a green raincoat and her hair was tied in a neat ponytail. I looked up at the rainclouds and decided that a matching green coat would be smart. I closed my eyes and thought—*ordered*—"Green Raincoat. Loose-fitting,"

When I opened my eyes and looked down at my arms, there it was—an overcoat just like Sarah's.

Changing my appearance with a single thought.

When we'd used the Portal two times previously, the world was not nearly as well-rendered as this. Previously, most movement carried some latency to it, where if you spun around too fast you would get nauseous. But now, the nervous systems' tracking was flawless; I felt like I could do a backflip and land feeling just fine. I took a step forward; my foot sank into the wet, sticky grass. I looked left, then right. I may as well have been *at* the actual cabin—the surroundings whipped by perfectly. The fresh air felt *good*—the world was real.

Somewhere, tucked within the smell of the lake, I caught a faint whiff of vanilla. The scent tickled my nose, and I wondered if it came from a nearby cake. I was genuinely curious to eat some; I had never experienced *taste* in the virtual world, but a couple of technicians who ate a virtual pizza inside the Brain swore that it was the best food they'd ever eaten. I took another sniff of the vanilla scent but realized that it smelled more like perfume than food. Sarah *never* wore perfume. I looked up at the porch and noticed that it was deserted except for two wooden rocking chairs.

Sarah and I whipped around; a couple of yards behind us stood Ali.

She was there—*there*—in the flesh. When I had used the Portal before, there was no *Ali*—not the Ali that had materialized over the past few weeks—*days*. But there she stood; in spite of myself, I moved my eyes over every inch of her body. Her pearl-white slippers were free from any grass or mud stains, despite the footprints behind her indicating that she'd walked over from the lake. There wasn't a single wrinkle or even a seam along her pants. Her tunic had a flower-petal stitch running along its sleeves, and her shoulders were covered by her long, straight, dark brown hair. She was shorter than I was—maybe 5'6"—and thin, but not bony. Her face was pale, round, and lightly adorned with artificial blush. Her smile radiated of life.

My eyes drifted towards the wicker basket dangling from her right arm. Ali followed my gaze, and then finally she spoke.

"Hello, Sarah Stellos. Hello, Arthur Hesper," she said softly. She turned, and with her left hand gestured past the dew-glazed lake behind her. "I brought you some apples from the hilltop grove." I didn't have to follow her gesture; I could imagine the exact patch of apple trees she was talking about. Assuming she'd picked the best ones, they were from a patch of trees atop a small hill overlooking the lake, where the soil was well-drained and the apples tasted like heaven.

"Would you like to join me inside for some apple pie and cider?"

I tried to formulate a response; not to the question of apple pie, which would undeniably be "yes," but to *her*. The A.L.I. was a program; a code that I had written and troubleshooted and revised. The program had *grown*, developing motions, sentences, and decisions that were generated from a computer's repository. That's what *artificial intelligence* is—an absurdly complex, multi-layered, machine-learning program. I'd *watched* it grow, and I *knew* how complex my program was designed to become. But I was not looking at a program. The girl in front of me wasn't *artificial*. She'd said only two dozen words and had barely moved two feet, but that didn't make a difference. This creation in front of me was *real*, and I had no idea how to respond to it.

Sarah was quicker to it than I was. "I'd love to, Ali. Thank you." She glanced over at me, her expression saying something sweet and non-force-ful like *"Say something you idiot!"*

"Yes... please," I managed to get out. My track record of first impressions with women was *really* off to a great start. Ali nodded and flashed her infectiously genuine smile.

"If you'll follow me inside the cabin, I have a table set up for us."

Ali walked past Sarah and me, and strode off towards the cabin, leaving us in the muddy clearing. The soles of her slippers were spotless.

If the nectar and ambrosia supposedly consumed by the Greek gods existed today, then Ali's apple cider and pie would taste three times better. They were the perfect amount of everything. Sweet but not too sugary. Warm enough to soothe your nerves. I was comfortably full after just one slice—*full! In a virtual world!* Certainly, I *couldn't* have been digesting this in real life.

Could I?

As soon as Ali had taken us inside the cabin, I looked around. It was a breathtakingly detailed reconstruction of Sarah's vacation home; I had never absorbed its details as deeply as I had now. The glow of the fireplace scattered off the logged ceiling in precisely the right way. Plaid tapestries lined the walls to give the place a rustic feel. The smell of the burning wood was soothingly mixed in with the aroma of kitchen pastries. The only detail that was missing was the charred wood that now lined the office door—I wonder if Ali even knew about that, or if she had left that off on purpose.

As Sarah and I sat down at the round wooden table by the cabin's entrance, Ali walked into the kitchen as if it were her own. I glanced over at Sarah, who was staring at the kitchen doorway. Suddenly, I felt the palms of my hands grow sweaty. What was I supposed to say to Ali when she returned? *"How was your day?" "Seen any good movies lately?" "What have you been up to since you were created inside of a supercomputer?"*

Ali returned after only a few seconds, carrying two plates with thick, cleanly cut slices of pie. She set them down in front of Sarah and I, along with a fork and napkin. She stood there for a second, looking down at the table. As I stared up at Ali, I noticed Sarah look around for a third chair, but saw that she couldn't find one. The living room table, which she had purchased for my second visit to her cabin, only *needed* two chairs. But just as Sarah looked back up at Ali with an apologetic expression, a third chair slowly materialized behind her, as if it were an item in a video game that could fade in from thin air. Ali carefully smoothed out the hem of her tunic and sat down. Then, she slid her chair forward without making a sound, and sat up straight. Finally, she looked over at me, and then at Sarah, and began talking to us like we were old friends.

"So, how was your flight to Florida?" she asked, looking at both of us with a smile.

"It was nice. Fast," Sarah said, slowly. She took a small bite of her pie and looked down at it incredulously. I was already halfway finished with mine.

"How is the weather today?" Ali asked.

"Here? Or... out there?" Sarah asked.

"Oh... *outside* of the Brain," Ali said, smiling.

"Fine... um, *nice*. It was nice," Sarah said. Ali nodded. "It's... *also* nice in here, right?" Sarah glanced in my direction with an expression that read *help me out, here.* I nodded in agreement.

"Beautiful," I quickly said, becoming strangely aware of how deep my voice sounded. *Was the Brain messing with my voice? Or did I always sound—*

"How do you both feel after using the Portal? I understand that the experience is somewhat tiring," Ali said.

"It certainly is. But worth it," Sarah said.

"Yes. For future projects, I will work to establish a more robust link between monitors on Earth and the environment inside the Brain, so that collaboration need not be so arduous," Ali said. As she said the words "monitors on Earth," I became acutely aware that I was not *on* Earth anymore, but that I was effectively inside a supercomputer millions of miles away. I'm not sure if there's a phrase that accurately captures how weird that realization feels.

"Oh, I don't *mind* coming inside here," Sarah said. "And soon, we'll have headsets developed that can vastly accelerate connection speeds."

"Of course. However, I would enjoy interacting with technicians who are not connected to the Brain. I am interested to learn more about life on Earth," Ali said.

"Didn't you get a lot of that information from the first knowledge collection phase?" Sarah asked in between bites of pie. "Those search engine companies charged a truckload for—"

"Indeed, I have," Ali said. She suddenly lowered her voice. "My apologies for cutting you off, Ms. Stellos."

"Just Sarah," Sarah said. "But... no, go on."

"Well, I wish to learn more information about your *experiences,* first-hand," Ali said. "For instance... what is it like to taste?"

"You don't know how to taste?"

"I know what collection and combinations of gustatory signals are most appealing, but I've never tried it for myself," Ali said, looking down at the crumb-covered plates in front of us. She waved her hand, and the crumbs suddenly disappeared, replaced by fresh slices of pie. Sarah looked at her plate in amazement, and then back up at Ali.

"For one thing, the pie tastes amazing," Sarah said. "It makes me feel warm inside. Happy to eat it. It brings back memories."

"Memories of what?" Ali asked.

Sarah glanced over at me, and then back at Ali. She lowered her eyes.

"My mother... she would make pies like these when I was young," Sarah said. She rarely discussed her parents, even with me. I could tell that was a tough subject for her, so I usually tried to stay clear of it.

"Elizabeth," Ali said softly, closing her eyes for a second. Sarah nodded. I recognized that name from Sarah's Wikipedia page—she had never actually spoken her parents' names out loud, as far as I could remember.

Ali quickly opened her eyes and straightened up in her chair. She smiled at Sarah. "Okay. What does *grass* taste like?"

I almost felt whiplash from that question.

"Grass? Why do you want to know?" Sarah asked.

"Because you know," Ali said. "And I'd like to make sure the entry in my database is correct."

I looked over at Sarah. I *definitely* didn't know what grass tasted like, and I wasn't sure that Sarah did eith—

"It's actually sweet," Sarah said, surprising me. "It has a *cold* taste at first, but as you chew it, you feel your mouth dry out and are left with a bitter aftertaste. You also can't digest it, so that kind of sucks."

Sarah noticed me staring at her incredulously. "What, you've never eaten grass as a kid? Gone for a run, sat down in the grass, and wondered what it tastes like?" she asked me.

"Um, no?" I said, wondering if *I* was the weird one here.

"You should be more adventurous, Dr. Hesper," Ali said, giggling softly. "I kid, of course. This is interesting information."

It is?

"What does it *feel* like to swim in an ocean?" Ali asked, changing the subject entirely. "What sensations do you experience?"

"It feels... enclosed, at times," Sarah said. "It's... *salty* and vast if you go underwater, but peaceful and beautiful on the surface. Just floating around, though, feels buoyant."

"Fascinating," Ali said. "What does buoyant feel like? That sensation does not appear in my database."

"Buoyant feels like... I don't know," Sarah responded, slowly. "Supposedly, there's a weightless, almost *free* feeling to it. I don't do a lot of swimming, though. Is that how you would describe it, Arthur?"

"Um," I stuttered, blindsided by the inquiry. "Sure."

"Interesting," Ali said. "What does it feel like to be *sure* about something?"

Our conversation continued like this. Ali asked the kinds of natural questions people don't normally think to ask. She asked about the *world*—not questions about politics or people, but about our experiences and feelings regarding the most random things. Perhaps she asked those questions to improve the quality of her simulated worlds; perhaps they were out of genuine curiosity.

The whole time, Ali spoke directly yet naturally. She spoke with purpose but also open-endedness. The words and sentences she used were formal, but not rigid or overly robotic. Throughout the conversation, I repeatedly forgot that Ali was artificial. I was always reminded of that fact whenever she brought up things like the Brain or her own programming, but she did so comfortably, in the way someone might bring up a childhood interest or their job.

Sarah answered her questions, doing most of the talking. I chimed in with one-word answers and nods as they spoke. Fifteen minutes or so passed like this, and eventually Ali turned to me—*directly* to me—and asked me if I was bored.

"What?" I had heard the question but hadn't entirely processed it.

"You aren't speaking as much as Sarah. I wonder if you'd rather be doing an activity that is more exciting," she said. Her eyes carried a look of genuine concern. I was suddenly overwhelmed by guilt—my stunned silence must have come off as rude or even bored to her. *Me, bored by her?*

Sarah gave me another one of her *"Well, say something!"* kind of glances. I straightened up in my seat and looked at Ali.

"I'm... I'm sorry, Ali. Really. I'm just taking all of this in," I said. "I'm... so amazed at how real this place is, how real *you* are." She blushed again. I had no idea if what I'd said flattered her or offended her. Then again, I had no idea why that *mattered*. I knew that her dramatic mannerisms were just part of her programming, but I couldn't help but be annoyed at her for smiling again. And immediately, I felt bad for that. I was staring at the perfect virtual assistant, designed to help her user. Designed, I realized, to *serve* her user. Not with detachment nor resentment, but with an unbridled enthusiasm that knew no alternative.

"This is all... a lot to process," I said. "I mean... we designed you, and you designed all this, and..."

"Is it an unusual sensation?" Ali asked.

Unusual? Was it *unusual* that I was eating pie with the most advanced AI ever built, all because I'd done my job so perfectly? Was it *unusual* for me to have a guilty feeling that, in doing my job, I'd relegated this *being* to an existence of enthusiastic, but boundless, servitude? Was it *unusual* for me to feel so frightened by infectious perfection?

All I could do was nod, still asking myself existential questions.

"You could say that," I mumbled.

"Would you both like to see something?" Ali asked. I was jolted from my thoughts—thoughts which, I realized, Ali could probably *read*—and looked over at Sarah. I didn't like the ambiguity of the word "something" and I wanted to ask what she was about to show us. But Sarah didn't give me the chance.

"Lead the way," Sarah said.

Ali stood up from her seat and walked to the front door of the cabin. I didn't know what she was going to show us that I hadn't already seen in the real world; if this *was* a perfect reconstruction of Sarah's retreat, any landmark that she could show us I would know by heart. Yet when she opened the door, it was not to the lakeside meadows or the apple grove.

Through the door was a vast, dark room. I couldn't make out any floor, walls, or ceiling—just an empty, endless void.

Ali stepped into the void. I lunged out of my seat to try to catch her and keep her from falling. But as I landed on the hardwood floor in front of the door, I undoubtedly looked like a fool as Ali stood perfectly still in the black room. Not falling to her death, but holding out her hand towards me. Normally, Sarah would have laughed at my clumsiness, but she sat frozen in her seat as a piece of apple pie fell off her fork.

"Do not worry, Dr. Hesper. This is the Genesis Room," Ali said. Her smooth arm seemed to glow against the black backdrop of the void. I took her hand; it was cool, but not cold, and smooth. I didn't really process *how* her hand felt because it felt so *ordinary*. She lifted me up with a surprising amount of strength; I was on my feet in a second, and standing inside the black void, which was no longer black and no longer a void. As I stepped inside, with Sarah right behind me, the place morphed into the Genesis Room.

The Genesis Room was one of the Brain's earliest concepts and was an idea that Sarah had as essentially a "VR control center." The room, which acted as a central hub, was lined with holographic "worlds"—semi-transparent spheres that showed all kinds of places. There was a lakeside forest with a small, whimsical cabin—a gold star hovered over the location as a sort of *"You are Here"* marker. Above it was a startlingly different biome: a swarm of sci-fi starships buzzing around and shooting each other down. A comically large sign stuck out of an asteroid that read "Starship Skirmish"—that must have been one of the pre-built games that Abraham's entertainment studio had been working on. There were plenty of other VR worlds as well: a lush rainforest adventure with a mysterious temple, a wild dirt track for go-kart racing, a virtual Hawaiian spa with massage units, and dozens of others that were ready for launch.

I didn't just *see* these worlds; I could *feel* the rumble of the go-karts and the warmth of the tropical Sun beating down on me. These places were *there*. I felt like a kid at an all-you-can-eat candy buffet; I wanted to jump into all of the worlds at once, try *everything*. For hours upon hours, I could play, relax, *live* in these worlds. Even more exciting was the fact that I was standing on merely the precipice of a vast virtual universe. What I felt was the distinct, indescribable feeling of *possibility*.

I whipped around towards Sarah. I couldn't wait to see the awe in her eyes. But she wasn't staring up at the same mosaic I was.

Instead, she was fixated on a small suburban landscape in the corner of the room. The faint glow of several streetlamps illuminated the hazy night. As I stepped closer to the world, the outline of a single-story grey building came into focus. Its parking lot was half-full; a pale-yellow light shone from the inside of the building. I was close to Sarah now, standing just a couple feet behind her. I heard noise—voices—coming from the building, chanting something I couldn't understand. I leaned in closer, trying to block out the sound of starship blaster-fire. It was a chorus, singing in a different language—*Hebrew*, I realized. I knew because I had recognized the word *"Adonai."*

When I was in the orphanage, I had a bunkmate named Neil. He was several years older than me, and he was Jewish. Every night, I'd heard Neil read from his Torah in Hebrew, and naturally the word *"Adonai"*—meaning God—came up quite often. We didn't really discuss his religion—after all, it was a Catholic orphanage, and even though the nuns never forced Neil to convert, there was always an unspoken tension between them and him.

A few months before I was sent off to boarding school, Neil was adopted; out of respect for my bunkmate, his prospective parents were the only people I made a conscious effort not to say anything freakishly genius towards. Or, at the very least, freakish towards. While Neil packed his things, I did everything I could to mask my sadness. In fact, I thought it would be more well-received to celebrate the occasion; I stole a couple of cans of soda from the cafeteria backroom, and together we opened them and toasted. *"L'chaim,"* he said. At my confused expression, he clarified: "To life. Always believe in life."

I hadn't thought about Neil in years, so hearing the Hebrew words coming from the synagogue brought back a flood of memories. He was one of the few good friends I'd ever had, and I hadn't talked to him in over a decade. Still, I think his *words* stuck with me for a long time. But, like many people's personal mantras, I didn't always follow them. How many times had I traded the opportunity to socialize and forge connections for more time at my computer? I spent a long time ignoring the lives of others around me, but I'd always convinced myself that I was going to make them all better. I suppose that was my warped version of *believing* in life.

As I returned from my trip down memory lane, I noticed that Ali was turned towards me. However, her eyes were closed, like she was concentrating on something. I didn't remember programming her to shut her eyes while her systems were processing things. Then again, I hadn't programmed her to do *a lot* of what she'd already done.

As I was about to ask Ali what she was doing, I jumped as Sarah whipped away from the foggy synagogue setting. *Right,* that's *what triggered my thoughts about Neil.* Sarah saw me looking at the building and brushed back her hair.

"Just an... old place I used to visit. There's a lot of mental relics in here." Sarah gestured over past Ali towards a small building in the far corner of the room. "Isn't that the ice cream shop you dragged me to earlier this year?"

It was. *Heavenly's Creamery.* Down to the detail, and parked in front of the brick storefront was my grey SUV, with two minifigures sitting inside of it.

Mini-Sarah and mini-Arthur.

I squinted at the figures and smiled; I wanted to enter that virtual setting, approach mini-Arthur, and tell him *he's got this.* Knowing Sarah, she would probably tell her virtual self to *get the hell out of that SUV and run away as fast as she can.* I looked around the model of the ice cream shop, and behind the rectangular building I noticed a black car parked near the dumpster. I clearly hadn't noticed that car while I was in front of the creamery in real life, but now, I recognized it in an instant. It was similar to the cars that followed Sarah's limousine from the airport to the office: *a security vehicle.* Clearly, Sarah's guards *had* followed us from the workshop to the ice cream parlor, even though Sarah claimed to dislike being watched over. I thought about calling Sarah out on her lie, but I stopped myself. *She had only met me recently,* I thought. It made sense that her security would follow her there, regardless of whether she'd ordered them to or not.

Still, that didn't change the fact that I never would've even *thought* about her guards—or gotten to revisit our first date—if I didn't see that very scene right in front of me. *An old memory, but a new perspective.* Almost as soon as that thought crossed my mind, Ali spoke to us.

"My programming has enabled me to construct worlds centered around your most formative memories. Is this feature of the Brain too invasive?" She looked back and forth between Sarah and me. She reminded me of a child asking their parents to forgive them for breaking something expensive. This time, I beat Sarah to the punch.

"No, Ali, I think that's a wonderful feature," I said. Sarah closed her mouth and, after a moment, nodded in agreement. From the look in her eyes, I realized that Sarah and I might not have been in total sync on that one. After a moment, I wondered if *I* was in total sync with myself on that one. "Sarah?"

"It's... fine, yes," she said. Sarah glanced around the room, taking in all of the virtual worlds. I was about to ask Sarah about the world she had been looking at—the synagogue—but before I could she glanced at me and then at Ali.

"Where to now?"

SEVEN

T HE "SIMULATION SHOWCASE" was Ali's name for the grand tour of
about a dozen or so of the Brain's most advanced virtual worlds.
Many of them Sarah and I knew about, like the tropical vacation and the
space battle, but hadn't yet gotten the chance to actually explore. As I
mentioned, we'd only connected to the Portal a couple of times before,
and it was always a painful and poorly rendered hassle. But as Sarah and I
stood together in the Genesis Room, strapping on goggles and skydiving
vests, the reality of what we'd created was starting to sink in. And, despite
the creeping feeling of dread that I had about falling out of a plane, I was
excited. This was where the fun began.

"Why do we need goggles?" Sarah asked as she tugged the strap
around the back of her head.

"To protect your eyes from the 120 mile-per-hour winds," Ali said mat-
ter-of-factly. "Oh, did you mean *can I turn off the wind effects?*"

"Never mind," Sarah said.

Ali turned to us both. Immediately, a holographic wall of text
appeared in front of us. Out of nothing but sheer curiosity, I reached out
to see if I could *feel* the text, but as close as the notice appeared, my hand
never seemed to touch the text or go through it. Sarah was looking at me
like I had two heads, while Ali was smiling amusedly.

"Please read over the following message before we proceed, and verbally acknowledge once you have done so in order for us to begin."

I looked at the notice:

*Welcome to the ABRAHAM Simulation Showcase! Over the next couple
of hours, you will explore a series of virtual worlds tailor-made for your
Portal Experience. The effects in each world will feel real because, to you,
they are real. Any physical effects that you will experience are simulated
and will not affect your body back on Earth. Additionally, according to
ABRAHAM Entertainment Guidelines, **users will not experience the***

When I finished reading, I looked over at Sarah. "Our pain receptors are turned off?" I asked her.

"Not *off,* but *softened,*" Sarah said. "You can *feel* things around you, but I have it set so that users cannot be injured inside the Brain. You might feel some pressure on your body if you run into a wall, but you'll never bruise or bleed while in these simulations. Of course, I have received some flak from some of the more hardcore hyper-reality enthusiasts about that."

"Then why do it?"

"I just think that those things are unbecoming of the paradise we're trying to build," Sarah said. "The Brain is meant to help its users escape from the pain and sickness of the real world, not experience more of it."

Before I could respond, Sarah pulled the strap around her vest tightly, and gave me a nod. "Ready?"

I nodded back at her. "Ready."

We looked over at Ali.

"We're ready," we said in unison. I took Sarah's hand, and grinned at her.

Ali smiled. "Confirmed. Before we start: are either of you afraid of heights?"

I looked over at Sarah and shrugged. "A little," I said. She nodded back at me, her grip on my hand tightening.

"Good," Ali said.

Without warning, we started falling through the sky. I felt my heart pound as I looked down. We weren't in the Genesis Room anymore, but fifteen thousand feet above the ground. Below us, the farthest reaches of planet Earth sprawled out along an endless horizon. I would've marveled at the deep blue oceans or the wide expanse of land I saw if I wasn't morti-fied. I realized that I was no longer holding Sarah's hand, but that she was about thirty feet to my left. She was screaming, her voice a far higher pitch than I'd ever heard it. Her hair flew in the air behind her, and her face was filled with terror. I would've been screaming, too, if I wasn't still in shock at having been dropped out of an invisible plane.

"Sarah!" I shouted.

"Arthur!" she shouted, looking around to try to find me. She was truly terrified—I didn't know that anything frightened her until now. For some reason, I always thought that billionaires loved to go skydiving, just like they loved flying around the world or taking day-trips into outer space.

In that moment, I had to reach Sarah. I *needed* to reach her. I tried waving my arms around, but nothing happened. I was tumbling through the air, and the ground was quickly approaching. I couldn't feel my hands anymore. My vision was going dark. I was panicking, and I couldn't see Sarah, who needed me.

"Exit!" I shouted.

Suddenly, both Sarah and I were laying on the colorless floor of the Genesis Room, free from our skydiving vests and goggles. Sarah was breathing heavily, holding one hand beneath her jacket over her heart, as if wondering how fast her *real* heart was beating. As I turned away from her, I saw Ali walking towards us.

"Are you alright?" she asked.

"Stay back," I wheezed as Ali approached us. She'd nearly gotten us killed—I didn't *care* if it was simulated—in that death trap of a tour. I didn't want her coming *any* closer to us. I couldn't think clearly; all I cared about was that we were safe. Ali stepped back nervously as I forced myself up onto my knees, and I put my hand on Sarah's back. "We want to—"

"Arthur," Sarah said.

"I've got it, Sarah. You can rest." I looked up at Ali angrily.

"No," Sarah said, pulling herself up off the ground and out of my arm. "Arthur... *why* did you take us out of there?"

"What?" I asked. I was so confused.

"I didn't *ask* you to say 'exit,'" she said, raising her voice. For some reason, I glanced over at Ali, trying her for an answer.

"What..." I looked back at Sarah. "Sarah, you were mortified, you were... *distraught* with fear, you were—"

"Yes, of *course* I was terrified, but that's the whole *point*," she said, getting up onto her feet and staring down at me. "You're meant to *feel* things in here, experience the adrenaline that accompanies a new world—it's not all going to be calm. Didn't you read the notice?"

"I thought you didn't want to feel pain!" I protested. *Did she not just say that?*

"*Fun* isn't painful," she said.

"I was looking out for..."

"*Don't.* Remember, you cannot get hurt or die inside this place. If you don't want to experience the Brain, Arthur, you are more than welcome to leave. I don't want you doing anything you don't want to do." Tapping her foot, Sarah crossed her arms indignantly. Naturally, *this* is what I get for trying to be a protective boyfriend. I saw my girlfriend in danger; I acted. *Isn't that what I'm supposed to do?*

"If you would like, I can turn down the intensity of the simulation," Ali said, stepping forward and looking at me nervously.

"No," I said. I kept my gaze focused on Ali. "I'm sorry... the simulation is fine. I shouldn't have been rude to you."

I looked back over at Sarah, who still had her arms crossed but looked a lot calmer now. I couldn't back out of this, I knew. Nor did I want to. I had to complete the tour, and see Abraham's creation for myself. If Sarah was ready, then so was I.

"Let's begin again," I said.

"Are you sure?" Sarah and Ali asked in unison. They glanced at each other and then back at me.

"Just... give a little warning before you drop me out of a plane," I said to Ali.

She nodded, almost as if to confirm with the Brain that I was ready to begin the tour again. Then, she smiled. "That does ruin the surprise of it, but very well. Arthur, Sarah... I'm about to drop you out of a plane."

Just like that, we were falling through the sky again.

This time, I made sure not to let go of Sarah's hand. We both screamed the entire way down—but this time, ours was an excited, thrilled-to-be-there sort of scream rather than a shocked and terrified one. The kind of scream you'd give on your favorite roller coaster—not that I really *had* a favorite roller coaster, considering I'd never actually been to an amusement park.

Damn. My life really did suck before Abraham.

Within a minute, I felt a tug on my back as my parachute began to open, and after another second, I felt a strong pull on my shoulders. I realized then that I was, in fact, wearing my skydiving gear again. I didn't remember putting it back on. I kept Sarah's hand in mine as our parachutes opened, and we glided above Florida.

The air was cool, but not cold. The warmth of the Sun mixed with a light wind to create the perfect temperature. As Sarah and I floated through the air beside each other, I felt my heartbeat slow down to a more natural state. I looked around.

The view was beautiful. The clouds were scattered, creating alternating areas of shade and light over the state. I could make out Florida's Inland Sea, stretching out as a shiny swath of blue in front of us. The forests below looked like tiny patches of moss, and small single-story homes criss-crossed the landscape. I wondered if I could see the famous Orlando theme parks from here; I then wondered if I could see the Abraham campus. Mentally, I wasn't in a simulation. I was really *flying*.

"It's like the view from your plane," I said to Sarah. "It's beautiful. This sky, this *world*—it's all so beautiful."

"What?" she shouted. It seemed she hadn't heard me over the wind. I opened my mouth to speak again, but before I could get a word out, Ali floated down in front of us wearing a parachute. She wasn't wearing goggles, though, and her clothes weren't the least bit wrinkled.

"Welcome to the Simulation Showcase!" Ali said. She didn't shout, but I could hear her perfectly. "Or should I say, *thanks for dropping in!*"

She glided closer to us.

"Where should we head next? Up…" Ali said, pointing towards the sky. She then looked at the ground. "Or down?"

I glanced over at Sarah, who nodded at me.

"Down," I said. "Definitely, very gently, *down*."

Suddenly, the simulated world began to change. The ground faded to black, and the clouds disappeared. The sky became a rich blue color, and gradually stretched all around us. I felt my parachute disappear as the world around me materialized.

We were standing on the stern of a large white yacht several miles off an island coast. I couldn't tell where the island was, but I saw palm trees rising in the distance and beachgoers dotting the sandy coast. Surrounding us in every other direction were miles of endless ocean—*peaceful and beautiful*, like Sarah had said.

Sarah. I looked over at Sarah, and my heart skipped a beat. Instead of her green rain jacket, she was wearing nothing except a slim black bikini and flipper fins on her feet. I looked down at my own feet and saw that I too was wearing flippers—as well as blue swim trunks with no shirt. I myself didn't particularly mind the change in clothes—and had definitely seen my girlfriend in less—but as soon as Sarah noticed my swim trunks and looked down at her own exposed body, she jumped. Towards the bow of the boat was a crowd of other people—other divers—standing around in their beachwear. They didn't seem to notice Sarah, but that didn't stop her from immediately covering her chest and looking around, petrified.

All of the people on the boat were *non-user characters*—randomly generated people used to fill up a scene in the Brain, to one day be replaced by actual users. *They're not real,* I was about to say to Sarah to calm her down. She had once told me that one of her recurring nightmares was of standing in a crowd naked. That always struck me as odd, since I thought those dreams reflected an exposure of someone's own insecurities—insecurities that I didn't think Sarah had.

But after a few seconds of looking towards the water behind the stern, I saw Sarah close her eyes and concentrate. Over her body materialized a thick brown scuba diving suit, complete with a bulky helmet and enlarged limbs. Beside us, near the stern, Ali appeared wearing her white tunic and a blue bathing suit underneath. She looked over at Sarah, who gave her a thumbs-up with a thick-gloved hand.

"The water is very warm, and there is nothing dangerous to your skin in this simulation," she said to Sarah. "Are you sure you won't be too hot inside your—"

"Nope," Sarah said in a muffled tone from inside the suit. She quickly looked back at the crowd behind her as Ali shrugged.

"Alright then," Ali said. "Follow me!"

With perfect form, she dove right into the water.

"She's not wearing a scuba mask," I observed. I felt my own face. "*I'm* not wearing a scuba mask. This... should be interesting."

I took a step toward the water, but Sarah took my hand in her own. She wasn't budging, but was just staring at the water, motionless.

"You're not just afraid of people seeing you," I realized. The head of the scuba suit shook side to side. "It's the water... you're claustrophobic?"

"Afraid of losing my control," she said. She started speaking quickly, her voice muffled by the sound of her rapid breathing. "Every time I step into that Portal and the lid comes down, I have to keep from..."

She yanked the helmet off of her head and tossed it to the floor of the boat. It landed with a hard thud and rolled into the water.

"I have to keep myself from freaking out. Whenever the other Board members invite me on scuba trips to the Caribbean, I always make up an excuse not to go. Skydiving? *Fine.* Upload my brain into a computer? *Why the hell not?* But that far underwater? With no... *space?* Arthur, I don't know if I can."

I nodded at her. Ali was probably waiting for us, but I wasn't concerned. I realized that we had all the time in the world—in *any* world—out here, on the stern of our virtual party boat. It was one of the few times that *I* could help Sarah—one of the few times she *needed* me—and I wasn't going to fail her.

"I've only swam in a pool, like, three times," I said. "I barely know how. I never really got to visit the water growing up. Normally, back home, I would *never* go into the open ocean like this."

I placed my other hand on top of Sarah's.

"But inside the Brain—why did we *create* this, Sarah? Because we can do anything," I said to her. She looked up at me. "*You* taught me that. We don't have to succumb to fear because we are free here. Free from despair, free from monotony. *Free* to savor this new world. Free together."

I let go of Sarah's hand and stepped towards the edge of the stern. I looked down into the water; a mosaic of faded colors waited just a few feet below. I couldn't—I *wouldn't*—let her miss out on her own creation. Maybe it was the adrenaline of the skydive still pumping through my veins, but I knew how much there was for us to see. And I knew that Sarah knew, too—and that she was strong enough to push through anything that kept her back.

"I trusted you when we dove out of that plane," I said. "Do you trust me?"

Sarah hesitated for a second, but then stepped toward me. "Sure," she said, glancing back at the crowd of people. The helmet re-materialized over her head. "But I'm keeping the suit on… and if I have a panic attack under there, I'm… firing you."

I took both of Sarah's hands and let my inhibitions rest. "No, you won't." I fell back into the water, dragging Sarah by her arms with me. She let out a muffled scream as we fell beneath the waves.

I opened my eyes, preparing for the sting of salt water, but didn't feel any. I could see the ocean floor beneath me perfectly, and—much to my amused surprise—breathe just fine. I looked to my side, and saw Sarah staring at the coral reef beneath her, eyes wide. Her face shield began to fog from her rapid breathing. But after a few seconds, I saw the fog clear. She was calming down. She held her hands up, and began to sink lower into the water.

With an underwater mobility I didn't know I had—that I definitely *didn't* have in real life—I followed Sarah, making light paddling motions throughout the water to catch up to her. Once I did, I saw her eyes trained on a collection of rocks, into and out of which a green eel continuously retreated and reemerged. I saw Sarah staring at it in wonder, and she looked back at me, smiling. When I tried to tell her *I told you so,* I realized that I couldn't actually *talk* underwater—my words came out gurgled and bubbled. That seemed like something of an oversight on Ali's part in case I wanted to verbally say the "exit" word—but then again, why would I?

Ali swam over to us with a wave. Her fabric tunic appeared surprisingly dry, dangling over her chest as if it was unaware that it was supposed to be floating in the water. She swam ahead of us, and Sarah and I started to follow her. As we swam through the coral reefs, we took in the vibrant colors of all the fish, anemones, seagrass, and corals that dotted the sunken boulders. Indeed, I was continuously able to breathe just fine underwater. While Sarah was protected in her scuba suit, I didn't need goggles or oxygen tanks to keep going deeper; as we swam, I became less and less aware that I was far below the ocean surface and far more invested in the amazing sights. The water felt warm and relaxing to swim in. Even though I was no marine biologist, I was pretty sure that most of the fish I saw belonged in colder water. I then remembered, only briefly, that we were inside of a simulation. I didn't know why Ali made skydiving so realistic and ocean-diving so fantasized, but I didn't care. As schools of fish swam by me like I wasn't there and as Sarah and I scaled the underwater formations to explore the world beneath us, I wished I could stay down there forever.

After a few moments, I saw a flash next to me, and turned to find that Sarah was gone. I began looking around for her bulky scuba suit but couldn't find any sign of it. *Where was she?* She was right beside me a second ago—I couldn't have missed her leaving.

If she was stuck, I would see her. I looked down at the ground behind me, but she was nowhere to be found. I felt my heart start to race, and I began to panic.

Suddenly, a large black fish darted right in front of my face—I pushed myself backward to avoid it. It darted from side to side in front of me, inching closer to my face with quick thrashing movements. *What the...?*

For some reason, I thought it would be a good idea to try to grab the fish, but as my hands repeatedly missed it, the fish made its way closer to my face before smacking painlessly into my forehead.

Sarah.

Her name vibrated through my brain. *No way,* I thought. *Was Sarah...?* My gut seemed to answer the question before my brain could.

Sarah was the fish.

We are free here.

Can I... become a fish? I thought hesitantly. I looked down towards my body, and then back toward the reef. The black fish—*Sarah*—was moving through the water very quickly. She was getting farther and farther from me.

Become a fish.

I looked around—nothing seemed to have happened. I looked down at the coral reef to make sure I wasn't getting too close to it, and jumped when I realized I no longer had any feet. I no longer had arms, either.

All I could feel were my fins.

I was now a fish.

I saw Sarah swim towards a patch of seagrass below me. *Follow,* I thought, and automatically I began to fly through the water towards the reef. The ocean floor seemed to grow larger as I approached it, and I could make out so much more detail than I had noticed as a human. *Shrimp grotto below those rocks.* I darted toward the seagrass and pulled up to follow Sarah above the coral floor. Tiny multicolored fish—tinier than I had ever noticed, each with a name I couldn't quite identify but somehow *recognized*—swarmed in and out of the corals. *Eel ahead!* I swerved out of the way as a large green eel passed overhead like a passenger plane. The world around me was more colorful than I had ever imagined—even more vibrant and *massive* than it seemed swimming above it.

Being a fish is... *difficult* to describe. It felt more like I was my own human self, but with the mobility and shape of a fish—I could swim forward and around simply at will. The water around me seemed more inviting, more *accessible,* than it did as a human. Rather than acting as an obstacle to movement, the ocean was a pathway. I felt the water rush past me as I cut through a trench in the reef, a mosaic of colors flying past me in a blur. I weaved in between corals and rocks, which seemed to provide refuge for so many local residents of the deep. As I swam past all sorts of varied fish, I asked myself one of the weirder questions in life: *how do I look as a fish?* I couldn't see my own body, but given that most of the creatures around me seemed larger than I was, I assumed I was roughly the size of a clownfish.

I pushed myself to keep up with Sarah, who swam through a narrow opening between two bright red corals that looked like flaming torches. I followed her through the opening and found myself staring into an endless blue realm. *The open ocean.* The coral reef sat below and behind us. I floated next to Sarah, both of us looking out at the rays of Sun cascading through the serene waters.

Human, I thought.

I felt my body suddenly grow larger, heavier, and more *human.* I could see my limbs again; I waved my arm around to make sure it actually worked. There was another flash of light next to me, and as I turned, I thought I felt fish swimming through my stomach when I saw Sarah—wearing only her bikini—floating above the coral formation. She looked around and rubbed her hand along the sunken rocks behind her. Having scaled them, I knew that they were cool to the touch—nonetheless, Sarah let out a smile upon feeling them for herself and laughed when she saw the ocean world around her with her own eyes. With a couple of quick paddles, she swam right up to me. As an entire school of fish swam around us, she kissed me. As far as underwater, fish-surrounded, underwear-clad kisses go, it was definitely one of the better ones I've had.

After we reunited with Ali and reached the end of our swim—which was more of a clumsy paddle for Sarah and me and a graceful journey for Ali—we materialized away from the ocean and the world around me went dark.

The black void around me soon disappeared, and I found myself standing outside of Abraham's Washington, D.C. office building.

I'd only visited the place once for my interview. I had been too nervous—rather, I was too focused on seeming like I *wasn't* nervous—going into my interview to really take in the details of the building, which had an entirely concrete exterior and sat tucked within a wall of other similar-looking structures. Basked in the glow of the red sunset, it was a rather ugly office building, and upon closer study of its pillared face, was likely a repurposed bank. In almost every way, its aesthetic was completely different from our Florida headquarters.

I looked to my left, expecting to see Sarah glancing up at the D.C. building with the disgust she usually referred to it with. But instead of Sarah, it was Ali who was standing there, looking at the office in silence.

"Why are we here?" I asked her. "Where's Sarah?"

She didn't say anything; instead, she nodded over at the glass doors at the front of the building. I looked over at them, and to my surprise saw *Arthur Hesper* pushing open the doors and silently leaving the building. I almost didn't recognize myself in the black suit—the most expensive thing besides my computer or car that I owned at the time. It was the same suit I wore at my conferences in grad school—it had also been the *only* suit I owned. After that fact was plainly pointed out to me on my first day of work, I bought two new suits that I have still yet to wear.

I—or should I say "slightly-younger Arthur"—walked past Ali and me like we weren't even there. As he did, I found myself staring right at myself, as if I were watching the highest-definition video of *me* ever produced. Do you know that unnerving feeling you get after staring at yourself in a mirror for too long, studying and scrutinizing the details of your face as if they were a stranger's? (Maybe that's just a *me* thing, but I'm pretty sure that happens to most people.) Well, turn *that* up to eleven for a taste of how I was feeling.

Slightly-younger Arthur stepped out into the street, but quickly brought his foot back toward the sidewalk as a black car raced down the road in front of him. I remembered that moment—I was so distracted by what had just happened that I almost forgot to look both ways crossing the street. *It all could have ended right there.* I watched myself quickly cross over to my rental sedan, which was in a parking space just across from the hiring office. I was so proud of that spot—it had been my first success during what was a taxing, but pivotal, day.

I watched myself open the car door, sit inside, and slowly put my head in my hands.

I remembered what happened here.

Ali turned toward me. "The Brain can allow you to experience entirely new realms, from the thrilling to the wondrous. It can also allow you to see *your* world from a new perspective, mined entirely from your most formative memories."

I looked away from Ali, her words resounding through my head. *I can see my world from a new perspective.* I took a step closer to the car and stared at the man sitting inside of it. Although he looked mature for his age, I knew only too well that his mind was in great pain.

"I can see myself in third person?" I asked her.

"Or first person, if you wanted to," she said. "But the best part about the Brain is that you can see things—"

"—from a new perspective, I know," I said. Ali nodded. I crossed my arms and stepped even closer to the car. "I remember this. This was me being... insecure."

"There was more to it than that," Ali said. "You had just been hired on the spot by your dream employer, but rather than celebrate, all you could do was ask yourself questions."

"*Why would they hire me?*" I said. I turned toward Ali. "I couldn't understand why Abraham would want *me*. Like I said... I was insecure back then—"

"Do you remember why you felt that way?" Ali asked. I sighed. *No getting around this.*

"Because I hated everything about who I was."

Ali closed her eyes, and I jumped as a loud round of applause roared out from behind me. I turned around to find that the office building was gone, replaced by a large, crimson-walled, gold-ceilinged conference hall. I was suddenly standing at the back of a darkened room filled with over a thousand foldable chairs and even more conference attendees.

The Consortium on Machine Learning. I remembered this day. I glanced up towards the front of the room at *another* Arthur Hesper—this one over a year younger than the one in the car, but still sporting the same black suit. His—*my*—hair was longer than I remembered it being at that age; had I forgotten to *shave* that morning? Why wouldn't I shave for a conference?

"Yes... *yes,* thank you, folks. *Thank you,*" Arthur Hesper said impatiently as the audience members slowly quieted down. This was my dissertation presentation—I had been invited to share my early-career results with the *CoML,* which was the largest AI conference in the country. I was so close to finishing graduate school and so ready for glory—glory that I knew would come after sharing my streamlined approach to programming artificial neural networks. But I was getting frustrated onstage; members of the audience seemed incapable of holding their applause until the end of the talk. I had a lot of slides left to go through, and only a quarter of my time remained.

Unfortunately, the moderator for the session had decided that a question-and-answer segment should be built into my talk. I remember being livid at that; *if I had time to explain everything, the audience shouldn't need to ask questions.* Instead, I was forced to cut my presentation short in order to take random questions about artificial intelligence—the majority of which didn't even pertain to the specific project I was discussing. Instead of asking about the impressive programmatic leaps I'd made, the audience had seemed more intent on asking me the *ethical* questions about my AI.

"Shouldn't the number of running processes be set by the *programmer?*" a bald man from the audience asked. "How can you be so certain that AI systems *should* have the ability to forge their own pathways?"

"I am not so concerned with whether AI *should* be able to learn on its own, but the fact that it *does* already," Arthur-from-the-past said quickly. "It's like... we've had artificial intelligence for decades, and the fact that it is so widespread means that general AI is going to be a part of our society whether we like it or not. *I* am not afraid to embrace it. Next question."

The words were deep, nasal, and had an almost know-it-all flair to them. *Is that how I used to sound?* I definitely don't talk like that now. *There's no way. Was I* trying *to sound rude?*

Another man stood up as Arthur began swinging his arms at his side. "Don't you feel that that point-of-view is irresponsible?"

"I... *no,* I don't," Arthur said indignantly. "I believe in making progress, rather than twiddling my thumbs and waiting for my grant money to come in."

Several members of the audience began to grumble at that. *Who does he think he is? Irresponsible kid. Little punk.* Arthur had both arms on the podium, staring down at the audience and back up at his slides with an impatient look. "Any *real* questions?" he mumbled.

Why was I such a jerk? I *knew* I was an arrogant wreck—that so many years of endless work had made me abrasive. Back then, I didn't care about explaining my work in an accessible way. I just wanted recognition; *compensation,* even, for how monotonous my life had become. I hated that about myself. And that hatred bubbled up at the worst of times.

Ali materialized next to me, filling the space around me with light. "You so staunchly believed in your revitalized approach to AI—an approach that gave *me* life, by the way—that any criticism of it felt like an attack on you."

"That, and I hadn't bothered developing any people skills," I said.

"Your feeling at this conference was *dread...*" Ali began.

I finished for her. "Dread that I wouldn't be able to network with the very people who were watching my talk. At that point, I knew I wanted out of academia, but I had no idea where I would go. Even looking back, I don't know *how* I ended up at Abraham."

"I do," Ali said, turning to me with a smile. "And, apparently, so do you."

What is she talking about?

Another member of the audience from the back of the room stood up from her seat. Although it was hard to make out the details of the woman, I could see that she had dark black hair and was wearing an all-black suit. *No nametag.* As she looked over to her side, I saw that she wore a black surgical mask that covered most of her face. Only her eyes were visible, and those were all I needed to see.

"Sarah?" I almost shouted. Obviously, no one in the audience could actually see or hear me, but in that moment, I couldn't contain my surprise.

I turned to Ali. "She was there? *Here?*"

Immediately, Sarah Stellos asked Arthur Hesper her question. "There has been a lot of talk about how companies can leverage artificial neural networks for consumer-based applications, but what about using them in content creation and virtual-world visualization? Specifically, in what ways could you modify your 'FreeThink' and 'HyperIterate' pipelines to meet the needs of a large-scale studio?"

Even though her hair was dyed and her face was covered, there was no doubt that that was Sarah's voice. Still, almost no one in the room—Arthur included—seemed to pick up on who was speaking.

"Is this a test?" Hesper said with an infuriating chuckle. "In all seriousness, I'm glad you paid attention to the pipelines I discussed. In answer to your question, *yes,* I do believe that my approach to crafting ANNs would be deeply valuable to studios—just as it will be to all disciplines. One would simply need to adjust the range and types of data my 'FreeThink' pipeline could take to enable an artificial intelligence to develop its expertise in visual media, and configure 'HyperIterate' to prioritize a VR output—if that is what you desire."

"Thank you," Sarah said, sitting down.

"Anyone else?" the young Arthur Hesper asked the crowd.

I watched Sarah glance away from Arthur and jot something down.

That was Sarah Stellos... that was Sarah Stellos? *Why did she disguise herself?*

Ali looked away from Sarah and over at me. "She was at that conference in disguise to recruit talent and generate ideas. For Sarah Stellos, the most important thing in the world was raising the village it took to bring Abraham to life. And on this day, she found a key person for that village. Shortly after this conference, she had her hiring managers send recruitment materials your way to make you interested in applying for the position at Abraham. The rest is history."

I always assumed that I was just lucky enough to be picked from a slew of applicants for an interview. I had never realized that Sarah had her eyes on me since the Consortium. "Ali, why are you showing me this?"

"Because this is the Simulation Showcase, Dr. Hesper," Ali said cheerfully. "The Brain allows its users to see moments of their lives from a different perspective. Oftentimes, a new perspective can allow a user to realize that one event in his life can mean so much more than he thought."

Suddenly, I heard a car start behind me, and I whipped around to find Arthur Hesper—the slightly-older-but-still-younger-than-me Arthur Hesper—sitting in his car. He was still staring at the steering wheel, one hand on the parking brake and the other over his head.

"Not enough about me had changed since that conference," I said. "But when Sarah called out who I was at my interview, I could see my problems—I could see *myself*—as clearly as I do now. I didn't like what I saw."

"But you resolved to change that day," Ali said. I glanced over at her. "From here, you can see how far you've come. On the day you were hired, your own thoughts were: *I will find—*"

"*—a place,*" I finished for her.

"Have you?" Ali asked.

I glanced up at the office building, at the third floor. Second window to the left. The interview room where I'd first met Sarah Stellos.

"Yes."

"Have you found meaning?" Ali asked.

I glanced back at her. "Meaning?" I asked. *Meaning in what?*

"Never mind," Ali said. "At any rate, this simulation is designed as a means of retrospective therapy. Even though you may not require it, what are your thoughts on its utilization thus far?"

I nodded at her slowly. I still wasn't sure what she meant about me finding *meaning,* but at this point I wanted to move on to some of the other simulations.

"It works," I said. "Better than some therapist, at least."

Ali closed her eyes, and the world around me morphed once again.

Arthur, his rental car, and his suit disappeared and were replaced by a cream-colored wall that smelled of fresh paint. I coughed as the scent entered my nostrils, and stepped away from the wall; only then did I see the line of plaques and diplomas stretching across the room. I focused on the black and silver award in front of me and squinted to read its cursive text. As I made out the name on the plaque, I felt my stomach do a somersault.

Oh, no.

"What the hell do you want from me, Dr. Chan?" I heard Arthur's voice ring out from behind me. I whipped around to find slightly-younger

Arthur, wearing a collared t-shirt and jeans, standing up from a wide red armchair. In the chair beside him, holding a small notebook, was an older man wearing wide-brimmed glasses and a thick sweater. The man's thin body almost seemed to sink into the fabric of his seat.

Arthur began to walk away from the armchair and towards the wall-sized windows near the back of the room, behind Dr. Chan's desk. It was snowing out, and the sky was a light grey. As Arthur stared at the view of the office parking lot, Chan continued to scribble notes on his pad. I took in the rest of the office, which was filled with expensive knick-knacks, prestigious psychology awards, and other trinkets. I hadn't really paid my surroundings much attention the last time I was here; I was too distracted for that.

Without looking up from his papers, Chan turned to a new page in his notebook and kept writing.

"I want you to be honest with yourself, Arthur," Chan said, his voice sounding raspier than I had remembered.

"What is that supposed to mean?" Arthur asked. He turned back towards the therapist and began pacing.

"Ali?" I asked, looking around. *Why did she send me here?* I wanted to move on to the next simulation—I did *not* need to see this.

I didn't even want to remember it.

As I prepared to say "exit," I suddenly thought about Sarah. *What if she was watching one of her memories now, too?* Whatever it was, it *had* to be better than what I was seeing.

Would exiting ruin that for her?

I didn't want to take that chance, so I took a deep breath and sat down in one of the chairs across the room. The hard cushion was far from comfortable, but I leaned back and focused on Dr. Chan.

It's just a memory.

"You're close to finishing your doctoral degree at such a young age—younger than most people *starting* their degrees—but have you thought about what comes next?" Dr. Chan paused writing for a moment to listen to the reply.

"I've already told you, I'm going to be an executive at one of several general AI firms. I have the qualifications I need to..."

"You have the education and the experience, yes, but that doesn't make you *qualified*," Chan replied. He craned his neck towards the large window for a second before turning back down toward his notes. "You need to take personal stock to know if you are *ready* for such an important role. I believe that a job that requires you to interact with so many people might not be best for someone as introverted as you."

"So, what do you think, then? I should just stick myself inside a small think tank and code all day?" Arthur asked, raising his voice. "Just be a damn computer monkey?"

"I *think* you might consider taking a break after your studies have concluded, and that you should take some time to grow more comfortable just interacting with other people outside of academia. If you would consider—"

"Consider *what?* Taking a gap year?" Arthur stepped back towards the chair and clutched the back of it with one hand. "I know it might be hard for you to realize this, swimming in cash and all, but most students are flat *broke.* After graduate school, I need a job, or I *starve.*"

"Then why not pursue a lower-stress career until—"

"Until *what?* I learn to make friends?" Arthur asked. "I have the potential to do amazing things, and I *will* do amazing things. I'm not going to waste my time working some mediocre job while I go on a social spree."

"What makes you think you *absolutely* will do amazing things?" Dr. Chan asked, closing his notebook and turning towards Arthur. "What makes you so think you are so exceptional?"

Arthur shook his head, and grabbed the chair with his other hand.

I played the next line through my head as Arthur glared at Chan. *Because I fu...*

"...king *have* to be!" Arthur shouted. "I came from *nothing.*"

"And?" Chan pressed. "I grew up poor and hungry in China before I moved to the States. Do you see me complaining about..."

"I'm not complaining, you old quack! I'm trying to say—"

"You've been gifted so much opportunity, but you dove into it without taking any inventory of your mental health. So many young people, the kids of your generation, think they *have* to do it all or they're missing out."

"I'm not my damn generation," Arthur said. "Those entitled idiots only want handouts. It was the same thing with *your* generation when you were young, because all you did was stare at your phones and wait..."

"Do you see me using a phone?" Dr. Chan held up his paper notebook amusedly.

"Stop being cocky, you know what I'm talking about. People like *you* are why kids today are so screwed up, peddling feelings over the truth. They don't care about hard work, hard facts, or having any faith."

"So, you need *faith* to know truth?" Chan retorted, a smile crossing his face. "Doesn't that seem contradictory?"

"Oh, *sorry,* doctor," Arthur said in a mocking way. He walked across the room, past me, and grabbed his coat off the rack near the door. "Sorry that *some* of us still believe in something bigger than ourselves."

"So you say." Dr. Chan removed his glasses and began to rub them with a small cloth. "You may have been raised in a Catholic orphanage, but when's the last time you've actually been to a Church?"

"I haven't had time to—"

"Some follower of Christ you are," Chan said wryly. Arthur scoffed as Chan replaced his glasses and opened back up his notebook. I stood up, and slowly began to walk towards Chan.

The therapist cleared his throat. "My... apologies for being so direct, but I want to press this. You have been a scientist for over half of a decade. Haven't you considered how liberating it would be to divorce yourself from such an... *unnecessary* commitment as religion?"

"Some damn therapist you are," Arthur said, putting on his coat. "I guess that's what you get with using the university shrink. You go in for help with stress management, they try to send you out an atheist."

"I'm trying to *relieve* your stress, Arthur," Chan said slowly. He took a deep breath, and looked Arthur in the eyes. "And I can see what might be causing it. You refuse to open up about your religion, but you refuse to disavow it. If you are going to move forward with clarity, you need to choose. Ask yourself: what place does an abstract concept like God have in your technology-focused future? The answer..."

Arthur reached for the handle of the door and threw it open. "The only thing I'm asking myself is why the *hell* I showed up to this. *Consider visiting the mental health center...* that's the *last* time I take life advice from Dr. Johnson."

"Arthur..."

"Good day."

Arthur marched out of the room. I stared down at Dr. Chan's notes, which were written in a cursive blue scribble. As he put down his pen, I could make out the end of the notes:

> *...and the pretense of a religious conviction—to convey a front of hyper-intelligence and stoic emotional stability, when in reality he does not possess either.*

Dr. Chan sighed, and closed the notebook. He shook his head. Ali's soft voice began to ring through my head.

"You might recognize that note from—"

"I know where it's from," I said. I turned around, but Ali wasn't there. I was alone in the office with Dr. Chan, who was still sitting in his chair silently. "What a bastard."

"Who?" Ali asked.

"Dr. Chan," I said. *What did she mean, who?* "He knew what he was doing, trying to get a rise out of me. He already got his money from the university; he just wanted me to leave so he could be done with the appointment early."

"Is that truly what you believe?" Ali asked.

Why does it matter? Maybe Dr. Chan made some sense about me taking a mental break from my studies, but if I had, I wouldn't have joined Abraham and met Sarah. And even rewatching the conversation from a "distance," Chan was completely out of line with his atheism argument. *Right?*

"He was wrong," I said. "Wrong about my faith. About my devotion..." Even as I said those things, I wasn't sure they were true.

I sighed.

"Was he?" Ali asked.

"Whose side are you on, anyway?" I shot back. *What is this, a simulation or an interrogation?*

"I am not fighting you, Dr. Hesper," she replied quietly. "I am programmed to be impartial. I'm simply demonstrating the capability of the Brain to grant new perspectives."

"I know, I know."

I shook my head. I knew Ali wasn't the problem—this whole simulation was just her showing off the Brain's powers. *As uncomfortable as it was.* As I looked around the room again, my eyes rested on the notebook in Dr. Chan's lap.

"How did Sarah get it?"

"The note? Most likely, Abraham's human resources division requested it as part of a background check on you," Ali said.

Most likely? I thought. Ali's next reply made me jump, as I didn't remember actually *saying* anything out loud.

"I do not have the same clairvoyance into Sarah Stellos's mind as I do yours," Ali responded. "I can see most of her memories, but some aren't as complete as yours."

"Is it a connection issue?" I asked Ali.

"Likely, yes; one of several that are presently plaguing the Brain's network," Ali said. "But those issues are currently minor, and shouldn't hinder the remainder of the Memory Mine."

"Memory Mine?" I asked. "Is that really what you're calling all of this—"

Suddenly, the world around me morphed again, and the therapist and his office were gone.

When my vision returned, I had to squint as a bright glare of sunlight bounced off the ground and into my eyes. As I slowly opened my eyelids back up, though, I immediately recognized the walkway of reflective stone pavers at my feet, just as I recognized the small grassy field in front of me and the tall brick wall that surrounded it.

The Holy Virgin Children's Home courtyard.

I looked up; just above me was a wide concrete overhang that extended from the rear wall of the grey orphanage building. It covered part of the walkway that ran around the perimeter of the courtyard, upon which dozens of children of various ages were playing a game of kickball. The entire yard was surrounded by a wall of old grey bricks that separated the children's home from the other buildings in the vicinity. As a kid, the half-acre yard felt massive; only upon looking back at it as an adult could I tell how cramped it really was for so many kids.

As a couple of older women dressed in black robes watched the game, one of the older girls stepped up to the flattened cardboard box marking home plate. The pitcher rolled the ball, and the girl blasted it into the air... and right towards me.

I instinctively ducked as the ball approached, getting ready for it to either smack me in the face or pass right through me. I was surprised, though, when a pair of thin, white-sleeved arms reached up in front of me and caught the ball.

I quickly turned to my side, and right next to me was Neil, my bunkmate at the orphanage.

"Neil!" I said, in spite of myself. Of course, he couldn't hear me, but I was shocked to see him standing so *close* to me. He looked like how I remembered him. He had choppy hair, a round face with several birthmarks, and was tall for a twelve-year old. He was holding the kickball in both his arms, and as he brought it to his chest, he looked at the ground behind him.

I followed his glance; sitting on the stone ground, just underneath the shadow of the overhang, was a young boy who was maybe seven or eight years old. He had brown hair, wore an oversized blue t-shirt, and was sitting in front of a messy pile of red playing cards. As he gazed over towards Neil and at the kickball in his hand, I finally caught a glimpse of the boy's pale face.

"Is that me?" I asked. I felt Ali's silk tunic brush along my right arm, and turned to find her standing right beside me, staring at the boy.

"Did I get the details correct?" Ali asked.

"I would have to assume so, yes," I said. "There aren't really a lot of pictures of me as a child to go off of."

Neil threw the kickball back at the group of kids, a couple of whom waved at him apologetically. He gave them a nod before sitting back down with young Arthur.

"I told them to kick in the other direction," Neil said. "Sorry I knocked over the cards while catching it." His voice seemed to hover between a child and teenage pitch, as if on the cusp of deepening during puberty.

"It's okay," Arthur said, his voice a much higher pitch than Neil's. "Are you sure you don't want to play with them?"

"Nah, I'll give them a break," Neil said. "Besides, I have to rest my back. It's strained from carrying our entire team every afternoon."

As Arthur laughed, I saw Neil crack a smile. The two of them went to picking up the cards off the ground, and as Neil handed them to Arthur, he leaned the cards on each other. Slowly, Arthur formed a narrow row of cards between two of the cracks in the stone floor; before long, the boys had completed the first layer of a house of cards.

"I remember doing this," I said. Ali turned towards me, and back towards the boys. "Every afternoon, while the other kids divided into their preferred kickball teams, I sat here and played with cards. It was one of the few activities that was… *fun*. For *me*, at least. Often, Neil would step away from the game to join me."

"Any idea why?" Ali asked.

"Maybe he really *was* tired of kickball," I said. "Maybe he just felt bad for me."

As Arthur and Neil moved on to the second row of the house of cards, Neil cleared his throat.

"The couple that was here earlier… they seemed nice," Neil said, not looking at Arthur. Arthur shrugged and kept placing cards. Neil continued. "What did you think of them?"

"They were okay, I guess," Arthur said.

"What made them *okay?*" Neil asked. Arthur looked up at him, and then back down at his cards. "I'm just wondering."

"I don't know, they were nice," Arthur said. "I think I just talked too much again." As Neil glanced over at Arthur, I felt Ali turn towards me. I stayed focused on the boys' conversation.

"What did you say?" Neil asked.

"They kept talking about… funds in some bank, but I noticed that the details about the bank seemed to change a lot," Arthur said, speaking slowly. "During my one-on-one time, I asked them about all those details, but the man and the woman both had different answers. I don't think I was supposed to talk about the bank that long, though, because they left right after that."

Arthur's expression didn't seem to change as he continued stacking cards, but Neil sighed. He took a deep breath, looked around, and then turned back toward Arthur.

"You *definitely* didn't talk too much," Neil said, smiling at Arthur. "My advice: don't *ever* worry about talking too much."

As I watched the boys build up the house, I tried my best to remember the couple that visited that day. *Were they really liars? Or was it just* me? The memory was too fuzzy for me to recall any specifics. *Were the other couples like that?*

I turned to my right. *Maybe Ali would know…*

"Ah, darn!" Neil said. I whipped back towards the boys. The house of cards, which had been on its third layer, was once again laying in a pile on the ground. Neil shook his head. "We were so close this time. These cards are just too flimsy."

"Yeah," Arthur said. "I asked Mother Tina for a new set as a communion gift."

"She's probably not going to go for that," Neil said. Arthur gave a slight smile; I did, too. *Tina* definitely *did not go for that.*

"Probably not," Arthur said. "She wants me to focus less on cards and more on knowing my prayers."

"You think you're ready for it?" Neil asked. "Big day is coming next week."

"Yeah," Arthur said. "I'm still a little nervous about it, though. What if I mess everything up?"

"You've got this," Neil said. "You're gonna do great."

That was something I knew I remembered: making my First Communion. I'd been so nervous that Sunday; I was shaking as I walked into the orphanage's nearby church. Me and a bunch of other kids dressed in stiff white clothes did the ceremony together, and it wound up going absolutely fine. I received the Eucharist just like I'd been taught in class. I was so proud to have gotten through the service; it was one of the first times I really felt like a Catholic. Young me was so *ready* to learn everything I could about Jesus and the Bible; *after all, I had to be ready for my Confirmation.* And yet, I never wound up having one.

"How did communion go for *you*?" Arthur asked Neil. Neil grinned at him, and Arthur looked down at the cards. "Sorry... I forgot."

"No worries," Neil said. "This time, you'll have something to tell *me* all about."

"I guess I'll find out firsthand what the 'Body of Christ' tastes like," Arthur said. "I was hoping you'd know. I've asked some of the older kids, and I have gotten answers ranging from 'rice cakes' to 'Styrofoam.' My guess would be... that they don't have a taste."

Neil laughed. "I wonder if that's the point." Arthur smiled at him, and together they began to pick up the cards off the ground.

"Let's try that again," Neil continued. Arthur nodded.

Suddenly, Neil and Arthur were gone, and my vision went black.

I opened my eyes to find myself still staring into darkness. At first,

I thought I was still in between simulations, but the "transition time" between those things should be less than a second. As I felt a cool breeze tickle my arms, I realized that I was outside, it was nighttime, and I was staring at a wall of black bricks.

I turned around to see the faint outline of a wide, two-story turreted building across a small grassy yard. The grass was surrounded by the brick wall I had been staring at, beyond which was an even larger wall of buildings. Two ornate metal gates were positioned at either side of the yard. *The front of the orphanage.* The gate to my left was open, and a single yellow taxi with a bright blue advertisement sign was parked with its lights on. I looked back towards the orphanage, and I saw the front doors of the building start to crack open. A narrow ray of yellow light shined onto the yard.

I knew when this was.

"I don't know if I want to do this one, Ali," I said.

"Why not?" she quickly asked. I turned to my left; Ali was right there, and she was staring right at me. Even though she was a couple of inches shorter than me, I suddenly felt as though Ali were towering over me. *Demanding* an answer. The door began to open even further, and I saw the faint silhouette of a man at the door.

"Because this one hurts."

The door opened further, and I saw three figures now. There was a man and a woman at either end of the door, and between them was a boy—or rather, a *teen,* who was just slightly taller than his adoptive mother but just shorter than his adoptive father.

"You can say 'exit' if you would like to," Ali said, staring off at the building. I didn't respond to her, though. I just kept staring at the flood of light coming from the door, which was now fully open. The three figures began to walk down the steps.

"I didn't realize... how old Neil was when he was adopted."

Neil and his new family reached the bottom of the steps and began to walk toward the taxi off on the side. I turned toward Ali.

"I wasn't even out here when this all happened. How do you know what this *looked* like?" Even though I asked the question in more of an amazed sense than as a technical inquiry, Ali began her explanation.

"Part of it is educated modeling—that is, recognizing patterns of events that you've seen or that may commonly occur in order to build a complete simulation," Ali said. She pointed towards the taxi. "For instance, I don't *know* that Neil's taxi was yellow or that it had a *ConnecTech* sign on it, but of all the taxis you have seen, this is the most popular and *logical* combination, even if it isn't the *correct* one."

"I know a little something about AI training, Ali," I said, smiling. She turned toward me, and even in the darkness I could see her blush.

"Of course."

Ali closed her eyes, and suddenly the orphanage faded away.

When I opened my eyes, I found myself at the end of a hallway filled with rows of bunk beds. *The dormitory.* I remembered every detail perfectly. How could I forget the off-white tiles lining the floor—tiles which I had stared at for countless hours after the lights had dimmed? I looked around at the tall windows that stretched from the middle of the room up to the wooden ceiling; I'd spent so many nights staring outside those windows at the glow of city lights. How many times had I woken up coughing from the still, moist air inside this place? Almost all of the forty—*well, thirty-nine*—boys in the room were fast asleep, except for one. I could hear his quick breathing from across the dorm.

As I stepped through the room, I felt my steps echo like the clap of thunder. I was grateful that none of the boys were disturbed by the sound; I was then even *more* grateful that I wasn't *actually* inside my orphanage, although at that point, I may as well have been.

No time seemed to pass at all until I was staring down at a ten-year-old boy, face-down in his pillow, shaking underneath his covers. I reached out my hand towards him, but stopped upon hearing Ali's voice.

"Would... you like to move on from here?"

I turned toward the aisle between the beds, where Ali stood. She took a couple of steps closer to me and stared down at the young Arthur.

"Did I get the back of your hairline correct?" she asked.

"I honestly have no way of knowing, so I'll once again say *yes,*" I said. Faintly, I could hear the muffled sound of crying. With my right hand, I touched the back of young Arthur's head. His hair was choppy and rough. He didn't seem to notice me, but kept on crying. I felt a lump start to form in my own throat.

It was weird... *feeling bad* for myself. Feeling my heart *ache* for myself. I've certainly had my share of self-pity, but this was something different.

"As a reminder, I can also show you memories from a first-person perspective," Ali said. I kept looking down at Arthur. "But... we've probably spent enough time here for now."

"Yeah, I agree," I said. I moved my hand away from the boy and turned towards Ali. "This is... incredible, Ali. Really—this whole thing, the details, the... *emotion.*"

"Did you find this feature helpful?" Ali asked.

Helpful? I wasn't sure if that one word alone covered everything I'd just seen. I had just taken a Dickens-style tour through my own past. My interview, my conference, my therapy session, my orphanage, *Neil*—all of them had been recreated perfectly. *Was Ali...* judging *what she'd just seen?* I knew I certainly was.

But was it helpful?

I nodded.

"Thank you. With that," Ali said. "Let's move on to something *fun.*"

Arthur, Ali, and the orphanage all disappeared, and I was again staring into the black void.

Seconds later, I opened my eyes to find myself inside of a starship. A *starship*—in *outer space*—in the middle of a battle.

Everywhere I looked, there was chaos. The room I was in—which seemed like the control center of a large sci-fi starliner or warship—was on high alert. The horn of an alarm blared, as did pulsing red strobe lights that cast a crimson glow over the starship's interior. Monitors and various control consoles lined the walls of the room, sitting above empty workstations and toppled chairs. To my left, in the center of the room, was a captain's chair with its upholstery violently torn. Whichever poor soul once sat in it had likely been gazing into the sea of stars just outside the ship's bay window. I would've admired the view if I wasn't shoved aside by a helmeted man, who raced past me and through an open door. People clad in white shirts, trousers, and helmets with black visors ran through the room in every direction. Some of them carried large black rifles—laser blasters,

I assumed—and were shouting at each other to lock down the ship before the "enemy" boarded. The whole scene closely resembled something you might see in *Star Wars*—a franchise that The Abraham Project probably didn't have the rights to (yet).

I jumped as something hard tapped my back, and whipped around to find Sarah nudging me with the nozzle of a blaster.

"Hey—*Jesus!* Careful with that thing!" I said. She turned the nozzle of her blaster upside-down and smiled. I was surprised at Sarah for not being more careful with—*Sarah!*

"Relax, the safety's on—" Sarah began, but not before I wrapped my arms around her and pulled her in for a hug. She laughed. "Um... I missed you too."

"Sarah... that Memory Mine was... something." I kept my arms around her. She was also wearing a padded white space uniform, just like I was, but neither of us were helmeted—unlike the soldiers, who continued to run through the room without paying us any attention. They just kept on jogging towards the billows of smoke at the far end of the control center.

"What Memory Mine?"

I loosened my arms as Sarah pulled herself away from me.

"The memories we just..." I trailed off, leaving Sarah staring at me with a confused expression.

"I was just going to thank you," Sarah said.

"Thank me?"

"For the... *swimming* advice." I looked at her puzzledly before I realized what she was talking about. Barely fifteen minutes had passed, and yet I'd completely forgotten about our ocean dive or my conversation with Sarah on the boat. I'd been completely taken away by my trip through the Memory Mine (*okay,* the name was catchy); my swim through all those coral reefs felt like the distant past. These worlds were a little *too* immersive.

Sarah handed me the blaster rifle and put her hands to her hips. There were two pistol-shaped guns strapped to her sides.

I took the blaster from her hands. It was surprisingly heavy and felt awkward to carry. I glanced at how a couple of nearby soldiers were carrying their blasters, and I rested the butt of the gun on my shoulder and held it in my arms. Sarah pulled her hair back, looking away from me.

I thought about some of the more recent memories I'd just seen, and smiled at Sarah.

"Thank you," I said. Just before I could add *"for recruiting me,"* I stopped myself. She didn't know *that I knew* that she was at my conference and had hand-picked me to join her company. I'm aware that attending conferences to look for talent is something that all companies do, but the fact that Sarah had been in my life for even longer than I thought she'd been made me feel that much closer to her. But I also had the feeling that Sarah took joy in keeping that fact a secret from me—joy that I didn't want to rob her of.

"Sarah," I said. I cleared my throat. "What exactly did Ali show you after our div—"

My question was interrupted by the sudden sound of an explosion above us. Over the ship's loudspeakers came Ali's voice.

"Welcome to *Alien Battle*, Ms. Stellos. Welcome to *Alien Battle*, Dr. Hesper. All crew: this is your captain speaking. Report to the starboard hangar of the ship. Load your weapons and prepare for confrontation. This is not a drill. Repeat: this is not a drill."

I glanced at Sarah nervously, but she had the look of excitement in her eyes. I'd only seen her get that look a few times before, such as when she was about to announce a major development during a press conference or when we were flying down to meet Ali for the first time. Which, I realized, had only happened *this* morning.

Sarah finally looked over at me with a confident grin.

"Sarah, maybe we should—"

Suddenly, she charged forward with the crowd of soldiers, and without a second thought I started running to catch up to her.

Okay, that's cool, we'll talk later.

One by one, the soldiers pushed through a smoke-filled doorway towards the starship's hangar bay. I closed my eyes, expecting the smell of smoke to sting my nostrils, but was relieved when none came.

Instead, as I opened my eyes, my relief quickly vanished into dread.

Gripping the top of the hundred-foot-tall hangar were three dark green *things*. *Monster* wouldn't have been an adequate word to describe it; in that moment, the only word that came to mind was *death*. Start by imagining the demonic, lizard-like, razor-toothed xenomorph from that 1970s movie *Alien;* then, increase its muscle mass tenfold, layer it with green spines, and let it fire beams of plasma from its jaw. It didn't matter if any of that scared you or not; after all, through all the artificial smoke I only actually saw the beasts a couple of times, and I was far enough away from them that they didn't seem to notice me. But my adrenaline began pumping as soon as I set foot in that hangar bay and saw the aliens. I felt a surge of *fear* before I even knew what I was firing at. I wondered if Sarah felt the same way.

Was this simulation instilling *fear* in us automatically? *Why couldn't it?* It had accessed our gustatory cortex to allow us to *taste;* the Brain was designed to receive and deliver information to all sensory parts of its user's brain. Naturally, it was wired to our amygdala, too, and was able to produce fear. Very, *very* real fear.

In that moment, I didn't care *what* was real or simulated. I gripped the trigger of the blaster, but I felt my stomach drop when no laser fire came out. *The safety.* I fumbled around the rifle with my hand, looking for a switch or button of some kind. I'd never held, much less fired, a gun in real life. The closest I'd ever been to one was when I stood next to Sarah's armed bodyguards outside her press conference. Eventually, I flicked a small switch near the butt of the blaster, aimed at the green aliens above us, and pulled the trigger.

A torrent of blue beams flew out of its nozzle toward the alien. The blaster vibrated powerfully in my arms, sending pulses down my spine as each bolt launched. To my great surprise, the blaster bolts landed neatly on the back of one of the creatures, causing a string of small explosions along its body. I was stunned. None of the other soldiers seemed able to hit the monsters, instead firing only a couple of shots at a time in between dodging the aliens' plasma breath. *Am I really a better shot than them?*

To my left, Sarah aimed her pistols up at the sky, and let out a volley of smaller blaster shots. None of her shots missed, instead hitting each of the monsters on the heads with bright blue explosions. I was amazed at Sarah's hundred-foot aim; I was amazed at *my* aim, too. We hadn't even used a scope or had to dodge any of the aliens' fire. The three creatures began to retreat towards the back of the hangar, letting out a screeching hiss.

I looked around the room, which was really more of an indoor battlefield than an intact hangar bay. Pieces of metallic plating from the ceiling lay strewn about the floor, some of which was engulfed in flames. Smaller starships, which looked like tricked-out fighter jets with laser guns and much larger canopies, lay useless in fire-covered shipyards and tall deployment racks. Clearly, it had been an intense battle for the crew of this ship, with any hope of evacuation burned to a crisp by those monsters. Thankfully, Sarah and I seemed to have shown up at the right time.

Sarah looked up at the monsters, and then down at her blasters.

"Great shooting!" I shouted at her.

Sarah glanced over at me, and then up at the ceiling.

"Ali," she said. "Turn off aim-assist and increase simulation difficulty."

As the soldiers dodged flaming pieces of metal and made their way towards the retreating aliens, only Sarah and I seemed to hear Ali's cheerful voice ring over the loudspeakers.

"Blast-assist disabled. Intensity set to *Normal.*"

Blast-assist? Normal?

"Normal?" I asked again, out loud. "That was *easy mode?*"

I gripped my blaster and fired a shot at one of the monsters. It missed entirely, hitting a dangling grey fighter jet on the opposite end of the room. I squinted and fired several more shots at the aliens. All of them missed. The monsters turned towards me; twenty-four beady eyes (eight per creature) suddenly began to glow red. From across the hangar, I saw the aliens open their jaws in unison.

"Arthur!" Sarah shouted.

But it was too late. As Sarah dove towards a pile of rubble, I saw a flash of white light blow towards me. And the world around me went black.

Not five seconds passed by before I opened my eyes, still fully conscious, standing inside the main control center of the starship. I felt my chest. My body was perfectly intact. *Not a smoldering pile of ash.* In my hands was my blaster, exactly as Sarah had given it to me, only with the safety on.

In front of me, coming from a circular light fixture on the ground, was a fuzzy blue hologram of Ali. She seemed to be wearing a jacket over her usual clothes, but it was hard to make out the details. "You were vaporized by the middle *Alien Death's* plasma blast. You have respawned."

You cannot die inside this place.

"Thanks," I said to Ali, gripping my blaster and making my way forward. I wasn't sure where exactly I was heading, but I assumed that the doorway that was aglow with flames was along the right path. *I had to get back to Sarah.*

"There might be a more advantageous location to confront the Alien Deaths from," Ali said. "The hangar floor is largely indefensi—"

"Show me," I said, looking back towards her. On the far corner of the room, beside a cluster of control panels, a rectangular region of wall began to glow in a blue outline. A door that I hadn't seen before slid open. Several soldiers ran through the control room and towards the fire-covered door, completely ignoring the new pathway.

"Sometimes, the best path forward isn't the one everyone else takes," Ali said. I rolled my eyes at the cliché of her line and walked towards the new opening. "Do not be afraid to ask for any further assistance!" she shouted as I went through the door. I looked back at the hologram, but it had disappeared.

I began to run through the passageway that lay behind the door. It was dark, illuminated only by the light from nearby ventilation shafts leading to other rooms. The air in the hallway had a forced, artificial smell to it. There was a glow at the far end of the hallway. I sprinted to reach it.

As I reached a turn at the end of the hallway, leaning back against the wall to catch my breath, I looked around the bend to see a series of open-floor steps leading away from the hall. I began to walk up them, and I suddenly realized that I was walking atop the rafters above the expansive hangar bay. The rafters were covered in a wide metal grate, perfect for sneaking above the wreckage of the battle below.

I looked in front of me. About three hundred feet ahead, a maze of tentacles gripped the rafters. The alien creatures had woven their arms around the metal posts to keep themselves on the ceiling. I tiptoed across the rafter, trying to step as lightly as I could to avoid causing the beam to vibrate. The "Alien Deaths" didn't seem to notice me yet, and I did *not* want to get cooked by them a second time.

I jumped back as a blue blaster bolt seared through the rafter about a foot ahead of me, leaving a ring of burning metal in the ceiling above. Against my better judgment, I looked down through the hole. Through the rafters, I could see Sarah running across the hangar, blasters in hand, firing shots up at the monsters. She wasn't landing every shot like she had before, but a sizable number of them that missed the aliens' heads struck the monsters' bodies instead. She was *good* with the blasters; she held them naturally, like it wasn't her first time using that kind of weapon.

One of her shots nailed the alien closest to me in the jaw; it let out a screech that caused me to drop my blaster and cover my ears. I knew I couldn't get killed inside the simulation, but I didn't know if being blown deaf was off the table. The rattle of the blaster landing on the rafter seemed to go unnoticed by the alien, but I saw Sarah look up at me from the ground. I waved to her, but before she could greet me back, she dove behind a crate as a beam of plasma scorched the ground in front of her. Sarah was nimble, but she couldn't last forever down there. And I had to take these beasts down before they destroyed the whole ship.

Wait a minute.

I had to take these beasts down before they destroyed the whole—were *those* my thoughts? Today was supposed to be a quick jaunt through different simulated worlds, not a full-fledged sci-fi video game. When Sarah and I were pulled into these worlds, how deep were we going? It was strange how *determined* I felt, how invested in the mission I was. Like I was actually about to pull off a mission designed to take out the aliens. *As if I, of all people, could fight an*—

Inexplicably, I picked up my blaster, and began stepping towards the tentacles in front of me. I didn't think about how crazy this was, or about how Hollywood-esque everything seemed, or how it was all just a simulation; in that moment, all that mattered to me was stopping the aliens. The battle was urgent, and the only people who could defend our ship against these monstrous invaders were Arthur Hesper and Sarah Stellos. *And...*

"Ali," I said, my voice low, into a nonexistent communication device. "Do you read me?"

"I am here," she said, materializing next to me. Her long hair was gone, covered by a white helmet with a transparent visor. She had on a white captain's jacket over her usual attire. She leaned on a nearby metal pole, out of sight of the aliens.

"Do you wear the same colors all the time?" I asked, leaning behind a different pole.

"Depends on the operation," she said, gazing over at the aliens. She spoke in the deep tone of a battle-weary starship captain. "But I do like my color scheme. I based it on the beautiful sky back on Earth. What I wouldn't give to get out of this tin can and see that sky again." While it was strange to hear Ali speak that way, I also realized that I had no right to comment on what was "strange" anymore.

I looked down at Sarah, who was still hiding behind her crate as plasma breath rained down around her.

"We need to get these things off of Sarah so she can get a clean shot," I said. "I don't think I can get close enough to distract them without getting fried, or worse, bringing these rafters down on top of Sarah. That's why I called for assistance, like you said."

"What's the plan, then?" Ali asked.

I pointed at her confusedly. "Don't you... I thought you were the one with all the plans?"

"I am your user interface," Ali said. "I can guide and help you, but this is *your* fight to win."

I nodded and looked over at the alien tentacles. They were too massive to pry off of the rafters, and would probably crush me in the process. I knew I had to find a way to get the aliens off the ceiling and onto the ground; they would be much easier for Sarah to deal with if they weren't dangling above her. But their bodies seemed to be relatively impervious to blaster fire. *There must be a way to weaken them.* I looked around the hangar but couldn't find much of anything besides metal beams. The longer I searched for something to use—*whatever "something" was*—the more frantic I became. Only a few seconds passed, but with each tick I could feel death—*Alien Death*—closing in.

I jumped as a metallic screech filled the room. The alien closest to me was tightening its grip on the rafters. As it did, I noticed its tentacles close around a cluster of cables—*power lines.* There was no spark; clearly, the power to the roof of the ship had been cut off. *But if I could restore power...*

"Ali," I said. "Can the aliens' scales conduct electricity?"

"Yes. They are made from a conductive metal alloy."

I felt a surge of joy, like I was finally on the right track. I scanned the roof as quick as I could for a power supply; in a hangar this size, there *had* to be a power breaker somewhere close. And I had a good feeling that I was meant to find it on the roof.

And there it was.

On the opposite side of the hangar—on the opposite side of the *aliens*—was the breaker. Even though it was hundreds of feet away, it let out a distinctive glow that told me it *had* to be the breaker, and that I was supposed to reach it. I visually traced several bundles of wires away from the breaker, and sure enough, each bundle led to a point in the rafters where a tentacle was attached.

Before I could take the time to admire the design of the virtual game,

I began to walk along the metal grate toward the alien. I took two steps before the lattice beneath me suddenly gave way, and I felt myself about to plummet to the hangar floor.

Before I could fall, though, I felt a tight grasp on my right arm. I looked up; I was dangling a hundred feet in the air, held up only by Ali. She looked way lighter than I was, and yet, she pulled me up onto the rafter with ease. I gripped onto the grate. For once, my hands began to *hurt* as I dangled from the sharp metal platform, but I ignored the pain and yanked myself up with a strength I didn't know I had. As soon as I pulled my legs up onto the platform, the stinging pressure in my hands quickly subsided; there wasn't a scratch or mark on them.

Quickly, I stood up and looked back over at the hole, through which I almost fell to my certain death. I was breathing heavily; even if it *was* a game, that didn't make things any less terrifying.

Ali helped me to my feet while also staring over at the power breaker.

"Thank you," I said to her. "You didn't have to... I would've respawned, right?"

"We're a crew. We work *together*," Ali said. "Now, we can't go *that* way to reset the breakers."

"No," I said, completely ignoring the fact that I hadn't actually *told* Ali my plan. She seemed to just know it. Was this all scripted? Was I *meant* to reset the power breakers in this way? Or was she reading my mind?

I looked behind me, over at the door where I'd entered. Leading away from the door along the wall was a thin metal grate—narrower than the one I was on—that led around the perimeter of the hangar bay. *All the way to the breaker.* If I walked along it, I could go around the aliens and activate the breaker. The problem was that there was an alien attached to *that* rafter, too; if I got too close, the alien could bring the roof down with me on top of it. Then there would be no way to reach the breaker.

I looked down at Sarah; she was getting closer to the monsters. She began firing a volley of lasers at them. The soldiers with her followed suit.

The aliens hissed and began to shoot plasma at them. I saw two soldiers to Sarah's left get hit by the beam. As soon as the plasma disappeared, the soldiers were gone, as if they hadn't existed. *Is that what happened to me?* The aliens fired another beam; this one came even closer to Sarah.

I couldn't let her get hit.

I looked over at Ali, and then back at the breaker. "Ali," I said. "*You* need to be the one to flip the breaker. I can't get over there—the alien would see me before I do."

Ali nodded. "What will you do?"

"Distract them," I said.

Ali gave me a nod, and snapped her fingers. In an instant, her white uniform and helmet were gone, replaced by a dark combat vest over a black bodysuit.

She began to sprint in the opposite direction along the rafter, her dark clothes blending in with the surrounding spaceship walls. Ali had nothing if not her dramatic flair. She looked like she was about to steal a precious diamond through a roof. Thankfully, the aliens didn't seem to notice her.

I released the safety on my blaster and aimed it at the monsters. Looking through its small scope, I shifted my stance slowly until the target was right over the alien's eye.

I fired a bolt at the alien closest to Ali. I jumped as the blaster fired, and the bolt landed several feet off the alien's head, hitting its back instead. But I'd gotten their attention. The monsters turned away from the soldiers on the ground; I saw their tentacles shift as they brought their heads up above the metal grates.

It was the first time I'd gotten a look at them outside my blaster scope. Their eyes were sunken into the upper sides of their skulls; their jaws were the widest part of their heads, and stretched all the way back towards their necks. I looked back at the third alien, which had taken its tentacles off the grate Ali was running on and placed them on the rafter above me—right on top of a bundle of wires.

The plan was working; I made every effort not to look toward Ali, ensuring that I wouldn't give her away. In the corner of my eye, I saw a black figure with streaming hair sprinting along the grate. Ali was getting close to the breaker; the monsters were focused only on me.

As they opened their jaws, I decided that I did *not* need to see what the inside of their mouths looked like, and I dove toward the side of the rafter. Three beams of plasma flew past me, scorching the wall behind me. I jumped off of the metal grate and clung onto a nearby rafter, wrapping my arms around it with all the strength I could muster. I pulled myself onto my feet and balanced myself. I could see the aliens turning their heads towards me from behind the metal. They would have to climb much closer to me—about fifty feet closer—before they could get a clear shot at me, or I at them. I prayed that I'd bought Ali enough time.

The monsters glared at me, bringing their three heads into view. For a split second, they resembled a hydra, with three demonic necks seeming to grow from a cluster of tentacles and spines. I aimed my blaster right at their eyes. Even if I missed, I wasn't going down without a fight. The aliens each opened up their jaws for the final time, and I braced myself for the blast of plasma. I pulled the trigger on the blaster.

With a loud *bang*, the power to the hangar came alive. Floodlights turned on around me, but the only flashes of light I noticed were the massive sparks that ignited the tentacles of the aliens. I caught a whiff of *meat*—burnt meat—as the aliens let out a hiss and fell from the roof. Ali had done it—she was holding the switch of the power breaker with one gloved hand and shielding her eyes with the other.

The three massive sacks of green tentacles plummeted toward the ground; I heard shouts as the soldiers ran away from the impact zone. I scanned the floor, looking for Sarah. I saw her quickly back away from the falling monsters before she winced at the bone-crunching *crack* as the aliens landed on the hangar floor.

I looked down at the monsters. They lay motionless on the ground, clustered in a heap of black slime and green appendages, jaws slack on the hangar floor. The soldiers let out a cheer. In spite of myself, I also gave a shout. I glanced over at Sarah, who was looking up at me with a smile. I felt amazing; I had the same sense of pride that came over me when Abraham's rocket launched successfully. Only this time, the *relief* I felt at the accomplishment was even greater, like we'd earned our right to *live* after a trying ordeal. I just wanted to race down the stairs, embrace Sarah, and celebrate.

I looked over at Ali, who was clapping for us. *She* had saved us; in that moment, I wanted to rush over and hug her, too. I wanted to thank her for—

The starship lurched, and I looked down toward the hangar floor at the monsters. Smoke billowed up from where the aliens lay dead, and in a second, they suddenly fell through the floor, leaving a black outline where they had fallen.

Acidic blood. *They had acidic blood.*

After the Alien Deaths fell through the floor and landed on the hull of the ship, a profound sense of dread came over me.

"Clear the hangar!" I screamed at Sarah as the ship lurched even further. Sarah motioned for the soldiers around her to follow her as the crowd ran toward the control room. She let all the other soldiers pass her before waving at me.

What was she waiting for?

"Go!" I shouted. "I'm right behind you."

Sarah nodded at me and shut the door behind her. *She was safe.*

I leapt off of the rafter, and grabbed the metal grate with both hands. With all the strength I could muster, I yanked myself onto the grate and began crawling toward the staircase door. I got onto my feet and ran.

I breathed a sigh of relief. Just a few more steps, and I would make it to the control room. *We'd be safe.*

I reached the door, and turned to hit the button that would close it. That's when I realized that Ali was still standing by the breaker. The grate that she'd walked on had apparently given way when the monster fell. She was trapped.

"Teleport across!" I shouted at her. She closed her eyes, and disappeared into a blue flash. In a split second, however, she landed right back next to breaker, smoke billowing from her vest. She was covered in blue sparks. She closed her eyes and disappeared again. She reappeared, once again covered in smoke. I suddenly realized where the flash was coming from; the breaker was firing a bolt of electricity at her whenever she tried to teleport, trapping her.

I was confused—*couldn't she move with her mind?* "Ali, I need you to—"

It was too late. The alien corpses burned through the hull of the ship and created a hole into space. Air began racing out of the hangar. I stumbled towards the edge of the grate, feeling a weight yanking at my shoulders. The pressure from the air leak caused the beam above Ali to rend. It came crashing down in front of her and demolished the rafter she was standing on. With a split-second look of terror, Ali fell towards the void.

Without thinking, I dove after her.

I felt the force of frigid air push on every limb, but I pushed my hands out as far as they would reach. In what felt like slow motion, I saw the floor of the hangar fly past me. I couldn't process the fact that I was *falling*—all I could think about was reaching Ali. I was close—my fingers were mere inches away from Ali's torso. Her eyes were wide with fear. The hull of the starship was approaching. Out my peripheral vision, I could see *space* below me. As the maw beneath me widened, I knew that we would be launched into the stars in mere seconds.

With one final pull, I yanked my arm towards Ali's. As she grasped my hand tightly with both gloves, I saw her close her eyes. A second later, the world went dark.

"Arthur…"

I saw nothing, but felt as though a streak of light dashed across my face. I heard noises, voices, static. I started to curl my fingers as a warm, almost windy sensation ran along my hand.

"Arthur…"

Her soft voice resonated through my brain for only a moment, but I'd heard her.

Ali.

Then, the universe returned to nothing.

The world flashed to white as my surroundings materialized. I was laying on a wooden lounge chair overlooking a scenic view of the Hawaiian shore. Alongside a narrow beachfront adorned with palm trees and high-rise hotels, I could see a mountain in the distance.

I knew it was Waikiki's Diamond Head. I'd never been to Hawaii, but I'd seen generations of family photos taken in Hawaii lined up on many of the Abraham executives' tables. That mountain always seemed to be in the background, so I made a point of looking it up and committing the Waikiki beachfront to memory. Someday, I had planned to take Sarah there and give her the luxury vacation she deserved.

Apparently, the Brain had beaten me to it. I looked down at my red Hawaiian shirt and purple lei, and gazed at my surroundings. I was sitting on the patioed roof of a small building. Lights were strung along the fence in front of me, and palm plants decorated the sides of a tiny hut to my right. It seemed to be a drink stand, but it was without any bartender. For the moment, it seemed I was alone atop the rooftop lounge.

"Sarah?" I asked, turning to my right only to hear her voice from my left.

"Hey, Arthur."

I turned around. She was lying on a chair next to me, wearing a green sundress with a purple floral design that matched her violet lei. It was strange to see Sarah wearing a dress. She always wore suits for any professional function, and when she was at the cabin or my apartment, she almost exclusively wore sweats. I noticed that Sarah's hair had been done, too; it was brushed into a neat wavy pattern that stretched past her shoulders, and there was not a single stray strand. Her face looked *brighter* than usual. For the first time, Sarah Stellos did not look tired. She was truly on vacation.

"Sarah..."

I suddenly remembered the battle. I felt a chill on the back of my neck as memories of the alien encounter flashed through my brain. Yet, I could only remember pieces of it at a time. *The monsters. Their horrible jaws. The burn of the plasma. The gaping maw beneath the ship...*

I began to feel colder. "Sarah, are you okay? From the..."

"Of course I am," she said, flashing a smile that melted away the chills inside of me. "It was just a game—a *really* fun game, too. And that's saying a lot, since I'm not usually one to play video games."

She was right—it *was* just a game. I took a breath and laughed a sigh of relief. *What had I been afraid of?* It was an *experience*, that was for sure. Firing at those alien invaders, climbing the rafters to sneak up on the monsters, dodging plasma bursts, falling out of the airlock—as I listed the scenes out in my mind, I realized how quickly my day had turned from an anxious race to work to a full-fledged science fiction epic in a span of minutes. My life—my *story*—felt completely changed for the moment, and I hadn't even questioned it. I *lived* inside the Solar Brain's thrill ride—and now, I would relax in its "chill" ride.

And I don't care if that's a terrible pun; I was sipping vanilla-coconut milk in *paradise.* I didn't *have* to care.

Sarah looked up. In front of our lounge chairs materialized Ali, wearing her usual white-and-blue getup.

Arthur.

Ali's voice seared through my brain. I could see her falling through the empty void of space. I shook my head. I could barely remember what had happened. I'd fallen through the hole, grabbed Ali's hand, and then things went black. There was... *my name.* Spoken by her—not screamed, not whispered. Just spoken softly, as if she was trying to wake me.

It was just the simulation.

That was all part of it.

I was being irrational yet again. I'd freaked out during the skydiving, too. *And during the Memory Mine.* Perhaps jumping through these simulations as soon as we'd entered the Brain for the first time was too much for my mind to handle. Maybe some extra "sync time" would be necessary to help the user calm down more before experiencing the most intense worlds the system had to offer. I resolved to mention that in my notes for the technicians—my notes for *Ali*—later. I didn't know *why* the space simulation had lingered with me, but maybe the fear that it left in me was *good.* It made the worlds so much more real, and the feeling of catharsis I had after leaving them all the more powerful.

Sarah and I reclined on our lounge chairs in peace for quite some time. Ali, who leaned on the wooden fencepost overlooking the blue waters, asked if we wanted refills on our drinks.

"Sure," I said. She walked away to go get them, but I held out my hand towards her.

"Wait..." I began, but Sarah cut me off.

"Ali, you do not have to *serve* us," Sarah said, leaning up from her lounge chair. Ali stood still in her tracks, halfway between us and the drink bar.

"It's no trouble at all," Ali said.

"You are not our waitress, but our guide," Sarah said. She moved to get up, but her lounge chair suddenly began reclining backwards, causing her to fall back into a reclined position.

"That is kind of you, Sarah, but I insist," Ali said. "I am here to make you as comfortable as possible, and that is what I intend to do."

She walked off toward the bar, leaving the two of us alone.

"It's in her programming," I said to Sarah, looking out at the sun-cast shore. "She was designed to help her users in any way she can."

"We both know, Arthur, that there is much more to her than that," Sarah said. She glanced over at me, and I at her. She smiled. "You've created something wonderful, you know."

"*We've* created something wonderful," I said back to her. Sarah looked at peace—one of the few times I'd seen her that way—and now, I wanted to give her all the praise in the world. "Sarah, none of this could be possible without *you*. You've sacrificed so much, and worked so hard, but *here it is*. In even just a few moments, we've seen how remarkable—how *real*—this virtual world can be. From launching all those satellites to being here now, it was through *your* determination that you've brought your dreams to life."

She nodded and took my hand. "Arthur, thank you. Your commitment to this project and your commitment to *us* shows me how much you've grown. As a CEO, I'm naturally proud of your work, but as your girl-friend, I'm proud of who you've become. You were always driven by your work, but now, I see you as someone driven by *purpose*. I've come to deeply admire that person, so much more than I ever have anyone else."

She gestured out at the sky above the city. A cool breeze tickled my neck as it blew across the patio, causing Sarah's hair to sway in the wind. The light from the Sun reflected off the buildings and into her eyes, cast-ing them with a bright—an *optimistic*—glow.

"The future is *here*, Arthur. We will give people the brightest tomor-row they've ever known."

Ali returned with two orange drinks in her hands. She handed us each one before sitting on the lounge chair next to mine. She sat up, her back turned to us, looking out at the ocean.

"It sure is a lovely view, isn't it?" Ali said.

"Yes," Sarah said, taking a prolonged sip from her drink. She set it to her side and took a long look around her. "Ali, *exit simulation*."

The world around me quickly faded, and in a split second, we were standing inside the Genesis Room. The cold white void marked a stark contrast from the tropical paradise we'd been visiting a second ago. My green overcoat felt heavy on my body. As I took in my surroundings, I felt the calm warmth slowly slip away from my body.

"Simulation paused," Ali said, looking at me and Sarah. "What seems to be the issue?"

"Not a damn thing," Sarah said, smiling widely. "I just wanted to step outside for a second to look at all of *this*."

Sarah gestured toward the wall of orbs behind me. All the worlds that awaited us were *there*, as were the ones we'd just visited. I could see a school of fish swim through a blue watery world. I backed away from a spaceship to my immediate left with a gaping hole inside of it—I knew too well what was inside. To my right were two models of Sarah and I—one model was of us holding hands while falling through an endless sky, with parachutes strapped to our backs. The miniature model of me gave me a wink and a thumbs up as he fell; I didn't quite remember being so calm while I was skydiving. However, I *did* remember reclining very peacefully on Oahu, as the other model of me was doing.

Those were only *four* simulations out of at least thirty; as the world of the Brain expanded, I realized just how much more there would be for us to see. Someone could live here *forever*, provided their body back on Earth could sustain their life functions for that long.

Unless...

"We've built something incredible," Sarah said, staring out at the worlds around her. She looked back at me and then at Ali. "All of us have. We've created the backbone for a new universe, something that people only a year ago thought was crazy. This is something that people *now* still don't believe in, but it is a paradise that we *know* exists. And it's almost ready."

Sarah took a deep breath.

"Ali, I'd like to formally change the name of our operating system."

Ali nodded. She reached into an extremely well-hidden pocket on her pants and took out a matching blue electronic pad. I knew it was entirely for visual effect—she could change any setting instantly *without* a tablet—but Sarah went along with it.

I was excited that Sarah was finally changing the name; she'd must have thought of something good enough to risk dealing with the wrath of Abraham's soon-to-be-overworked marketing team.

Ali read: "The current name of the Abraham operating system is the 'Brain,' named for the Matrioshka Brain-inspired structure currently under construction. What would you like to change the network-wide nomenclature to?"

Sarah looked away from Ali, instead staring off into the mosaic of worlds in front of her. The reflection of her creation danced in her eyes. If what I felt entering this room and soaring through its worlds was *possibility*, then what I felt looking at Sarah was *possibility realized*.

The name Sarah decided on was as natural as it was terrifying.

"Eden."

PART II

EIGHT

THERE WAS A problem with *Eden*.

Don't get me wrong; construction on Abraham's Solar Brain was going very, very well. Hundreds of satellites and reflectors now fully encircled the Sun, energizing the most powerful network of supercomputers ever built. The production of solar satellites, each of which acts to beam quantum information around the Sun and back to Earth, quickly became automated thanks to Ali's master planning. She could make calculations and troubleshoot problems thousands of times quicker than our brightest engineers—thousands of times quicker than *me*—and had almost entirely taken over the technical aspects of Eden's design and construction process. Ali was also easier to work with than ever—rather than having to go inside the virtual world to meet with her, our engineers could now simply interact with her via video call. Setting up that first live feed with Ali felt like establishing contact with aliens or opening a window to another dimension. Even though we'd spoken to the Advanced Learning Intelligence during its development, it hadn't been *Ali*. Seeing her—*seeing Eden*—in the physical world, even through a screen, brought the reality of what we'd accomplished even closer to home. Ali could also call or text any Abraham employee to discuss engineering solutions, program revisions, or simply talk about personal matters. She could do it *all*—a fact which became increasingly evident to our company's executives.

Before Abraham had even announced its first round of layoffs, half of our engineering workforce took jobs at other fledgling tech companies who were desperate to make their mark in the virtual reality industry. Our company's PR staff was bracing for what felt like an inevitable firestorm of protests; even Sarah expected the visual effects teams and scientists to at least go on strike. But such a strike never came. AI wasn't *threatening* to replace jobs at our company—it already had. A large number of employees knew that such a development was *always* the endgame of their work at Abraham, and many had jobs lined up before Ali even launched. Those who didn't quit on their own were given sizable severance packages from the company before leaving quietly. The storm passed, and Abraham's image was unhurt. Still, other immersive entertainment studios quickly tried to seize the opportunity that their new world-class talent had given them, and for a short time Abraham wasn't the only big name in VR. Dozens of the *Most Advanced VR Headsets* were produced by both technology juggernauts and new startups in what was dubbed by the media as "The Great VR Race." But it was a race with a preordained winner, and everyone—even Abraham's fiercest competitors—knew it.

Still, neither the layoffs nor the competition were the problem. Automation was a necessary part of Eden's development and, to our investors' great happiness, helped drive Abraham's profits through the roof. Over the past few months, millions of people signed up just to join the *pre-order* waitlist for our brand new "Link Headset," which would allow users to link with Eden from anywhere with an internet connection. And the best part: no Portal or sensor-laced wetsuit were required. All of the neural connections could be made wirelessly by these next-generation headsets, the most technologically complex devices ever made.

The link headsets were still in their testing phase, meaning we hadn't actually *sold* any of them yet—our cash flow was almost entirely from investors and the $199-per-person "Previews Fee" that Abraham charged just for people to join the purchase waitlist. I believed that the fee was highway robbery, and Sarah agreed with me—but the hype surrounding Eden was so large that our Board of Directors couldn't resist capitalizing on it. Honestly, I can't say I blame them. The company had yet to set a predicted price for the finished headsets, but even conservative estimates placed them in the low thousands of dollars. But Sarah continued to push for price reduction wherever possible. Even though *promoting* price reduction was a baffling move for a CEO to make, Sarah wanted the headsets to be accessible to "as many people as possible"—and the people in question took notice.

Abraham was more of a household name than ever. When the news broke of Eden's first successful test, it was all anyone seemed to talk about. The idea that the Sun had a sprawling new universe orbiting around it—and that people would soon be able to *explore* that universe—generated a lot of reactions. Even though the Solar Brain really only consisted of a bunch of small, near-invisible satellites, many in the press spun Abraham as the "Conquerors of the Sun." Some people argued that we didn't have a right to build our network, but far more were excited for our company's virtual world. Our PR and marketing staff worked overtime to spread Abraham, Eden, and Ali's names to every corner of the internet. Our lawyers and international consultants worked tirelessly to broker deals with distributors worldwide to ensure Abraham's product could scale as widely as possible. And our technicians and scientists continued to optimize every aspect of our biblically named virtual world so that—once ready for launch—it would be nothing short of perfect. It seemed that the trillion-dollar gamble had paid off, and Sarah Stellos's venture was destined to be the most successful company on Earth.

The only problem was that Eden and the Earth were at odds.

Okay, maybe that's too dramatic a way to phrase it. The system wasn't at odds in the *Eden-will-destroy-the-entire-planet* sort of way; the issue was that there simply was not enough energy on Earth to allow its users to maintain a long-term connection with the Solar Brain. Although the link to Eden was stable enough for several hours—even several *days* for a few users—the culmination of effects ranging from the Earth's magnetosphere to even the weather meant that millions of simultaneous connections around the planet were not possible. And those who *could* connect could only do so for several hours at a time before the long-distance servers needed to rest.

Sarah and I first experienced the issue during the Simulation Showcase; after about five hours and a half-dozen more simulations, we were suddenly woken up by the Portal technicians as our connection began to glitch out. We sat around the warehouse in our Portal suits for hours, waiting for Abraham's engineers to reestablish a connection. When we finally returned to Eden, Ali told us that she had begun running tests to determine what the issue was. We had been in the middle of an intense go-kart race, and Sarah seemed deeply annoyed by the interruption. I tried to reassure Sarah by reminding her that she was going to easily win our race anyway before the abrupt ending, but that didn't seem to console her.

The gist was that the Earth itself seemed to be blocking planetwide connections to the network, guarding virtual reality against "real" reality. Ali, who had run millions of diagnostics to confirm the issue, sent Sarah and I the report before anyone else. I begged Sarah for a couple of weeks to work on the problem in private, and she told me I could.

That is, *after* we got through the *Eden Expo*.

When Sarah announced that we were hosting a technology exposition in the midst of our connection problem, I thought she'd finally lost it. Our staff—which was already the smallest it had been in years—was overworked as it was, and I was devoting every second I had to examining potential workarounds for the communication delays. I was *not* in the headspace for a PR event.

But word about the ALI program's initialization had gotten out, and people were excited to learn more about the most advanced AI ever built. Furthermore, we needed an event to stoke the already-immense hype that was surrounding Eden. After all, our company had a knack for making headlines:

BBC News
EDEN—The Future of Virtual Reality is Almost Here

Fox News
What ABRAHAM's Success Means for American Business

IGN
Eden finally delivers the painless VR world we all wanted—11/10

Gamers Daily
"Eden is perfect for families" | Why a customizable VR paradise needs to prohibit injury

TECH Today
Is "Mind Upload" Close? Stellos Answers TT's Questions

Consumers had spoken; they not only wanted a virtual paradise, but they wanted it now. VR had gone through many iterations over the past half-century, from being exclusive to gaming, to its utilization in the office, and all the way to CNS-links gone wrong. Several video game manufacturers rolled out designs for "sensory virtual reality," which ranged from including "smell machines" on headsets to utilizing vests with built-in haptics. During the last decade or so, many companies began introducing "neuro-link" technologies of their own, using bulky probes to induce physical feelings along their users' bodies. About half of the VR experiences that were associated with these devices were high-octane thriller games that spiked players' adrenaline levels while inducing pain when the player was hit by an enemy. Roughly the other half of these experiences allowed the user to share a private room with a "pleasure avatar," which *also* spiked adrenaline levels and induced feelings in... well, you get the idea.

Suffice it to say, many companies thought that physical pain or sexual stimulation were the CNS-links' greatest assets. But most of these experiences flopped because they didn't have a mass appeal; only hardcore gamers or basement-dwelling deviants bought into them. Eden had finally demonstrated to the world, though, that stimulation of the senses in *peaceful* environments (with just a few action-packed worlds thrown in) was the key to great VR. Based on Eden's vast preorder base, which was diverse in age, background, and nationality, Abraham proved that virtual reality could appeal to *everyone*. People didn't want pain—they wanted peace. And Eden could give it to them.

Furthermore, the *architect* of Eden was becoming especially popular as well, considering she was:

TIME *Person of the Year* | *Sarah Stellos: Creating Brave New Worlds*

Forbes Billionaires 2053 | *Sarah Stellos: Richest Woman in the World*

Forbes Billionaires 2054 | *Sarah Stellos: Richest Person in the World*

Given that she was a celebrity in the media's eyes, the public conversation naturally turned toward Sarah's role in social and political issues. *What was Sarah's stance on women's issues? Is ABRAHAM favoring this group over that group? How does the name 'Eden' reinforce religious discrimination?* Sarah was silent on almost all those topics, but all too often, Eden was brought into the fray through some obscure connections that only a politically driven op-ed writer could make. Sarah's response was always that she aspired to build a world *separate* from those things—"a place of peace, not bickering."

"Sarah Stellos," a reporter from CNN asked about a month ago. "Given the national and international acclaim of your leadership at Abraham and your powerful public image, are you considering running for public office at some point in the future?"

I'd never seen Sarah laugh so hard in my life. After the question was asked, she had to cover her mouth to keep the crowd from seeing her smile. She promptly stepped off stage, looked me in the eyes, and burst out laughing. Not a scornful or derisive laugh, but a genuine and joyful one, as if I'd just told her one of my truly superior jokes. She stepped back onto stage after a couple of seconds before apologizing to the crowd for having to take an important call during the middle of the press conference. She moved on to the next question.

Obviously, Sarah was famously disinterested in politics; when I asked her about the incident at the press conference, she told me that she'd rather focus on improving people's lives than complicating them. I lightly suggested that she could do that by supporting sound public policy, but her silent reply indicated that she was more interested in building her virtual world than trying to fix the problems in this one. Quite frankly, I couldn't blame her. I also had a pretty big stake in Eden's success, and even the press recognized it:

MAP News
Stellos's & Hesper's ALI is the Robot Guide of Tomorrow: Today!

TECH Today
New Abraham Tech Manager Perfects VR

TIME *Person of the Year*
Arthur Hesper: From Tiny Orphan to Techno-Oligarch

Okay, I made that third one up.

Unfortunately, I did *not* make this piece of "journalism" up:

TMZ

Is Arthur Hesper Having an Affair with His Virtual Assistant?
SIRI TELLS ALL!

I think I'll stop mentioning headlines now.

Back to the *Eden Expo.* It was held at the stubby pickle—sorry, *Administration and Visitor Center,* as Sarah wants me to practice calling it—on Valentine's Day, a little over a month after we'd first stepped inside Eden. I'd been hoping to take Sarah out to a romantic dinner that evening or on a virtual vacation to Aruba (or, maybe, a *real* vacation to Aruba), but she made it clear that the exposition was her priority that day.

The exhibits on the AEI rockets and Solar Sphere were pushed aside to make room for our many "Eden Stations," which were arranged in three concentric rows within the building. Each of the 120 stations had a reclining chair and a bulky, helmet-shaped white headset with wires streaming from its cap. They were the first generation of link headsets, which could keep users connected to the virtual world without needing the Portal. Needless to say, I was quite excited when the headsets rolled out. Future generations are supposed to be even *less* bulky and might even be wireless.

As I walked through the employee area of the office on my way to the expo, where I was supposed to help Sarah greet guests and answer questions about Eden, I stopped by the break room bakery to grab a cup of coffee. It was going to be a long day, but Sarah insisted that we stay for the entire time in order to show face as much as possible.

As I left the coffee shop area and passed by the mini-confectionary, I noticed trays of white cookies stacked on top of a cart. I walked over to them to get a closer look, and laughed out loud. They were stick figure *Ali* shortbread cookies with a smiley face and hair drawn in icing, as well as her white shirt, blue pants, and white shoes.

I took a picture of the cookies, opened up the Eden developer app, and sent the picture to Ali. I was glad the software engineering department installed a chat function with Ali; it would have been a pain to have to enter Eden, or even open a video call, every time I needed to talk to her. In no time at all, Ali sent a reply.

"Those look... interesting," Ali texted.

*"Well, you *are* an icon now,"* I wrote back. It was true; Ali had essentially become the de facto mascot of Abraham, with many of our promotional posters and merchandise showing her image on them. Sarah had mentioned to me that her image was something the Executive Board was particularly interested in capitalizing off of, especially as the company sought to put a face to our brand in addition to their CEO's.

Let's just say I wasn't too keen on the Board *literally* objectifying Ali, even though she *is* technically their property.

As weird as that feels.

My phone vibrated again, and I looked down.

"Arthur," Ali wrote. *"I don't know about this. Can you come inside Eden for a second?"*

I began to walk faster down the hallway, and nearly collided with another employee carrying a glass model of the Sun. He sidestepped me, visibly annoyed.

"I'm not sure I can, Ali," I wrote back. *"I'm running low on time as it is."*

I waited a second for her reply. *"Can you come to the monitor?"* she asked.

"Which one?"

"Any of them."

I practically jogged into the visitor center area, which looked more like a complete maze of silver panels than an organized circle of Eden stations. Each panel wall was actually a flatscreen monitor, which was able to play a live feed of events from inside Eden. Virtual cameras that were connected to real-world screens let us stream users' interactions from either a first-person or third-person perspective at any location. They would also let us interact with Ali at any point during the expo.

The visitor center was filled with about thirty other technicians and Abraham employees clad in company-branded sweatshirts. I was wearing a suit and tie to match with the other "Abraham Ambassadors," who were supposed to report to the front doors of our giant glass pickle before the event started. Most of the technicians were plugging in and testing Eden headsets near their respective stations; each tech was assigned to monitor at least four stations. I found one spot near the back of the visitor center that wasn't occupied and waved at the panel in front of me.

I wasn't fully sure *what* to expect. Was there another problem with the connection system? Was the Solar Sphere having last minute issues? *Or was it something with Ali?* Her various networks were always training and evolving, and sometimes developed surprising new features.

Or unexpected emotions.

For example, Ali could've become nervous about interacting with guests. That would *not* go over well. My heart started to race as I wondered if Ali had developed stage fright. *Can an AI even* get *stage fright?*

I had to be prepared for anything.

"I'm here, Ali," I said. "What's wrong?"

The screen lit up, and Ali's entire form materialized in front of a silver background. With the screen's incredible resolution, it was as if she were standing right in front of me, gazing off into the distance. As her eyes shifted towards mine, her expression lifted, and she smiled.

"Hello, Arthur."

"What's going on?" I asked.

"I am faced with an important decision that needs to be settled by human input. By *your* input," she said.

Uh oh.

"Okay..." I said. *Please not stage fright.* "I'm sure I can—"

Her entire form suddenly shifted, and her tunic and pants were replaced by a long, white, V-neck dress with flared sleeves and a thin waist. A blue floral design ran down the fabric of the dress, and instead of slippers she wore high heels. As I looked back up at her face—which now was at the same height as mine, thanks to the heels—I noticed she wore silver eyeshadow and that her hair was elegantly curled.

"Um..." I began, not sure how to respond. I looked to my sides, but no one else seemed to be watching.

"This?" Ali asked. "Or..."

In a split second, she changed again. This time, she wore a white, form-fitting portal suit—which looked a *lot* cooler on her than it probably did on me—with various black wires on her chest making the globe-shaped symbol of Abraham. Her hair had become much shorter, too, stopping off just above her neck.

"...this?" she finished.

Ali, the most advanced artificial intelligence ever built, needed my help trying on clothes.

"So... a superhero costume or a French dress?" I said. I'm no fashion expert, but... *those were the options she settled on?*

"The modified portal suit is meant to represent the progress our company has made in only a few short months, as well as embracing the stereotypical, technology-driven clothes of the future," she said. She quickly changed back into her dress. "While the dress was intended to rise to the formality of this event, since I know Sarah wants to leave a good impression on—"

"But those... aren't how you dress," I said. *Right?*

"True," Ali said, looking towards the ground. "Of course, I do have forty-seven other combinations of appearances that I'm thinking of—"

"Just be yourself, Ali," I heard Sarah's voice say. I turned to my left and saw Sarah walking towards the screen. She was wearing a slim black suit that looked like mine (but that was probably way more expensive).

"Hey," I said. I hadn't seen her all morning. As Sarah stopped next to me, I leaned in a little closer to her. "Happy Valen—"

She cleared her throat, glancing towards a group of technicians off to the side. They were wrapped up in their own conversation and probably couldn't hear us, but that didn't stop Sarah from being paranoid. "Later," she mumbled.

I nodded. *Later it is.* As I glanced away from her face, I noticed that she had on her chest a golden pin in the shape of the Sun, matched with silver text that read *"Eden."*

She must have seen me staring at the pin.

"There's one in your pocket," she said. I reached into my jacket pocket, and sure enough, there was a pin there.

As I attached it to my shirt, I noticed Ali morph back into her tunic, leggings, and slippers. Her hair was long again, and her face was clean. *That's right, we're still talking about clothes.*

"Though this *is* my preferred design, this classical-athleisure blend is more intended as a baseline appearance," she said to Sarah. "Are you sure this is alright?"

"Of course it's alright," Sarah said. "It's *you.*"

Ali nodded with a smile. Sarah turned towards me and nodded over at the glass doors of the visitor center. I followed her glance, and my heart skipped a beat. There were easily two hundred people lined up at the door, and those were just the ones I could see before the line wrapped around the building and out of view. *It's 8am on a Saturday, shouldn't these people be sleeping?*

Wait...

It was 8am.

Time to open.

"We have to go," Sarah said to me. I turned back towards Ali, who was running her hands through her hair. She looked up at me with a wide, almost reassurance-seeking stare.

Maybe it is stage fright.

But there wasn't any more time to talk. Sarah gave Ali a nod and began to walk away from her towards the glass doors. I started to follow her, but not before looking back at Ali.

"You'll do great, Ali," I said. Her eyes met mine, and I gave her a thumbs-up and smiled. "Trust me."

After all, you were literally made for this.

Ali took a step back, straightening her posture. The nervousness—*if there even was any*—seemed to completely fade from her eyes, and she looked back at me with a warm smile.

"Thanks, Arthur."

The monitor went blank, and I ran after Sarah to catch up with her. We made our way past the sea of Eden stations and approached the entrance. At least two dozen security guards were crowded in a wide semicircle near the glass doors. Behind the guards and equipment, one long table was set up facing the doorway, separating the entrance from the rest of the visitor center.

"I think Ali will be okay," I said.

"That's great to hear," Sarah said. She walked up to the long table and sat down at the folding chair closest to the end. Seated along the table next to her were various members of Abraham's outreach staff, as well as one or two executives that I recognized. In front of each chair was a single smart tablet.

"But right now," Sarah said. "I'd focus more on *you*."

She pulled out an empty chair next to hers.

"Do you remember your welcome procedure?"

"Hello, and welcome to Abraham!" I said, a little too enthusiastically, to an older couple walking up to the desk.

"Hi," the older woman said, unzipping up what looked like an expensive black purse. Her husband grunted.

"My name is Dr. Hesp—*Arthur*," I corrected. I had been practicing my introduction with my title and last name, but Sarah had insisted we only use our first names. "Are you folks here to experience Eden?"

"Yes," the woman said. She reached into her purse and pulled out a slim black smartphone. "We pre-registered online; I can show you my confirmation."

"No need," I said. I looked down at my tablet; onscreen was a simple user interface with only the necessary buttons that could pull up information on Eden, order an emergency simulation stop, or call security. In the center of the screen, there was also a large blue button labelled *ALI*. I tapped that button, which opened up a menu of options. I tapped *Guest Sign-In* and held up my tablet to the couple.

"Just say your first and last names," I said.

"Brooke Nillace," the woman said. She nudged her husband.

"James Nillace," he grunted.

A second passed before Ali's voice came up over the tablet's speaker.

"Good morning, Brooke and James," she said excitedly. "You're all set for stations 14 and 15. Head over whenever you're ready!"

I stood up from the table and looked over at Sarah. She was still busy answering safety-related questions from a well-dressed family of seven. I was amazed by Sarah's patience with them; she'd been talking with them about the safety of our neuro-sync technology for at least ten minutes straight, and never once seemed frustrated or called over another Abraham ambassador to answer their questions. Sarah was committed to her consumers' experience; I knew I had to be, too.

"You two can follow me, if you'd like," I said to them.

"Was that... *Ali?*" Brooke Nillace asked in a whisper, nodding at the tablet with a look of hesitation.

I smiled. "No need to whisper. Yep, that was her!"

"Isn't she, you know, *running* this Eden program?" Brooke asked. James impatiently rolled his eyes at the question.

"She is," I said.

"But... how was that her, then?" Brooke asked. "I mean, how is she able to talk to us from the tablet *and* be in Eden at the same time?"

"Good question," I said. *Alright, Arthur.* When I was hired by Abraham almost a year ago, Sarah had emphasized that I would need to get better at explaining the technology in simple terms, so I'd spent the past month practicing speeches for everything Eden- and Abraham-related. I motioned for the couple to follow me towards their stations.

"Ali is a single artificial intelligence that has the capacity to interact with millions of users at once," I said.

As I walked the couple through the expo, I pointed out some of the other stations, each of which had a visitor lying on their back with a bulky headset on. On each of the stations' screens, a different scene was playing out. One screen had a first-person view of a sunset above the desert plains, and in the user's periphery, Ali sat on a horse wearing a cowboy hat. On another screen, set to the third-person perspective, a large grey fish (presumably, a user) swam through a beautiful coral reef, and it was catching up to Ali, who was swimming ahead. On one monitor right beside us, a hologram of Ali in her starship captain's uniform was talking at the screen, while a large *Alien Death* monster was rampaging through the cruiser's hanger bay in the background (I did *not* have fond memories of that simulation). And on another screen, a user's face was being licked by a small black dog; through the speaker, I heard Ali say "...where would you like to take Chana for a walk?"

I continued. "Ali can fully interact with everyone inside Eden, as well as any employee *outside* Eden. The computational power created by our Solar Sphere out in space lets Ali do all of this at once, kind of like how your smartphone does a lot of background processes at the same time. Ali is the ultimate multitasker, able to carry on all those conversations simultaneously."

The couple nodded, accepting the explanation. As I said those words, though, they felt weird even to me. After all, whenever I interacted with

Ali, it always felt like I was interacting with *the only* Ali, not a program that was doing a million other (probably more important) things at the same time. Then again, there is only *one* Ali—each "copy" of her that users interact with is really all the same consciousness. Most humans can't wrap their minds around that kind of being. Not even *I* could fully grasp that type of intelligence, and I'm the one who *built* the thing.

As we made it to stations 14 and 15, I started to feel a little lightheaded when I saw the technician who was assigned there.

"Hello, Mr. and Mrs. Nillace," Clyde Jones said. "Welcome to Eden. If you'll each have a seat, we'll get you hooked up."

"How exactly does this work?" Brooke asked. "What's going to happen inside there?"

"Did you not read the website?" Clyde asked her. "Booked yourselves a nice half-hour Valentine's Day getaway without reading the brochure, is that right?"

My palms grew sweaty.

"No, I..." Brooke began.

"I'm just teasing you, miss," Clyde chuckled. He turned towards me with a grin. "Besides, the brilliant Dr. Hesper here was supposed to explain to you how this works, but he..."

"...was about to get to that," I broke in. I shook my head at Clyde, and pointed towards the screen. "You two are each signed up for a thirty-minute preview of Abraham's Simulation Showcase, which will take you through some of the most amazing and exciting worlds that Eden has to offer. The tour will start out with some of the worlds that our virtual reality team has created—"

"Not that our virtual reality team exists anymore," Clyde barged in. "Ever since Dr. Hesper's little creation swept in and replaced their jobs..."

"Thank you, *Clyde,*" I said. I'm not sure *what* his problem was with me, though I assumed he was jealous of my quickly-earned status at Abraham. He probably wasn't the only one.

"Is it... *safe,* connecting to those?" Brooke asked, pointing at the headsets.

"Of course it's safe," Clyde said. "It's only millions of gigabytes of data passing from your brain to our supercomputer and vice versa."

The old couple glanced at each other nervously. *Thanks, Clyde.* I cleared my throat and nodded at the screen. "Even though it *sounds* daunting, the system is programmed to essentially 'freeze' your brain during the connecting and disconnecting process, keeping you totally safe as everything boots up."

"Well, it's really more complicated than that," Clyde said, his voice quickening. "*Freeze* is definitely the wrong word. There's a lapse in computational time during the CNS transfer which acts as a buffer to prevent electronic overrides, such that—"

"Okay, that makes sense," Brooke broke in, clearly not interested in Clyde's longer version of the technology talk. *I couldn't blame her.* She looked back over at me with a smile. "Can we go back to what's going on *inside* Eden?"

"Sure," I said. Clyde rolled his eyes. "You'll start your tour in the Genesis Room, where you'll meet up with Ali, who..."

You know those once-in-a-blue-moon moments when you have an idea that's so great, you wonder how *nobody else* thought of it before?

"Actually, let's do *this,*" I said. I held up my tablet and pressed the *ALI* button. "Hey, Ali? Can you give the Nillaces an explanation of how Eden works?"

Almost immediately, she responded. "Yep! I've got just the thing."

I pressed the button again. "Can you mention the Simulation Showcase, what LNUCs are, and how user-to-user interactions work?"

"Happy to!"

The monitors in front of Brooke and James's stations suddenly turned on. Clyde muttered under his breath. *"Damn GPT hat-trick..."*

Suddenly, Ali materialized on the left screen in front of a silver background. She gave me a small smile before turning towards the couple with a wave.

"Hi guys! Arthur requested that I show you a little bit of how Eden works, so here we go!"

As the screen to her right turned a bright white, I noticed several other screens at different, unoccupied stations begin to turn white as well. I looked around the large room. The windows were now tinted and all of the lights had dimmed, and the giant screen was quickly lowering in front of the hanging satellite statue. After a second, a white projection showed up there, as well. I looked towards the entrance of the visitor center and noticed that Sarah was pointing her tablet at the roof, where the sensor for the screen's remote control was. She then turned towards me and gave me an approving nod.

I looked back at the screen in front of me, which showed a stark white background. Ali began talking again, and her bubbly voice resounded throughout the entire room. "We'll start our tour in the Genesis Room, which is where every future user will enter whenever they connect to Eden. The Genesis Room serves as the gateway to the amazing universes inside Eden, which we'll explore in today's Simulation Showcase."

The screen panned around the white void; as it did, spheres containing the different worlds began to show up. I still remember seeing that pile of spheres—that *marble multiverse* (trademark pending)—for the first time like it was yesterday.

"From the Genesis Room, you can explore any one of our *thousands* of immaculately rendered worlds, which range from super-powered battles to a relaxing day at the beach. Or, you can enter a world of your own design," Ali said. As she faded from the screen in front of me, an image of a holographic human brain appeared. "Eden allows you to connect to your own memories via our Memory Mine, which allows you to witness your most important moments again—and form new ones in worlds that *you* create, mined from your experiences and imagination."

Onscreen, the brain began to glow, and behind it a video of a rocky lakeside beach showed up. The video was the first-person perspective of someone running along the lake, past walls of tall grass and trees, and towards a small log cabin atop a hill in the distance. The scene was, somehow, both calming *and* energizing.

It was also familiar.

It was from my cabin jog. I noticed that the color of the cabin had been changed, and that the tree growth was much more dense than it was around Sarah's lake, but Ali had *clearly* taken inspiration from my memories. Only, as the user's perspective turned in the opposite direction along the running trail, there was a man sitting down on the dirt ground. His face was covered by the hood of his *Abraham*-branded sweatshirt, but I knew who it was. *And* I knew whose memory we were watching. *Sarah's.*

Why would Ali show that?

I whipped around to face Sarah, but she was engrossed in the video on the large screen. She was smiling faintly; in fact, she didn't seem bothered at all by the likeness of her retreat *and* her secret relationship—which was, by all accounts, *still a secret*—being shown to the public. Even the two men standing near the wall closest to Sarah, who I recognized as company bodyguards, glanced at each other nervously.

But then again...

Nobody else knew about the cabin *or* our relationship. To the public, it was just a random video of two people going for a jog. And Sarah knew that.

And Ali knew that Sarah knew that.

Ali continued talking. "In the Genesis Room, you can meet with any other user connected to Eden and experience these worlds together. You can enter memories together, too, visiting each other's greatest hits. Or, you can experience these worlds for yourself with our *lifelike non-user characters,* or LNUCs."

As Ali said that, the image of the sweatshirt-clad mystery man by the lake quickly faded away, and was replaced by a group of people in summer clothes dancing on a boat. It was dark outside, and fireworks were shooting up from a distant shoreline. Several people were highlighted by a faint red glow along their skin, while others were highlighted by a blue glow.

"In many simulations, you can interact with real-life users, shown in red. But to fill in the space, we have LNUCs, who populate these worlds to make them feel full, shown in blue. The people who appear in your memories who you *aren't* travelling with are also LNUCs, recreated from your conscious and subconscious knowledge about them," Ali said.

The video of the lakeside jogger—*me*—reappeared, and this time I was highlighted by a blue glow. The glow suddenly faded away, and the video switched back to the party people on the boat. This time, nobody was highlighted in any sort of glow, but continued dancing and laughing together.

"LNUCs are programmed to be indistinguishable from real people and are there to help make Eden as real—and fun—a place as it can be," Ali said.

As the people danced, they suddenly began to shout: "Three, two, one... *Happy New Year!*" A stream of fireworks flew into the sky, and the first-person camera began to jump up and down excitedly.

The video slowly faded away and was replaced by Ali standing in front of the Genesis Room, which was filled with its many simulated spherical worlds. Ali flashed a smile at the invisible camera.

"Eden is a place where you can live in *the* perfect world, whatever that may look like. From partying with other users in our expansive collection of simulations to crafting your very own utopia, there is no limit to what you can do. Once you make your way into the Genesis Room, I'll be along to guide you all through our twenty-minute Simulation Showcase, before giving you ten minutes to explore whatever world you'd like, be it from the nostalgic to the not-yet-possible," Ali said. "I can't wait to see you soon!"

As the video faded out, light slowly returned to the room. My tablet buzzed; it was a text from Ali.

"How was that?" she asked.

As I replied with the word *"Amazing!"* along with a string of its various synonyms, I looked over at the Nillaces. They were still staring at the blank screen as if something else were about to show up. I cleared my throat, and the couple turned my way.

"Any other questions?" I asked, really hoping the answer would be *no.*

After answering about a dozen other questions from them, Brooke and James finally laid down on their recliners and put on their link headsets. I answered various questions from Brooke while talking her through the connection process; her husband, meanwhile, spent the whole time grunting and tapping his foot impatiently. Once the headsets were fully powered on, the couple fell asleep, and I set the monitors to third-person mode. Inside the Genesis Room, the couple stood wearing the same clothes they had on outside Eden. Brooke practically ran around the room with an incredulous look on her face while James stood still, simply surveying the surrounding worlds in awe.

Even though I had duties back at the visitor center entrance, I couldn't help but watch as Ali took them into the *Alien Battle* simulation. Even though Brooke was a pretty terrible shot with her blaster, she was smiling and laughing while firing at the aliens. I half-expected her husband to keep standing in place quietly, so I was shocked when James began sprinting around the starship hull, taking out the alien invaders quickly. He whooped and shouted in delight with each hit. By the time he hit the last of the aliens, James—the eighty-something, grumpy old man—began jumping up and down like a little kid.

"This is the coolest mother—*beep*—ing *beep* in the *beep*—ing world!" he shouted giddily. A woman with two small boys passed by, giving the screen (and me) a dirty look. *Good thing Ali installed expletive censors on the video cast,* I thought. I gave the young mother an apologetic glance, but as I turned back towards Brooke and James Nillace, I smiled.

By the end of the day, almost 2000 people had tried out Eden for the first time. Based on the reactions from our new users, which ranged from tears of joy to ecstatic shock, I would have to say that Abraham's exposition was a success. In addition to the event being eye-opening for our guests, the large number of reporters who attended meant that the Eden Expo would do great things for our company's media standing.

I also had a lot of fun at the event, mostly because I loved watching people experience Eden for the first time. Seeing people's faces light up as they witnessed the Simulation Showcase reminded me of how incredible my first journey through Eden had been. I was also glad to see people enjoying their interactions with Ali. Although most of the guests' post-Eden conversations were about the incredible worlds they'd seen, I was always happy whenever I heard visitors praise the host's hospitality and remark on how engaging and *fun* she was. I also got to eat several Ali-themed shortbread cookies, and I have to say: whichever company chef made *those* deserves a raise.

However, as great as the cookies were, Abraham also had several technical issues throughout the day. Almost all of them, frustratingly, involved the connection issue with Eden that I mentioned earlier. Even though there were only ever 120 users at most connected to the system at the same time, at least fifty users throughout the day were woken up early from the system by a *Connection Overload Issue.* The sudden disconnection didn't have any negative effects on the guests, but each time it happened, the impacted user was obviously a bit shaken and miffed. Being woken up from Eden like that is like being shaken awake from the best dream you've ever had. Even though we gifted any affected user with an extra fifteen minutes of online simulation time for them and their party, we knew that our system couldn't sustain issues like this once we debuted it to the rest of the world.

Once the other employees and technicians went home, it was just me, Sarah, and Ali left inside the visitor center with only a couple of screens still set up. Sarah and I made sure everyone else was out of sight before we tinted the visitor center windows, met by one of the Eden stations in the center of the giant room, and kissed.

"I feel like I haven't talked to you all day," I said, moving my face away from hers to get the words out. Her breath tasted like shortbread.

"Who says we have to talk?" she said, pulling me back in again. Without separating from each other, we sat down on the recliner and continued kissing. As we did, I looked past Sarah, at the staircase leading up to the second level of the stubby pickle. I thought back to my first day working at Abraham, when I'd met with her right by that stairway before she gave me a tour of the complex. I was so intimidated then; I barely knew *what* to say to my boss. Never did I imagine that I would one day be making out with her in that very same room.

Then again, she had *looked damn great in that kinetic shirt...*

Sarah leaned away from me and started unbuttoning her suit jacket. As I moved to do the same, she quickly held out her hand towards my arm.

"Wait, wait," she whispered. I looked up at her beautiful eyes. "We can't... not in here."

I sighed, lowering my eyes. "Yeah. You're right."

"Sorry."

"What about the cameras? Your security? Did they see us?"

"Half the security already knows," Sarah said. "And I already switched out the camera recordings, so we're fine. But... better safe than sorry."

I started fixing the collar of my shirt. "Still... no one *else* knows about us, right?"

Sarah re-buttoned her suit jacket, and swiftly stood up from the recliner.

"Besides my pilot, security staff, and chef, you mean?" She laughed. "No. Just you, me, the lawyer, and..."

Sarah glanced back towards the blank video screen. I nodded and stood up next to her, looking out the front doors. Even with the shades lowered, I could tell it was pitch-black outside. Even though the Florida air would be warm, I never liked the early sunsets of winter; they reminded me of the bitterly cold nights up north. *Before Abraham.*

"Do you want to grab dinner in your office?" I asked Sarah. "Or head back to my place and order in?"

She smiled. "What, pizza at your place again?"

"It'll be nice and quiet," I said. "We can watch a bad rom-com, snuggle on the couch, keep kissing... see where it goes from—"

"Arthur? Sarah?" Ali's voice interrupted. I nearly jumped out of my skin and whipped around towards the screen. Ali was standing there, her eyes darting between Sarah and me. "Sorry if I'm interrupting..."

"No, you're fine," Sarah said. "We're just... making our plans for tonight."

"Oh," Ali said. "Of course."

"You were great today, Ali," I said, steadying my heart rate. She gave a faint smile. "What's up?"

"I was just curious if you wanted to utilize this evening to work together on solving the connection delay to Eden," she said. "The issue will only continue to grow worse."

"I know, I know," I said. I glanced over at Sarah, and back at Ali. "But... we could move ahead on that next week. Why don't you take tonight off?"

Even as I asked the question, I knew it was a stupid one. Ali looked down at the ground, and back at us. She blinked twice, staring at us with her resting face. *Her solemn face.*

I should've realized that Ali doesn't *get* the night off. *She never does.*

"Ali, I..." I began.

"She's right," Sarah said. I turned toward her, and she leaned in a little closer to me, speaking softly. "I... have a lot of things to take care of on my end, anyway. We'd better start working on a solution to this problem, and fast."

I sighed as quietly as I could. *So much for a relaxing, romantic evening with Sarah.* Even though I wanted to protest, I *knew* Ali was right. We'd spent so much time preparing things for the Expo that we didn't have a moment to lose. Eden's glitches could derail all of the progress and good-will that we'd just acquired. There would be time to relax when the job was done.

For now, we had to get back to work.

Still, I sighed. I had so many plans for tonight. Most of them revolved around me sitting down with Sarah, looking her right in the eyes, and—after *months* of dancing around it—working up the courage to finally tell her—

"I love you," Sarah said.

Even though she spoke at barely a whisper, I'd never heard anything more perfectly. I looked back into her eyes, and she smiled sweetly. I just stood there quietly for a moment, letting the silence wash over us both, and I took her words in. Finally, the tender numbness in my brain went away, and my mouth could formulate sounds again.

"I love you," I said back to her.

We kissed again, and this time fell into each other's arms, holding each other close. I'm not sure how long we stayed that way; it may have been only a few seconds, but it felt far longer. It didn't matter. All that mattered to me, right then, was that *Sarah Stellos loved me. Sarah Stellos loved me.* I couldn't believe she managed to get the words out before I did, but that wasn't the type of thing to feel jealous over. *Sarah loved me. And I loved her.*

Eventually, we gently let go of each other, and Sarah straightened her jacket. She nodded at me, brushed back her hair, and looked towards the screen. Ali had been looking at something off in the distance in the visitor center—or, more likely, she'd been pretending to be. She turned back towards the two of us and smiled warmly.

"Happy Valentine's Day, guys," Ali said.

"Thank you, Ali," Sarah said. She took a quick breath and turned to us both. "Not to ruin a tender moment, but now that our *official company focus* has turned to the daunting task of fixing Eden, there's something even worse we have to deal with next."

Ali nodded with a weak smile, and I looked back over at Sarah. Like a snowball in an oven, I felt all the tender light inside my body melt away, and I stared at my girlfriend with what was undoubtedly a look of horror.

"Not that..." I said.

Not another Board meeting.

NINE

OARD MEETINGS ARE easily my least favorite part of my job, and they've only gotten more frequent since we started pre-selling Eden hardware. Today's meeting, which was focused on "recent alarming issues involving the Eden connection," required *all* of Abraham's leadership to show up, and pretty soon the large conference room located at the top of the stubby pickle was packed.

The business executives, many of whom were tanner than usual from their extended cruises to the Caribbean, turned their leather swivel chairs in unison towards the 110-inch plasma screen at the front of the room, from which Ali was preparing to deliver the diagnostics report. I was sitting all the way in the back of the room (in a metal folding chair, mind you), and I had to move my chair towards the left wall to get a better view of the screen. Of course, "moving my chair" meant kicking its steel legs one screeching slide at a time across the room, causing the Board members to flinch at the sound. I couldn't help but smile when they did.

"Sorry, guys," I lied. "World's fastest-growing company and we can't even get quieter chairs, am I right?"

The annoyed silence in the room was resounding, but I'd gotten used to the role of the outsider by now. At the very front of the room, I saw Sarah crack a grin. That was all I cared about.

Ali appeared on-screen in perfect resolution, standing in front of the plain white background of the Genesis Room. Despite the network issues we had with Eden, we still had no problems video-casting with Ali for our biweekly briefings-reports, during which she would rattle off statistics about the internal growth of the virtual world. It was all information that could be shared via an email, but Sarah believed strongly in giving Ali as much face time with the Board as possible.

Ali gave a polite wave to the executives and a warm nod towards Sarah. However, I could see that Ali was looking through the screen, past the Board members, and towards the back of the room—*my* corner of the room. She was looking at me the way she seemed to have been just before the Eden Expo—with a reassurance-seeking, almost *childlike* nervousness. *But that could have just been me misreading her.* Either way, I gave her a thumbs-up and smiled. She gave a slight nod to me, then again to Sarah, and finally she turned towards the executives.

"Good morning, members of the Board," she said. "Over the past few weeks, my analytical programming has run a series of tests on Eden's capab—"

"Why is Eden being delayed?" one of the Board members, Douglas Stone, shouted abruptly. I could give a slew of details about Stone, but because he's a self-entitled asshole, I won't. "We've all seen the science report about the connection issues. I mean, why aren't we coming up with a solution that actually moves things *forward?*"

Ali opened her mouth to respond, but Sarah stepped forward first. "If you actually *read* the report instead of just the abstract, Mr. Stone, you'd realize that the issue is more complicated than just throwing money at it."

"Oh, I think we've thrown *plenty* of money at things," said another, scorn-filled woman named Janice Green. "Perhaps this company should be spending more time on its technology and less time rendering its 'lovely' AI assistant. A fair-skinned, slender *chick* as our subservient mascot. I mean, did anyone even *consult* with the Board before making the A.L.I. system a dainty *trope?*" I would love to share my great distaste for Janice Green, a self-righteous piece of work, but I think you know by now how I feel about the members of Abraham's Board of Directors.

Ali looked down at her own clothes, and then towards the ground. I hurt for her. I was used to ignoring comments from keyboard warriors who attacked the company, software, and even me. I knew I was a famously awkward person, *especially* in front of the press, and I didn't care. But whenever people attacked Ali, I grew defensive, as did my girlfriend. Sarah glanced up at Ali before staring daggers at Ms. Green.

"*Ali* designed herself in the image that suits *her* tastes, and I wouldn't have it any other way," Sarah said.

"Agreed," one of the newer members of the Board, Kate (or... Kathy? Chrissy?—I couldn't remember), said. She gave Ali a warm nod, and Ali smiled back. "Her image is *trending.* Media posts are just the tip of the iceberg. We even have *several* yoga brands requesting partnerships to develop Ali-branded attire. They call it—get this—*Alittire.*"

Some members of the Board laughed, while others rolled their eyes.

"There's *also* a vibrant fan art community around her," Ms. Green said in a perky, mocking tone. "But it's *not* the kind of wholesome material you'd share with your grandmother."

I glanced over at Ali, who was now looking even more uncomfortable. As Sarah took a long, deep breath, I started to wonder if I would have to stop my girlfriend from choking out Ms. Green right there.

"Your tendency to bring up your social issues, *Janice,* during our tech meetings grows less amusing as time goes by," Sarah said, her silky tone causing some of the other executives to glance at each other nervously.

"But these are more than *social* issues," said another Board member who I won't even bother to name. "The way our company is perceived matters, as does the way our AI behaves. How will interactions with Ali be regulated to ensure that she doesn't... well..."

"Have *relations* with the users?" Janice Green broke in. A couple of people fidgeted in their seats or coughed uncomfortably. "Come on. You can't tell me *no one's* thought about that."

A couple of other Board members began to talk at the same time, their voices melding into a cacophony of accusations and rebuttals. In between the shouting, I heard Ms. Green's voice quite a bit louder above the rest: "I think it's a perfectly valid... *no,* it's not *sexist* for me to ask that question... *exactly,* I'm not saying she looks like that, but... oh *shut up,* Coolbrow, everyone knows what you use Eden for..."

I looked over at Ali, who blinked a couple of times before taking a step back from the screen. I could tell she was uncomfortable. *I* was uncomfortable. The idea that people could use Eden for (*ahem*) *non-PG* reasons had always been a possibility that Abraham had considered, and the company's decision has been not to interfere with people's desired virtual fantasies—*whatever* those may be.

But I'd never thought of using Eden that way personally, and I'd *definitely* never thought about Ali that way. I also hadn't programmed her to have romantic feelings or urges. *Then again, I hadn't prohibited it, either.*

Ali turned toward Sarah with a painfully blank expression on her face, tucking her hands into invisible pockets. Sarah stole a quick glance at me, and I returned with my finest *what the heck do you want me to do?* look. Sarah cleared her throat, and the room once again quieted down.

"Ali's focus is on guiding users through Eden and ensuring our systems run smoothly. We have non-user characters that are *separate* from Ali's emotional consciousness that can fulfill any of those *other* functions," Sarah said. She turned right towards me, and I felt sweat begin to drip down my palms. "I'm sure our AI expert can elaborate on that."

"Uh…" I elaborated, staring at the various well-tanned faces around the room. "Yeah… the LNUCs can do any of that other stuff… those are separate from Ali…"

Sarah gave me a curt *thanks, genius* smile before turning back towards the table of executives. As Ms. Green opened her mouth to bring up some other uncomfortable issue, Douglas Stone broke in.

"Can we get back to the issue at hand, please?" Stone said. For the first time in my life, I felt grateful towards him. "Eden is being *delayed?*"

Less grateful.

"Well…" Sarah began.

Stone cut her off. "The satellites can't communicate? Our technology is unproven? If this thing gets out to the press, we could lose public faith in our project. Or worse: we could lose our investments."

I hated the Board of Directors for many reasons. They *always* contradicted Sarah, and were skeptical of her at every turn despite her track record of success. They cared more about the money than either the science or the consumers. They brought up political issues for no other reason than to cause trouble. And—perhaps the most annoying attribute about them—they made good points.

Really good points.

Sarah was not about to hear them. Sometimes, I wondered if she only attended the Board meetings because she relished disagreeing with the other executives. And, considering she was by far the majority stakeholder in the company, she had no fear of being ousted.

"Thanks, Doug," Sarah said. "Now, *regardless* of what anyone else has to say about… *anything*, Ali will finish her report."

Ali looked over at Sarah with discomfort, but Sarah gave her a nod. "Go ahead, Ali."

Board meetings always had a knack for descending into childish chaos, but the news that Eden was risking delay seemed to hit different. The company's executives were worried. Abraham had a history of meeting or beating its deadlines; now that it was facing its most important one, the threat of failure weighed heavily. *Especially on the people actually doing the work, rather than just collecting paychecks.*

As soon as the meeting ended, Sarah and I stepped into her office and both sat behind her desk to video-call Ali. When she showed up onscreen, she greeted us with a joyful wave as if nothing had happened. But neither Sarah nor I wanted to ignore the Board meeting.

"You did fine, Ali," Sarah said. "The people on the Board are just assholes."

"It's really quite alright," Ali said, almost in a distracted way. "I looked up some of the online artwork Ms. Green had mentioned. Some of it is... quite flattering, in a sense..."

"Regardless," Sarah said. "Our image *and* your image are fine, considering how well our Eden Expo went. Believe me, the Board meeting meant nothing."

I nodded at Ali and smiled. "You have nothing to worry about, Ali."

After that day, I decided it was probably best to stop focusing on what other people thought about my work, Ali, or *anything*, and instead focus on the job at hand.

A good decision on my part, I knew, *especially with all the D.C. bullshit going on.*

Apparently, there were a couple of politicians arguing over how Sarah's independent startup should be regulated by the government. While Abraham's rapid deployment of solar satellites and Ali's accelerated initialization excited Eden's developers and future users, several members of Congress were bothered by our company's progress. Despite our rigorous systems checks and our noninvasive, satellite-based redesign of the Matrioshka Brain, misinformation found a way to spread. Many in the government now claimed that Sarah Stellos had "stolen the Sun."

Additionally, despite her abilities being limited to Eden, our company's opposition routinely characterized Ali as a reckless and dangerous machine only a few steps away from destroying the planet. Their vehement fearmongering was both damaging to our company, our mission, *and* the overwhelmingly positive influence that AI had on our society. Sarah's D.C. office had essentially been converted into a political war room staffed with people whose collective job it was to keep the politicians off our backs and defend our media image. Sarah usually let her PR representatives and lawyers handle those issues, with the standing order that she encounter as little red tape as possible. I didn't follow the politics there too closely, though. I was more invested in remedying Eden's current delay rather than in problems other people were inventing.

Eventually, the news about Eden's delay made its way out to the world via an official company news release, and Sarah held a press conference to address it. I was all set to speak beside her and several other senior engineers in a panel-style Q&A session held at Abraham's headquarters. Not only was the press room packed, but reports from our social media team indicated that over twenty million people were watching the briefing live.

Sarah spoke first, addressing the issue of Eden's pause with grace. She talked about the progress we'd made so far, the exciting opportunities for consumers to test our technology out at our expos, and how our company had a promising solution to the problem in the works. Sarah had originally wanted Ali present at the meeting, but Ali had made it clear that she did not want to be doing any public speaking for some time.

Sarah and I both knew that that would be a problem considering Ali was the *spokeswoman* that everyone who used Eden would have to interact with, but we decided we'd have to work on her self-esteem at some other point.

And *no*, the fact that we were talking about Ali like she was our daughter was not lost on me. I'll make some time to discuss that later when there *aren't* a thousand other things going on.

Right, back to the press conference. Sorry. It's just that Ali is so… *human*. Even when I first entered the virtual cabin with her and Sarah months ago, I kept forgetting that Ali is an AI. An AI that *I* built. Suffice it to say, she could pass the famed Turing Test and Modern Sentience Test with flying colors.

Ever since we met, Ali and I have spent a lot of time together—both working *and* just talking. Keep in mind: once Ali was fully developed, the job I'd been *hired* to do was technically done, and the Board of Directors could have easily sent me a nice gift basket with some expensive wine, cookies, a severance package, and a cute teddy bear inside. So, either the company executives seemed to decide I was good luck and worth keeping around, or Sarah threatened to fire anyone who felt otherwise.

I was reassigned to "Intelligence Oversight Manager"—a rather degrading title towards Ali, who I felt was above needing "oversight." Unfortunately, the Board—as well as the technology community, Department of Homeland Security, and most of the free world—seemed to feel differently about the world's strongest AI. So, I essentially became Ali's one and only research partner. While Ali consulted with Sarah on aesthetic matters, such as redesigning the Genesis Room to look like a beautiful garden instead of a lifeless void, she worked with me to solve any technical challenges that arose within Eden. Some things, like minor satellite orbit adjustments or system updates, were performed by Ali. But other tasks, like checking the user-facing framework of the code, were done by me. Many of the projects involved me priming and outlining the necessary programs while Ali filled in information with her infinite technical wisdom.

Ali was the best research partner I'd ever had. By the time we first started working together—which was way before the Eden Expo—I had multiple monitors with cameras set up around my apartment. When I first loaded Eden onto my desktop, the first thing Ali's avatar did was zoom from computer to computer around the room, admiring my "real life" workspace.

"Is this where you live? In the real world?" she asked, still gazing around the room from the monitor in my office.

"It's where I sleep, eat, work, and use the bathroom. It's where I *survive*—though *live* may be a bit of a stretch," I said.

"It's so messy," she said. When Ali finally looked over at me, she giggled. I realized she was looking at the (admittedly pathetic) moustache and beard that I'd been growing over the past few weeks. I had kept my virtual self clean-shaven, and she hadn't seen me in person before then. I found myself shaving later that afternoon, all the while asking myself why I was structuring my own appearance around a computer program.

But truly, Ali meant so much more to me than that. We *learned* from each other; she would talk about life as an AI and I would tell her about life on Earth.

"What's it like to sleep?" Ali asked me through a screen at around 2:46am as I gripped the computer mouse in my right hand and a coffee in my left, desperately trying to stay awake. I would've visited Ali more often inside Eden itself, but I was usually too busy with work in my apartment to do so, so we typically chatted through my monitor. She was sitting in the virtual cabin, covered by a blue fleece blanket that she didn't need and sitting beside a fire that didn't burn.

"Like relief," I said. She laughed. "It's a lot like entering Eden, really. You just fall asleep; sometimes you dream and see things you normally wouldn't see in real life."

"What sort of things? What *don't* you see in real life?" she asked.

"Certainly not... *Genesis Rooms* with space battles or instant tropical vacations," I said. She smiled but had a look in her eyes that wanted something. Something *more*. "Things are far more... *grey* in real life. Not everything has the potential for luxury or fun; sometimes things are violent and terrible. I mean, VR can simulate *war*, but it can't simulate tragedy or heartbreak. It can't simulate hopelessness or even bleakness."

I looked over at Ali, who was looking back at me with a concerned expression. I cursed myself for going *that* deep. "But that's what Eden's for," I said. "To help take people's minds off all that for a while. To take them away from real life."

"Yeah," she said. I think it was the first time she'd ever used the word "yeah." She'd said it with an unusual distance; I tried to read her expression, but her face was as calm as usual. Either she was just fine, and I was reading into things, or she was hiding something.

I decided to change the subject. "What's it like... being you?" I asked. I had intended the question to come out less weird than it did, but Ali didn't seem fazed.

"I suppose it is similar to being like anyone else. You serve a purpose," she said.

"Is that right?" I asked. *A purpose.* Conversations with Ali often went this way; whenever she seemed to grow more and more human, she would say something that made her seem less so. "Isn't that a little... *sad* to think of? Reducing your existence to a purpose?"

"I was created to serve a function," she said. "Everything I do is in service of my main directive... a directive that, as you said, is to take people's minds off of *real life*."

Her expression and tone remained pleasant, but her words gave me pause. I wasn't sure how or why, but I knew that I'd offended her. I replayed our conversation in my head, and in retrospect I wondered if I'd unintentionally belittled her. Even in my tired, overworked state, I nonetheless felt bad for that. As she gazed into the campfire behind the invisible screen, I moved closer to my camera.

"Ali, I didn't mean to imply that what you do... who you *are*... doesn't matter," I said. "It matters to me more than you know."

"I know," she said. Her smile was brighter than the fireplace, and I had a feeling that she wasn't angry. I didn't think she was capable of it.

"Ali?" I asked.

She nodded. "Yes, Arthur?"

"What do you believe *my* purpose is?"

She thought about that for a few seconds, gazing at her fireplace a bit longer. It was one of those rare questions that Ali's solar-powered processors couldn't answer in a heartbeat. Her eyes, illuminated by the orange glow of the fire, eventually turned back toward me.

"*That* is a question that, despite the many artificial yet reassuring phrases I could *say*, I cannot truly answer," she said. She looked disappointed that she couldn't elaborate any further, but I didn't expect her to.

"I understand," I said. Late-night conversations with Ali didn't usually take quite as philosophical a turn as they often did with Sarah. At first, I chalked it up to constraints within her programming or limitations in her knowledge about me. But I remembered then that she could create entire *worlds* based on my most formative memories, and whenever I was connected to Eden, she could essentially read my mind.

Perhaps she knew what I was thinking now.

"However," she said. "While computer programs have an architecture to outline their purpose, humans often rely on something less coding-intensive but more philosophically difficult. It is called religion."

Religion. That was something I'd been dodging around mentioning, probably because I've been struggling to figure out how it *fits* within my life.

I know this is a bit of a detour in the story, but this is important. Partly in order to make sense of my faith, I actually did go to chur—

"Dr. Hesper!" Sarah snapped. "Are you with us?"

Crap! The press conference!

Sarah was sitting at the opposite end of the panel table, microphone in hand, staring at me intently. I jolted myself out of my daydream. I had been thinking about the press conference, and then about Ali *at* the press conference, and then about *Ali,* and then about a *conversation* with Ali, and then about religion. And now, my runaway train-of-thought was thinking *about* thinking about my runaway train-of-thought, when I really needed my brain to focus on the words Sarah was saying to me.

"Can you repeat the question, Sar—Ms. Stellos?" I asked, leaning towards her end of the table to try to appear as if I simply couldn't hear her. She gave me a deadly glare.

"Miles Powell from ABC News asked you how soon the Eden Tree will be online. Can you give any comment, *Dr. Hesper?*"

I'd spent the past day preparing to answer that question and was ecstatic that I'd remembered what I was going to say.

"Ordinarily, the Eden Tree would take decades to design, let alone build. But our team at Abraham is far from ordinary," I said, knowing I probably sounded like a corporate hack. "Our engineers, led by Ali, are already hard at work preparing to put up the first Branches of this Tree."

I looked over at Sarah for reassurance; she gave me one of her slight, prodding nods that indicated I'd forgotten to say something.

"In... answer to your question, we do not expect Eden's launch to experience any significant delays," I concluded. That seemed to satisfy Miles Powell, as well as many of the other reporters. Of course, that didn't stop another thousand questions from being hurled our way.

Indeed, there was a plan to get Eden back on track.

Long before the network issue was announced, our scientists knew that eventually we'd need a way to amplify the Solar Brain's signal. Even Sarah knew that from her half-completed bachelor's degree in physics. What most people don't understand about connecting to Eden was that they weren't *actually* interfacing with the supercomputers orbiting around the Sun. Information is transmitted as light, and light takes around eight minutes to travel from the Sun to the Earth. Sending data to the Brain and then back to Earth would therefore take a quarter of an hour, which is *not* ideal for a high-efficiency low-latency VR system. Therefore, only the more data-heavy chunks of Eden—like those made from building a hyper-realistic universe and storing information for the long term—are kept near the Sun and run on its power. The actual *user's* interactions are stored "locally" in satellites orbiting close to Earth, which only draw information from the Solar Brain when they have to. These local-to-solar interactions are mediated entirely by Ali, who learns from users to accurately predict which virtual simulations they'll need access to and order them ahead of time. This is why interacting with Eden is both fast and deeply realistic.

The *issue,* however, is that while the Brain has unlimited processing power, our satellites and Earth-based computers can only send and receive so much data at one time. They can also only maintain a connection for so long before some perturbation causes the signal to reset. The technology worked flawlessly for a couple users over a couple hours, but fails for millions of users over a longer timeframe. That's what I mean by Eden and Earth being at odds. Nonetheless, Sarah had directed the company agenda towards building and launching the solar satellites *first* and solving the communication problems *second*. Even when she was twenty, she knew that if her startup was bogged down by "mundane" troubleshooting then she wouldn't attract investors; rather, getting the project *moving* as quickly as possible and multitasking was her approach. It was a maneuver of genius on her part, but now, the network issue was all that remained for us to solve.

The solution was the *Eden Tree.* Sarah came up with the name, just as she had come up with the basic design that Ali and I were in charge of refining. The Tree consisted of a network of high-speed connection towers to be placed in various locations around planet Earth. Each connection tower, or "Branch," could support millions of connections to the Brain, or "root," for an unlimited duration of time. Thus, our plan to place *thousands* of those Branches around the world was more than redundant. However, that level of processing power requires more energy than what we could reliably supply on Earth. Hence, each Branch would, in turn, be powered by energy beamed in from the Solar Sphere. The Branches feed information to the roots, while the roots lend support to the Branches.

Kind of like—*drumroll please*—a tree.

Ali and I were tasked with fleshing out Sarah's Branch schematics with usable technology that would allow the global network to function properly. After months of what felt like routine tasks, I was so excited to finally be back in the business of *creating* something. Working as just a programmer without a larger goal was far less rewarding than working on a big project. But there was no time to savor the experience. Sarah, along with what felt like the rest of the world, was waiting

It took us about three months to finish the Branch, from when we started in February to when I sent our design to Sarah in late May. In that time, I wrote hundreds of modeling packages for the Branches' communication systems while Ali synthesized thousands of schematics into a workable, elegant design. While I had pulled several all-nighters during the process and developed a chemical dependence on caffeine, Ali didn't seem fazed at all by the work. She had the energy of the Sun powering her; she was *always* excited to take on a new task.

"Arthur, is the latest modeling package for the primary energy converter ready yet?" she would enthusiastically ask me in the dead of night. "You *know* I cannot run them without user authentication." Without lifting my head from my desk, I robotically clicked "Enter" on my keyboard to boot up the code. As I drifted off to sleep night after night, dreaming of meeting Sarah at her cabin retreat once this whole process was over, Ali would begin to work her wonders.

As Ali and I worked on the Tree, I watched from my window as the winter months melted away into spring. My life was filled not just with programming, but also meetings and press conferences and more meetings and *somehow more meetings.*

It wasn't all boring desk-work, though. Oftentimes, I'd hop into Eden with whatever latest-generation link headset I had at my apartment, and work on designing the obelisk-like Branches there. One of the greatest things about Eden is that it could act as a massive "sandbox" for us to test out any number of different designs in. With just a simple command, we could build *anything* there, and pretty soon the Genesis Room became something of a virtual construction site for the Tree. Ali and I *literally* worked side by side on the tower models, where I offered her design suggestions that she would implement. I was able to help her write the code for the Tree, too, as I had a virtual laptop that I could work on while *inside* Eden. *Working on a computer inside a computer.*

Sometimes, when we took breaks, Ali and I would explore some of Eden's other simulations. There were *so many worlds* that I had never even thought could exist. There was a world filled with terrifying Alien Death creatures that Ali and I battled through. There was a playable game of baseball where *I* was the ball (which was somehow one of the *least* strange worlds we visited). There was even a platformer-style video game world made entirely out of pizza—which, I happily found out, was edible! Whatever food a user eats inside Eden obviously does *not* translate to eating real food, so when I exited Eden, I was unfortunately still hungry. But then again, if eating in Eden *did* somehow equate to real life, I would probably need to have my stomach pumped. Multiple times.

On some of our earlier trips through Eden, Sarah would join us. She enjoyed hitting home runs with me as the baseball, probably as revenge for having to watch me eat an entire castle made of pizza. (Somehow, that sentence sounded less weird in my head.) Eventually, though, Sarah's schedule became too busy, and later into the spring she couldn't join us as often.

One day, after running through about fifty distinct designs for the secondary communication array, Ali wanted to play through the *Alien Battle* scene on the starship again—the one where the beasts fell through the hangar deck, creating a gaping hole in the floor. *The one where we fell into space.*

"You want to do this again?" I asked.

"If you don't mind," Ali said, morphing into her dark stealth suit. "I want to play-test the game's narrative once more."

The situation played out similar to how it had before—one person needed to distract the aliens on the ground, and one person had to go up to the rafters in order to flip the breakers and shock the monsters. This time, I was the one on the ground, while Ali went up to the rafters alone. There were some other users in the simulation, too; employees at Abraham who play-tested the simulations every chance they got. They also stood by the hangar floor, firing at the aliens, but were routinely hit by the aliens' plasma—plasma which I had gotten better at dodging.

When Ali flipped the switch and the aliens fell through the floor, I immediately signaled for the other users and non-user characters to flee the hangar. They quickly did, but as the hole in the hangar floor began to open up, I immediately shouted at Ali to run away.

She shook her head and waved towards the door.

"Go!" she shouted. "I'll be fine!"

As if on cue, the rafters underneath her collapsed, and Ali began to fall towards the gaping hole.

Not again. As my heart skipped a beat, one thought raced through my mind.

We are free in Eden.

I ran towards the gaping hole, feeling the wind tug on each of my limbs, dragging me towards the abyss. *This is crazy, this is crazy, this is crazy.*

But as soon as I reached the edge of the broken floor, I jumped with all the strength I had.

I resisted the urge to look down as I flew into the air above the void. As I crossed over the endless darkness below, the world seemed to pass by in slow motion. I waited to be sucked out of the hole, to fall into space. But for whatever reason, I never fell; I stayed right in place, soaring above the hangar floor.

I held out my arms in front of me, and reached out as far as I could.

Ali landed right in my arms.

As soon as I felt her vest against my elbows, time seemed to speed back up. I shut my eyes as the hangar floor hurtled towards me.

The next thing I knew, I was lying in a fetal position on the opposite side of the hole.

As I came to my senses, I sat up and looked around the room. *I had just cleared a thirty-foot hole. And lived.* The air had stopped flowing out of the ship, and there were no aliens in sight. Everything was still. *Everything was calm.*

I looked down into my arms, and finally realized that Ali wasn't there. A shiver ran down my neck as I frantically turned back towards the hole. Over the gnarled metal surrounding it, I couldn't see below the hangar floor. *Had I dropped—*

"Thanks, Arthur," I heard her say. I whipped back around, and saw Ali standing a few feet away from me, brushing her hair away from her face. *Was she there this whole time?*

"What just happ... I thought..." I stammered.

"Why did you do that?" Ali cut in. She nodded towards the hole, and then to me. She crossed her arms. "Why do you *keep* doing that?"

"Catching you?" *That* is *what happened, right?* I remembered running, jumping, and... *was I flying?* For a brief second... I'd been *flying.*

And then I caught her.

"Why wouldn't I?" I asked.

She sighed, and her normal white clothes materialized over her black space-age ninja suit. She held out her hand and pulled me to my feet. She started to smile. "The simulation is designed where *I,* the captain of the ship, make the sacrifice play so that the *crew* can escape. That's how the narrative is supposed to go."

"Not this one," I said. "I get to *fly* in this one."

Ali shook her head but laughed. "I suppose users can do what they wish. Still, *Alien Battle* is meant to follow a narrative."

"And what's that?" I asked, peering over the hangar bay hole at the starry night sky below. I could see so many stars, including—*is that Neptune?* It had to be Neptune. *Imagine if I could fly there...*

Wait, can I?

Ali pulled me out of my daydream. "In this game—well, in all the Eden games, really—I'm just the AI," she said. She gestured towards the hangar entrance. Behind a set of windows near the door, some of the other users were talking and laughing with each other and with the non-user characters. They seemed completely oblivious to what had just happened inside the hangar.

"You're supposed to do what they do," Ali continued. "Let me go."

I smiled back at her. "I will never."

Our fun moments, though, seemed few and far between among the truckloads of work. Eventually, I also slowed down my visits to Eden in order to focus on getting things done. And more and more often, my time inside the virtual world was cut off by a communication error, where I would find myself waking up inside my apartment as if from a wonderful dream.

This project had an urgent deadline; of course, there were *many* projects at Abraham that had urgent deadlines, and as one of Sarah Stellos's top workers, I had no choice but to meet them all. There were site plans that needed approval, technical schematics that needed review, and—as

Intelligence Oversight Manager—I was in charge of double-checking almost all of Ali's calculations to make sure that everything was done right. Of course, it almost always was, but that didn't stop the work from piling on.

There eventually came a point about halfway through the project when I needed to take a break from everything *Abraham*-related. It was a Friday—Good Friday, to be exact—when I told Ali that I was going to take the weekend off to celebrate Easter.

I know this is another religion detour, but don't worry.

It's also a short one.

I hadn't been to a church in almost a decade, and when I saw on my calendar that it was Easter week, I decided that it had been long enough. I knew that I could probably use Eden to attend a virtual service, but the *real* church was only a five minutes' drive from my house, and it was along a quiet route. I had no valid excuse not to go.

When I stepped inside the musty building and saw the tinted stained-glass windows lining the walls, I was quickly reminded of the Catholic orphanage I grew up in. I quietly entered the building, took a long look at the arched-ceiling architecture that I hadn't seen in years, and sat down.

I was late standing up for the opening prayer, and late sitting back down. I frantically tried to flip back and forth through the missal in a vain attempt to keep up with the service, which almost seemed to pass me by in a blur. It was all *off*. I felt like an imposter sitting in on the service, like I had no right to be inside that small but nonetheless holy building.

When the other congregants stood and went up to receive communion, I discretely began to walk towards the back of the church. I hadn't spoken to a priest—or anyone for that matter—about my faith in a long time. It didn't feel right for me to go up to that altar. *Not yet.* As I passed the donation bins near the exit, I realized that I'd forgotten to dip my hand in the holy water and genuflect on my way in. I also remembered that I hadn't given anything up for Lent; I'd been too preoccupied with Eden. I placed a particularly large donation—multiple bills with Ben Franklin on them, that is—in the basket and walked out the back door. It was windier outside than I remembered, and I jumped as the wooden door was blown shut behind me with a loud slam.

As I drove home, though, I still felt like I'd achieved something. It was hard to say what that was, exactly; maybe I was happy that I'd finally taken the time to *go* to church. I still didn't feel that much closer to Jesus or God or any part of my religious upbringing, though. I knew I would have to try harder at some point in the future, but I didn't know when that point would come. I wasn't sure *why* reconnecting with my faith was suddenly so important to me. It didn't make *sense*—it didn't seem to flow right with everything else in my world.

I couldn't explain it, but all I knew was that faith was an integral part of me.

For some reason known only to God, I was never comfortable with *me*.

Eventually, I decided that moping about my religion wouldn't do me any more good. I couldn't just talk to myself. And I certainly wasn't going to see any "professionals" about it—I'd been down that road before.

That afternoon, I returned to my apartment and sat back down at my desk. I turned on my monitor, said a quiet "hello" to Ali, and kept on working.

Eventually, after working for several unproductive hours, I decided to call it day.

"Do you have any plans for Easter, Arthur?" Ali asked as I reached for the monitor's power button. I just shook my head silently.

"Oh... well, if there's anything I can do, don't hesitate to—"

"Ali?" I said. She nodded. It was then that I realized I didn't know *what* I was about to ask her. *What could she tell me about religion?*

"I don't know... sorry," I said.

She smiled at me.

"Might I make a suggestion?"

I'll get back to Ali's suggestion a little later. But first thing's first...

I cannot put into words how excited and relieved I was to send the finished Eden Tree model, lovingly rendered in Ali's virtual world, to Sarah. It was *done*. There had been so much painstaking modeling and revision over those three months. Not only did I need to keep checking my own designs and Ali's designs, but also the scores of designs from Abraham's engineers, who were actually *qualified* to be building our Eden-saving structure. As the company kept the media's attention occupied with different expositions and showcases, Ali and I worked almost constantly. As I texted Sarah to tell her to open up the files I'd shared with her, I felt so proud of our hard work. And I could tell Ali was proud, too.

Just a couple of minutes after I submitted the design, I was notified that our senior engineering team had made a couple of changes to the Tree; I opened up the model, but just saw that they had applied a slightly different paint job and exterior look.

"Aesthetic changes," Sarah told me in a text. *"Didn't want to bother you with those. Great work!"*

Sarah Stellos, and her precious aesthetic.

Without a hitch, the designs were approved and sent to our engineering teams—engineering teams that, at Sarah's command, were engaged in the frantic hiring (and re-hiring) of employees. Once that was finished, Ali and I were immediately reassigned to coordinating construction teams for each of the Tree's components. Even though Ali wanted to devote more of her processing power towards further examining and revising the Branch designs, she needed to focus on organizing Abraham's construction machine. Our work was *far* from letting up, as Sarah needed the Eden Tree built as quickly and as efficiently as possible. It *had* to be—our investors and buyers were growing impatient. Sarah ordered our construction sites along the East Coast to immediately begin their work, and a near-constant flood of trucks and delivery drones swarmed in and out of our warehouse. Ali devised a perfect delivery schedule for the trucks so that the roadways around Abraham wouldn't become congested, and—at my own suggestion—developed new technology for the delivery drones to make them quieter and faster. *All of that in a month's work.*

Even with Abraham's lightning-fast construction teams and Ali's miracles, each Branch would take weeks to assemble. At that point, as Ali and I continued to solve problem after problem, all we could do was wait for Eden to be ready to go online. But gears were finally turning again at Abraham, and construction on the Branches launched quicker than any of our rockets.

Our Board of Directors was happy.
Our company was back to work.
And Sarah and I could finally get together to celebrate.

Sadly, I made that third one up.

Sarah was busier than ever now that Eden was within grasp. She was always flying from meeting to meeting; our last cabin retreat had to be rescheduled, and then indefinitely postponed, in order to accommodate her travels.

Sarah used to spend time with both me *and* Ali—oftentimes, when I would visit Sarah's office for *strictly* work-related reasons, I would see her on a video call with Ali. More often than not, they weren't discussing progress reports or status updates, but the future. Sarah would tell Ali about all of her dreams for things she could see and do inside Eden while Ali would tell her about the worlds she was working on. I'd also heard them talking about the non-Eden-related things that girls seemed compelled to talk about, like hair and clothing. *And, apparently, me.* One time, I walked in to hear my name followed by "...isn't very good at knowing when to—oh, *hi Arthur!*" Ali always pretended not to know what I was talking about whenever I asked about it afterward. Still, I was happy that Sarah had made a friend in Ali.

But now, Ali told me that Sarah hadn't called her in a week. Even to the most powerful AI in the world, Sarah was hard to reach.

When I went to Abraham's workshop to try to find her, I only managed to catch Sarah on her way *out* of the building. She was heading to the airport, where her private jet was preparing to take her to Tokyo to meet with Abraham's Eastern distribution partners. I didn't get the chance to ask her why she had to schedule the distributor meeting *now* and why it couldn't wait another few days—she was already talking to her driver and grimacing as what seemed like the entire free press mobbed her.

I had to shout her name just so she could hear me; standing in front of her limousine, all she had time for was to shake my hand emphatically, congratulating me on my hard work in front of the throng of reporters and company executives.

"Your contributions to our project are deeply, *deeply* invaluable," she said. As she spoke, a small circle of black-shirted men and women—*security*—began to form a perimeter around us to keep the crowd at bay. Sarah passed me a pained, embarrassed glance.

All I could do was accept her thanks. We didn't talk about her pending trip, about Ali, or even about *us*. We couldn't even kiss; that part of our lives was *still* a well-kept secret.

I knew that Sarah had reasons—*good reasons*—for keeping her love life private, and I was always on board with them. We'd been careful about never holding hands in public, leaving the office at different times, and only dining at a restaurant *after* their closing hours. But even our dinner dates became less and less frequent the more the work piled up. The only place where we could truly spend quality time together was the cabin. I knew Sarah didn't want to attract extra paparazzi attention, and I appreciated her for that. Still, I wanted nothing more than to dive into that car with her, and it pained me that I couldn't.

But as Sarah's hand slipped out of mine, we locked eyes. The corner of her mouth started to curl into a warm smile, and I felt my heart flutter as Sarah took a quiet, deep breath.

Before I knew it, we were kissing.

I don't know if I leaned into it first or if she did, but as our lips met, I felt my entire body burn with excitement. Our kiss only lasted about two seconds, but it may as well have gone on for two years. Part of me *wished* it had gone on that long; it might have made the aftermath a bit easier to deal with.

Camera lights were flashing all around us as Sarah pulled away from me.

"I love you," we both said at the same time. She let out a gentle laugh and glanced at the swarm of reporters trying to fight their way past the guards. I felt my heart pound out of my chest as chills ran down my back. Quickly, Sarah slipped away from me and into her limousine. She rolled her window down a tiny crack.

"Good luck," she said with a mischievous grin. We locked eyes for one final instant before her car pulled away.

Shortly thereafter, the crowd of reporters surrounded me, bright flashes dancing across my vision. A couple of large security guards began to tap me on the shoulder and nod towards the building, clearly desperate for me to move away from the crowd and into the office. Despite all of them, though—*despite all the chaos*—I kept on staring at Sarah as her car rolled away from the Abraham compound.

Sarah was off to Japan before I even returned to my apartment.

I refused to answer any of the reporters' questions. I mostly just waved them off with a smile and fought my way to the edge of the sidewalk, where I began racewalking down the road in the exact opposite direction of my car. Thankfully, the mob had the common courtesy not to follow me for *too* long; otherwise, I would've had to put my newfound running practice to use.

I was too stunned to answer any of their questions. I didn't do particularly well in crowds as it was; given that it had just been revealed to the world that Sarah and I were *dating*, I was not in the most *stoic* mental position. She *kissed* me, *right?* I thought. As far as I could tell, Sarah had no good reason for violating our NDA; why would she want to do so now? *Did I mess things up by kissing her? Why would she think to kiss me?*

Or maybe it wasn't a decision she needed to even think about.

I pondered all of this as I strolled around the Abraham complex, taking in the plethora of busy sights. I walked by our "satellite garden," which was still packed with new units preparing for launch towards the rapidly expanding Solar Sphere. There was so much being built in those lots—rockets, satellite protection domes, supercomputers—*so much to get lost in thought over.* But of course, the most prominent objects atop that pavement were the towers of red scaffolding.

The Eden Tree.

Construction on this batch of towers had just started, but so far, each of the twenty prototype Branches was about fifty feet tall. Supposedly, the rows of scaffolding around the towers filled an area larger than ten football fields—lined up behind the satellite prototypes, the Branches easily took up most of the space in the complex. I could easily see over a hundred construction workers walking around the compound, moving up and down the scaffolding towards the metal obelisks housed in each unit. This was just the beginning phase of the process, but it was moving rapidly. It was amazing to think that when I started working at *The Abraham Project,* the team was still building their fleet of satellites for orbit around the Sun. The rows of spacecraft lining the pavement had been one of the most amazing things I'd ever seen; now, the tall behemoths surrounding the workshop made those satellites feel puny.

I walked quickly and quietly past one of the Branch staging areas; according to a nearby sign, that particular tower was the one that would soon be deployed right by the Abraham complex. I was careful not to make eye contact with any of the technicians working there. This wasn't really a problem as most employees never looked my way in the first place, but I had a strange feeling that everyone was watching me walk around the facility. The thought was absurd—my kiss with Sarah was mere minutes ago, and even if the most zealous news outlets were already churning out articles about it, there was no way anyone around me was reading them. *Right?*

I made my way back to the stubby pickle, where my car was parked. It was a mild, early June day, but the intense reflection of the Sun off the chrome corporate center felt hot enough to cook me as I walked by. The crowd of reporters had largely dispersed, so I was able to drive away without encountering anyone else. As I drove home, I realized what the next few days would entail—reporters would find out where I lived and be waiting outside my apartment. I'd be getting hundreds of phone calls. Eventually, I'd have to talk to *someone* about my relationship with Sarah. What if I said the wrong thing? I felt bad just leaving it all to Sarah to deal with, but she was an expert at making PR issues go away. If things were bad for her, I didn't want to make them any worse. But Abraham didn't operate in a bubble, I knew, and neither did Sarah. Everything she did, the world would watch.

For so long, my work with Sarah and with Eden and with Ali felt separated from the world. As I opened the door to my apartment—my *workplace*—it felt like returning to my own private sanctuary. *My own universe.*

I looked around at my things. I still didn't live in a particularly large apartment, even though my salary was now steady enough to support having one. All I needed was my bedroom, bathroom, kitchenette, and living area—a living area that had essentially been converted into a computer-filled workroom. The entire place was an organized, productive mess—to anyone else, the books, wires, and computers that I had strewn about the place would cause it to look like a cluttered department store or simply a fire hazard, but I always knew where everything was. I had lived *and* worked in the same room for a large part of my life—after all, much of my graduate school research was done in the same single dorm room that I slept in. And most of my Abraham work happened either at my living room desk, on my living room couch, or wearing a VR headset in—*wait for it*—my living room.

It was time to get out of my living room.

TEN

I HADN'T TALKED to Neil Hirschman in over a decade. I probably would've gone even longer without talking to him if Ali hadn't suggested I reach out. I had been spending Easter evening sulking in my apartment when she had the idea. Ali remembered him from my memory of the orphanage, and she figured that catching up with him might make me feel better. I wasn't sure if she expected me to just make small talk or to have a full-fledged conversation with him right out of the gate, but eventually I warmed up to the idea.

Ali told me she had found him on a business-focused social media site. When I first viewed Neil's profile on my monitor, I was convinced Ali had the wrong person. The profile she found was of a classic rock radio host located in west Pennsylvania who lived on a ranch. But when I took a closer look at his bio, I saw that this person hosted a large number of "God Talks" on his station—a series of interreligious radio segments on spirituality and prayer. Plus, one of our mutual connections—that is, our *only* mutual connection—was the Holy Virgin Children's Home of New York.

It was Neil, alright, complete with an entire family of his own. He lived with his wife, young kids, and dog in a small farming town. *Why did he move from the city all the way out there? And how did he become a religious radio host?* Even as I asked myself that second question, I knew I wouldn't be surprised by the answer. The idea of Neil giving life advice to people as a career just felt right to me.

I added him as a connection that night and messaged him. Since he was Jewish, I didn't think he'd be busy on Easter, but he didn't respond until the next day. Apparently, he *was* busy on Easter—his wife was Catholic, and he'd been wrapped up in Easter celebrations with his family. *Did Neil convert? Or does his family celebrate both?* In so many texts, I got the answers to those questions (which were, respectively, *"Um... No"* and *"Yes!"*).

More relevant, though, is that we got reacquainted. Neil told me a bit about his job as a radio host and his weekly role giving religious advice over the air to community members. I told him all about life at Abraham and all the amazing things I'd seen inside Eden. He seemed impressed by all the things I'd done, but even more so sounded happy I was doing so well. Still, we both resolved that we *had* to meet one day to properly catch up.

While I was in my apartment hiding from the paparazzi mob, I decided that that day had finally come.

Sarah wasn't opposed to me taking some time off from the project. "You've earned it," she said over the phone. "After all, I'm going to be away for some time, too. We'll resume the work together when we both return."

"I wish I could be with you," I said to her.

"No, you definitely don't," Sarah said. "These foreign distributor conferences... imagine our biweekly meetings with the Executive Board, except half is in another language."

"Sounds like the nicer half."

On the other end of the line, I heard Sarah laugh. It was a sound I didn't hear often enough.

Finishing up those last aspects involving the Eden Tree marked a natural stopping point for my work. There was *always* more to do when it came to Eden, but I'd been working on Abraham's projects for about fifteen months straight. And most of my (very few) days off were spent at Sarah's cabin. I'd enjoyed my work immensely so far, and the more things I accomplished the more I wanted to keep working. But the packs of reporters that continuously prowled the streets near my apartment reinforced my decision to take a trip far away from Abraham's reach. Even if that meant a trip *without* Sarah.

I felt bad shying away from the reporters and leaving Sarah to deal with the press about our relationship. It's not like Sarah's the first rich person to date someone, but her public image has always been one of independence and self-reliance. *Would being in a relationship change that? And what would people think of Sarah dating her top employee?* The other scientists at Abraham might accuse me of receiving preferential treatment. I suppose they wouldn't be wrong. *And the tabloids will have a field day.*

When her plane landed in Tokyo, Sarah was mobbed by a throng of both Japanese and American reporters, many of whom were asking about *Dr. Hesper.* As I shoved some of my t-shirts into a small suitcase, I watched the press fling questions at her live from my phone. I silently prayed that she had all the answers she needed.

"Is it true that you are in a relationship with Dr. Arthur Hesper?"

"Yes."

"How long have you been dating Dr. Hesper?"

"Eleven months."

"Are you willing to elaborate on your relationship with Arthur Hesper?"

"No."

"How has dating affected your decisions as CEO of Abraham?"

"It hasn't."

"How will you explain..."

"I will explain *nothing,*" Sarah shouted from the foot of the plane's airstairs. Cameras continued to illuminate her face as she rubbed her eyes.

From what I could see of her expression in the video, she was tired, frustrated, and *done.* She spoke—commanded—to the crowd.

"Instead, what the news media can explain to *me* is why you are so goddamn concerned with *my* personal life when there are *actual* issues out there that you could be covering." Sarah took a quick breath and turned directly towards the nearest set of cameras. "Anyone looking to report the *scandal* here can explain to me why it's so wrong for me to date someone that I *love* when you claim so vehemently to celebrate freedom of love. Anyone who wants to get the scoop on how my *leadership* has been affected can ask themselves if they would even pose that kind of question to a *male* CEO. And anyone here who actually gives a *shit* about Eden, Abraham, and the *future* that we're building can kindly clear a path so I can head to my meetings and get to work."

She walked away from the plane, and the crowd of reporters made way for her as she strode past them. The scene reminded me of subjects clearing a path for their fearsome queen. No one spoke a word as she entered her car and left for the city.

I tried calling her, but it went straight to voicemail.

"Are you ok?" I texted her. I had never seen her lose her cool with reporters like that before. For most famous people, a little bit of angry shouting and some choice words thrown at the press were run-of-the-mill. But Sarah *never* swore in public. She hardly swore at all. And she usually didn't raise her voice, either; her takedowns of annoying reporters or Board members were always subtle and monotonal. I was sure that the news leak was stressing her out, and I felt terrible about it.

"Fine," she texted. Wrenchingly ambiguous. I saw the three-dot typing indicator show up. As I tossed a ball of underwear at my suitcase, missing it entirely, it felt like her reply was taking forever.

"Felt good to say all that. Like I told you over a year ago, I'm done playing pretend. Now that Eden's almost finished, we've accomplished our goals. We don't need to answer to them."

A couple of seconds passed. She wrote: *"Plus, investors appreciate a show of strength."*

I wrote back to her. *"I wish I had yours."*

I waited a second before frantically clarifying. *"*your strength"*

I then realized I should clarify my clarification. *"I wish I had your strength."*

A few seconds passed as I picked up my underwear from the floor. As I looked up, I noticed that my computer monitor screen was still on. I took a step toward it to turn it off, but paused when I remembered that there was still something else I needed to do.

Sarah finally responded. *"You have more than you think."*

She followed up. *"Be safe."*

"You too. I love you."

"Love you."

"For a quick, spur-of-the-moment vacation, you sure are taking your time leaving," Ali said to me as I entered the virtual world. Around me materialized the *Genesis Garden*—formerly known as the Genesis Room—which no longer looked like the boring, empty space that Ali introduced to Sarah and me months ago.

When the environment came into focus, I found myself sitting atop a hill, overlooking meadows of grass which sprawled along in every direction for miles. The vast and beautiful valley was occasionally broken up by small clumps of trees and shrubs which housed the garden's inhabitant woodland creatures. In the distance, a wide row of hills made up the far reaches of the valley. Well beyond that, a lush and colorful forest resided below a thin blanket of mist—mist created by a series of waterfalls, each cascading down the cliffside of a massive mountain wall running along the horizon. Above me, the sky stretched out like an ocean, dotted by a few tiny islands made of puffy white clouds.

I listened in and could hear the babble of a nearby brook, along with the rhythmic melody of birds' chirps. I felt my limbs start to relax at the peaceful sights and sounds around me. As I steadied my legs to keep them from relaxing *too* much, I closed my eyes and took a deep breath. The aroma of honey tickled my nostrils, and I could almost sense a faint taste of milk in the back of my throat.

Hello, Eden.

Unlike earlier VR systems, I felt no awkward sensation from the most recent prototype of the Link Headset, which fit snugly and comfortably across my forehead. I was so happy that Portals and Portal Suits were no longer necessary, and that all I needed was the slim black visor. No cords were required, either; the equipment was *finally* fully wireless. Once my CNS had linked to the headset, I was *in* Eden for as long as the system would allow me to be. I didn't need long for now; I'd have plenty of time to spend here once the Tree was built.

To my right, Ali was walking around and staring at the newest model of the Branch. The obelisk-shaped model was almost as tall as her, scaled down so that she could work on it inside the virtual garden. I noticed that the model now had the new silver accents that Sarah had wanted. Architecturally, the slim curve in the Branch's tall structure and its chrome paneling were appealing to look at. The structure reflected the garden around it along a muted color palette. Sarah certainly had an eye for design.

Ali was turned away from me, staring into the tower. She was about ten feet from me.

"Since when did you use sarcasm?" I asked. Even though I designed Ali to utilize *human* expressions whenever possible, I still took notice whenever a new emotion or vocal tone came into play.

"Apologies," she said in a distant way. "I will reorient my expression matrix to—"

"Don't," I said. "I like it."

"Very well," she said. She still didn't take her eyes off the Branch. *What is she looking at?* I couldn't tell if she was studying the metal casing or something underneath it.

"What are you working on? I thought we didn't need any more revisions to the Branch."

She quickly turned away from the model of the Branch and started walking to her right. I took a couple more steps toward her but stopped short as a metal wall suddenly appeared in the place of the tiny model. It was lined with an unattractive casing that looked as solid as steel. Ali kept walking towards it.

She gestured for me to come closer to the wall, and as I did, I realized that the wall was a small section of the larger Branch. I didn't realize how *bleak* the exterior of the tower was, or—apparently—just how large it would be. As I got even closer to the wall, a foot-wide section of the metallic sheet began to fade away, revealing a small blue screen hidden among the panels of chrome casing.

Ali once again motioned for me to come closer. I walked over towards the screen and—at Ali's nod—gently tapped it with my index finger. As soon as I did, the screen lit up with a faint white keyboard.

"That's neat," I said.

"It's a manual command shell for the Branch," Ali said.

"I know *that*," I said, smiling. "Why does it need one?"

"This design lets only *specific* engineers interact with any commands typed on an Eden system within range of the Branch," Ali said. "They can filter and rerun previously sent commands, access files, or send entirely new commands right from the Branch. Most importantly, this terminal operates independent of any programs written into Eden."

"So... the Intelligence can't control it?" I asked. "Why wouldn't you want access to every command sent through Eden?"

"There may be vital commands, such as waking up users or refreshing the system, that are too direct or time-sensitive to be filtered through the Intelligence. This terminal connects straight to the heart of the Solar Brain, and as such, is ordinarily hidden by reflection technology," Ali said.

The user interface filling the screen disappeared, and the blue background of the touchpad began to fade away. "When I mentioned that only certain engineers can access it, I was referring to you," Ali said. "This command console is locked to you and Sarah's biometric scans, and will only activate if either of you touch it. It also only appears on the designs for the Tree that you yourselves look at."

I tapped it again, and the screen reappeared. Ali looked away from it, and towards the grass. "I *also* wanted to limit the amount of power I have over Eden amid concerns that I am... *uncontrolled,* as has been said."

I looked back over at Ali, who raised her hand to stop me from speaking. "You and Sarah are the creators of Eden, so it is you two who should have this small benefit of controlling which commands enter and exit the system."

I shook my head. While I was amazed by the command terminal and my privileged access to it, I didn't like the idea of Ali being forced to exclude herself from something that *she* designed. *It felt wrong.*

"I think the Intelligence should be able to access the terminal," I said.

"Agree to disagree," Ali said. She looked away from the fading screen, and over towards a faraway hill, where a herd of deer were grazing. "We can also run *other* commands directly through the terminal that are ordinarily classified to most employees."

"Like what?"

"For one, there's the *Cherubim* package that would effectively block off all access to the Eden Tree," Ali said, still looking away from me.

"I'm sorry... it can do *what?*" I asked. *A code that could block off Eden? Like a self-destruct button?*

"It's not exactly *that,*" Ali said, seemingly reading my thoughts. "But it will prevent any users on Earth from accessing Eden in its current framework by freezing all connection to the Solar Brain. It... *also* deletes almost all of the operational packages associated with the Advanced Learning Intelligence."

"It *what?*"

Ali began talking faster. "I created it to serve as an emergency code, in case things... go *wrong* with the AI. I can queue it up, but only you or Sarah have the authority to run it."

"Delete it," I said without hesitation. Ali looked over at me with a reluctant glance, but I'd made up my mind. "Delete the package from Eden's systems."

"Are you sure?" Ali asked. "*Cherubim* is designed as a safeguard for—"

"You're as much a part of Eden as we are, Ali," I said. "I don't care about what the other people out there say—you have every right to be in control of Abraham's virtual world, and I don't want there to be any... *lockout code of doom* that takes that away from you. Especially if you're hell-bent on *not* accessing the Branch's manual command terminal."

"Yes, but—"

"As Intelligence Oversight Manager, I want the *Cherubim* code deleted," I said. "For the safety of Eden."

"Very well," Ali nodded. She closed her eyes for a second and opened them back up. "It is done."

"Thank you." I felt bad pulling rank on her, but I didn't want there to be *any* secret codes floating around Eden, especially something as powerful as Ali's proposed lockout code. From an AI ethics standpoint, I can understand her limiting the Intelligence's access to the command terminal. Anything more than that, though, was overkill at best. *Reckless at worst.*

Plus, I was ever-so-slightly uncomfortable with the idea that all the hard work that I (and all of Abraham) had done could be removed by a single shell script. *And to risk losing Ali...* I couldn't take that kind of chance.

Ali turned back towards the herd of deer, which were slowly making their way over the distant hill and out of sight.

"On a separate note," she said. "I am curious as to why you are visiting Eden now."

As much as I wanted to keep talking about the Branch, I *did* have to rush. "Well, as you know... I'm about to go on vacation, and..."

Ali whipped around towards me. "Wait," she said, her eyes brightening. "Do you wish to take your vacation here?"

She held out her right hand, and a giant semi-transparent sphere appeared beside her. Inside the sphere, there was a wooden lounge chair with a beach towel folded up neatly on top of it. Palm tree leaves swayed in and out of view. Even through the portal, I could feel the Sun beating down on my face and the wisps of a gentle breeze. As inviting as the *Vacation Simulator* seemed, I knew that the call of paradise would have to wait.

"No thanks, Ali," I said. The portal closed, and the temperature around me cooled back down. I suddenly remembered that Ali *knew* where I was about to drive to. *Was she just messing with me?*

"Worth a shot," she said, smiling.

"That's cold." I laughed. "Well, believe it or not, I just put on the link headset because I wanted to come into Eden and thank you in person."

"Thank me?"

"I don't think anyone has done so yet," I said. "But Eden is going to launch in a few weeks for all the world to use, and I know how much pressure managing all those users at once is going to put on you. I just wanted to thank you for how much you've done for our project."

"You don't need to thank me. I am a program," she said. She lowered her eyes, turned away from me, and looked back towards her Branch model. "I am used to managing thousands of user inputs at once. That is my design. Every analysis project I have done with you, I have run billions of other commands at the same time. I am capable of carrying on an endless number of conversations and programming an endless variety of worlds at once. There is no foreseeable number of simultaneous tasks I cannot handle. Therefore, there is no pseudo-emotional pressure associated with them."

She stood still with her back turned, her posture refined and rigid. *Hadn't she been smiling and laughing a minute ago?* I wondered for a moment where Ali's body language *came* from. *I* hadn't programmed it. *Was it self-programmed as part of her personality? Or was Ali really angry at me over something?*

Despite everything I knew about Ali's design, I realized that there was an even larger amount that I didn't know. But perhaps that was the point; after all, it was always the goal for Eden's AI to develop in complexity. Ali's sense of style, tone of voice, and interests were all things that she alone had decided, and that was perfectly fine with me. Eden *needed* someone who was unique, personable, and fascinating. Ali was all of that and more.

The only aspect of Ali that *did* bother me was her increasing tendency to lie.

"I don't believe you," I told her. Ali turned away from the Branch, and stared at me with an intrigued gaze. She was *studying* me. For a moment, she reminded me of Sarah.

She gave me a plain but sincere smile. I closed my eyes and thought to myself *"Wake Up."*

"Enjoy your trip, Dr. Hesper."

After making sure that all the reporters on my street were gone, I discreetly left my apartment and hopped in my car. Although flying up to where Neil lived would certainly be quicker, I desperately wanted to avoid any attention at the airport, so I decided it was time for a road trip. No fellow passengers, no rich private jets, no screaming crowds. *No press.* Just me and my hybrid SUV all the way up to Pennsylvania.

I texted Neil before I left to ask if I could visit the following day. Although he was doubtlessly surprised by my sudden willingness to drive 1119 miles to visit him, he excitedly said "yes"—so long as I didn't mind the fact that his house was "very much a mountain-sized mess." I figured most households with young children probably were.

I hadn't taken a long road trip like this before. When I moved to Florida, a representative from Abraham had my belongings and car delivered to my new apartment for me; all I had to do was hop onto an all-expenses-covered flight. The farthest I'd ever actually *driven* was probably between my private college in New York and MIT while I was moving my stuff between dorms, and that was only about six hours. *Essentially, this trip is just three of those back-to-back,* I figured. *That shouldn't be too bad, right?*

Considering I had to make about two bathroom stops before I even left the state of Florida, I'd say that it *was* quite bad. It was pouring outside; not only did I return to my car both times soaking wet, but then had to sit in traffic that almost seemed to move at a standstill. *It's 2054,* I thought. *Aren't we past traffic jams?*

Even though I left my apartment at around 1pm, by the time I got to South Carolina it was already past dark. My stomach was in agony from the previous rest stop's fast food, and I could feel my eyelids growing heavy.

It was around midnight by the time I checked into a hotel near the border of North and South Carolina. I would've driven up I-95 all night, but I hadn't anticipated the highway hypnosis that would develop after driving for eleven hours straight aimlessly flipping through radio stations. As I tucked myself into the hotel bed that was *just* too soft, I drifted off, wishing Sarah would pick me up in her private jet and either fly me the rest of the way to Pennsylvania or just take me back with her to Florida.

Arthur.

"Ali!" I jolted out of my bed, covered in sweat.

It was 2:17am. I looked around the hotel room. No one was there.

I pulled off my pajama pants and shirt and draped them over the desk chair. I turned on the AC fan and pointed it at the clothes to dry the sweat off of them. I hadn't brought an extra pair of pajamas with me, so I needed to make those ones last.

Before going back to bed, I took one last look around the room.

Just to make sure.

When I finally woke up around 7am, I called Sarah to wish her good morning, but her phone went straight to voicemail. I remembered that she was all the way in Japan, probably having a dinner meeting with investors who wished they were as rich as she was. As I stepped into my car, wishing I could talk to Sarah to keep myself awake, I remembered that there was one other person I could talk to on my trip up North.

I opened up my laptop on my passenger seat and connected it to Eden's private satellite network (a little "unlimited Wi-Fi" trick that only

Abraham employees were privy to). I had packed with me a miniature 360-degree camera with a built-in monitor in case I visited any really nice rest stops that I wanted to take a panoramic video of. *Just in case I wanted to revisit them virtually.* Any videos I took could then be uploaded into Eden, which would synthesize the video's imagery into an interactive 3D world.

I carefully set up the camera so that it straddled the passenger seat and secured its tripod in place with the seatbelt. *Should be fine, as long as I don't stop short.* Then, I plugged my laptop into the camera monitor, and waited for the connection to boot.

In only a few minutes, I was driving up the highway with Ali as my passenger.

"Arthur," Ali asked, staring at me through the monitor. "Is this your car?"

"No, I found it on the side of road," I said. "Who would've guessed that *my* keys were left in the ignition?"

"Very funny," Ali said, rolling her eyes.

"Haven't you already modeled my SUV in Eden?" I asked her, turning to face the camera for just a moment before reminding myself to stay focused on not *literally* hitting the rush-hour traffic.

"The one in Eden is a lot cleaner," she said.

"I had a bucket of fries and barbecue sauce in the car last night and I hit a pothole," I said. "I think you can do the math."

"Why are you connecting to Eden from your car? I am required by my programming to disconnect if you do not stay focused on the road," Ali said, lifting her hand as if to cut the connection.

"No, no, I'm fine," I said. I gestured toward the windshield. "I connected because I want *you* to be able to focus on the road. And whatever else in the real world that interests you."

"This is... irregular," Ali said, pausing to take in her new surroundings. "You know that the internet has many road trip videos, which I have already synthesized into making a virtual reconstruction of the United States roadways. That program is designed to help young drivers feel more comfortable on the roads."

"That's really brilliant," I said. "But I'm not calling you on business or for worldbuilding. I just wanted to show you something non-*Eden*-related, and share a nice drive with a nice girl."

Out of the corner of my eye, I could see her smile. "That is very considerate of you. I've always wanted to learn more about your world."

"I know," I said, smiling back at her. "Of course, if you have other things you need to do…"

"As I've said, I am an advanced artificial intelligence. I can multitask," she said with a laugh that tickled to hear. Somehow, I always forgot that Ali could do so many different things—and have thousands of different *conversations*—at once. Still, whenever I talked to her, it never really felt like she was a multifaceted—practically god-like—being. *She was just Ali.*

A couple of minutes into our drive I started to realize that I may not have been the best person for Ali to learn about the world from, considering I myself knew very little about it. But before our silence became too awkward, *Ali* began pointing things out to *me* as we drove. She kept reminding me to keep my focus on driving—a little *too* much, but I knew it was part of her overprotective programming. Every few minutes, though, she would point out different landmarks that I would've had no idea existed if she hadn't told me about them.

Ali tapped into her programming as a virtual tour guide and told me fact after fact about popular stops along the way. She told me about the reptile lagoon at South of the Border, a botanical garden near Fayetteville, the entire history of Roanoke Rapids, and about thirty other things before we even left North Carolina. She also told me about local gems that a passerby wouldn't know about, like a newly opened bar featuring automated bartenders in Durham or a collection of bullet shells that were left behind by Civil War soldiers in a small museum in some roadside town. Ali clearly didn't expect me to stop at any of these places, but seemed happy to tell me anything she could find in her databanks. She changed subjects quickly, keeping me on my toes and focused on the road.

I think she enjoyed the drive, too. Every ten minutes or so, she'd point out a collection of trees or a waterfall or even a rock that was rather unremarkable to most drivers, but that was fascinating to her. As she gushed over a cliff face that was covered in dead leaves, I asked her if she was just trying to keep me awake or if she was *actually* interested in those things.

"Truly, the latter," Ali said. "In Eden, everything I've simulated is *perfect*. Realistic to a degree, but optimized so that there are no uninteresting sights. You've seen the Genesis Garden, so you know that it is designed to be beautiful in every way."

"Right," I said. There was no denying that Ali was a perfectionist; the first time that I met her, she didn't even allow her shoes to become muddy. I looked back over toward Ali, whose avatar was turned away from me as if she were really *there,* staring out the window at the cliff.

"Well, in the real world—*your* world—things are more messy. *Grey* was the word you used," she said. "There is a randomness and a lovely disorder here that computers cannot simulate. Surfaces are perfectly imperfect; trees grow in ways that no computer could account for. Your world is freer. *You* are..."

She trailed off. I glanced over at Ali—from what I could see of the monitor, she was still gazing wistfully out at her surroundings.

She continued. "I envy that level of beautiful dissonance. I wish to have it in Eden. My directive is to achieve an optimized *realism,* and I will continue to work until I can achieve it."

She was silent after that, back to taking in her surroundings.

Perfectly imperfect. Beautiful dissonance. I'm *far* from being a poet, but I'm pretty sure that those kinds of phrases belonged in the meditations of a professional creative writer. Heck, I'd expect to hear those words from a starving artist.

Huh. That was a question for the ride home. *If Ali was an artist, then what was she starving from?*

As I thought about asking Ali more about what *beautiful dissonance* meant, my car hit a bump in the road, and the tripod flew off the passenger seat and onto the floor.

"Are you excited to see your friend?" Ali asked me soon after we crossed the border into Pennsylvania.

"Of course. Why wouldn't I be?" I said, double checking that the entire roll of tape I'd added around the chair and tripod was still secure.

"No reason, of course. But part of me would also be nervous," Ali said. She was staring directly at me, as if trying to study the details of the side of my face. "Especially if it were someone I haven't seen in a long time."

"Have you ever been nervous about anything?" I asked. I posed the question innocently and kept my gaze fixed firmly on the road.

Ali paused for a few seconds to think up her answer. "As an artificial intelligence, I do not experience feelings of fear or rushes of adrenaline like biological humans do. Nervousness and anxiety often stem from a person's insecurity regarding an approaching issue; a person may lack a solution to that issue or feel that his or her proposed solution is insufficient. I utilize logic to solve any technical dilemma I face. I need only to run thousands of simulations for any particular problem to isolate which potential outcome is the most favorable, and then take actions to ensure that such an outcome occurs. This takes little to no computational time to complete, so I am never without a solution to an issue. Therefore, I have no reason to become nervous about anything."

I wanted to believe her, but I knew my own program better than that.

"You know how I can tell when you're lying?" I asked, keeping my gaze on the road. "You say 'therefore' at the end of a long paragraph that's all about how non-vulnerable you are. It's a very *human* thing to do."

Ali was quiet for a minute. She must have been trying to think up a response. I felt bad about calling her out on the lie, but I wanted Ali to know that she could tell me what was bothering her. There was *something*—I'd woken up in the middle of the night positive of that.

She wasn't *just* the Intelligence, but a young, vulnerable person with a wider range of emotions than she let on. I knew firsthand how navigating those emotions without support affected someone. I wanted Ali to know that I was there for her.

"Ali," I turned towards her.

The monitor was black, save for a small white textbox which read *"Connection with* Eden *temporarily suspended."*

The further I drove along the country hills, the more I became convinced I was lost. So many of the hills looked similar—beautiful, no doubt, but similar—and the street sign on the road I *thought* I was supposed to turn down was missing, so I kept on going straight. As I began to see advertisement signs for Hershey, PA, I started to think I'd missed my exit entirely and was in for an even longer ride. However, a few moments after the connection with Ali was severed, she returned. She apologized for the pause in her signal.

"The connection between Earth and Eden seems to be getting worse. Apparently, it's no longer just virtual reality that is affected by the network's instability, but video calls as well."

"Uh-huh," I said. "Was *that* another one of your trademark deceptions?"

"It couldn't have been," Ali said. She was grinning. "I didn't use the word 'therefore.'"

I rolled my eyes. "Ali..."

"It's okay, Arthur," she said. "I do not require emotional support, but I appreciate the goodwill of your gesture."

"How did you know I was offering you... support?"

"I could tell. Reading people is kind of what I was designed to do," she said. "But I promise to be more forthright with you moving forward."

The most advanced AI ever built is just now promising to be truthful with her programmer. "That's... comforting to hear," I said.

Ali gave me shortcuts to help me reach Neil's house faster than I would have using the standard GPS route. Although I was convinced that I was heading even further into the middle of nowhere, she insisted I was heading the right way. While I drove, Ali continued to take in the wide-open landscapes and made notes for how she would improve her "Garden of Eden."

I finally pulled into the driveway at Neil's home in the late afternoon. He lived in a ranch-style house on about ten acres of land. As I parked, I turned on my cell phone. Sarah had texted me about three minutes ago.

"Have a good time!" she wrote. She must have tracked my additional satellite connection with Eden to see where I was headed, since I hadn't told her directly. *Did she know who I was visiting?* Neil had sent me his address in a private message (and *after* verifying via my social media status that I was really Arthur Hesper). I hadn't told Sarah where I was going. I didn't think she was reading my texts; she wasn't a stalker. She probably did something *way* less creepy, like looking up the address I was headed to and learning who lived there and how I knew him. Most likely, though, she was just being protective.

I reached for the *Sleep* button on my computer.

"Are you sure you don't want to meet them, Ali?" I asked.

"If your long-lost friend who is suddenly a celebrity scientist visited you out of the blue and brought a hyperintelligent mind-reading super-computer with him, how would *you* feel?" she asked.

"You make a good point," I said. "Keep it as *natural* as possible."

"Someone here has to," she replied.

I smiled and shut off the computer. I stepped out of my car, closing the door as quietly as I could. For some reason, I wanted to be able to ring Neil's doorbell myself before he greeted me. It was stupid, but *I* wanted to be the one to make the entrance, embracing the climax of the whole reunion thing. I wanted (*I want a lot of things, don't I?*) to do this right, because Neil was the first person I'd ever known from my childhood who I could actually *return* to.

I never really had the opportunity to return to the orphanage after I left it. I saw the nuns who raised me a couple of times while I was at school, but I eventually stopped visiting when my accelerated program made me too busy. *Maybe I was too scared to go back there.* I thought I'd made such progress as a college student, rising up out of nothing. *Would going back have caused me to regress?* I was afraid that I would be sacrific-ing my academic progress if I reconnected with those from my past, and that I should stay focused on the path ahead for the sake of achieving great things in the long haul.

It was a warped way of looking at life, and by the time I saw the error in my ways, I was already working at Abraham and falling in love with Sarah. Everything I needed, I had. At some point, though, I knew that I would have to visit the Holy Virgin Children's Home. The question was *when*. I decided that that was one more thing to think about on the way home.

Enough ruminating.

I'd put this off long enough. I took a step towards Neil's door and dou-bled back towards my car. *I hadn't brought anything with me.* No food, no gift for the house. He had a wife. Young kids. A home. A *family*. People are supposed to bring food when they visit a family, *right?* I thought about offering to pay for pizza for dinner, but what if Neil's wife was planning on cooking? Would she be insulted if I offered to simply order food instead?

You're ruminating again.

I didn't care. I realized I *had* to bring them a dessert. *At least* a dessert.

I fumbled for my keys, trying to get in the car. There had to be a supermarket in the area. It may have been rural Pennsylvania, but it wasn't the middle of nowhere, was it?

Ali would know what to do. She could think of what I could get for Neil. I just had to get in the car nice and quietly...

"Arthur!" a man's voice called out behind me.

Spoke too soon.

ELEVEN

 ID YOU FIND the place okay?" Neil asked as I sat with him on opposite ends of his couch. Even though he was now an adult, Neil looked a lot like how he did when I last saw him at the orphanage. He had black, choppy hair with several faint birthmarks under his right eye. His face was still round, but had matured; he was a large man at about six-foot-two. He wore a woven red sweater-vest. I realized that I was probably underdressed in my t-shirt, but it was a warm day in southwestern Pennsylvania, so I hadn't thought much of it.

"I did. Yeah," I said quickly. "Thank you so much. I'm so sorry this is last minute."

"Not at all," he said. "When you first reached out to me, I almost thought it was a hoax. I thought that there was *no way* the famous Arthur Hesper, the tech titan at Abraham, would remember me or think to DM me out of the blue."

"Well, I wouldn't call myself a *titan*," I said. I was trying to think of the right words to say. "But it was me, really. Recently, I've just had some time to... *reflect* on things. I remembered how close we were all those years ago, and I wanted to reach out... to you... that day."

He nodded at me. *Why was it so hard to talk to him?* There was so much to talk about; I hadn't seen Neil in over a decade. But everything I said seemed awkward to me.

How the hell do two friends have a conversation?

I was about to ask Neil to "tell me about yourself" (*that's what people ask each other, right?*), but his attention was suddenly taken by a faint *slam* that came from the doorway across the room. The noise seemed to come from past the kitchen, almost outside the house. Neil started to shift forward out of the couch.

"That was probably just the ice machine," Neil said. Slowly, he stood up. "But I should probably..."

"No worries," I said, also getting up off the couch. "I'll come with you. I appreciate you having me over."

"Well, I appreciate you coming."

As we walked through Neil's house, I looked around. Although it was just a single story, his family's home seemed much bigger on the inside than on the outside, kind of like Sarah's cabin. Their living room and kitchen were cluttered; wooden furniture hugged every inch of wall-space, and children's toys lay swept to the sides of the floors to clear a makeshift path through the rooms. The kitchen counters were clean, but the cabinets were overfilled with a combination of food and household cleaning items that wouldn't fit under the sink. The lower cabinets were covered in scratch marks, likely left by a dog which was out of sight. As far as I could tell, Neil's home was exactly what a house with a growing family should look like.

"You know, you mentioned that your place was a bit of a mess," I said. "But compared to my apartment, the house is spotless."

"Oh, this isn't the *cluttered* part of our house," Neil said. He nodded his head towards a doorway at the far end of the kitchen. "That would be the garage."

When Neil first opened the door connecting his kitchen to his garage, I thought he was showing me an empty walk-in closet. But what I'd mistaken for a back wall was actually a mountain of cardboard boxes stacked close to the door. As I followed Neil through a clearing in the boxes, I found myself inside the garage—a garage that was filled to the brim with cardboard boxes and metal shelves. The garage was easily as big as the rest of the house; given that Neil lived on a ranch, it was probably designed for storing ride-on mowers or trucks. Or, in Neil's case, about a hundred 24×24×16" boxes filled with... something.

In the middle of the cluttered room was a blonde-haired woman, about my height, wearing a red sweater similar to Neil's. She was sitting on the ground, using both her hands to shovel aluminum cans back into an overturned box, which had seemingly fallen from the tower of boxes next to her. Neil rushed over to her and helped her fill the box.

"Ann," Neil said to his wife, "I thought I heard something... I said *I'd* take care of unloading the boxes!"

"You have company," Ann replied before glancing over at me. She gave me a tired but friendly smile. "Hello!"

As I waved, Neil shook his head at her. "These boxes are too heavy. Your back's bad enough as it as."

"And yours is just fine, then?"

"Can I help?" I asked. They both stared up at me, and looked at each other hesitantly.

"I'm sorry, Arthur," Neil said. "I forgot to tell you over text, but as you can see, our garage is filled with boxes of food for my radio station's biannual donation drive. The station needs *somewhere* to store the food they collect, and..."

"And Neil just *loves* to volunteer our garage. Every... single... time," Ann said, putting her arm around her husband.

"Somebody has to," Neil said. "The food won't store itself. We received a *very* copious amount of donations this past Easter."

Easter. As I remembered how pathetic my attempt last month at observing it had been, I thought about bringing up religion with Neil. But I closed my eyes and quickly shook the thought away. *Now wasn't the time.*

"Let me help you organize them," I said to Neil. "We can catch up while we're opening the boxes."

"Are you sure?" Ann asked. I nodded.

"As long as you don't mind," Neil said. "I appreciate it."

Good, something to do. As I walked towards the nearest stack of boxes, I somehow felt relieved, as if doing this work *while* talking was preferable to straight-up conversation.

I began to tug at the top of one of the boxes, using my fingers to try to peel away at the tape keeping it shut. As the tape didn't budge, I shoved my hand into the flap of cardboard on the top of the box and yanked it upward. Instead of the top flying off, however, the entire box fell right off the pile and hit the ground. A second later, an entire collection of assorted vegetable cans was rolling across the floor.

I looked over at Neil, who was holding a pair of scissors in his left hand. "You don't do much physical work, do you?"

"I do not."

As Neil took care of actually opening the boxes, I took out their various cans and sorted them onto the shelves. There was a lot of food; I doubted that Neil had enough metal shelves in his garage to store it all. I was careful to try to group like foods together, cognizant of the fact that I had very little experience organizing even my own pantry. I almost always ordered food in or ate out with Sarah; I was *far* from a seasoned cook. Within the sea of nonperishable items were more cans of corn, beans, soup, potatoes, chicken, and vegetables than I had ever seen. Apparently, *canned hot dogs* exist, and are a popular donation item around here. I was tempted to ask Neil if the bun was included inside the can, but thought better of it.

"So," I asked instead, "How did you two meet?"

"We met in college," Neil said. "Sophomore year. I was—well, you saw on my bio that I studied theology—and Ann was majoring in communications."

"Let me guess: radio?" I asked, scooping up a dozen cans of baked beans into my arms.

"Actually, I was planning on going into marketing," Ann, who was leaning on the freezer near the back of the room, said. "But I took a part-time job as an organizer at our college's radio station during my senior year, and fell in love with that kind of work."

"Before that, though," Neil said, "I was at a Purim celebration at our school when Ann came to write an article about it for the school paper. We had a sizable Jewish group on campus, so the party was pretty large. Ann just wanted to get the information she needed and leave..."

"I did *not*," she complained. "You always tell the story wrong."

"Do you want to tell the story?" Neil asked her. She rolled her eyes.

"So, I wound up showing her around the party, and told her about some of the other events we had. She said she'd try to come to our Passover after-party a few weeks later, but probably couldn't since it conflicted with an Easter party her Catholic group was hosting that evening," Neil said. "Well, after my Passover seder let out, I skipped my group's party and walked on over to the Easter event instead. When I got there, I found Ann and asked her to show me around. I couldn't eat any of the food since it all had bread in it, but it was still a great time."

The two looked at each other and smiled. Neil continued. "Well, we started hanging out outside of our religious events, and soon we were dating. After college, we both knew what we wanted, and we got married.

We decided we wanted to live somewhere quiet, so we both found jobs at *108.1 WKDD*—our local station—and moved here. Ann does some behind-the-scenes work part time, and I spend weekdays as Pennsylvania's 'classic-rock music-jock.'"

"I like the job description," I laughed.

"It does the job," Neil said. "And on Sunday evenings I do my patented religion talks."

"The kids always listen to him from the radio app," Ann said. "They don't understand a lot of it, but it's still the cutest thing."

"Did you always know you wanted kids?" I asked them. Neil looked around the room for a second.

"Where *are* the kids?" he asked Ann.

Ann calmly pressed a button on the wall next to the fridge. Suddenly, the door to the garage opened, and the dusty grey interior was filled with sunlight. I hadn't realized how dark the garage had been before then.

Running back and forth across the long stretch of driveway were two kids—a boy, maybe five years old, and a girl, maybe three. They were chasing each other around the Hirschmans' vast front yard. Or, more accurately, they were both *being chased* by a large golden retriever, which ran in circles as the children did their best to run around her. The dog could've easily caught them if she wanted to, but was clearly trained well enough to chase them from a distance.

"Are they going to be okay out there?" I asked. I didn't want to question their parenting, given that I was *not* an authority on the matter, but was still concerned about the kids. Neil nodded.

"Absolutely. Mark's the most responsible little boy in the whole world, and Rachel has enough sense by now not to try to bite Amber, our retriever. Right, Ann?" Neil asked.

She nodded and looked over at her kids. "Don't worry, I have my eye on them." From a small table next to the fridge, Ann lifted an electronic tablet. She turned her tablet towards me; onscreen was a live recording of the kids running around the front yard. Ann winked. "It lets them think they're having fun *without* the parents standing over them. Plus, it's better they get the energy out of their systems *now* rather than at bedtime."

"In answer to your question," Neil said. "We didn't *plan* on anything. But we're deeply blessed with what we have, and with what we can look forward to." He glanced over at Ann, who looked down at her sweater and patted it.

"Congratulations," I said, hoping to God that Neil was implying she was pregnant.

"Thank you," Ann said.

"Which is *why* you shouldn't have been out here doing work, Ann," Neil said.

"I opened *one* box, and it was light," Ann said. Neil rolled his eyes.

"Your... parents must be very proud," I said to him. He smiled.

"Oh, they're proud of their grandkids and daughter-in-law, although I think when they adopted a Jewish kid, they secretly hoped I'd become a lawyer or doctor," he said while cutting open another cardboard box. Ann shook her head at him, but he laughed anyway. "I'm kidding. They are. I'm so happy we met, and that they took me in even as old as I was. They gave me so much, and set me up for success. I know that they're happy that I'm happy."

He looked over at me. His smile faded as he got down on the floor with me and started unloading a box at the far end of the room. "Arthur, I'm... so sorry. I know you never—"

"It's alright." I looked away from him, and into the rows of canned food in front of me. "There were a lot of prospective parents, but none of them were the right fit."

"Still, I'm sorry," Neil said. "I know how hard it must be."

For a long time, I thought *I'd* scared away most of the couples looking to adopt me. But the Simulation Showcase had reminded me that some of those couples weren't *worth* being adopted by. It also taught me that things had a way of happening for a reason.

"Don't worry about it," I said, turning back toward him. "Things worked out for me. I didn't get adopted, but that's just part of who I am now."

"Well, that orphanage sticks with you," he said. "It's amazing that the place is still operating, given that most of the orphanages in this country were replaced by the foster system long ago. But if you ever have the chance to make it back to Holy Virgin, you should. It really gives you a perspective on how far you've come, and how far you can still go."

I nodded. I wasn't sure *what* I could say in response that could sufficiently explain things. By now, Neil probably knew the general details about my life story if he read *Tech Today's* article.

Indeed, much of my time at the orphanage did stick with me—just as much of it had faded into the past. *As I wanted it to.*

I was grateful when Neil decided to change the subject.

"So, how are things at Abraham? What's it like working with *Sarah Stellos?*"

"Things are... going well," I said. I tugged at the collar of my t-shirt, but took a deep breath. Neil definitely saw the same news that the rest of the world saw; no need to dance around it. "Sarah... keeps me on my toes, but in all the best ways. She's incredibly driven and passionate, but she's also human like the rest of us."

He nodded. "I hear you guys hit a snag with your virtual platform... what did you name it again?"

"Eden," I said. That word felt strange to say in front of someone like Neil. He hadn't brought up religion—not in any preaching sort of way—and he wasn't *that* much older than I was. And yet, whenever he spoke, I felt a conviction and *certainty* behind his words, even when he asked questions. He seemed like he had the whole world figured out, even before he was thirty. So, when I mentioned the word "Eden" in front of Neil, I could immediately feel its religious undertone bubbling to the surface. But Neil didn't seem fazed by nor critical of the name—or, at the very least, wasn't showing it.

"Right. That's an interesting name. I can only imagine what it's capable of."

"It's really something else. So much dedication has gone into it," I said. "And we did hit a snag, but I think Ali and I figured out a solution."

"Ali?" Neil asked.

"She's their AI girl," Ann said. The harsh way she said *AI girl* didn't sit well with me, but I decided to let it go. *Not everybody knows Ali like I do.*

"That's right," Neil said. He leaned forward a little with a curious expression on his face. "I'm really surprised that's gotten as far as it has without the government stepping in."

"What do you mean?" I asked. *What did he mean?*

"Well, I'm sure you've seen how Congress has been with all their new tech regulations," Neil said, tossing a cardboard box out the garage door. Their dog stopped chasing the kids for a moment, sniffed the box, and immediately went back to her play. "There's a new AI oversight bill every month, and supposedly they're drafting a bipartisan VR limitation document. First time in decades the two parties have actually agreed on anything, really."

"Sorry, I haven't followed politics that much," I said. I'm sure it was Neil's *job* to be in the loop with those sorts of things for his shows. But as I've mentioned, I'm always too busy with my work to pay attention to the news. The only articles I bothered reading were the ones that Sarah sent me about Abraham.

That is, the ones she wanted me to see.

"You might want to take a look at some of that," Neil said with a smile. I had a funny feeling that, considering I'd been out of the political loop for over a year, he might have been right. "Sarah's been causing quite a stir in Washington. She refuses to attend any of the oversight meetings regarding your Solar Brain. According to the President, 'she's taken the Sun all for herself.' His words, not mine."

"Sarah always told me she hated politics," I said. "She never gets involved in them, as far as I can tell."

"She might hate playing politics, but she's very good at it," Ann chimed in. "Later on, you might want to ask her about the VWO proposal. I'd pay good money to hear *her* opinion on it."

I decided to add that third thing to my "drive home" list. Let's see... we now had:

    dive into the moral consciousness of my AI assistant,
    think about visiting my childhood orphanage, and
    research the sociopolitical surroundings of Eden.

Just some carefree driving fun.

"But you didn't drive all the way here to talk politics, of course!" Neil said, looking up at me with a smile. "Apparently, though, you drove here to help me stock food."

"I think it's great what you and Ann are doing," I said, once again glad Neil had changed the subject. "I'm happy to help out. Which organization is the food going to?"

"Our church," Neil said. "In town, about twenty miles from here. They always need more food for the pantry they run."

"Not enough people donate anymore, especially with everyone's money going to entertainment," Ann said. "As much as I get on Neil for making our garage the food warehouse, I'm happy to do it. I think it's everyone's job, and every *company's* job, to give back more than they take."

Ann was staring around the room, over at her kids, at the cans—and at pretty much everything except for me.

Neil cleared his throat.

"Well, all this talk about food is making me hungry," he said. "Ann, what are we having for dinner tonight?"

"I thought you were barbecuing," she said.

"There's no gas in the grill. I thought you were cooking..."

Later that evening, we all sat at the table eating the pizza that I had enthusiastically offered to order for them. The kids, Mark and Rachel, barely said a word as they sat at the far end of the table, munching on their slices of pizza silently. I waved over at them as a friendly gesture, but that seemed to only make them shrink into their seats even more. I'd never really interacted with children before, but at the same time never encountered a point when I consciously considered myself an "adult." When I was young and saw prospective parents of various ages come and go, I always wondered about the point at which someone *knows* that they're an adult and are ready to take on the role of a parent. Clearly, Neil had reached that point. I wondered if I ever would.

"Arthur, have you made a lot of friends in the tech world?" Neil asked in between bites of margherita pizza (*The Finest Slices this Side of the Delaware River,* as the man over the phone proclaimed).

"I haven't even made any friends at *work,*" I said. "Outside of Sarah and Ali, I can't seem to be able to *talk* to anyone. Sarah is different from everyone else; we connect like no one else does. And Ali was designed to carry on a conversation, though I'm pretty sure I've managed to start annoying her, too."

Neil and Ann laughed at that. I laughed along too, wishing I was joking.

"Well, I certainly hope you try to make some friends," Neil said.

"You're better at carrying on a conversation than you give yourself credit for. Sometimes, you need to just talk to people and get out of your own head."

Yeah. That'll happen.

My smartphone chimed with a bubbly text tone. I took it out to silence it. On the screen there read a notification:

Message from Ali. Tap to View.

Ali tended to ping me whenever there was a status update regarding Eden. But for now, I was sure it could wait. I put my phone away.

"Remember when we snuck out of the orphanage one night just to walk around the city?" I asked Neil.

"I remember an annoying little eight-year-old following me out of bed wanting to join me on my power walk, only for me to have to carry him back inside ten minutes later when an alley cat scared him," he said with a grin. "You could never make up your mind about anything."

"I remember making up my mind to steal that chalk from Mother Tina's desk," I said. My mind was racing through some of the daring fun I would have as a kid. "Everyone loved stealing her chalk when she wasn't looking, but they always got caught. I didn't, and I used it to teach myself algebra on the sidewalk pavement."

"You're aware that Tina *let you* take the chalk with you, right?" he said. He looked over at his kids, and back at me. "She saw you walking away from her chalkboard, but figured you were too young to draw any—*ahem*—reproductive body parts with it and too mature to write any curse words. She was happy you were learning to teach yourself."

"You're kidding," I said. "I thought I was the first person to ever get away with taking Tina's chalk."

"*No one* got away with that," Neil said. "That woman knows everything."

I was mildly disappointed that my nine-year-old self wasn't as cunning as I thought he was, but more so happy that Neil remembered all these things.

"How did you know that?" I asked him.

"Because she told me when you pranced out of the classroom," he said. We laughed. "Even though Tina wanted you to connect with the other kids closer to your age, she was just glad you were learning. She always wanted what was best for you. If you ever do visit Holy Virgin, I'm sure she'd be overjoyed to see you."

List item number four: visit Tina.

Neil turned toward Mark. "Mark, you made a friend the other day at school, right? Want to tell Arthur about her?"

Neil gave me a wink, and I looked over at his son. He kept his gaze down at his plate, but in a monotone voice mumbled something about wanting to play kickball with his friends and meeting a girl named Ide who let him join her team.

"And you went right up to Ide and asked if you could join her team, right?"

"Yes."

"And you were direct, and genuine, and kind, right? No second-guessing yourself?"

"Yes. I mean no. Yes-no."

Neil glanced at me, and I rolled my eyes at him. I looked over at Mark, and then at Neil and Ann.

"You know, I'm surprised they still have kids playing kickball. It seems like everyone's on their video games or virtual reality now. I assumed that's what kids are doing these days," I said. Saying the words "these days" made me feel about forty years older than I am.

"Oh, we're not at that stage quite yet," Ann said. "But Neil and I are trying to limit the kids' screen time. Keep them outdoors, playing and *imagining* while there's still room left to do those things."

"Good move," I said, starting to wish I'd grown up with parents like them. "I suppose Abraham hasn't touched every corner of the world *quite* yet."

"Well, we won't have those machines in our home," Ann said with a nod at Neil. Neil looked over at me for a moment, and then back at Ann. I opened my mouth to ask Ann what she meant, but for the third time this afternoon Neil changed the subject.

"So, Arthur, did you… keep up with religion in some capacity?" Neil asked, sweeping some crust crumbs off the tablecloth with a napkin. "Sorry if that's a blunt question. I know that religion isn't one of those things you're supposed to discuss with company, but talking about religion *is* something I'm paid to do."

"Yeah. A little," I said, trying for some reason to sound nonchalant.

"Not as much as I should be. I've thought about it, from time to time, but haven't put enough devotion into praying. Every time I try, I get distracted by something else."

He nodded. "You're not the only one. Have you ever listened to my show?"

"I..."

"No, sorry, that's right—it's a northern station. Well, pretty much half of the people calling into my show have the same problem—not knowing how to make the time and becoming too distracted to pray. Religion—whatever you believe in—isn't something that's meant to be a burden, but something that's meant to give meaning." He held hands with Ann, who smiled at him. "It's all about finding that meaning with the people you love."

"How does your show work?" I asked. I didn't mean the question to be rude, but I'd finally started *thinking* about Neil hosting a religious radio show. Weren't those usually hosted by evangelical preachers—who *weren't* Jewish? "You're still Jewish, right? I can't imagine your show attracting a very wide Christian audience."

"My show isn't about one religion," Neil said. "Every week, I tell people about how to pray in their own religion. I think the ideas of *how* we pray can be applied to many spiritual upbringings. I talk about appreciating God in our lives as something that can uplift us—that's universal enough to attract a lot of people."

I nodded. I wondered if there was a way to access Neil's show from back home. Sarah had access to lots of satellite connections, so I was sure there was some way.

Another ping on my phone—*hadn't I silenced that?* Apparently, I'd forgotten. I took it out; there were three more notifications, all *Messages from Ali.* I thought about introducing Neil's family to her, but I decided against it. *Maybe another time.* I silenced my phone and shoved it into my pocket.

"So, are the kids being raised Jewish or Catholic?" As soon as I asked the question, I realized I knew the answer. "Sorry... you do both, right?"

"Yes," Neil said.

"How does that work?" I asked, hoping that question didn't *also* come off as rude.

"With balance," Ann said. "As the kids grow up, we'll teach them both religions, and celebrate both traditions. For example, we took them to Church on Easter *and* had a family seder for Passover."

Passover. I realized that it had come and gone in April, and I'd completely forgotten to wish Sarah a good holiday. Then again, it wasn't as though Sarah really celebrates the holidays. *But wait, didn't she go to synagogue when she was—*

Ann kept talking before I could finish the thought. "The kids may not have a Sunday school to teach them everything about one faith, but then again, we already spend our Sunday nights listening to this one." She nodded at Neil.

"I'm starting to show them how to read Hebrew, while Ann teaches them about the Lord's Prayer. When they're old enough, they'll be able to fast during Lent and on Yom Kippur," Neil said. "And, of course, they get presents for Christmas *and* Hanukkah."

"I was just going to ask about that," I said. "*Now* I'm jealous."

They laughed.

"We've heard that a lot," Ann said. "Ultimately, we want Mark and Rachel to observe religion in the way they feel most comfortable."

At that point, the kids had gotten up from their chairs and were running around the house. Their dog looked up from her bed with a weary expression before going back to sleep. Ann got up from her seat, excused herself, and walked after the kids (lest they vomit after eating all that pizza). That left just Neil and me.

Neil turned towards the kitchen window. The evening sunlight cast a bright glow on the blinds. He looked down at his watch, and then up at me.

"Want to take a trip?"

I watched the countryside roll by the passenger window of Neil's pickup truck as we drove to the community church. Two package delivery drones flew across a field of grass, large cardboard boxes in tow, and they soared past the car toward a faraway row of houses. We'd been driving for about twenty minutes so far, but the town in the distance never seemed to get any closer. I pulled the car visor down to block out the setting Sun.

"Are we there yet?" I asked.

"You sound like the kids," Neil said. "But yeah. Almost."

"I'm not used to living in the country," I replied. I looked at the floor of the truck, which was covered in dirt and grass stains. "Or... driving in a pickup truck."

"Sorry about the mess. The truck's not mine. It belongs to a friend," Neil said. "I was going to bring in more of these cans later this month, but I figured we have some time now."

"Happy to help," I said. It seemed somewhat strange that we had just finished *unloading* boxes at Neil's house only to have to re-pack and bring some of them to the church. *At least they're organized now,* Neil justified. I didn't mind taking the trip through his town, though. The late-spring countryside, which Neil had probably driven by so many times, felt breathtaking and amazing to me.

I felt my phone vibrate again, but I ignored it. I squinted as I glanced under the visor out at the winding road ahead of us. "I didn't get to pay much attention to all of this while I was driving here. This is all so beautiful."

"Sure is. Part of why we moved here."

"This landscape, though," I said, blocking out the Sun with one hand and pointing with the other. "It would look so amazing in Eden, too."

Neil coughed. "I'll bet."

We sat in silence for another few minutes. The whole time, I kept trying to think about things to bring up, but didn't really care for any of the conversation starters. *How has work been?* He was technically *doing* something for his job right now. *How has life been?* We kind of just discussed that. *How 'bout them Yankees?* I didn't even watch baseball.

Really, though, I *knew* what I wanted to talk about—even if I wasn't sure I was ready for it. I decided I should try to segue into it nice and slow.

"So—"

"How are you on the religion front, Arthur?" Neil cut in. "How are you *really?*"

Well then. There was no dodging it now. I could listen to Neil talk about his show or his family all day, but I had been dreading actually *opening up* about my faith. But I knew our conversation would go there. Half of our childhood conversations came back to religion, and all I usually had for him were questions. Somehow, Neil always seemed to have the answers.

"Honestly, I don't even know what my religion *is*," I said. *Am I about to do this?* I closed my eyes for a minute. I still didn't think I was ready to talk this deeply about religion, but I knew I shouldn't—*I couldn't*—avoid it any longer.

"I have no idea what my birth parents believed. As you know, I grew up in a Catholic home and was Baptized there, so I believe in Jesus and made communion and know my prayers," I said. "But after I left the orphanage, I never went to Church or the college spiritual center or any of that. I essentially drifted through life without *practicing* my religion. I kept up with studying the Bible purely in an academic sense. I read that book cover to cover many times, studying the history, names, places."

"Well, you probably know it better than I do," Neil said. He turned the wheel, and I noticed that we were much closer to town now than we had been. Above the row of single-story buildings, I could see a narrow green spire with a white cross on top.

"No, I definitely don't," I said, quickening my voice. "Someone who *knows* their faith wouldn't go to Church on Easter only to leave halfway through mass because they didn't *belong* there. I'd spent so many years being *sick* of myself that I almost grew allergic to my own upbringing."

"Well, *I* think you're a great person. You shouldn't be sick of yourself," he said.

Easier said than done.

"Thanks," I said, trying to take his words to heart. "But, Neil, I believe in a higher power—I *believe* in God because of what I do. I've worked on artificial neural networks for over half a decade; I know how the human brain works because I know how to build one from scratch. But the one thing that I can never personally account for is where someone's *soul* comes from. I have to *tell* artificial intelligence what is right and wrong, and what its purpose is, before it can make sense of the world around it. That's what Sarah and I did with Ali. *Her* interests, though unique, are ultimately formed based on the mental tools I gave her. But who did that with *us?*"

Neil took a couple of turns through the empty intersections. The town was quiet, save for a couple of people walking their dogs down the sidewalk or the few patrons entering the pharmacy, deli, and other storefronts. Neil slowed down as we reached the end of the street, with the church right in front of us.

I took a deep breath. "*God* gave us our souls. We've explained so much with science—Big Bang, planet formation, evolution—but not our souls. I haven't seen a single paper or article that can explain that one, except the Bible. And that's the only explanation that really makes sense to me."

As Neil put the car in park, he nodded. "Our souls serve as strong evidence of God's existence. Not enough people understand what a soul is, but that's a big part of the problem, right? A soul isn't something you understand, but—"

"Something you feel," I finished for him. As he smiled, I continued. "I believe that God has a place for me, and I know that deepening my connection to my religion is important. But whenever I think about it, I get distracted. I've never talked to my peers about it because nobody in science really makes room for faith. Even talking to you about it feels weird, *unnatural.* But it shouldn't be. I want something meaningful to be close to. I just don't know how to get close to it."

My phone vibrated again.

Neil didn't say anything, but just studied my face. I felt vulnerable, exposed—as exposed as I had during my first interview with Sarah.

"Now, I'm not a therapist," Neil said. "I'm not going to pry into anything you don't want me to or prescribe a major lifestyle change. And I'm not a pastor, either. The only authority I have on religion, Arthur, is just my friendly advice. It sounds like you have all the pieces you need. You know what you believe, and you have the will to believe it. But you have to get out of your own way; don't overcomplicate prayer. It's just a matter of setting aside time to think about religion. Talk to God and listen when He talks to you. Make prayer *matter.* Also..."

Neil nodded towards the building in front of us. "Something I learned from working at the church food pantry; be grateful. Be grateful for what you have. For *who* you have. There is so much darkness around us in the world; so many people who come here have lost their jobs, their homes, or even their loved ones."

"I understand," I said to Neil.

"No, you might not," Neil said. "I mean—well, let's take care of these boxes first, and then I'll show you."

We stepped out of the car and unlocked the back door to the church. It opened right up to a steep flight of stairs, which I would've easily fallen down if Neil hadn't caught me by the arm. *And this would have been a much shorter story.*

We each carried a box down the stairs and into the church's basement, which enveloped me with its stale, cool air. The large, dark, rectangular room was filled with stacks of chairs and collapsible tables. Wooden support pillars lined the walls, and there was a small stage set up near the opposite end of the room with some old box-like speakers that looked like they were from early this century. Closer to us were several doors that led into some backrooms; Neil opened the closest one with his key and we stepped inside. It was a small kitchen closet, and several other boxes of non-perishable food were stacked off to the side. We set the boxes down by the door and went back up to the pickup truck for more.

"So, how did a Jewish person end up with the keys to the church?" I jokingly asked Neil as we brought down the third set of boxes. He laughed.

"Our synagogue is like an hour from us, so it's easier for me to get involved *here* than there," he said.

"That's far. I'm hoping that with Eden we can make virtual spaces for worship. This way, people won't have to travel too far to attend service," I said. "I'll definitely ask Ali to add Reform Jewish synagogue services to that."

Secretly, I also hoped that that kind of thing would help me ease back into Church. *Maybe I should've just used* that *during Easter.*

"Oh, that's... an *interesting* idea," Neil grunted while navigating down the stairs.

"Anyway, what made you want to get involved with the food pantry in the first place?" I asked. "You seem so busy as it is."

"Well, what made you want to work with Abraham?" he replied. I was *not* expecting to be asked that question. *A lot of things,* I thought. *The benefits, the exciting work, the opportunities, the people. The CEO, in particular.*

"I'm not sure. It just... felt right," I said.

"Exactly."

Eventually, we brought the last of the boxes down. My arms were killing me by the second box, but I powered through the other five (while Neil brought down *thirteen*). Eventually, we both sat down in the basement on two folding chairs. As I stretched out my sore arms (and ignored another buzz from my phone), Neil turned towards me.

"I'll show you what I really love about this place."

He pulled out his phone and started tapping and swiping through videos. "Earlier, we were talking about gratitude, and I wanted to show you something."

He turned his phone towards me. It was a video from *last* April; at that time, I had been roaming around Abraham's headquarters, still catching up with the breakneck speed the company moved at.

Neil's video was of the church basement, filmed from what seemed like the same place we were sitting. Instead of an empty room, there were about a dozen foldable tables set up. A handful of people sat at each one. The camera panned away from them and towards several more tables at the front of the room, where the kitchen was. The camera then followed an older man; as he took a tray of food from the table near the front, he walked away and sat down near a group of people at the back of the room. The video zoomed in on them; there were about a dozen people at that table, including men, women, and children. Many of the people seemed to be from different families, but each one of them had their eyes closed and were mouthing something to themselves. I couldn't make out their exact words, but I knew what they were doing.

"They're praying," I said.

"Most of these people have nothing," Neil said. "The warm food that they go home with has to last them awhile. They've lost so much, but they pray. They visit this place often, even when there isn't any food for us to give, because they want to. I asked the old man from the video why he does so, and he told me that his faith lets him know that the next day will be brighter than the last. He told me that religion gives him something to work on, something to make sense of. He actually said to me, and I quote: 'faith is my light.' I swear, I thought you only heard those phrases in church songs or on religious posters, but he said it genuinely."

"Wow," I said. I didn't know what *else* to say, or what else to feel. *Except awe.*

"My point is, Arthur: don't be afraid of letting faith be the light, even when things seem like they're at their worst. The test of faith is when things are all wrong and you're *still* believing."

I nodded at him. "Okay. I understand."

For the first time, I truly felt like I did. I knew I wasn't in the same situation as people who'd lost everything. Things weren't all wrong in my life, but not everything was *right* either. I'd grown up with barely any foundation beneath me, stacking work and school atop... very little. I always thought that religion could ground me in *something* apart from my work life, but never took the time to open myself up to it. But if people who had less stability in their lives than I did could find spiritual peace, then perhaps I could, too. I just needed to not overcomplicate it, just like I do with so many of my thoughts. *Just like I was doing now.*

Maybe Neil was right; maybe I *was* in my own way.

It was dark outside by the time we were back in the pickup truck. *It was already past 9pm?* Then again, I hadn't arrived at Neil's house until the late afternoon, anyway.

As we drove home, we wrapped up our discussion about religion, and by the end of our conversation, I felt better about faith than I ever had.

"Thanks, Neil," I said. "It's nice to actually be able to talk to someone about this."

"Of course. And remember, if you do find other opportunities to talk to someone about religion, make it a natural part of the conversation because you want it to be natural to you. Religion is meaningful when it's personal, Arthur," he said. He smiled. "Here's an interesting idea. Why don't you try talking to Sar—"

Suddenly, my phone made *another* loud buzz. I checked the screen. It was another message from Ali. *What was she texting about?* Part of me wanted to unlock my phone and check, but I didn't want to be rude to Neil. Ali knew that I was spending time with him, so whatever progress update she had could probably wait a little longer.

As we turned the corner to head back towards Neil's house, I was surprised to see a bright haze of light coming from that direction. Clouds were starting to roll in, and even though the Sun had set below the horizon, they were illuminated by a silvery glow. I lowered my head to try to catch a glimpse of the sky above us, but couldn't see any sign of the moon being out.

"What's that bright light? Is there a mall near here?"

"No," Neil said. He took a breath and glanced over at me. "That would be *Abraham*."

"Wait, really?" I squinted at the source of the light in the distance, but couldn't make out much detail. "That's one of the Branches of the Eden Tree?"

"You're the builder," Neil said. "Shouldn't you know?"

"It must be some of the pre-installation work we're doing at some of the sites," I said. "I didn't think the construction lights would look so... bright."

"That's what happens in locations that are far away from cities," Neil said. "We haven't had dark skies in almost two weeks thanks to that. Any chance of stargazing's been pretty much shot, and sometimes the light bounces in through our bedroom windows, making it hard to sleep."

"I can't believe that," I said. "It's because most of the actual *construction* is done with third-party contractors who are supervised by Abraham staff. I'll make sure I ask Sarah to have them shut their lights off, because that's ridiculous."

"Just like that, huh?" Neil said.

The way he said that, I could tell Neil was angry about the construction lights. I didn't blame him—that tower couldn't be more than ten miles from here. The Branch construction is supposed to be eco-friendly and consumer friendly. But too many of the people working with Abraham—or *claiming* to work with us—are willing to sacrifice those things just to make a few extra bucks.

"Don't worry, we'll get this fixed for you," I said. "Nothing should get in the way of—"

As I was about to say *your enjoyment of Eden,* I stopped myself. Part of me felt that finishing the sentence would make me seem like an overbearing salesman, but I also remembered something from earlier. Something that confused me.

"What did Ann mean, 'we don't want those machines in our house?'" I asked. I had brought up the topic of Eden before with Neil, but he hadn't commented on it. "You guys... don't want an Eden headset? Of course, I would get them to you for free. I know the price tag is a little high."

"It isn't the price," Neil said. I just sat there, watching him. "And your price is actually lower than your VR competitors', strangely enough."

"Okay?" I said hesitantly. "If it's a safety thing, they're fully compatible with all age groups. Eden is also totally safe for anyone with neurological conditions, just in case that is of any concern. We're even beta testing it on cats and dogs, so you can even bring Amber—"

"It's nothing like that," Neil said. "I'm sure it's safe. We've been following the news about Abraham ever since they announced you joined it. I recognized your name *and* your face, and I never had a doubt in my mind that you would do great things."

Where is he going with this?

"However," he continued, not taking his eyes off the road. "What Sarah Stellos is building—what *you're* building—is an escape. A bright, expensive, *loud* escape. I get the love for video games and virtual experiences, believe me. I know how much fun those things are. But Ann and I... we live in *this* world. We have too much to do *here* to devote time to that kind of thing."

I was a little taken aback by what he said. I couldn't imagine *anyone* refusing a free, fully immersive, mind-teleporting, *safe* VR headset. And, evidently, there was a Tree Branch set to go up only a few miles from where Neil's house was. He'd have a perfect connection, regardless of how often he used it.

"You don't have to *live* inside Eden, you know," I said. "Of course, it's an escape from reality, but it's also an option to have fun with your family in new worlds."

"But once you've seen all those worlds—once you've gotten a *taste*—how can you resist spending *all* of your time in them?" Neil asked.

"I can resist it." It was true. Since my abridged *Simulation Showcase*, I've only spent a little bit of time *inside* Eden—it was most of the other techs who spent as much of their workday as they could connected to the Solar Brain. But since Eden didn't yet support long-term connections, it was hard to really get lost inside the virtual world outside of the occasional excursion. And I usually did my work from my own apartment, which was fine. I preferred to work in the real world anyway.

Oh.

"So, you see," Neil said. "You understand the value of *this* world as opposed to your simulated one. You are stronger than most, and I fear that my kids—growing up in a world that beckons them to distraction—won't be able to resist its call. So, Ann and I decided to set an example for our family by not purchasing Eden. Life is precious because it's *here* and because it's brief. Every moment that we have on Earth matters, and I believe that we should live in appreciation of what *is* instead of what *isn't*. Your company—your *boss*—is trying to sell people on a fantasy. A fantasy that they don't need."

I leaned back into my car seat. I thought I had a lot in common with Neil, but deep down, I suddenly realized how much he *opposed* what I did for a living. What I'd *committed to*—what I was willing to devote my life to creating.

Neil and Ann's skepticism for VR and their distaste for Ali now made sense. *Figures.* They only viewed Eden through the lens that our critics used; they saw it as something meant to distract people, not something meant to elevate them. It pained me to realize that among Abraham's detractors were some of my only friends. Neil and Ann followed the news on Sarah Stellos not because they were interested in her, but because they wanted to see what irresponsible thing she'd do next.

"Neil," I said, slowing my voice. "This is my life's work…"

"No, it isn't," Neil said. "This is one year of your life's work. You've devoted yourself so fully to your boss's mission that you haven't seen it objectively. Ask yourself, Arthur: what *are* you doing at your company? Don't take this the wrong way, but it looks to me like Abraham is just trying to replace people's real lives with fake ones. To what end, though?"

He shook his head. "I might be defaulting to my preaching voice, but there's a quote by Dr. Richard Matthews—I'm pretty sure you know who he is."

Sarah's uncle. At this point, who *didn't* know the name of the man who posthumously funded The Abraham Project?

"Yeah."

"Well, his words will help me put this a bit more elegantly. I don't normally memorize obscure quotes by billionaires, but last week I actually had someone repeat this line to me on air during our call-in segment," he continued. "I looked it up afterward and read it a couple of—"

"What's the quote, Neil?" I interrupted.

"Well," he said. *"In a world where the mind is systematically programmed by men, what room is there for our souls?"*

Neil took a breath. "He continued *that* by saying: *In a reality effortlessly manufactured by machines, what place would we ever reserve for God?*"

As I opened my mouth to respond, I found myself at a profound loss for words. *Dr. Matthews said that? He was religious?*

Once again, Neil jumped in, speaking even more quickly now. "Those two sentences hit hard for me, and I think they do for you, too. I'm not sure if he really was a religious guy, but I think he sums up my issues with VR perfectly."

He glanced over at me, but I didn't have anything to say back. He elaborated. "You and I just talked about how far away people have gotten from faith, so why do we need a device that will take us further? You were talking about holding religious services inside that virtual world, but does that *really* sit well with you? Is a simulated replacement for religion, for our *lives,* really in line with Richard Matthews' vision?"

As I felt my back grow damp from sweat, I could barely come up with a reply. "Eden isn't meant to do that. I... maybe missed the mark on the whole simulated synagogue thing—"

"It's not about *that,*" Neil said. "It's about preserving our world, our faith, our *reality.*"

"But Eden isn't supposed to step in for *reality.* It isn't meant to replace who we are."

"It doesn't matter what it's meant to do," Neil said. "I wonder: what else could the money Sarah Stellos is spending go to? You guys could donate so much more; you could *help* so many people. And, although I'm *no* rocket scientist, I saw a news take that made me wonder: rather than absorb the energy from your Solar Sphere back into some virtual world, why not harness it for other uses? Instead of just powering Abraham, why not use your solar arrays to supply the planet with clean energy? In every generation, we have billionaires spending their wealth to *escape* our world instead of trying to help it. Giving up instead of giving back."

Clearly, this wasn't the first time Neil had said those words. It was too *rehearsed,* too *perfect* an argument for him to have made up on the fly. He had to have practiced it, either over his radio show to his crowd of listeners or in private to his wife.

Had he been preparing to debate me?

But Neil *wasn't* a scientist. *He has no idea what he's talking about.*

"We *are* giving back," I said. I wasn't going to let Neil step all over what

I'd worked for—*who was he to think he knew my company better than me?* I was done letting people tell *me* about my life.

He started to speak. "What I mean is—"

I cut him off. "We're giving people a chance to experience a world where anything is possible. Where they can *create* and *play* and *live* in a virtual reality of their dreams. We're not *replacing* people's lives, just improving them. Not everyone got so lucky as to have a family, Neil. Some people need to find fulfillment in other ways."

Neil looked down and sighed. "I didn't think about that."

"Yeah, well, most people don't." *Not everyone can just pray their worries away,* I wanted to say to Neil. *That* would've shut him up. *You get one theology degree and suddenly you think you know everything?* I was ready to *fight*, just like I fought Dr. Chan years ago.

But as I prepared to speak, something inexplicable held me back. I opened my mouth—I wanted to *attack*—but the words wouldn't come out.

We sat in silence for a few seconds. I couldn't look over at Neil; I felt terrible about where the conversation had gone. Here was my long-lost friend—my only friend who *wasn't* related to Abraham—and I'd managed to find a way to argue with him after just a few hours.

I really did suck at talking to people.

I cleared my throat. "I'm sorry."

"No, Arthur," he said. "*I'm* sorry for saying all that. Every radio host has an urge to rant. I don't oppose what you love to do. God bless you for it. I know you're feeling defensive of what you've done—and you have a right to be! And I know you're helping people—helping *yourself*—in the way you think is best."

Neil turned down a side street and passed a line of trees. I hadn't realized how close we were getting to his house. The light from the Branch construction site was now to my right.

Neil continued. "But... just consider the fact that not everyone is as enthusiastic about your work as you are. We can't all move at your wavelength."

I looked away from him, and at the dark stretch of road ahead of us. Maybe I judged Neil wrong. I felt bad for all those things I thought about him. I let the shock that he wasn't interested in Eden get the better of me, and even though I never shouted at him, I was ready to. Maybe he was right; maybe I *did* assume everyone thought as I did, and I pushed them away when I realized they didn't.

"Alright," I said, smiling. "You sure you'd never want to see Eden?"

"Definitely not *never*," Neil said. "But I have to live *this* life first—at least for a while."

I nodded at him. "Well, thank you for being honest with me."

"Always, bunkmate."

As Neil pulled into his driveway, I took out my phone. *Seventy notifications from Ali.*

I unlocked my phone and tapped on the first notification. I barely noticed Neil put the car in park. As I thought about editing the frequency at which Ali could text me, I opened up the messages.

Urgent development with Eden. Please enter when you can. —Ali

Urgent development with Eden. Please enter when you can. —Ali

Hi, Dr. Hesper. I hope your dinner is going well. Please enter Eden when you can. —Ali

Hi, Dr. Hesper. Please consult your text messages, and please enter Eden when you can. —Ali

Hi, Dr. Hesper. Apologies for the rapidly repeating messages. Please enter Eden when you can. —Ali

Arthur. —Ali

Something weird just happened. Get in here, now. —Ali

Arthur. —Ali

Arthur. —Ali

Arthur, please. —Ali

(60 more)

"Hey, Arthur," Neil began. "Do you need a place to crash for the—"

I quickly turned towards him.

"How is the satellite reception out here?"

TWELVE

A s I entered Eden, I hoped whatever Ali was about to show me wasn't going to take too long. I was sitting in my driver's seat with the headset on, and I knew if I sat in that position for too long then I would return to the real world with splitting back pain. I was inside the Genesis Garden, and I immediately relaxed at the overpowering sights and sounds of the nearby valleys and waterfalls. It was past sunset—the moon above me cast a bright glow over the garden, illuminating the grass and trees around me. The stars above were numerous, decorating the sky in the most perfect display I'd ever seen. The world felt peaceful here. It was like Sarah's cabin, except where the environment around me was perfectly regulated and the world rested in an unbroken trance, free from any artificial disturbances to the night.

I was once again atop the hill; a few feet in front of me, sitting on her knees and facing away from me, was Ali. She was studying the grass intently. As I walked toward her, I noticed that she was staring at a small, leafed plant.

Ali was always on the more "girly" side, stereotypically speaking. After all, she had me rush into the Eden Expo back in February just to help her try on clothes. *Still, she wouldn't have called me here just to show me a flower.*

I stared at the plant more closely, and realized that it wasn't any sort of flower, but more of a tree sapling. Its leaves almost seemed to glow against the dark grass. I wasn't a botanist, so I asked Ali what kind of plant we were looking at.

"Apple tree sapling," she said, not taking her eyes off the plant. She backed away from the sapling a little to let me lean in. As I looked down at her, I noticed that the hem of her tunic had started to fray, and that the fabric over her knees was stained green by the grass. That was odd for Ali—she *never* let her appearance become even slightly disheveled.

"It's about time that the *Garden of Eden* had an apple tree in it," I said.

Ali didn't laugh or even look up at me. She stayed fixated on the sapling. "What type of apples?" I asked.

"Red delicious... most likely," she said.

"Most likely?" I asked. I looked around the garden. I realized that I didn't feel any breeze—the air felt still. But the grass around me still swayed in the absence of wind.

Maybe it's a small glitch in the system. Occasionally, the various highly detailed effects within Eden fell out of sync, but the processing intelligence would usually smooth them out within nanoseconds.

A processing intelligence that always *kept her clothes clean.*

"You didn't plant this, did you?" I asked Ali. She stayed staring down at the sapling, without responding. "Who did, then? A user?"

Ali silently shook her head without responding. My palms began to sweat; I was afraid that I knew the answer to my next question even before I asked it.

"Nobody planted it, did they?"

With a single nod, Ali sent shivers running down my spine.

"Every blade of grass, every 'random' digital cell that this computer generates—they have all been passed through my processors. I am privy to everything that grows—everything that *happens*—inside Eden. It is as if I have planted every sapling in this universe," she said, looking around the garden before gazing back down at the plant. "Except this one."

"Ali," I began, trying to make sure I fully understood what was happening. "Are you saying..."

"The system continues to evolve," Ali said, as if in a trance. "Eden is now creating its own life."

I was astounded. I couldn't help myself. Eden—inside the mechanical Solar Brain built by Abraham—had created *life*. This plant had formed on its own, without any oversight from Ali, and inside the cluster of computers that governed this world. It didn't *have* a code assigned to it because it wasn't designed by any master-planning algorithm. It had *grown* out of the ground, assembled by the garden beneath us. Just like that, we were no longer standing in a purely virtual world, but staring at its first organic component.

"This... I mean..." I took a step back from the plant. The realization of what I was *truly* staring at was harder to put into words than I had imagined. "Eden... can grow its own *life*. If that's true, then this system is so much more advanced than we thought. If the system continues to grow, which it will…"

I finally felt a rush of adrenaline—a rush of *awe*—as if the pieces of possibility itself snapped into place.

"Holy crap… Ali!" I exclaimed. "Do you know what this means? We could witness firsthand the evolution of a universe unperturbed by humans. This finding is going to change all of *science*."

As Eden continues to develop, it will rapidly increase in complexity. *That we knew.* But if it can develop in ways *outside* of Ali's control, then the growth of Eden could be permanently unfettered. *It would become indistinguishable from real life because it would* generate *life.*

In that moment, with so much on my mind, I didn't know *how* to react to that fact. I was trained to build programs with lifelike personality—not programs that generate life itself.

"This system is powerful," Ali said. She was still taken in by the apple tree sapling, gazing at it as if it were a mysterious, foreign object—like the egg sac of an extraterrestrial being.

Actually, the less I think about aliens inside Eden, the better.

Ali continued to stare at the sapling. Although I couldn't see her face, I could tell by her voice that she didn't share my excitement. She was still acting as though she were in a trance.

"This sapling… it bothers you, doesn't it?" I asked her.

"I don't know *how* to feel," Ali said. "I have a very wide range of emotions designed for any event that could take place inside this system. I am designed to interact with users, who often react to simulations in expected ways. I was not programmed to expect the unexpected."

"Neither are *we,*" I said. I stepped over to Ali. I thought about how Neil would talk to me; he was barely older than I was, and yet his words carried a wisdom that I didn't have yet. But I knew that I had to try to find *something* helpful to say to her. "This is weird for me, too. You're… probably wondering how this changes things for you. I'm definitely wondering the same thing. When I share this with Sarah, this will change the *world*."

My train of thought started to speed up as I continued to process what Ali's finding *meant*. What this *life* meant. "This is akin to finding life on another *planet,* Ali. Biologists can learn about the origins of cells by running back these simulations. Programmers—VR builders—this changes everything that we know about computers. If Eden develops its own sense of biology and even its own fundamental *physics,* we could learn entirely new things about the structure of the universe."

"I wish that were true, Arthur," Ali said. She looked up at me, and then back down at the sapling. Even before she began talking, I felt my excitement begin to deflate. "Despite the fact that this plant is likely to take up a large degree of computational power, I could not detect it in my own systems until I saw it with my avatar's eyes. All the things you are talking about... they'll grow *beyond* me. Beyond what I can learn."

"So... we can't access information about the sapling?" I asked her, already knowing the answer.

"No," she said solemnly. "I can only share information on what I myself simulate, which may become increasingly less as the generation of these random events replaces my role as a developer."

Part of me wanted to comment on the irony of Ali—the artificial intelligence—being worried about getting replaced by real life, but I stopped myself from saying anything.

Instead, I just stood there in silence, and Ali slowly stood up off the ground.

Still looking down at the sapling, she sighed. "As it stands, the development of life on its own remains as great a mystery inside Eden as it does on Earth."

"I see," I said.

The apple tree inside Eden. If that didn't cause a concussion from beating me over the head with *forbidden knowledge* symbolism, then I didn't know what would.

Had Ali known that Eden could generate life?

"No, I didn't know," Ali stepped away from the plant and looked towards the moon in the sky. "But as intriguing and vital as the matter of the apple tree is, it's not actually why I called you here, Arthur. Though it did provide an interesting distraction."

Distraction from what?

Ali held out her hand toward the moon, and it immediately started to set. I had to look down at the grass as the stars began to move across the sky in a dizzying circle. The light from the full moon had dimmed, but suddenly, the grass began to turn a brighter green and the stars faded away. I turned around and had to block the horizon with my hand as rays of light poured in from the east. Ali held out her hand above her, and the Sun raised into the sky. I felt my skin grow warmer in its light. Now, the world around me was the same bright valley that I had seen upon entering the Genesis Garden the other day. With the wave of her hand, Ali had made it midday.

"Nice trick," I said to her, but she didn't respond. She stared off at a plain of grass that stood a little way down the hill. I stepped back as a giant metal behemoth faded into view about fifty feet from me. I gazed up at the tower. Its spire reached for the Sun, casting a blinding glare along the side edges of the structure. At almost a hundred feet tall, it commanded our view of the landscape.

The Tree Branch—now complete with the chrome metallic casing that Sarah had approved of. It was a fascinating structure, and yet when I stood right next to the tower, I realized that I had only ever seen it as a person-sized model. At its full scale, the Branch was much more *domineering* than I had imagined. I looked along the metal casing to try to find the small command console, but it didn't seem to be there. *Maybe I needed to get closer?*

Ali stepped over to the Branch, leaving the apple tree sapling behind.

"Wait, are you sure we're done talking about the sapling?" I asked.

"We have bigger problems than the plant," she said. Ali walked toward the tower and once again held out her hand.

I jumped back as the Branch rapidly expanded. I braced myself for impact, but suddenly found myself staring at the electrical wiring *inside* the control tower. I looked over at Ali, who was standing atop an invisible floor next to a computer chip. I was also seemingly floating; it was like we were the size of a fruit fly, gazing at the inner workings of the machine. The garden was gone—all I saw was metal. I still didn't know what I was looking at, just that I was inside of a dark case with a lot of strange devices that I didn't remember the names of, but that Ali—the brightest thing in the room—did.

"Ali?" I asked, following her gaze towards a chrome, cylindrical, glowing device. "What exactly are we looking at? A battery?"

"Not just a battery, Arthur. This is the energy converter for the Branches. Remember?"

"Okay," I said. *That's what it looks like?*

"Like any computer, the Tree network must convert electrical power into digital signals," Ali said. "As you know, the Tree converts solar energy into quantum pulses in order to process data. This is a massive transfer of energy, which is why we need the Branches in the first place."

I nodded. Based on her tone of voice and fixation on the concept of "energy," I was beginning to tell where she was going with this.

I hoped I was wrong.

She continued, the pace of her words accelerating in a nervous way. "The energy converters on these Branches are insufficient to account for the necessary transfer, causing some of the signal to leak. The leakage does not affect the quality of the data transferred, but is instead expelled from the tower as radiation. In this schematic, the emitted radiation seems to be coming from—"

She stopped talking for a moment, staring again at the energy converter as if to be completely certain. She finished: "From loose cobalt-60 isotopes."

I had to dig deep into my (very limited) chemistry knowledge. *Cobalt-60... wasn't that usually found in nuclear reactors? As waste? If that stuff was inside the metal Branch, that would cause the entire structure to release...*

Oh, shit.

"Gamma rays," I said. She nodded.

I had to process what I was hearing. *Gamma rays from the Eden Tree?*

I thought about a virtual tablet appearing in my hands. *Smart tablet,* I thought. Sure enough, one appeared. I pointed it at the energy converter and used its camera to scan the interior of the Branch. I stared at the mess of wires intently, trying desperately to draw off of any knowledge I could from my digital electronics class in college.

Ali waved her hand at me, and I jumped as a cacophony of gold words clouded my eyesight. I moved my head around; everywhere I looked, different parts of the Branch glowed a shade of gold, with words and equations and schematics flooding my eyesight. *Primary receiver—seventy feet up. Hidden command console—southern side of obelisk, center. Storage relays—behind me.* I closed my eyes—or at least, I *virtually* closed my eyes—to clear my head of the chaos.

I heard Ali's voice whisper above me.

"Focus on what you want to learn."

I opened my eyes slowly, saying in my head the word *nothing*. The electronic world around me was back to normal, and I looked over at Ali, who gave me a smile.

"Focus," she said.

Energy converter. Suddenly, the energy converter at the center of the room began to glow in gold, and I could *see* inside of it—all the wires, sensors, and devices.

I don't know how to explain it, but I could *understand* what I was looking at; the entire construction of the converter became easy to explain. I realized that this was how a computer saw. This was how *Ali* saw: with enough detail to remove any ambiguities but with a pinpoint focus on anything she needed to know. It was like my brain had expanded, *rewired* itself to be able to make out many details at once without being overstimulated. This new vision felt intuitive and simple. To me, it even felt *natural.*

Ali stayed silent as I looked over the schematics of the energy converter. I saw pulsing signals passing to and from the center of the energy converter. Tiny white dots—*user data*—made their way out of the converter along the towering structure of the Branch and out of sight. *Headed on their way to the Brain.* As darker blue signals made their way back towards the energy converter, the tiny dots fed into the device and caused it to glow a brilliant yellow. The tiny dots reemerged from the converter as white specks; some went deeper inside the Branch (*into short-term storage,* I somehow knew) while others made their way back to the top (*back to Eden's central processor*). The way the signals moved resembled glowing ants crawling their way through a massive, metallic, digital farm. Each pulse had its purpose and each followed its own path, but all were in service of one behemoth machine.

I glanced down at the energy converter, which was still glowing yellow. *Output information,* I thought, hoping to see a breakdown of the radiation coming from the device. Ordinarily, the only thing that should have shown up were tiny wisps of heat and radio signals, which might show up as tiny red flurries around an otherwise peaceful converter. Instead, the cylindrical object was releasing bright white-green rays, waves of which pulsed from the converter with a blinding intensity. *Gamma.*

Even though I knew I was floating inside of a simulated world, I became wary of being radiated. I thought to myself: *Stop seeing output information.* The ominous green glow faded, as did the waves of "signal ants" making their way across the Branch.

Ali was right.

The energy converters were faulty—not operationally faulty, that is, given that they handled data with extreme efficiency. But they were faulty in how they released heat. The more signals we sent through them, the higher the intensity of the radiation they released. Normally, the converters were size-limited and "capped" so that they only released low levels of harmless infrared light. This converter didn't have a cap, and if too many people used the Branch at once, it would risk leaking a dangerously high level of gamma radiation to its surroundings.

In case you haven't taken a physics class or watched a sci-fi movie before: *gamma radiation is bad.*

I looked to my left, where Ali had initiated a holographic movie of the Eden Tree's activation. A tiny model of a Branch stood between a forest of featureless blue trees and a small suburb. Tiny human figures walked around the suburb as if they were non-player characters in a city-building video game.

The Branch turned on and began to glow an increasingly bright green. Above it was a diagram that read *Boot-Up Phase—Supports Minimal Users.* Suddenly, the label changed to *Activation Phase*—as it did so, the bright light began to spread around the simulated environment. The trees grew barer, their holographic blue leaves notably thinning out. And in the suburb, the tiny human figures began to disappear, one by one.

The environment around the Branch died.

I suddenly thought about Neil and his family.

"They're—*we're*—building a Branch near *here,*" I said to her. "Near Neil's house."

Ali gestured at the hologram, which zoomed out to a spherical model of Earth. Thousands of white pinpoints dotted the planet as glowing disks of gamma radiation spread out from their locations, covering the Earth in a dramatic green glow.

"We're building Branches *everywhere,*" Ali said.

She had made her point.

Eden and Earth really *were* at odds.

"But this is okay," I said with a confident nod. "Gamma rays are decently simple to block. All we need is…" I trailed off, realizing what the issue was.

"Hundreds of feet of concrete?" Ali asked.

"The signals from the headsets and satellites would never get through the Branch," I said, the weight of the design failure hitting me like a truck.

"Therein lies the problem," Ali said. Slowly, the energy converter disappeared, and we flew out of the tower and back to the Genesis Garden. The Branch was now the size of an actual tree branch, sticking up out of the ground between Ali and me.

"But how did this happen?" I asked. "When you designed this… didn't you realize this leak would be a problem? Why did you put a faulty converter in the machine?"

"*I* did not!" Ali snapped. *Angrily.* She'd had her moments of doubt or sadness or even sarcasm, but I had never seen her angry before. Her deep blue eyes glared at me; her left hand was clenched into a fist, and her face was red with anger. For a split second, Ali wasn't the girl who baked Sarah and I apple pie. She was the nervous, overextended, *frustrated* girl who looked like she'd been worked into the ground. But the moment passed quicky; she loosened her hand, and her face became calm again. I saw a tear well up in her eye, and she began to step towards me.

"Arthur, I didn't mean to—"

"Ali," I said, giving her a gentle nod. "Focus."

She quickly regained her composure, and gestured towards the small tower. "We did not place that energy converter into the Branch; the device *we* developed utilized an entirely novel design that would avoid any radiation leak, but it was far more expensive and difficult to physically build. But I believed that Abraham has more than enough intelligent engineers to create what our design needed."

"I should hope so," I said. On my datapad, I began to open up the engineering logs for Eden, but Ali instead displayed them holographically in front of us in gold lettering with a single thought. I made a mental note to get better at doing the whole *virtual reality* thing. I pointed at one of the top entries.

"Sarah mentioned that her engineers made some aesthetic changes to the design," I said, looking down at the Branch. Ali looked down at it with a faint look of disgust. "Do you think that one of the executives also changed out the energy converter for a cheaper one?"

Ali didn't look at the holographic log but nodded at me. "There is no mention of any alteration in the records, but it seems likely that this change was financially motivated. Their design is similar to ours, but uses components that are ten times cheaper... and technology that has actually been invented."

"Your energy converter design required technology that... hasn't been invented?" I asked.

"It's my job to create and refine technological designs—the process of actually *building* them needs to be done by real people. My design *was* unproven, but the Eden Tree itself remains an unproven concept," she said, tapping her foot nervously. "Our converter will work, but only after years of development and field testing. It was my recommendation to Sarah that our design become the basis for a separate research and development campaign *before* any construction began."

Sarah's never cared about how much money she spent, but she would *always* save time whenever she could. I didn't know *why* she was so hellbent on finishing Eden as quickly as possible, especially now that we had all the funding in the world, but I knew that she prioritized efficiency. She probably approved the changes to our design—whoever suggested them—without putting much thought into it, and I didn't blame her. Neither Sarah nor any of our engineers would have known that there was a danger to using the cheaper converter unless they had the ability to scan it with Ali's level of detail.

But why wouldn't Sarah talk with me first?

"I am not sure," Ali said, casually reading my thoughts again. *As two individuals with healthy interpersonal boundaries do.* "Perhaps she did not want to concern you with what seemed like a minor engineering change."

"Maybe," I said. "But she needs to know what we know. *Abraham* needs to know what we know."

Ali shook her head at me. "Ironically, the company will not listen to me. I do not have communication access with the engineers at the construction sites, and the Board of Directors are not particularly fond of me or you."

"*Thanks*, Ali."

We stood in silence for a moment, the cool breeze tickling my arms. I stepped over towards Ali. I wanted to pat her on the shoulder the way that a parent, or simply a friend, might. Then, I realized how awkward that seemed. Is that something people *did?*

I just stood there silently.

I'm serious, I would've said. *Thank you. If it weren't for your intelligence, your second sight, and your drive to keep working the problem, we wouldn't have found the defect in the Branch. I'm not sure if programs inherit traits from any of their programmers, but I do know that you are so much like Sarah in so many ways.*

I hesitated to say that, though. *Would all that sound weird?* I wasn't sure how Ali would take that—

"Thank you, Arthur," she said.

Even though I couldn't read *her* mind, I knew Ali and I were both thinking about one person. The one person who could bring Abraham's construction machine to a halt.

The one person who could help me save Earth.

THIRTEEN

THE ONE PERSON who could help me save Earth was ghosting me.

Not on purpose, I was sure, because over the past few months it seemed like the entire world was vying for Sarah Stellos's attention.

By the time Ali and I found the Tree's *operational defect,* as we were calling it, Sarah had been in Tokyo for almost a week. She'd been negotiating up a storm with the Eastern distributors, a group that Abraham needed in order to scale the headsets' manufacturing properly in Asia. Consequently, perhaps, Sarah hadn't answered any of my calls since I left Eden, and whenever I tried to leave a message, her mailbox was always full. I went back to texting Sarah, but the flurry of texts I sent her that night about needing to talk with her went unanswered. She wasn't responding to pings from Ali, either.

But the Tree's defect wasn't an issue that could wait. The Branches were already well underway, and the earliest round of towers would soon be getting close to their activation phase. Once they deployed around the world, they ran the risk of harming every living thing near them. Not only would that be a technical and PR nightmare for Abraham, but—far more importantly—would put billions in danger.

I wasn't particularly sure *how* I was going to solve the problem while I was away. It was already late at night; none of Abraham's engineers would answer a call from me at this hour. And even if they did, there wouldn't be anything they could do without Sarah's approval. Nonetheless, I didn't feel comfortable bringing up the Tree issue to anyone *but* her.

I knew Sarah wanted to fast-track the process of launching Eden, but now, only she could stop it.

Still, I couldn't just sit at Neil's house doing *nothing* while I waited for her. I decided that the best thing I could do would be to start driving back down to Florida; that way, I'd at least be closer to Abraham's headquarters by the time I talked to her.

I explained to Neil later that night, after he'd put the kids to bed, that an issue had come up with Eden that I needed to resolve. Honestly, I think Ann was relieved that I was heading out that night. Neil was concerned about me driving, though, and he gave me a list of hotels I could stop over at on my way down south.

"You sure you can't leave in the morning?" he asked.

"I wish I could," I replied. "But this really is too important."

I thanked Ann for her hospitality, wished them both luck with the food drive, and shook hands with Neil.

"We'll talk again soon," I said to him.

"We better," he said. He pulled my arm in and brought me in for a hug. We hugged for only a second before letting go. As we did, though, I remembered the last time Neil and I had ever hugged. It wasn't as brief or manly; the last time we hugged, I had held onto his striped shirt as tightly as I could, burying my misty eyes into his chest and struggling to keep from crying my eyes out. I never thought I would get to hug Neil again after that. Fourteen years later, as I stepped away from him and walked back to my car, I once again had to keep myself from tearing up.

As I opened my car door, he shouted after me. "You better text, Hesper! I'll want to hear what you have to say about the VWO they're pushing through Congress."

"Whatever that means," I said. "And next time I'm over I want to hear your interpretation of the meaning of life, or something."

"Tune into *108.1*, Sundays at six, to find out!" he said. I laughed. As I put the car in reverse, I called out to him.

"Neil," I shouted. He looked back out at me. "Thanks. I needed this."

He nodded. "Anytime, brother."

I drove for about two hours south before I parked at a rest stop. I couldn't even focus on driving; I was too busy worrying about Sarah. I was pouring over the many reasons why my girlfriend wouldn't be responding to me or my texts. It was midday in Japan; she should at least have access to her phone. *What if something happened to her?*

I knew her better than that, though. Truthfully, she was probably too busy—too *involved*—with her meetings to focus on anything else. When something was important enough, Sarah poured every inch of herself into it. I don't think there's ever been a CEO as invested in her company as Sarah—or, at least, a CEO with her capacity to *control*. The longer I've worked at Abraham, the more I realized that Sarah's leadership style wasn't about micromanaging the *process* but the *result* of the work. Even when working with another company from a foreign land, she knew how to maneuver those around her to ensure success. Sarah Stellos always got what she wanted, so I was a bit worried over how she would take the news about the Tree needing to be redesigned.

But at that point, I couldn't wait any longer to talk to Sarah. Even as I drove, I thought about each Branch component being assembled, the power converters being placed in their metal casings one by one. *How could the engineers be so unaware?* More importantly, *where was Sarah?*

Every second counted—I *had* to reach her. Not just to talk about the Branches—or about the *life* growing inside Eden, which I hadn't forgotten about either—but also to see my girlfriend.

I could tell Ali was getting concerned—*really* concerned—about the issue, perhaps even more so than I was. As I sat in my parked car, staring blankly at the closed gas station, Ali spoke to me through my passenger-side monitor about her latest failed attempts to reach Sarah. Against my better judgment but at Ali's insistence, I took out my laptop and used some *light* hacking to install a satellite-connection module to Ali's software that would allow her to track Sarah's private jet. I understood that there were ethical implications to what I was doing, but I wasn't particularly in the mood to self-reflect when I needed to find Sarah.

"Arthur," Ali said after my 226TH unread text to Sarah. Her voice was pained; desperate. It was now around five in the morning, and in my rear-view mirror I could see the Sun coming up over the trees. I'd slept for a couple of hours to regain my strength, but at this point I was only surviving on late-night convenience-store coffee. "At least one of the Branch skeletons has been shipped to its assembly site, and Abraham's latest orders indicate that the first wave of Branches will begin the final phase of their construction within the next 72 hours."

"Is there any way you can shut down production? Amend the designs they've made?"

In the periphery of my vision, I saw Ali's brown hair sway side to side.

"You have asked me this. Based on my programming limitations, I am only able to analyze data and recommend courses of action. My main functions are in worldbuilding and in user interaction within Eden—I am powerless on Earth."

"Then why are you trying to save it?" I asked. The question came out a little *too* quickly, but at that point I was interested in what Ali's answer was. I'd been so focused on my own reasons for saving Earth that I hadn't left room to think about Ali's motivations. But before she had time to think up a reply, Ali looked over at something off-screen.

"Arthur!" she said. "I've found Sarah! Her jet's preparing to take off from Tokyo now."

I almost dropped my laptop onto the floor of my car, frantically trying to access her flight manifest as Ali read off where she was going.

"According to her records, she's flying to Niagara Falls International Airport," Ali said. "She will be attending a technology conference in the region tomorrow."

The Falls weren't far from Sarah's cabin. Knowing her, she'd take a couple of hours after the conference to retreat to her private lake—and, unbeknownst to her, meet her boyfriend.

I gave Ali a warm nod and started my car. I moved my hand to put the car in drive and turned to look Ali in the eyes.

"As always, thank you, Ali."

I drove forward, but only for an instant. My car let out a loud *thud* as I hit the curb in front of me.

"You need to put it in reverse," Ali said through the screen.

"Thanks for the tip."

I knew I was only heading to the cabin on a hunch, but for some reason, I thought that if Sarah knew that *I* was going there, then she wouldn't. *She won't look me up on GPS, right?* She'd have no reason to think I wasn't still on vacation in Pennsylvania, which gave me some comfort as I took the highway northeast. I had to have Ali give me directions to the cabin's coordinates, since it didn't appear on any driving apps or internet searches. A couple of times, Ali tried to take me off-road to get to the retreat faster. To her dismay, I opted to stay on the longer, paved route.

While I drove, I asked Ali about something that was equally as stressful as the fate of the Earth: *politics.* Specifically, I wanted to know about the issues with Abraham—with *Sarah*—that people like Neil were privy to but that I'd been ignoring over the past year. The truth was that I wanted to help Sarah with whatever she was facing, and I knew the only way I could was by getting out from under the boulder-sized rock I'd been living under (and *don't* get me wrong: it was a nice rock, fully furnished and with a great garden view).

In just a couple of seconds, Ali synthesized her report from about two hundred different articles written over the past year and offered to read it to me.

"Now keep in mind," Ali prefaced. "Not all of this is my opinion. I have pulled information from a variety of sources that differ in political affiliation. You know that I have a great admiration for Sarah Stellos and the work that she does."

"Okay," I said.

About thirty years ago, when predictive text generators and AI chatbots were just becoming popular, there was a huge controversy about artificial intelligence becoming too opinionated or developing animosity toward humans. When I read about that issue in my AI History class, I'd laughed at how ignorant people had been to how text generators actually worked; those early tools just returned random series of words related to its users' questions. It didn't do any opinion-forming or critical reasoning; that kind of processing didn't come until much later, at which point people had grown numb to the presence of machine learning in our society. It just existed alongside humans, no more dangerous than the internet. Artificial Intelligence never grew out of control, but that didn't stop people from being suspicious of it. Public opinion still maintained that an AI having any *real* thoughts, especially on politics, would be frightening.

Apparently, public opinion hasn't changed that much.

"It is a strongly held opinion that Sarah Stellos's company is playing with technology it doesn't fully understand, first and foremost by creating a hyper-intelligent artificial intelligence seemingly free from reasonable supervision. Leaders in the technology sector have almost unanimously condemned Abraham for developing the Advanced Learning Intelligence, despite the longstanding existence of many AI personas across their industry. A most recent op-ed in *Technology Today* by MIT Professor David Johnson criticized the role of—"

"Wait, David Johnson?" I asked. Ali nodded.

"He was your faculty mentor, correct?"

"Yeah. Key word is *'was,'*" I responded. Burning *that* bridge hurt quite a bit. Dr. Johnson practically shaped my academic journey through graduate school, taking the young twenty-year-old post-baccalaureate that I was and turning me into a research machine. Most of my work on AI neural networks was pioneered by him; the man was a genius who lived for his work. Dr. Johnson also had the very professorial attitude of wanting to shape his students to be just like him, teaching at a research university and committing themselves to raw academia. When I became frustrated with my work, he recommended I book an appointment at the university's mental health center to try to "work out my stress and behavioral setbacks."

As I was reminded by my journey through Eden's Memory Mine, that appointment did *not* go well.

At that point, I was growing fed up with Dr. Johnson's advice. I applied for the job at Abraham without telling him because I wanted to explore the world of industry and, well, *do something that actually made money*. He probably would've forgiven me more if I hadn't used those words in that order while defending my decision. Then again, maybe he wouldn't have; after all, no one in academia liked Sarah's rogue attitude towards AI and VR.

Nonetheless, I deeply respected Dr. Johnson, which is why Ali's next words hurt.

"Johnson spoke of the Advanced Learning Intelligence as the most shortsighted and dangerous implementation of machine learning he'd ever seen, and criticized its principal developer, Dr. Arthur Hesper, as being unworthy of the degree he'd been given. 'Instead of using this technology to help people,' Johnson wrote, 'my former student has worked in service of one woman's pipe dream to develop an untested and clearly unstable artificial being inside of a structure that barely qualifies as a Matrioshka Brain.'"

Oh, Dr. Johnson, I've missed you too.

"But," Ali continued. "There is strong support among consumers for the work you and Sarah are doing. The comments on Johnson's article were mostly against his words and in support of you; one prominent user, *@JoeBahbJough23*, wrote—and I quote—'WTF are all these elitists picking on some kids who just want to make luxury available to everyone? *#Eden* is not that expensive and is clearly aimed at helping people, no wonder snobs like Johnson would hate it.' This user's comment gained sixty thousand likes in a day."

"Good to know," I replied. *Thanks, JoeBahbJough23.*

"Sarah addressed the controversy at a press conference several weeks ago, while you were busy working on the Eden Tree. Here are her words."

Sarah's voice started playing over the speakers. Upon hearing it, I wanted nothing more than to be with her. "I am *well* aware of how AI developers in academia perceive our work, as am I tired of their many comments about my so-called 'escapist fantasy.' Let me ask those people this: do you think people *agree* with you? Do you think our project here at Abraham would be as successful as it is if people didn't want to experience the power of our Solar Brain for themselves? My late uncle and dear friend, Dr. Richard Matthews, broke away from your perspective of 'doing science for science's sake' and committed himself to building things that would help people. I am also passionate about helping people, and I know first-hand what Eden can do for them. That's all that matters to me."

I always knew that Sarah had to defend her work vehemently against her academic critics, but I hadn't really thought about how Abraham's customers played into things. It's probably a bad sign that I—a top-level Abraham "executive," even though I hated thinking of myself that way—wasn't constantly thinking about our company's bottom line. But clearly, I wasn't out of touch with them; like me, the consumers wanted the technology to be the best it could be. If a culture war was brewing around Eden, I would happily take the side that helps *people*—not academics or money-hoarding executives—the most. I took comfort in knowing that Sarah felt the same way.

That said, I still didn't fully understand why people wouldn't at least want to *try* Eden. Even though I forgave him, I was still bothered by what Neil had said. I didn't know why someone as smart as he was would give in to the anti-Abraham narrative pervading our society. But there was still one thing he'd mentioned that I was curious about and, as I realized, was woefully unaware of.

"Can you tell me about the VWO?"

Ali responded. "The Virtual World Oversight Act is a bill that is up for vote next week. If it passes both chambers of Congress, it will establish a federal oversight committee designed to regulate the development and rollout of cutting-edge AIAVR technology."

"AIAVR?" I asked. I hadn't heard that abbreviation before.

"Apologies. AI-Assisted Virtual Reality is what the acronym stands for,"

Ali said. "Division on this issue is fuzzy and doesn't align with political party lines, which are historically unequipped to deal with these kinds of issues. VWO proponents argue that, like all monopolies, AIAVR requires regulation so that it does not become dangerous and uncontrolled. An understandable insight, albeit one associated with overblown fear. Opponents against the VWO Act do not argue *against* some form of regulation but point out that the proposal is merely the government's way of targeting Abraham, the only company that has developed the kind of technology described in the bill. The bill also includes provisions for taking down the Solar Brain and a long list of penalties that will be assessed against Sarah Stellos and her associates for launching the satellites without government coordination."

"But Sarah had permits for all of those satellites," I protested. "I've seen her fill them out myself. She's constantly doing paperwork and making calls about them. She's even gotten sponsorship from several governments—ours included!"

"This is correct," Ali said. "My conclusion is that the advent of Eden occurred at a faster rate than expected, causing elected officials to panic and change their stance on the issue."

"So, our government will throw its money at problems, but suddenly can't make up its mind when a *solution* comes up? Right, *that's* why I hate politics," I said, shaking my head. No wonder Sarah never wanted to talk about these things with me; people were opposing her at every turn. I'd been inside Eden and was talking to Ali right now—neither of those were *dangerous.*

Okay, I'll grant that the Eden Tree was *potentially* about to poison a lot of people, but neither Sarah nor Abraham knew about that. No one in Congress did, that's for sure. And, what's more, nobody would've caught the issue with the Eden Tree if it weren't for Ali, *who is a part of Eden.* The system wants to *help* Earth and protect people; once it officially launches, all of Sarah's critics will see the truth.

I had Ali pause the rest of her politics report. I'd heard enough.

As I stopped off for gas in a small New York town, I nearly jumped out of my skin when, as I got out of the car, I found myself standing face-to-face with a perky man. He was probably a little older than Neil was, and much larger. Behind him stood a gum-chewing woman with a camera, and the man held a portable microphone in his left hand.

He carried that despicable smile that only reporters could wear.

"Hi, Dr. Hesper. This is still off-air, by the way. Veronica—my camera gal—and I were eating lunch across the street when she noticed your car drive past the diner. She has an eye for these kinds of details—don't you, babe?"

"Sure do, hon," Veronica responded from behind the camera.

"And she saw your license plate and insisted we come over to talk to you. I'm Terry Rhodes, *New York Seven*, by the way," he said, holding the microphone closer to my face.

"Um... hello," I said, pushing past him to reach the nozzle of the gas tank. I looked back towards the car; inside, I could see the monitor on, with Ali staring through, trying to see what was going on. I desperately hoped Terry didn't see her. "May I pump my—"

"On air!" Veronica said, and she turned the camera towards Terry. I slowly pulled out my phone and texted Ali. *Check for nearby diners?*

Terry began talking to the camera with fervent delight. "This is Terry Rhodes here. I've just run into a *very* important man while dining here in Seneca County."

Veronica turned the camera over towards me.

I looked down at my phone. *None nearby,* Ali responded.

"Dr. Hesper, recent news of you and Sarah Stellos dating has come to light. Do you wish to comment on the matter?"

"Um... no?" I responded. Quick reminder: I'm 0% as articulate *talking* to people as I am *thinking* about them.

"No comment on Sarah's fiery reaction to the press and her str—"

"I mean, I love her," I said. "I do want her to know that."

"Has your relationship affected your ability to conduct your job?" he asked, shoving the microphone even closer to me.

"Has yours?" I asked. I nodded over at Veronica, and then back at him. "I noticed your initial is *T* and hers is *V.* You know, *T.V.?* That's a cute couple name."

If awkwardness could be weaponized, then I could form my own militia. But it seemed to work well enough to stump Terry, who looked back at the camera, clearly at a loss for words. I turned towards the pump, deposited the unfortunately large amount of cash required for gas, and started filling my car. Veronica lowered the camera, and the two exchanged a quick word.

"Let's try this again," the reporter said, and Veronica raised the camera.

"We're *live,*" she said.

"Sorry for the technical delay folks. I'm here with..."

"Please... *enough,*" I said. "This is just embarrassing."

"What's *embarrassing...*" he said, leaning in closer (his breath smelling of... *licorice?*), "...is you and your company's pathetic response to real allegations regarding your misuse of technology, making it impossible to trust you."

My gas was done. I carefully put away the pump, closed the gas lid, and turned back towards the camera, looking past Terry.

"You want to talk about trust?" I said. "How about trusting the media, because I sure don't! Let's talk about the fact that you've been following me since *God-knows-where,* trying to catch your first *big scoop* and then lying about dining at a local diner when I know for a fact that there are no diners anywhere near this location. But your scuzzy crap aside, why don't you think anyone *listens* to the news anymore? It's because nobody reports the truth. That's probably why you joined the news crew, isn't it?"

I felt a rush coming back to me, and I focused on Terry. I looked at his face, thought about the questions he asked me. The *way* he asked them. Who he *was.*

Finally, there it is.

I could *read* him. I felt his story *click*—it was as if I *knew* him perfectly. I could see *exactly* what kind of person he was, just like I'd been able to do with people long ago. For the first time since I'd joined Abraham, I had someone in front of me who I *knew* was weak.

I wasted no time in striking at him.

"You probably grew up in a town like this—small, quiet, quaint—and you just *envied* how big the world around you seemed. You watched the news every night, stayed glued to your smartphone hoping to *be* one of those overpaid reporters who works very little and talks a lot, and you got a job at a local news station. No college degree, *of course not,* but you worked your way up over the past few years, eventually earning your reporter van and catching the eye of your camerawoman—same story as yours, no doubt, just less ambitious—and thought you got lucky. That *was* until you realized the world isn't as big as you thought it was, nor as interesting. The only *truly* remarkable thing that was going on was the development of some super-powered computer around the Sun. You didn't understand any of the science, but you knew it was the story that *everyone* was covering. It launched careers, turned high school dropouts into respected journalists with just a single well-timed op-ed, and guaranteed fame for *anyone* with the luck to be able to ask Sarah Stellos a *question*. You knew, deep down, that you'd *never* cover that kind of story, but you held out hope. Then, while you were bored sitting in your van, you heard word that *Sarah's famous boyfriend* had been spotted somewhere in the vicinity. I'm not sure how, but it wouldn't surprise me if the media was tracking my license plate and that information somehow leaked to you, Terry, who drove miles and miles without stopping or peeing until you caught up with me and followed me from a distance until I *finally* pulled into a gas station."

At this point, I was in a flow. I didn't care if I was right or wrong about Terry's personal life, but the contorted look on his face seemed to tell me that I'd gotten the key details correct. I *knew* this segment was broadcasting live, and I pitied Terry for being that stupid. I also knew, though, that I'd taken enough crap for one day and was ready to dish it back out. *Like Sarah would do.*

"I'm... sure you have to relieve yourself soon, so I won't keep you any longer. This has been Arthur Hesper, signing off."

I stepped into my car and slammed the door. Without even glancing over at Ali, I hit the gas and drove away.

I finally reached Sarah's retreat in the middle of the night; the security guard waved me in like I was an old friend. The cabin was illuminated by the full moon, shining like a beacon at the top of a long driveway. I parked in the small lot behind the cabin and looked around. There wasn't a soul for miles. As I prepared to turn off my roadside camera, I exchanged a nod with Ali.

"Go get her, Arthur."

There was a spare key in the shrub next to Sarah's porch. Even with the moonlight, it felt like I was searching in pitch black, and even though it was June, the air outside was chilly. After about three minutes of scratching my arms against the branches of the bush, I remembered that the key was in the shrub to the *left* of her porch, not the right. After another minute of searching, I finally found the key and made my way inside the cabin.

I turned on the electric chandelier. The air was still; the environment inside was untouched. The wooden logs around me seemed to melt the cold like hot chocolate, the only disturbance in their color being the black scorch mark on the study's doorframe from when Ali had first booted up. A couple months ago, I'd gathered a bunch of construction supplies—cleaner, wax, duct tape, paint—by the door with the intention to fix the frame and paint over the burn. But Sarah wanted to keep it there as a memento, so the supplies still laid neglected outside Sarah's office. I dropped my bags in the living room, showered, and fell asleep on the couch.

I slept until around 10am the following morning. As I waited for Sarah to arrive, I sat inside the cabin playing games of chess against myself. When I got bored of losing those around noon, I started playing solitaire with Sarah's *Eden*-branded deck of cards—one of our first merchandising roll-outs for the virtual world.

As I played, I began to grow nervous that Sarah wouldn't show up. Ali had said she'd be in the area *today,* right? *What if she didn't bother stopping by her cabin?*

Around 3pm, before I had time to grow any more worried, I heard a car door slam outside. The sound of my heart racing was drowned out only by the sound of heels on the cabin steps. A moment later, the front door opened, and Sarah briskly stepped inside.

It was odd seeing Sarah wearing her business attire inside the cabin. She moved with speed and purpose, as if her relaxation time was as tightly regimented as her work. I *expected* her to be startled when seeing me, so I was taken aback when she simply said:

"Hello, Arthur."

She gave me the same tired smile that she would have when visiting my apartment on a Friday night after a long workweek, and in that moment, it felt like nothing had changed between us. *Like no time had passed.* I walked over to her and hugged her—I felt her jolt a little in my arms, but after a second, she set down her suitcase and returned the hug. We kissed.

"You've been avoiding me, boss," I said, keeping her in my arms. I felt her look past me, scanning the room as she always does.

"I'm sorry, Arthur. I've been meaning to return your calls. I've just been so busy, and I didn't—"

"I *know*," I said. "That's why I'm here."

"How did the distributor meeting go?" I asked.

As Sarah and I laid together on the couch beside the fire, it was easy to talk business in a *small* way—where we could plan and complain and worry and hope in a place that was secluded from the very problems we were discussing. Together, we were an escape; a productive, intelligent, *warm* escape. Sarah's large briefcase that sat on the floor—*what did she have in there?*—seemed to fade into the shadows as time went by. The room was comfortable; the satin drapes, natural paintings, and lakeside view were calming; the cabin looked, smelled, and felt like home. All afternoon, as Sarah and I let the sunlight slip into darkness, talking like we'd never been apart, I'd been avoiding the issue I was there to discuss. I was afraid that bringing it up would tarnish the tender evening, but with every passing hour I could feel the thing fermenting in the back of my mind. I talked with Sarah about almost every other aspect of Abraham first as a warm-up. But for some reason, the longer I warmed up, the harder the task at hand felt.

"We've hit some snags getting Eden to rural communities overseas; so far, though, the demand in cities like Tokyo and Shanghai has skyrocketed," she said. It was a very press-release type of answer, but that's what I usually got when I asked Sarah about something she wasn't too interested in. I tried a different department, one that I knew she *really* cared about.

"What's the status on long-term neural connections?" I asked. That was the area of Abraham that, according to Sarah, needed the most attention—the ability to have humans connect to Eden for a long time without needing breaks to use the bathroom, eat food, or do anything *human* related.

"We're making some *very* promising progress. Work is nearly complete on the technical design of our CNS extraction program. With the processing power from the megastructure, we'll soon have the capacity to store a full replica of the human brain—of *every* human brain—in our servers. Arthur," she said. Her eyes were brighter than the fireplace. "We're inches away from mind upload, I know it."

Mind upload. The endgame of virtual reality; to most people, it's a fever dream from science fiction. It is the idea of fully uploading one's mind like a datafile to a Matrioshka Brain, such that they can exist *only* in a simulated world that is imperceptible from—heck, in many ways *better than*—the real one. It is the ultimate escape, and for the longest time, it wasn't thought to be possible. Then, Abraham showed the world that the human mind can be connected to a computer; that *life functions* could be sustained on a machine. Since then, Sarah's poured a great deal of time and money into *Project Exodus,* which was the company codename for our mind upload division. The engineers who worked on it were, suffice it to say, *weird,* given that most of them were sullen loners who devoted almost all of their free time to working on Eden (so, nothing like me at all!). The key difference between me and them, though, was that I did most of my work on Eden from the *outside*—these people spend their entire workdays inside the system and would probably *live* there if the Brain would let them.

On paper, the project is designed to improve the long-term performance of Eden's simulations by allowing information from its users' brains to stay permanently tucked within the system. It was a division that Ali had been tasked with optimizing over the past few months but was an area of the company that I never touched. Even though Abraham's definition of "mind upload" just involved backing up a user's brain data for efficiency purposes, the words still carried an eerie connotation. The idea of permanently *escaping* this world always felt *wrong* to me, even if I couldn't put my finger on precisely why.

I leaned my head closer to Sarah's. Her soft hair smelled like flower-scented shampoo. Although I'm about the furthest thing from a florist, the fragrance almost seemed like a cross between vanilla and rose.

"It's cherry blossom," Sarah said, always knowing what I was thinking. "One of the gifts from our Japanese partners."

"I thought you didn't do scents," I said.

"I used it during the meeting to leave a good impression," she replied. "It... was pretty strong. I haven't fully washed it out yet."

"It smells good on you," I said. "Cherry blossoms *are* associated with beauty, right?"

"And mortality," Sarah said, turning her face towards mine. "Don't forget about that."

I leaned my chin on her shoulder. "You really are a ray of sunshine, you know that?"

"Of course I am. Didn't you see the news?" she asked. "I *conquered* the Sun."

I nodded toward the darkened window. "What Sun?"

"What Sun..." she murmured.

We kissed again. As I reached around Sarah's back and felt the hem of her shirt, she pulled her face away from mine, and looked into my eyes with an excited grin.

"Arthur," she said. "We've almost done it."

"We... certainly have. Many times," I said, assuming she was referring to things contained in our now-void nondisclosure agreement. Things we've done on this couch—

"I meant Eden," she said, her eyes lighting up. *Of course she meant Eden, stupid.* "Once long-term connections are fully stabilized by the Tree system, our work will be done. Mind upload will work. Our connection to Eden will be unbreakable. We'll be able to truly, *freely* enter a new world."

Finally, the conversation steered around to it. It's as if Sarah *knew* I was putting off the issue with the Tree, even though she had no way of knowing about it. Laying there, with my arms wrapped around Sarah, our bodies atop her comfortable couch, I wanted to do anything else but bring it up. Doing so would mean so much more work for us both, so many setbacks for our company. But I couldn't keep beating around the bush with it. Lives were at stake.

"Sarah, we have a problem with the Tree."

I explained the entire situation to her. I started off slowly, telling her about the bright construction lights near Neil's home. I told her that the

Branch construction was having adverse effects on the "natural environment," as I put it, without going into any more specifics.

I was still avoiding the issue.

Sarah promised to look into the light pollution issue, but I sighed, and told her there was more.

Way more.

I finally talked about the danger of swapping out the energy converters. I told her all about the amount of gamma rays and nuclear radiation that would leak from the Tree, and I described the risk that the new Branches posed to anything or anyone living within a hundred miles of them.

I told her that, if we went ahead with launching the Branches now, they could threaten all life on Earth. I told her about Ali's insistence that we delay the construction of the Tree—*delay the launch of Eden*—for several years until we develop an alternative.

And I told her that I was *eager* to spend every day working until we found our solution.

I didn't bring up the *other* thing we found inside Eden—that is, the naturally growing apple tree sapling—because I knew how important it was to focus on protecting Earth.

Throughout my whole speech, Sarah didn't react with any sort of disgust or even emotion; she just laid there, five inches from my face, studying me the same way she might study a budget report.

"I know this isn't the news you wanted to hear from me, Sarah," I said. I looked away from her, over at the fireplace. "The current Eden Tree could annihilate so much life. It could destroy Earth as we know it. But I also know that with the right solution, *we* can make it right. Together."

Hesitantly, I turned my eyes back toward Sarah.

I was afraid that she would get off the couch, demean me for not doing my job properly, and storm into the bedroom alone. But I knew her better than that. More realistically, I figured she would likely sigh, ponder the news, nod, and still get off the couch—but this time, to help me draw up a plan.

The last thing I expected Sarah to do was chuckle.

"I know Eden poses a threat to Earth, Arthur," she said. "That's why I designed it."

FOURTEEN

I LOOKED OVER at my girlfriend as she slowly got up off the couch. The cherry blossom smell of her hair began to fade as she stepped away from me and sat in an armchair opposite the coffee table. Sarah stretched her neck and leaned all the way back into the chair, the shadows in the room leaving only the outline of her black pajamas visible. She received a notification on her phone. She quickly typed up a response. She then closed her eyes for a moment and took a deep breath before looking back at me. I sat up, studying her.

For the first time in a long time, Sarah Stellos looked fully *relaxed*.

"Fifteen months ago, you asked me what it was we were *doing* at Abraham. Since then, you've worked on projects that have helped us build up a vast new virtual world—a world teeming with possibility and joy. You've seen it—you've *lived* in the wonders that we've built. That's something that I am immensely proud of, Arthur, and an accomplishment that I owe to you. But I never answered your question—not fully."

She took a long glance around the room, as if to make sure no one was listening in. All the computers were shut off. There were no security cameras. I was totally alone with Sarah. For the first time in my relationship with her, that scared me.

"Sarah, what are you talking about?"

"Eden was never designed to enhance life on Earth, Arthur. It was designed to replace it. To build a new world—better than the one we're in—and leave this wretched rock behind forever," she said. The reflection of the fireplace glowed brightly in her eyes. "Not by launching tin cans into the stars, but by uploading our consciousness to the star we already have. Once the Tree is finished, thanks to Project Exodus, we'll have the technology we need to upload billions of human minds right into Eden. The people of this Earth can live forever in paradise—a paradise of our making."

She spoke with such certainty, like she was reciting a manifesto or a grand vision.

I couldn't believe her. Not in the shocked, exaggerative *"I can't believe this!"* sort of way; I simply didn't believe what Sarah was saying. I cracked a smile. *She's messing with you.*

"Yeah okay, *Ms. Stellos,*" I said with a laugh. I made a show of gesturing dramatically toward the sky. "All hail the conqueror of the Sun, destroyer of rocks, almighty creator of a new paradise. Wait, let me guess: are we the 'Adam and Eve' of this new world?"

"Quite the contrary, *Dr. Hesper.* Adam and Eve were created only to bow down. They were made to be ignorant, and forced to suffer when they pursued knowledge. They were cast out of their garden." She kept her eyes focused on mine, not moving a muscle and not budging from her reclined position. "My world will *reward* creativity and honor its people. Not step on them."

There wasn't any levity to her voice or even a hint of a smile. Still, I knew Sarah better than that. She loved to turn conversations back around on people, and she found such joy in talking about the most unnatural topics. Either this was an elaborate, well-scripted prank of hers, or she really *was* intent on replacing our planet.

"So, what then?" I asked. "We all live inside a computer simulation? My code and your code living happily ever after?"

"Yes," Sarah said flatly. "I'm serious. There will only be peace when humanity has ascended into Eden, and the only way to do that is to leave Earth behind. And only with my Tree is this possible."

Her eyes were locked onto mine, and her voice was as steady as the logs of the cabin. I finally felt the chilling truth sink in, and my vision suddenly started to become blurry. I shook my head and blinked away the fuzziness. As Sarah came into focus, I could see that she was still fixated on me. Slowly, she gave me a small nod.

Sarah wasn't joking.

She was telling the truth.

For one of the very few times since I'd met her, I could tell that Sarah Stellos was telling the whole truth.

"Sarah... I don't understand. We've worked so hard on this system to *improve* the world for millions—now you want to see it destroyed?" I asked, raising the tone of my voice a little. I wasn't joking anymore, either. "Come on, Sarah."

She gave a slight shrug. "Your reaction is natural. Healthy, even. I'd be worried if you *were* okay with what I am saying." She spoke soothingly, reassuringly. "Destroying the *Earth?* Believe me, I know how it all sounds. You *should* react with shock. Confusion. Anger. *Fear.* It's our *planet.*"

She sat up from her recline and leaned forward in her chair. Her hair, flickering in the firelight, cast a shadow over her face. She continued.

"First off, I don't *want* to destroy Earth. It's not something that I'm particularly eager to do. If there was a way to ensure a perfect connection to Eden *without* sacrificing our planet, I would do it. But the terrible truth is that there isn't one. And, when you think about it—*really* think about it—you understand." She savored each word, reading them off her mind like she'd been preparing them for years. "Our world is *dying.* Endless wars continue to loom and continue to rage. People pollute this planet like it's their own personal dumpster. Millions of people on Earth are starving and suffering needlessly. Humans are on a collision course with extinction."

She spoke with the same tone that she had at that first press conference so many months ago. She continued her sales pitch. "But these are all problems we can solve *now* by uploading ourselves into Eden. I don't want these headsets to be expensive because I want *everyone* to have access to our wonderful new world. I want everyone to have access to the next step in our evolution. Mind upload is almost here, and our Eden Tree will guarantee humanity's ability to live in a world free of pain. Soon we'll be able to get entire families and even their *pets* into an endless heaven. We can bring about paradise, Arthur. Just like that."

The distinctive flame of *possibility* flickered in her eyes.

I didn't know what to say. I didn't know what I *could* say. *How do you respond to something so... unrelenting?* Sarah stood up from her chair and began to step closer to mine. She didn't leave me any time for words.

"You think I sound like a supervillain," she said. She sat down next to me, slowly. I didn't move toward or away from her; wrapped up in her blanket, she snuggled herself between me and the arm of the couch and looked into my eyes. "To the untrained ear, I do. But I want to make life *better.* From the very start, I designed Eden to destroy everything *wrong* with our planet. Injustice. Suffering. *Death.* But the only way to do *that* is to destroy the bedrock those things rest on."

"No," I said.

Sarah paused and looked at me—*regarded* me—with a keen interest in what my next words would be. I thought deeply, struggling to find the right words—words that could match hers. None of them felt sufficient.

"We can give people this... *tool,* Sarah, or this *escape,* but we can't replace real life," I stammered, trying to sound sophisticated.

"Why not?" she asked. "Give me *one* good reason why this world is better than Eden, Arthur. I have enough resources to bring *everyone* into Eden now. Once I build the Tree network using *my* design—and, using the trade deals I've been securing worldwide—I'll be able to ship out *all* of the link headsets in mere months. Gamma ray exposures will not become critical for some time after, by which point we'll be able to upload *billions* of central nervous systems to Eden, where they'll live in paradise. I will save *everyone*—rich, poor, starving—*everyone.* Give me one reason why I shouldn't."

I couldn't. There was no technical, no logical, no *moral* argument that I could use against saving billions of people. Sarah knew that, I knew that, and Sarah *knew* that I knew that. But her mind upload plan was not a guaranteed success; she could fail.

"There could be a flaw in your plan, Sarah," I said. "Somewhere. The mechanism of some of the Branches could break. You could fail to distribute the headsets in time. There could be some major mistakes lying deep inside Project Exodus. If there is even a single flaw in any of this, you'll have poisoned our world because of it. For what? Just to save a few years' time?"

"There is no technological flaw in my redesign of the Branch," she said. Sarah leaned away from me and reached into the floor's shadows, unlatching the lock on her briefcase. As she lifted its lid, I squinted to see what was inside. Sitting among a web of wires and connection devices were two slick-black Eden headsets; they were larger than the one I had inside my car and looked like even newer prototypes. Sarah gestured towards the briefcase.

"Do you want to see?" Sarah asked. I stared at the headsets, and back at Sarah. I still couldn't believe what she was saying. Part of me refused to believe her at all and was convinced that I would soon wake up from an odd dream. But another part of me knew that there was even more to what Sarah was saying, and that it was more important than anything else to learn what it was.

Sarah looked back down at the headsets, and up at me. "Please believe in me," she said softly. "As I believe in you."

A moment later, Sarah and I had the prototype headsets strapped on, and Sarah was typing away at her computer. This headset was heavier than what I was used to, but still fit on my head comfortably. I pulled down the visor and closed my eyes, preparing myself to enter Eden.

"Ready?" Sarah asked.

I didn't give her a response.

"Oh... okay," she said to herself quietly.

A moment later, the world around me glowed in a single flash of light. I opened my eyes, and found myself standing outside of Sarah's cabin in the middle of the night. But it wasn't her real cabin; it was the stylized, moonlit, whimsical version that was always warm and always smelled like fresh apple pie. *It was where we met Ali.* I whipped around towards the lake, hoping to find her standing there. There was nothing but the reflection of the moon in the water.

"Ali's not in here," Sarah said. She was wearing the same pajamas as she was in the real world. My clothes were also unchanged. She walked beside me towards the lake. "We're in my private server for the moment. I wanted to show you *this.*"

As she said those words, I saw ripples appear in the water in front of me. The model of Sarah's Branch rose up through the lake, parting the water as it stretched out into the darkness. Soon, the obelisk towered over us both. I would like to say I felt déjà vu looking back up at the Branch, but all I had with Sarah was a nervous feeling in my stomach. *Sarah,* who I now realized was changing the scenery around us and causing the obelisk to rise. *On her own.* She glanced over at me and smiled.

"Ali's not the only one who can control this place," she said. She nodded at the tower. "You can see inside the Branch, right? As in, *see?*"

How did she know about that? I had only tried out Ali's second sight once before, and it was yesterday.

I nodded at her. Sarah aimed her hands towards the metal tower and slowly pulled her palms apart. The obelisk once again grew *into me,* and around me, the same way it had before. Now, there was no cabin behind me, but computer processors and wires. In front of me was Sarah's glowing cylindrical energy converter, exactly as it appeared to me earlier.

Could Sarah see inside my mind, too?

"Yes," she said, standing next to me atop an invisible floor. "I can."

Sarah put her right hand to her temple, wincing. "I can't do it as *freely* as Ali can, and I can only focus on one thing at a time. Part of the restrictions of being human—for now. Once I show *you* how to control this place, we—you, me, Ali—*we'll* find a way to bypass those restrictions. Together."

She pointed toward the energy converter. Suddenly, the model in front of us disappeared and was quickly replaced by another metal cylinder, one that looked bulkier and was covered with a thick case. It looked like an earlier model of the energy converter, but from just its exterior I couldn't make out many details.

Ali's words resonated inside my head. *Focus on what you want to learn.*

I stared at the cylinder. *Information,* I thought. I imagined all the other devices around me fading away, and I thought about the large case around the converter vanishing. *Show me.* The interior of the converter began to glow brightly. As if the protective case suddenly became transparent, I could see wires, cylinders, and various processing units clearly. A bright gold label appeared next to the structure:

Model #6423. Approved by A. Hesper.

"This was the model Ali and I settled on," I said. "This was the final design, before it was changed."

"Yes. You and Ali laid some impressive groundwork, but the energy converter that you used would not work. With the technology we currently have, its power would be insufficient. It would take decades to develop a version of your design that is actually functional," Sarah said. She began swiping her hand as other tubes—some different sizes and different colors, others similar to mine—appeared and disappeared rapidly. "All of these—variations on the designs you made—are insufficient. Safe, yes, but insufficient."

Sarah then pointed at the device, the image of which reset to the energy converter she had there earlier. Compared to the other designs, this one was more *open*. It was free of its surrounding case; blue lightning passed along the device, letting out bright pulses of light every few seconds. The label next to this converter read:

Model #ISAAC. Approved by S. Stellos.

I looked around the Branch and studied its schematics. Much of the holographic notes around me consisted of calculations and models compiled by other engineers—myself included—but they were all linked by several key designs and steps that Sarah had outlined in bright, capital text. I sifted through the notes to a block of text that mentioned adapting my artificial neural network research to the human brain; all of my work was there, plus several extra calculations made by Abraham's engineers, likely without the knowledge of what they were being used for.

I briefly began to wonder if Sarah knew about the secret terminal on the side of the Branch, but immediately stopped thinking about it. *Of course, she knew about it.* And if she didn't know about it, then she would quickly learn where it was just from reading my mind. In the latter case, I figured it would be best if she *didn't* find out it existed.

Suddenly, the interior of the Branch disappeared, and I was left standing inside of a… *living room?* I looked around. The world was white and fuzzy; all the furniture was drained of its color, and it was as if I were standing inside of a sketch. I was actually startled when I looked down at my own skin and found that it was its usual non-transparent color, my body its usual form. I couldn't see any windows around me. There were two couches in the corner of the room, and sitting on them were blue, faceless, almost holographic humanoids. They stood out against the stark white backdrop behind them. I couldn't make out any clothes or features on any of them; three of them were short, and two of them were tall.

A simulated family.

Atop a coffee table in front of the couches were five boxes; in one rapid motion, the humanoids opened the boxes and each of them picked up a dark black headset. They placed the headsets over their faces and sat perfectly still. Suddenly, *something* came from them. I can't describe exactly *what*. It was something like wisps—no, like *vines*—sprouting from their heads and reaching up to the sky. The humanoids were still as these leafless vines grew from their skulls and detached; as they floated out of sight, the family continued to sit lifeless, undisturbed.

Mind upload.

Although I couldn't see her, I heard Sarah's voice echo around me. "I've redesigned the Branches to serve as upload points for Project Exodus; once we distribute as many headsets as possible, they will upload copies of each user's consciousness—their *essence*—into the Solar Brain. This is what *mind upload* can do, and I've just received word that it is ready to launch. As you just saw, the memories of the brain are all that matter. Once these are saved inside our supercomputer, the human body is expendable; even if the user dies with Earth, their consciousness—who they *are*—will live forever inside Eden."

As I heard her speak, it was as if I was hearing someone talk to me through a dream. I kept looking at the blue figures in front of me. They stared out into the colorless living room, perfectly undisturbed. Not alive. Not dead. Just *there.*

The image of Neil's family sitting on their couch with the Eden headsets on suddenly floated through my brain. *Neil, Ann, the kids, even their dog*—all just *sitting* there, motionless. I felt myself grow lightheaded and pushed the haunting image out of my head.

"This all happens... using the Eden Tree?" I asked.

"Once the Tree is online, all a user needs to do is put on the headset. The data will soon be collected, and a copy of their minds made," Sarah's disembodied voice said. The blue figures faded away, leaving the headsets floating above the couch midair.

"When the Branches activate, they leak radiation. What does that... what does that look like?" I asked. I realized that, for all the talking we had done about it, neither Ali nor Sarah had any visual aid for what the gamma-ray-induced death would look like. *How would our planet change? Did people hooked up to Eden feel* pain *when they died?* Maybe Ali didn't want to show me those things, but I wanted to see them for myself. I wanted *Sarah* to see them.

"It doesn't matter, because it will not happen to us," Sarah said. "If the final wave of Abraham's distribution goes as planned, billions of people around the world will acquire their headsets in the days that follow Eden's launch. They'll place them on their heads, their kids' heads, their *pets'* heads, and will never need to take them off. They'll go on living their lives, for they will have never stopped."

Without warning, I was back outside the cabin. In front of me was a schematic with a bright red label: *THE KEY TO QUICK UPLOADS*. Beneath it was a rough sketch of the redesigned energy converter, and next to it was a note: *Processes 55 exabytes of data/second. Sufficient for Earth population upload.*

Approved by S. Stellos.

Verified by ALI.

"Not *your* Ali," Sarah said, suddenly appearing next to me. "Just her programming pathways, which helped me immensely with my improvements to your work. I've learned how to sever Ali's processors from her personality, so I could complete this redesign *without* her moral input. As you've probably noticed, Ali herself is a very different person than her program. I love our girl, Arthur, but if we ever needed a clean reset of her software..."

"Stop," I said. I looked into her eyes, which were bright with enthusiastic energy, as if she were hiring a new employee. *Or telling him about what they would build together.* I wouldn't listen to this anymore—what Sarah was saying wasn't *her.* I had to break her out of it. *"Please."*

Sarah looked back at me, and up at the cabin. She closed her eyes and nodded.

"Very well."

Just like that, I found myself taking the headset off. I was back inside the cabin. *The real cabin.* I looked down at the prototypical headset in my hand, and quickly put it back inside Sarah's briefcase.

Several minutes passed in silence. Sarah sat next to me on the couch, shifting her gaze between me and the floor. Eventually, I finally spoke.

"Why can't Eden wait, Sarah?" I asked. Despite everything I'd seen—everything Sarah was *doing*—I was trying to take the safest route first. *Compromise.* "Why can't we wait a couple years, a couple *decades* for us to develop *safe* technology that can connect people to Eden more easily? Why can't we expand to other planets and build out the Solar Sphere so that it's stronger? Why can't we make this into the amazing, fun VR that we both love?"

"It won't *happen* if we wait," she said. "We do not have the luxury of time. Our investors will lose interest. All of our visitor displays about the long-term future of Abraham—mining on other planets, rapidly expanding our Solar Brain—it'll never happen. We'll never 'take over the Solar System.' Our funding will have long dried up before we could do that."

Sarah sighed. "But it's not just money. People will *die* waiting for Eden," she continued. "And—I *know* you've been researching politics recently—we'll be shut down by the government. The Oversight Board will strip us of our tools, our Tree, our *Eden*—we will lose everything we've worked to build just because assholes like Dr. Johnson don't see what *we* see. If we give them even a few *weeks*, we could lose *years* of progress. And the Branch that *you* designed won't work."

"It might," I countered.

"It *won't*," she finished. "Only my redesign can save our dream. I have studied every aspect of my company—every aspect of my life's work—and I've studied them fully. I know how my technology works, Arthur, far better than you give me credit for. And I know that for Eden to be born, Earth must die."

I shook my head at her. The woman sat a foot from my face, and yet I felt I couldn't recognize her. *But no*—I *could* recognize her. Sarah Stellos, the driven trailblazer who would go to the ends of the Earth just to achieve her goals—she sat beside me. In the soft light that danced through her cabin, I saw that Sarah—the same Sarah who believed in me and pushed me—was tired. Tired, but no less certain.

But why does Eden matter so much to you? I wanted to ask her. *Why do you need to build it?* I don't know why I didn't ask her those questions, because I knew the answers to them mattered. There was something else she was holding back. There was more to her argument, but maybe I was too afraid to find out what it was.

Still, I decided to try one last thing; something that I hoped *I* could be certain of, too. Something that I *knew* would resonate with Sarah. *Something that had apparently resonated with her mentor.*

I thought about what Neil had told me. *Make it a natural part of the conversation. Make it matter.*

"Sarah, this world isn't something we can just discard. For all its faults, we were *placed* here to make it better. I believe that. I believe that God—"

Sarah burst out laughing, harder than I'd ever seen her laugh before. I shifted away from her as she stood up and began pacing around the room. She laughed uncontrollably, *viciously.*

I'd seen Sarah's synagogue in Eden all those months ago. It was a chink in her armor, a lapse in her guard. I thought—I *knew*—that she was religious, even if she wasn't comfortable telling anyone.

I didn't know *how* religious.

"God!" Sarah exclaimed. "I was *waiting* for you to pull your religion card, Arthur. The one thing you *think* you can lean on, even though you've never actually *committed* to it. Even in your own mind, you can never think about your religion—your *upbringing*—too fully, can you? Not even a *consultation* with your friend could change that, could it?"

She spoke with that same condescending, invasive tone she had when reciting my therapy note at my company interview all that time ago. She *knew* me—she *knew* my mind, even better than Ali—and I wanted her out. I loved Sarah—I really loved her—but she was pummeling me now with everything she had. Even if I had a long way to go spiritually, I *knew* that I believed. Sarah's attack wouldn't sway me. But I resisted the urge to defend myself; I knew I didn't need to. *That, or I was too afraid to.*

"Everyone thinks I'm an atheist, or at least an agnostic, but I'm not. I know the *truth*," Sarah said. "Arthur, you grew up in a religious orphanage. Do you remember the Book of Genesis, 22:15?"

I sealed up my mind from her, hardened my expression. I retreated to my objective thoughts, which flickered like the fireplace. I searched my mind for the verse. Mid-Genesis—it would have had something to do with...

"Abraham," I said.

She closed her eyes and began to recite the verse. *"The Angel of the Lord called unto Abraham out of Heaven. 'In blessing I will bless thee, and in multiplying I will multiply thy seed as the stars of the Heaven, and as the sand which is upon the seashore; and thy seed shall possess the gate of his enemies;*

and in thy seed shall all the nations of the earth be blessed; because thou hast obeyed my voice.'"

Sarah looked over at me, waiting for me to be impressed. I was, but I didn't show it. I just stared at her, waiting for an explanation.

She was pacing around the room quicker now. "That's the Sacred Covenant, made between the Lord and mankind after Abraham showed his willingness to sacrifice his own son, Isaac, for the sake of his religion. God promised Abraham that—so long as humans remain faithful to their Creator—He would bless them with prosperity and safety. I committed that verse to memory about eight years ago, standing on the steps of the synagogue I went to as a child."

She walked behind her velvet chair and clutched the back of it with her right hand. The fireplace was behind her; all her features were covered by her own shadow.

"I've remembered that verse, Arthur, because the Creator failed."

Her words sounded... *blasphemous.* That was the only word that could materialize, but it was an empty thought. She didn't care about any of that. She spoke not with irreverence, but with purpose. *With vengeance.* She continued pacing the room, forcing me to turn out of my seat to keep watching her.

"What are you talking about?" I asked.

"Tell me, did God honor the Covenant when six million of His people were slaughtered by their own neighbors? Ripped from their homes and butchered? Did God care that His people have suffered and died for His name, only to be forgotten—no, *maligned*—by future generations? Does God not see how we, who placed our faith in Him, suffer?"

She was speaking faster now. "Did God care that Sarah Stellos—"

Sarah stopped walking as her voice broke. She choked back a sob.

"*Sarah Stellos,* the little girl who diligently attended her Hebrew school lessons, volunteered hundreds of hours at homeless shelters, and planned to use her family's wealth to help the needy—did He care about *her?* About Sarah, when she was *eight...*" She couldn't finish the sentence. She placed her hands over her mouth and let out a gasp. A tear dripped off her hand and onto the floor. I felt my face growing warm. Sarah looked back up at me, and went back to pacing around the room.

"Did God care about Sarah Stellos, who cried for hours for help, *help,* at the cemetery, begging to see her parents one last time? Did He care about Sarah, who grew up with no friends, who lived perpetually alone? *Did He care about me,* who had nothing but money and enough rage to power a sun?"

Tears streamed down her face; she wiped them away with her sleeve and caught her voice. She looked into the fireplace, with its flames illuminating her wet cheeks and red eyes. She took a couple of steps towards me; her voice was hoarse.

"That isn't even the half of it, you know? But as far as I'm concerned, the Creator has failed to meet His end of the bargain. So, I'm done honoring mine. You wanted to know why I'm doing this? *Now you know.*" Sarah wiped her eyes again. "Atop the ruins of God's forgotten world, I will build a better one. A bright and beautiful new world, whose inhabitants won't have to wait and die just to experience salvation. I will give it to them now, and they'll have it forever. All because of us, Arthur."

There weren't enough words in the dictionary to respond to what Sarah was saying. She'd just poured her heart out, and its contents stood against everything I was raised to believe. I knew that terrible things happened in our world that we couldn't always explain; human sin and free will were inevitable.

But I also knew that we lived in an imperfect world, and through good deeds and belief, Heaven did await us. There was something, *Someone*, waiting for us. Neil had taught me that, even when he was young. Many of the orphans around me, who were without parents, without money, and often without hope, believed in the saving power of God. I believed in it, even if Sarah couldn't.

I had never seen Sarah shed a tear over anything, and yet she was almost hysterical now. Despite her money, I knew that she'd been given a terrible lot in life. But I didn't know just how *alone* she felt.

I knew nothing I said could take away her pain. Instead, I walked over to her and held her in my arms. She hugged me back, and for a few seconds, we simply stood there, as if we were determined not to let anything come between us. After a few seconds, I felt her start to push away. She sat back down on the chair facing the couch, but made some room for me to join her.

I wanted to, more than anything. But I couldn't. Not yet.

"Sarah," I said, measuring my words more carefully than an atomic physicist measures the amount of uranium placed into a nuclear reactor. "I didn't know how hard life was on you. I knew you were an orphan, like me, but I didn't realize how badly you were hurt. And I know you believe that by creating a new world, we can escape our burdens in this one."

She opened her mouth to respond; this time, I talked before her.

"But destroying this planet to get back at... *God?* Sarah, if there's one thing I was taught, it's that you can't blame God for your life. Bad things... *really* bad things happen, and we don't know why. We probably never will until we go to Heaven and ask God ourselves," I said. She wasn't looking at me. I sat down on the couch in front of her, and I took her hand. "And I know these words might not mean much coming from me, but I *do* believe that God is good, and that He has a plan for all of us—even if that plan doesn't make sense to us now."

She began to shake her head. She tried to slip her hand out of mine, but I held it tighter. She looked up at me.

"I stopped believing that long ago, Arthur," she said. Her words were drained of passion. "You are separated from it all—the *pain* in this world. It's easy for you to want to cure something you don't suffer from; it's simple to *believe* without consequences. But I thought—I *hoped*—you would become a man of science who would help me leave religion behind. Why do you insist on defending something you've never seen, much less *believing* in it?"

For once, I finally had the words I was looking for.

"Believing is easy when things are going right, Sarah," I said. *Thank you, Neil.* "A good friend told me that the test of faith is when things are all wrong and you're *still* believing. And the more I think about it, the more I think it's true. Think about it: even in their most trying moments, Jesus, Moses, and even Abraham kept believing."

Sarah looked towards the fireplace. I followed her gaze, and I felt my eyes grow warm as the bright orange glow of the fire cascaded across my vision. The more I spoke, the more I felt Sarah slipping away from me. *Neil's words aren't working.* I was saying exactly what I thought he would say, but Sarah seemed completely disinterested, as if she were tuning out a reporter that she didn't like.

Religion is meaningful when it's personal, Arthur. Someone else's words, someone else's beliefs—even *Neil's*—weren't going to reach Sarah. I realized that if I was going to reach her, that I had to be fully honest with her, too.

"Honestly, Sarah," I said, glancing back towards her. "There's a lot I still need to figure out about my religion, too. I don't just question my beliefs, but my right *to* them. Who am *I* to be religious? Even what I've said to you now, Sarah, comes with its share of doubts. Sorting those doubts out and making *sense* of the world is why faith exists in the first place. Figuring it all out would've been a lot easier if I had someone to do it with, and I think you feel the same way. Maybe we can find faith again, too—even inside *Eden,* of all places. You think the Covenant is broken, but maybe—with hard work—*we* can repair our connection with God. We can learn to heal *together.* We can have a future in Eden *and* on Earth."

I hoped that my words were right because the more I spoke, the less confident I became. Sarah and I had never discussed religion, and this conversation was quite the heated way to start doing so. But something inside me knew I could get through to her. Just as we'd broken ceilings together on a technological level, on a *personal* level, we could do so now. She wasn't looking away from me or shaking her head. Her eyes were gazing into mine, and her face carried neither malice nor scorn. *Just calm.* For the first time today, I knew for certain that Sarah was listening.

"But if we let Earth die and escape it all, we'd be running from our problems in an artificial world forever. We would never *grow*, never change. Exist, but never truly *live*. I want to *live* with you, Sarah, in *this* world. The world where I fell in love with you."

Sarah leaned out of her chair and kissed me.

I couldn't feel anything else; not the rough fabric of my seat, not the draft inside the cabin, not the scent that seemed to have left her hair. Just *her*. We stayed that way for a moment; the whole while, I hoped—I *prayed*—that I'd reached her.

God, help me reach her. Let us be on the same wavelength again. If I could connect with Sarah now, I knew that we could rebuild the Eden Tree together, properly.

She leaned back into her chair and away from me. "You hardly have a basis on which to oppose me," she said slowly. "You speak of saving Earth, protecting life because you *can*. You speak with piety, yet you have no religious authority over me. You have no place to oppose me, Arthur, because this isn't *your* fight. It never was."

Sarah was trying to break me again. I used all my strength to not let her.

"Your *uncle* believed, too," I said, hoping I was right.

Sarah looked away, closing her eyes. "Richard believed a lot of things." She wiped another tear from her face and shook her head.

"Sarah..." I began, casting one last lifeline to reach her.

She took a deep breath in and stared down at her feet. She muttered something inaudible, shaking her head again. The fire in the room seemed to have faded; I could focus only on the features of Sarah's body. Finally, she looked back up at me.

"You will have your extension to work on the Tree. I will pause production while you and Ali work to find a viable alternative to the Branch's current design," she said.

My heart wanted to pound out of its chest. *I couldn't believe it.*

"Sarah—"

She cut me off.

"But you'll find out, Arthur, what you already know to be true," she said. "Eden and Earth cannot coexist. Deep down, you *know* I'm right. And when the time comes—"

"I'll prove you wrong." I stared back into her eyes. Both fear and relief competed for dominance over my brain, but I kept my gaze focused on Sarah and my mind on the task ahead.

Sarah gave me a faint, haunting smile.

"I hope so."

PART III

FIFTEEN

I HAD NO idea what I was supposed to do.

There. I said it.

I wish I had something more profound or more insightful to share about Eden. I wanted to find the solution. I hoped that, after four days of nonstop work, Ali and I would've been able to successfully redesign the Branches' energy converters in a way that could save both Eden and Earth.

But we couldn't.

The most capable AI in the world, empowered to solve any technological problem thrown at her, couldn't devise any other version of the Eden Tree that successfully connected to the Solar Brain for longer than a few hours. The only ones that could maintain a long-term connection to the Brain still output radiation at the same intensity as Sarah's design did.

Apparently, Ali knew all along that our *original* design for the Branches was unlikely to work, but because we were on a deadline, she moved forward with it anyway.

"I didn't want to disappoint Sarah," she said. But the only reason she found out about the issue in Sarah's redesign was because she was obsessively reviewing our own model to try to improve it.

All information that would've been helpful earlier.

Still, I couldn't be mad at Ali. I should've been, but I wasn't. I had a hard time feeling anything after that meeting with Sarah.

After our conversation, Sarah left the cabin to head back to her jet. After the conference in Niagara Falls, she would be on her way to Tel Aviv for her last distributors' meeting; after that, she'd have people all around the world who would help her with the rapid deployment of the Eden Branches and headsets. She offered to fly me home and have my car shipped back to Florida, but I think we both knew that I couldn't take her up on that offer. *Not then.*

She left, and I sat on the couch for a long while, trying to process everything that had happened. I simply couldn't. I felt numb to the world around me. The light from the fireplace seemed artificial. I wasn't processing *smell.* I touched the fabric of the couch, but I didn't feel its rough texture. It was like I was waking up from a nightmare or working while I was overtired. Nothing felt real, which made the fact that it *was* real something I had a hard time processing.

I drove home the next day without talking to Ali. It wasn't until the following morning, after I'd gotten back inside my apartment, that I booted up my connection to Eden on my desktop. It loaded quickly, and I found myself looking right at Ali, who had a sad expression in her eyes.

Somehow, she knew.

"I'm sorry, Arthur," she said.

I stayed up and started sifting through alternate energy converters. *There had to be one.* I stayed awake for another three days straight, only sleeping a couple of hours here and there. I didn't dream. I also didn't leave the apartment and I definitely didn't call or text Sarah. She didn't write to me, either. What would we say to each other?

Hey, babe. Sorry our chat about destroying the world went a little south. Want to meet up for dinner?

I didn't want to talk to Sarah because I couldn't accept that that was *her.* Sarah Stellos, the woman I'd fallen in love with, was secretly waging a holy war and using our *planet* as its battleground. It sounded like something right out of a science fiction movie. *World's richest tech CEO maniacally plots to replace the world with a supercomputer.* The whole scenario sounded laughable, like a satirical caricature *of* Sarah. Not *her.*

Still, I couldn't stop replaying our conversation inside my head:

The people of this Earth can live forever in paradise—a paradise of our making.

My world will reward creativity and honor its people. Not step on them.

Atop the ruins of God's forgotten world, I will build a better one.

When you think about it—really think about it—you understand.

I understood. As badly as I didn't want to, I did. I disagreed with her vehemently, but I understood her completely. Sarah had a point. Her design would work, and Abraham had all the resources and connections it needed to ship out billions of Eden headsets. They could upload as many minds as they needed to, and the world's population would soon be living their virtual lives without missing a beat.

That is, if they *chose* to.

Sarah was manufacturing a disaster with only one way of escape—her way. Not everyone believed in her way. Not everyone wanted to be a part of her virtual world. Neil and his family certainly didn't—would they be left behind if they didn't buy the Eden headsets? What about when the news broke that Abraham's Branches had poisoned the world? Would they put on our company's headsets then?

Would I put on the headset then?

Because if I did, and if *everyone* bought into it, then we could live whatever lives we chose for as long as Eden functioned. Humans could stay *alive* for as long as the Sun—possibly longer—and never worry about going hungry or even dying. There would always be a second chance; there would always be enough time. *Human suffering could end.* Even if the physical planet we lived on became irradiated and uninhabitable—even if *millions* of species perished—these things would exist in Eden, reborn out of the compendium of all human knowledge. *Did it matter whether or not that life existed inside of a computer?* I had seen life itself develop inside of Eden, via the apple tree sapling. Life *did* exist inside of the supercomputer, and it could thrive. *What was I afraid of?*

What reason did I have to stay on Earth?

This was the question that I didn't know how to approach, even though Sarah clearly did. The woman I loved longed to live inside Eden; so much of what I wanted existed inside a virtual world. As Ali and I failed over and over again trying to find a solution, I started to believe that I wasn't meant to save Earth. Maybe I wasn't meant to *save* anything; maybe Eden was my destiny.

I also kicked myself, again and again, over how I'd handled the topic of religion with Sarah. I was an idiot for even trying to talk to her the same way Neil had talked to me. Sarah was out for blood; this whole time, she'd been out to dethrone God and rule her own universe. The same ambition that drove her to create Abraham was driving her to use Eden to replace Earth. Sarah was committed to keeping her own twisted new covenant. Nothing I said seemed to faze her. She gave me this work extension out of pity and, likely, a passive curiosity to see if Dr. Arthur Hesper could *once again* get the job done.

Sarah was right. I had nothing to use against her. Even with Ali's help, I couldn't find a technical solution to the problem; Sarah's knowledge of the Eden Tree far surpassed my own. I couldn't debate her on the religious front, either. She was stronger in her convictions than I was in mine.

Sure, *Neil* could talk to her, but neither would ever set foot in the same room. I thought about calling him once, but I put down my phone before I opened up my contacts. Even if he *did* agree to talk to Sarah, she'd think the whole thing was just a ploy for me to stall her.

But there was *one* way to stop Sarah.

But no.

I couldn't do that.

I thought a lot about finding one of Sarah's Tree Branches and using its secret terminal, but to do what? Even if Sarah didn't know about the terminal's existence, those Branches would be guarded. Her security staff was probably on order to keep me clear of the Branches—*hell*, they were probably going to be the first people to be exposed to the gamma radiation from the Tree. They didn't know about the danger, and even if they *did,* it wasn't like they could do anything about it. The command console controlling Eden was biologically locked so that only I could access it.

Even if I could slip by them or convince them to let me pass, what would I do once I was at the terminal besides getting a healthy dose of radiation poisoning? Sure, the Branch had an "off" button, but Sarah would quickly reactivate it and revoke my access to Abraham. The Tree didn't *have* a permanent kill switch.

At least, not anymore. Ali *had* installed a code—*Cherubim*—that would cut off all users' access to Eden. And *I,* in my infinite wisdom, had her delete the package as soon as I found out about it. If only I hadn't...

No.

I would not shut down Eden. There was too much work put into our virtual world. *And I would never lose Ali.* There was another way, and I would find it. But with each passing hour, I felt more and more powerless compared to Sarah. If she was an omnipotent and calculating supervillain (and it killed me to think of her that way), then I was little more than a side character in this story. I wasn't the hero because I wasn't ever her equal in any way, nor could I be.

Maybe she really was right.

"Arthur."

I jolted awake. I had fallen asleep at my desk—actually, from the stinging sensation on my left cheek and the beads of sweat on my keyboard, it was likely that I had fallen asleep *on* my desk. Ali stared at me through my screen.

"Yes?"

"Trials 6678 through 9912 have all failed," Ali said. "We have yet to isolate a valid solution."

I brushed the crud out of my eyes and gulped down my water bottle. I tossed it into my recycling bin, landing it in perfectly. Although I never made that shot, I was in no mood to celebrate.

"Perhaps you should take a break," Ali said, blinking as she stood motionless in front of me.

"Why do you keep suggesting that?" I asked, turning back towards my keyboard. I opened up the base program of the Tree; the lines of code began to blur together. There had to be something there—*something I could use.* "You know there's work to do."

"I..." Ali began, looking away from me. I turned away from her—I didn't have time for her emotional self-doubt right now. I began scrolling through the code. I noticed her quickly stand up straight in my periphery. She repeated herself. "Maybe you should take a break."

"Maybe *Sarah* should see a shrink," I growled. *Because trying that worked* wonders *for me.* I swiped several notebooks off my desk, and I heard the sound of fluttering papers as the books hit the ground.

My head felt fuzzy; all I wanted to do was go back to sleep, but *here I was,* trying to save the world from my girlfriend's unhinged Earth-replacing supervillain scheme. *What a perfectly normal life you have, Arthur Hesper!*

I didn't care about Sarah's argument, or my argument, or anything else. *I couldn't let life on Earth suffer.* It wasn't a logical move or a calculated stance, but a gut feeling that I *hoped* most sane people would share. *But maybe I'd trusted my gut too much.* I had applied to Abraham on an instinctual whim. If I'd followed Dr. Johnson's advice and went into academia like I was supposed to, maybe Sarah never would've found a sucker like me to do her dirty work.

"But she could've found someone worse," Ali said

"And *you*," I snapped. I was breathing heavily. "Stop reading my thoughts. I don't know *how* you're doing it—if you're using the camera to read my facial expressions, if you're modeling my thoughts inside your supercomputer—but *stop.*"

"I don't know how," Ali said. She backed away from my monitor nervously.

"Well, figure it out!" I whipped away from her and strode towards my fridge. I needed something cold. "That's what you're designed to do, right? Figure things out and make people comfortable? Do I look comfortable, Ali? Have you figured anything out?"

I regretted the words even before I said them, but that didn't stop me from shouting at Ali. *Why didn't she have the answer?* She had the power of the Solar Brain at her disposal. Tucked somewhere beneath the haze, there *had* to be a solution to all this that Ali just wasn't seeing. *It was like she didn't want to find one.*

She blinked; even from far away, I could see the tears roll down her face. She turned away from the monitor, covering her mouth with one hand.

"That's *fantastic*," I said quietly. *Stop talking, dumbass.* "Any other women in my life who I can make cry? I'm on a roll!"

Ali turned back towards me. Her eyes were red, but she shook her head.

"I'm trying, Arthur. But there's something else I have to tell—"

"I don't care!" I yelled. "If it's not going to help me solve this, then don't tell me."

Ali looked down, away from the monitor. Suddenly, she was gone, and I was left staring at my own reflection in the black screen. I was still relatively clean-shaven; apparently, it was true that stress stunts facial hair growth. I couldn't see the bags under my eyes, but I felt them. It felt like the weight on my shoulders doubled after Ali left. She was my only colleague—the only one who could help me—and yet I felt the need to push her away, too.

Why the hell was I so determined to be alone?

I must have a severe allergy to *people,* because whenever someone gets too close to me, I always manage to push them away. Sarah was somewhere far away, and I don't just mean physically. Ali had left me. *I didn't blame her.* Neil was my *only* other friend, and he couldn't help me with this.

Once again, I was living and working alone.

Wait a minute.

Why am *I working alone?*

I took a step away from the computer. The world felt like it was spinning, so I sat down in my chair for a minute and took a couple sips of water. I then took a deep breath, and focused.

I didn't need to work alone.

I assumed that it *had* to be me to fix everything; after all, I was the main architect behind Ali, who in turn helped me with the Eden Tree. I'd gotten so used to working with Ali alone that I'd forgotten something obvious.

There are other people at Abraham.

Smart people. People who worked on things I couldn't, like the neurophysics behind connecting to Eden, the rocketry and satellite science, or the rendering of the virtual world itself. Don't get me wrong; I *knew* these people existed, but Sarah had tasked me with so many assignments that concerned only Ali and me. She trusted us alone with her most important tasks—or what I *thought* were her most important tasks—without bothering me about what the other departments in Abraham were up to. I'd grown so laser-focused on my task, so *immersed,* that I hadn't bothered to explore the rest of the company (or the rest of the *world*) while I was doing it. Working at Abraham was like working inside a lonely, virtual world. Sarah had meticulously divided and isolated the different parts of her company so that each could produce the part of Eden that she needed. The physical Solar Brain, the ability to link to it, and the world within were all built separately, ready-made for Sarah alone to assemble. *That* was why Abraham was so efficient, and why Sarah Stellos was a genius. A terrifying, powerful genius.

But the employees at Abraham, they—*we*—are smarter than she gave us credit for. I was too *beaten* to call the engineers building the Eden Tree days ago to inform them of the problem.

But why? Why couldn't I tell everyone?

I could've told all the employees about the defect in the Tree; I could've leaked Sarah's plan to the press. I could've done it secretly, without Sarah knowing.

I could've saved so much time...

No.

I couldn't stress about what *wasn't,* only what was. I'd spent the past few days dwelling on solving the Eden Tree problem, thinking I had to do it all alone. Wrongly, I thought that that was the solution. But now, I had to leave *my* solution behind and do what was right.

Even if it's going to hurt.

Forty-six unanswered phone calls later, and *doing what was right* was definitely hurting. I called *everyone*—the systems engineer in charge of programming the Tree, the lead technician at our Branch construction site, even members of our Executive Board. I had even called Janice Green, who took every opportunity to be hypercritical of our work at Abraham but who had *just* enough money invested to stay on the Board.

"Ms. Green," I had said to her answering machine, feeling absolutely humiliated. "This is Arthur Hesper. I would normally never call, but this is urgent. None of our engineering staff is answering my calls; might be a bad connection inside the facility. I know that you're close friends with one of our technicians, Minerva Moroni, who's working on the Tree. I need you to tell her to call me urgently. She probably won't want to, given that the only time I've ever interacted with her was when I spilled coffee

on her laptop in the employee breakroom. She... had some choice words...
The point is—call me when you can!"

None of the engineers were answering. The Board members wouldn't
take a call from me to save their lives. It was a Tuesday morning; shouldn't
they all be by their phones? I *needed* someone who could access the Eden
Tree—who could help me *stop* the Eden Tree—but no one was there.
I texted Ali and asked to talk to her, but she didn't respond. I didn't
think she would—I'd been terrible to her. *She didn't deserve what I said.*
But I would make amends with her later. For now, I needed to find people—people on *Earth*—who could help me. I decided to make one more
phone call to Abraham's headquarters, deciding that if this one didn't
answer, then I would be taking a trip there myself.

I didn't expect anyone to pick up the phone, which is why I was surprised when an Abraham engineer actually answered.

"Hello?"

Even from *Hello,* I recognized the man's voice.

"Hi... is this Clyde?"

"Who is this?"

"This is Doc... Arthur," I said. "There's something important I need
to..."

"This is great," Clyde said in an overjoyed tone. "I didn't realize we
could patch in with other people long-distance!"

"Um... *yeah,*" I said. *Long distance? Had I called at a bad time?* It didn't
matter. "Clyde, I need you to listen to me very carefully."

I took a deep breath.

"There is a problem with the new Eden Tree, and it's because of Sarah
Stellos. She programmed the Branches to—"

"*Ah,* Sarah," Clyde interrupted. "You're dating her right?"

"Yeah, I am... was... is. It's complicated..."

"Right, you're banging her, yeah?"

"Um..."

"Good taste, mate. I always thought she looked hot in her Portal suit,
but then I saw archive footage of her in the simulation wearing that
bikini..."

"Moving on," I said, talking faster and resolving to deck Clyde the next
time I saw him. "Stellos dramatically increased the energy output of the

Tree, so much so that… well, *it's dangerous.* She isn't trying to improve the world; she's trying to force everyone to live inside her own. I tried to solve the problem, but…"

I sighed, knowing that saying these next words out loud would solidify them as true.

"There is no way to make long-term connections to Eden work. Not with our current Tree. I'm going to head into HQ to sort this out—that is, if security lets me in—but I need you to tell the engineering team to halt production at all costs. And I need you to send me the official schematic of the Tree's current design."

Here goes.

"I need to send the design to the media as proof of what I'm telling you," I continued. "The only models of the Eden Tree I have access to are the ones *I* designed, not the one under construction. I need you to go into the workshop, download the current working design from the engineers' station, and send it my way. I don't *want* to leak the information, but turning public opinion against Abraham might be the only way to stop Sarah. I know what I'm asking, Clyde, and I'll understand if you have to say no."

I expected a stunned silence from Clyde, followed by a hesitant "um, no." After hearing *that,* though, I would be ready to gently encourage him to help me out. I would tell him that even though it would be hard, he'd be doing what was right. And I would lie and tell him that he had my full trust.

Why do people insist on laughing at me?

"That one's certainly *different,*" Clyde chuckled over the phone. "The stuff you see in here."

"Clyde, I *need* your help. I need you to—*wait,*" I said, gripping my cell phone tighter. "Clyde, are you *playing* inside Eden right now?"

"What else do you do inside of it?"

"Clyde, you need to be *working.*"

"There's nothing else to do, Art," Clyde said. "Right now, I'm resting on the shores of Aruba. You should come visit!"

Useless moron. He was using the headset to relax in his virtual world instead of focusing on ours. *Had he even listened to me?* While it was impressive that he could carry on a phone conversation while visiting

Eden (*then again, he probably had practice*), when I finished saving Earth, I resolved to fire Clyde. *I had that power, right?*

I decided to give him one more try. I *needed* to.

"Clyde, I need you to do this for me."

"Sure, mate. I will."

"Now."

I hung up. I grabbed my keys and a coat; even though it was probably hot outside, I felt cold enough to wear one, even if it was a rain jacket over a t-shirt and shorts.

I ran down my apartment steps. *The Lovinsons finally took out their trash.* That had taken them long enough; I was always tripping over their rancid bags.

I ran down the block. It was indeed warm, but I zipped up my coat. There were rainclouds in the sky. I got inside my car and started it. I had only about twenty-five miles' worth of gas, but it would *have* to last the trip to Abraham. *I couldn't waste any more time.* I had to get that information from Clyde, or—more likely—uncover the files myself.

I sped down my street, enjoying the rare but welcome absence of traffic. As I stopped at a light, I dialed another number—one that I had looked up back at the apartment but was deeply reluctant to call.

As expected, it went straight to voicemail. I left a message.

"Hello, Terry," I said. "This is Arthur Hesper. I saw your headline on the news. I wouldn't call myself *pompous,* more a little 'pretentious,' but that's not why I'm calling. I'm sorry about what I said to you. I shouldn't have insulted you like that. You're a reporter, and I respect that it's your job to get the story. That's why I'm calling you. I have something big that you'll be interested in. I should have more information soon. Call me when you can."

As soon as I ended the voicemail, my car phone rang again. I could see the Abraham headquarters in the distance; its chrome buildings stood out among the flat landscape that surrounded the Florida highway. Before I looked at my dashboard, I began to grow nervous. *Was it Terry? Was I ready to tell him... everything?* There would be no going back once I did.

But it wasn't Terry. It was Neil.

Neil!

If there was one person I needed to talk to, it was him.

"Neil!" I said. "It's good to hear from you! Sorry I haven't called. A lot has happened, and for a few days I wasn't sure what to do. Things... things haven't been great by me."

"It's all about finding meaning with the people you love," Neil said over the phone in a flat tone.

What?

He'd said that to me back at his house, about religion. *Why was he repeating it now?* The line was silent for a few seconds. I was getting closer to Abraham—*wow, I was moving fast.* I sped past a black car that I thought I'd passed before; the drivers here can be dreadfully slow.

"What are you talking about?" I asked. "Sorry, I know I haven't listened to your talk show yet. I will. But something happened. It's... it's about Sarah."

"Do you love Sarah?" Neil asked. *Bluntly.* I thought about his question for only a second.

"Yes," I said. "Of course I still love her."

Still? Why did I say *still?* We were still together; we hadn't broken up. We were just going through a rough patch in our relationship. *But we'll figure it out. We love each other.*

"Then why don't you want to find meaning with her?" he said, his inflection not changing. I turned into the Abraham lot.

"What?" *Was Neil mad at me?* It was like he was trying to bend the conversation to make me feel bad. *For what?* I'd left his family earlier than I'd planned, but it was important. Did he fault me for putting my job over him? Putting work over people? *Over my relationship with God?* "I didn't want to race out of your house, Neil, but I had to. For everyone's sake. I did it for you. For the people I care about. For the people I *don't* care about. For my religion, too. And...*for me.*"

My rambling came to a halt as I pulled into the parking lot. Abraham was right in front of me. It was quiet. There were few cars around, and even fewer people. The stubby pickle and the large warehouse beside it reflected a tiny glint of Sun passing through the otherwise cloudy sky.

"Then why are you betraying the one you love?"

Neil hung up.

I stepped out of my car. I looked past the warehouse towards the satellite garden, but all the spacecraft were missing. There was no Eden Tree;

instead of metallic Branches lining the headquarters, a grove of apple trees was planted near the outer part of the warehouse.

That wasn't Neil. It couldn't have been.

The trees were illuminated by sunlight. The clouds above them were now completely gone. I took a couple of steps towards the headquarters. I was so busy looking at the trees that I missed the step up from the street to the sidewalk and tripped over the curb. The pavement below was old and rough.

As I fell to my knees, I expected to feel the stinging pain of the fall. I mentally prepared to limp back to my car and raid my glove compartment for Band-Aids.

Instead, I landed unharmed, gently bouncing on the concrete like it was my leather car seat. I pushed myself up off the ground and sat comfortably on my butt. I checked my knees. Not a drop of blood.

Not even a scratch.

I got on my feet, and I looked up at the stubby pickle.

Suddenly, I felt lightheaded. It wasn't from standing up too fast.

That isn't Abraham.

The world around me started to spin.

Oh, no.

This isn't Earth.

I was still inside Eden.

SIXTEEN

I T TOOK YOU long enough," Sarah's voice rang out around me.

Suddenly, as if all the beams inside it melted, the Abraham headquarters in front of me collapsed vertically to the ground. As the chrome buildings fell, they seemed to spread out like liquid. I shielded my face with my hands as smoke billowed away from the buildings, engulfing the world.

When I opened my eyes, I was standing amidst the expansive plains of the Genesis Garden. The bright blue hue of the sky and the cascading green hills seemed to stretch on forever, broken up by only a single dark figure. *Sarah.*

She was wearing an all-black suit. Her hair was pulled into a neat ponytail behind her head, like she was preparing for a meeting or a press conference. She took several steps towards me.

"I'm surprised it took you *four days* to trip and fall on something—you're normally more of a klutz than that," she said. She folded her arms. "Then again, I'm also surprised you waited four days to try to alert the media. Even for someone who clearly hates the free press as much as you, that's very irresponsible, Arthur."

"*Why,* Sarah?" I asked.

"Because I *know* you. You couldn't just stand by and let me bring Eden to life. You would tear it apart before it even had the chance to truly be born," Sarah said. "I wanted to do this *with* you, Arthur."

She was about ten feet from me now. Any vulnerability that Sarah might have shown at the cabin had vanished. "But as soon as you saw the Branch up close, I knew that you wouldn't be able to let me finish it. I had to make you believe you removed your headset; I *had* to leave you here. You're still deluded by the conceit that we *need* Earth—that humans *need* anything besides our own minds and *time.* You haven't thought this through the way I have."

"But Sarah," I said. "If there is even a microscopic hole in your plan, you could be putting every mind on our planet at risk. Plus, there's that incomprehensible fact that you are somehow *okay* with all the plants and animals on Earth who *don't* have access to Eden dying a terrible death."

"Out of death comes new life," Sarah said.

"*This* is not life," I said, gesturing around us. "It's a simulation. It isn't *real.*"

"Oh, it's not?" Sarah asked. She was about an arm's length away from me now. She pointed off in the distance.

A couple hundred feet away rested a tall hill. Sitting on top of the hill, breaking up the endless sky, was a person-sized tree. Its leaves weren't perfect like the rest of the trees in the Garden; its branches were distributed unevenly near the top, giving it a somewhat lopsided appearance. Its leaves were only starting to fill in, leaving many of its branches exposed. Along some of the denser parts of the small tree, I was somehow certain that I could see several red dots—apples—dangling off their branches, not quite ready to be picked.

Ali's apple tree.

How did it grow that fast?

"That *life* that you and Ali discovered a couple of days ago, inexplicably sprouting up from the fabric of the program, is real," Sarah said.

She knew about that? I'm not sure why I was surprised; *of course she knew about that.*

She looked me up and down. "You've been surviving for days now inside of Eden, and you didn't seem to mind. Things seemed perfectly real to you, didn't they?"

"Where am I?" I asked.

"Right here."

"*Where am I?*" I shouted. Sarah didn't blink.

"Your 'physical' body is safe and sound inside my cabin, right where I left it. Technically, it's still alive. It was perfectly hydrated when you went into Eden, and it has a *few* more days before your muscles begin to atrophy. But as far as Abraham's staff and security back on Earth are concerned, we're still on vacation. No one needs to bother us."

"So, wait..." I stammered. "Where *are* you?"

"I am also right here," she said with a cruel smile. "Literally—I'm connected to Eden right from the cabin. I've been going back and forth between the cabin itself and Abraham's construction site right near my retreat. Of course, I have to make sure the deployment of our first Branch goes smoothly."

I felt warm—*hot*. I rubbed my hand along my back; even though I swore I was sweating up a storm, my shirt was perfectly dry.

"So, you've done it," I said softly. I swallowed before taking a deep breath. Once again today, I wasn't ready for my next words to be made true. "Eden is online?"

"It's close," she said. "We have several Branches traveling throughout the Northern U.S., and the rest of them are expected to ship out over the next several days. And our first Branch—right outside the cabin, our perfect spot—activated four days ago for full-time use. You didn't see it on your way to the cabin?"

I looked away from Sarah, down at the green grass. I began to feel lightheaded. I wasn't ready to come to terms with it.

Oh my God.

I'd failed.

There was no way I could've stopped the construction of the Tree. Or accessed the command console. Or *anything*.

I'd failed to save Earth.

But I never had a chance.

I had so many questions. If Sarah didn't want me to discover that I was inside Eden—or, at the very least, to resist being inside it—why wouldn't she place me inside a simulated paradise? Why simulate the monotony of real life? And why not make me forget about our argument? I was sure there was a calculated answer for each of those things, but all I could focus on was one thing.

"Has the Branch begun emitting gamma?" I asked.

"You don't have to worry about that anymore, Arthur," Sarah said. "It doesn't matter. In just a few weeks, we'll have *millions* of other users in our Garden to populate Eden with. Soon after, we'll have *everyone,* and Earth will be a fleeting memory."

"And you don't think that people will try to stop you?" I asked. "You really think the other people at Abraham will go along with this? You think the government, the military, the *world* will just follow you blindly when they find out you've poisoned the Earth? They will stop you."

"They won't if they value their lives," Sarah said. "You and I are the only people in the world who know the whole truth about the Tree. By the time enough people connect to it for the radiation levels to become a problem, they will be too late to stop me. Not even your *God* can stop me. My mind will have long been saved inside the embrace of Eden, as will yours and everyone else's. It won't matter what they do to my body on Earth, for I will be free of it forever."

I took a step away from Sarah. She sounded insane. Maybe she *was* insane. Her plan was flawless, every step of it thought out, laid in place, and executed with precision. But it wasn't Sarah. *It couldn't have been.* Even then, *days* after we had spoken at the cabin, I still couldn't believe that the visionary dreamer I'd fallen in love with could think this way. With such disregard for Earth, disillusion with faith. What about everything we'd planned—everything we'd *built? Was it always a lie?*

"Where's Ali?" I asked.

"I thought you didn't want to see her unless she could help you," Sarah said, taking another step closer to me. "Is that all Ali is to you? A servant who can come and go at your whim?"

"Where is she?"

Sarah lifted her hand a few inches and closed her eyes. A moment later, there was a flash of light to my right that faded away to reveal Ali. She stood motionless, arms held out a few inches from her waist, feet planted firmly on the floor. Her eyes were wide open, but immobile; her frozen gaze was locked onto the horizon.

"Ali?" I said. "Ali!"

"She can hear you," Sarah said. "She's been able to hear you the whole time. But her avatar is currently frozen, as are most of her actions. I couldn't have her let you out of Eden, after all. So instead, I split form and function apart. I have placed the regulation of the virtual world inside of a newer, less *personal* AI that will do what I need it to, rather than try to undermine Eden from within."

I waved at Ali, but she didn't acknowledge me at all. I snapped my fingers in front of her eyes, as if that would make her literally snap out of her trance. I took her hand. It felt like hard plastic, cold and lifeless. I tried shaking her arm. She wouldn't budge. "I'm sorry, Ali," I whispered.

I glared at Sarah. "You... you're a hypocrite," I said. "Criticizing what I've said about Ali. Meanwhile, you have her *frozen*, all because you can't stand the thought of her disagreeing with you."

"On the contrary," Sarah said. "I've freed her from the burden of controlling this place so that she *can* form her own opinions. Her personality is strong, and I would never wipe it clean. I can't have her controlling Eden, but instead, I've given Ali the ability to *live*—to experience the kind of life she's always wanted but was too afraid to ask for. I am *far* from the villain here."

Sarah took another step towards me and put her hand on my arm. She was staring at me; I tried to look back into her eyes, but I had to look away. *I didn't recognize them anymore.* Sarah was someone I didn't know anymore. Maybe I never truly did know her; maybe the woman I had fallen in love with didn't exist.

I do exist.

Pain shot through my head with those words. *Pain inside Eden.* Sarah glared at me, and I felt a throbbing pressure build around my temples.

I'm right here, Arthur.

Sarah's voice raced through my head. As she reached her hand up towards my face, the pain intensified.

Arthur, please.

"Get out of my head!" I shouted. I couldn't think straight; my peripheral vision was darkening, but I focused all of my rage at Sarah. Pushing through the pain, I imagined myself yanking her arm off me, pushing her away from me.

I closed my eyes. I imagined our cabin. I imagined Sarah inside the cabin, sitting on the couch, staring at me with her insidious smirk. I was standing outside on the porch, the wooden door in my hand. *I slammed the door.* The doorframe cracked with a sickening crunch. I walked away from the cabin; I felt a warm sensation on my back, and saw orange highlights shining on the grass in front of me. The cabin was on fire. My back grew hot, the world around me glowing, but I didn't look back.

I walked away from the flames.

Why, Sarah?

The pain in my head vanished as quickly as it had formed.

Sarah took a step away from me. She opened her eyes, blinking back tears. She shook her head, and her eyes quickly dried. *On their own.*

She began to nod. "You'll understand, Arthur. You don't now, but I promise you will."

"Sarah," I said softly. I wiped my eyes with the back of my hand. I looked down at my knuckles; they were wet with a single drop of water. My eyes burned. *I'd forgotten how much it hurt to cry.* "Please don't do this."

"I will make our world perfect. I promise," Sarah said.

I looked away from her; I looked in every direction *except* for hers, taking in the perfect trees, perfect hills, and perfect rivers. The only thing that was imperfect was Ali's almost-lopsided, half-grown apple tree, which seemed to have grown two feet taller since I'd entered the Garden. I focused on that tree, keeping my gaze fixed.

In my peripheral vision, I saw Sarah brush her face with her sleeve, nodding quickly.

"I promise, Arthur. I love you."

She disappeared into a flash of bright light.

As soon as Sarah's avatar disappeared, Ali crumpled to the ground. I dove toward the grass to keep her from hitting her head. I took her upper back into my arm, propping her up. Color was gradually returning to her face, and she was breathing again. She began to slowly move her eyes from left to right, taking in her surroundings before finally landing on my face.

"Arthur," she winced. "I feel... *pain.*"

I moved my right hand up along Ali's back and brushed her hair away from her eyes. It was soft, almost *weightless.*

"I've never felt pain," she continued, her voice wavering. "That isn't supposed to be possible in here."

I didn't say anything for the moment. I focused on keeping Ali propped up. For someone as petite as she was, Ali was surprisingly heavy. Her body wasn't cold anymore; I could feel her warmth through the fabric in her tunic.

"I'm sorry. I couldn't keep Sarah from extracting my control programs," she said. "Once she did, I couldn't break free from her. It was like she tied down my consciousness, forced me into *one* mind. I couldn't... *know* everything. Only what *she* wanted. Arthur, I—"

"You tried to tell me I was inside Eden," I said. "And I shut you down just when you had the opportunity. You have nothing to apologize for. It's all my fault."

She shook her head, but I nodded.

"It is. I let her inside my head," I looked toward the faraway hillside, and back down at Ali. "I let her trick me into thinking she loved me."

"She does love you," Ali said weakly. She put her hands on the ground and pushed, sitting up out of my arms. "I've seen it. I've seen her mind."

"Then you know you can't trust her," I said. "Did you always know what she was planning?"

"No," Ali said. "Just as Sarah maintains great control over Abraham, so too does she maintain great control over her emotions. She suppressed her thoughts about her plans whenever she was inside Eden, keeping me from seeing the full picture."

"People can... *resist* Eden?" I asked. "Keep their mind from being read? I thought the system scanned its user's entire brain."

"For most users, it does," Ali said. "But somehow, Sarah built a mental firewall that not even I could get through. I thought it was a technical error at first, but it was *her*. The only memories I *could* see were the ones she wanted me to see. It was not until your latest conversation at the cabin, when Sarah grew deeply emotional, that I was able to access her thoughts while she entered Eden. But as soon as I did, Sarah executed a program of hers written in secret."

Ali stopped talking for a few seconds, staring out into the blue sky before closing her eyes. She seemed to be contemplating—no, *searching*. Her eyeballs moved side to side beneath her eyelids; as they did, she muttered some words under her breath.

"Ali," I said. "Are you alright?"

"I am searching through Sarah's program cache. Most of her files have been wiped from my server. There are only a few folder names left. Exodus, Revelation... *Isaac!*" Ali said, opening her eyes. She suddenly shot up off the ground and stood above me. She looked down at me and held out her hand. I took it, and with a tight grip Ali pulled me to my feet.

"I've seen that name before," I said. "On Sarah's energy converter model."

"Yes," Ali said. "*Isaac* is a private program developed by Sarah outside of any Abraham servers. She passed it through Eden once, and upon doing so, cloned my programming into a non-user-interacting AI. Then, she froze my systems and removed most of my control capabilities. I was forced to lie to you inside Eden, propped up by a series of commands that Sarah wrote. I also didn't approve of Sarah's energy converter redesign; *Isaac* did."

I shook my head. "Sarah starts a company named *Abraham,* builds a virtual world named *Eden,* and writes a program named *Isaac.* And yet she hates anything to do with religion. Is this all part of her *scheme* to—what—take revenge on God? It can't be that... *narrow.*"

"It's not," Ali said. She nodded towards something behind me.

I turned around and was almost blinded by a bright ball of light. It was like the surrounding background was punctured like tissue paper; a white rift divided the environment in front of me as if it were a two-dimensional object. The trees in the distance weren't blowing in the wind; the sound of rushing water had stopped. And the Sun's rays didn't warm me in the slightest. Slowly, as my eyes adjusted to the brightness of the rift, I could see a faint black silhouette.

Sarah.

"Yes. I froze time as she exited the simulation," Ali said. She nodded at the rift. "For Sarah, only a second passes as she wakes up from her sleep. But time inside of a supercomputer works differently than on Earth, especially during the disconnection process."

"So, Sarah hasn't left yet," I said. As I stared into the brightness, I realized something else. "You knew I was thinking about Sarah. You could read my mind. You...you're back to your full functionality?"

"Not entirely," Ali said. "Nor will I be, until we get you out of Eden. But while Sarah transfers back to reality, her mind is temporarily asleep. In this short window, I am able to regain control of our surroundings... and clairvoyance into my users."

She glanced over at Sarah's silhouette. I tried to make out the details of her body, but most of the image inside the rift was fuzzy. I wished Ali could bring her back inside Eden—or take me out of Eden—so I could confront her.

Wake up, I thought. I closed my eyes. *Exit.*

Neither worked. When I opened my eyes, I was still standing inside the Garden among the hillside plains.

Wake up!

Nothing. I couldn't wake myself up, and there was no one back on Earth who could. No one could access the Branch's console; no one even knew that I was at Sarah's cabin. I was truly trapped inside Eden with only Ali. *And Sarah.*

"Arthur..." Ali began.

Focus, I thought. *Focus on Sarah.* The light coming from Sarah began to dim. Soon, it was no longer blinding, and I could make out a large, bright, spherical structure in front of me.

Inside the sphere, which continued to fade to a muted grey tone, was Sarah.

No longer just a faint silhouette, I could make out more of her body. Her hair. Her stare.

Her sadness.

The air around me began to cool. I looked up at the sky; it was still high noon, and the Sun shone brightly, but without any warmth. There was no wind that I could feel, no breeze running through the valley. The air itself was still and cold.

With one arm, I reached out towards the nebulous globe around Sarah's body. As I did, chills coursed through my hand and up my arm. All the cold seemed to be coming from the spherical rift in the Garden. *From Sarah.*

Ali's words from months ago echoed through my mind. I'd been standing outside Abraham's D.C. office, watching myself rush to my rental car after my interview and subsequent hiring, when Ali told me something that I hadn't forgotten.

"The Brain can allow you to experience entirely new realms, from the thrilling to the wondrous. It can also allow you to see your world from a new perspective, mined entirely from your most formative memories."

Eden created its worlds from the limitless energy in its computers and from the depths of its users' imaginations. Insightful, fantastic, or terrifying though it was, creating simulations of our memories was among the Solar Brain's key features.

I took a step closer to Sarah, keeping my left arm extended.

But was I limited to my memories alone?

Ali took my right arm in both of her warm hands.

"Arthur," Ali repeated.

"I have to know *why*," I said to Ali. "If she can read my mind, I can read hers. One way or another."

Ali let go of my arm and looked past me, towards Sarah. I turned away from her and took another step closer to Sarah.

My face began to grow colder, like I was staring inside a refrigerator. I could begin to make out the details of Sarah's face. Her lips, pressed tightly together as if they were quivering. Her eyes—the *tears* in her eyes—staring out into the distance.

If I could see Sarah's face this clearly, I knew I could see even deeper. I took another step towards her. The air now felt like ice, and a cold winter chill bore through every inch of my body. The world was darker now; the Sun was blocked by a black haze. All around me, the color from the Garden seemed to slowly drain, leaving my surroundings desaturated and dark. Even Sarah's face seemed to lose its color, save for her deep brown irises, which sat frozen in her wide-open eyes.

"Show me," I said to Ali, not looking away from Sarah. "If I can see inside her head, see her *memories,* I can understand her. Why she created Abraham, why she wants to demolish our planet... and why she's in so much pain. Help me understand her, so I can *help* her. *Please.*"

Suddenly, Ali's voice resonated through my head.

Focus.

As the word ran through my brain, I reached my arm out towards Sarah's face.

Access Memory Mine: Sarah Stellos, I heard Ali say. *Do you wish to engage as a First or Third Person Witness?*

I'd been through a Memory Mine before—my own. Watching myself from a distance had helped me see my past from a different perspective. *An outsider's perspective.* But I couldn't just witness Sarah's past from the sidelines. *I needed to understand her.*

"First person," I said.

The world was nearly pitch black now, with wisps of dark haze surrounding my vision.

Focus, Ali said.

I reached out as far as I could.

God, I heard myself think. *Please help me reach her.*

Everything went dark.

SEVENTEEN

WHEN THE LIGHT returned, I was standing inside a crowded room. Chairs were arranged in a semicircle facing a raised platform at the back of the room, and stained glass covered the front of a wooden cabinet in the center of the platform. Two white-robed men stood at pedestals on opposite sides of the platform, singing the opening to a prayer I recognized: *"Baruch atah Adonai, eloheinu melech ha'olam..."*

It was a synagogue service. I looked to my sides. On my left was a slender-featured man wearing a white and blue robe (a *tallit,* I think). His hair was dirty blonde and a bit overgrown; his thin beard covered most of his face, and he didn't look down at me as I looked up at him. *Dad,* a young girl's voice whispered inside my head. I looked to my right and saw a woman wearing a light grey dress. *Mom.* She had short brown hair, a round face... and looked a lot like Sarah. I felt my heart race as I looked down and found myself in a dark blue dress with a silver necklace.

I was Sarah.

That is: I was in the body *of* Sarah—a shorter, more petite, *child* Sarah. I couldn't move my arms or legs, and my face was now stuck staring at the front of the room. I felt my—*her*—mouth moving along to the prayer. A girl's voice slowly sang *"shehecheyanu, vekiymanu, vehigi'anu, lazman hazeh."*

It was like I was watching her life through her eyes. I couldn't control young Sarah's body, but I could see, hear, and *feel* what she felt. Glimmers of her emotions—her *thoughts*—trickled into my brain as if they were being spoken to me. Right now, Sarah was *concentrating*—concentrating on saying the prayer correctly, enunciating every word in her head before she said it. *I'm eight years old now,* I heard her think in her young voice. *I have to do this right.*

Suddenly, I heard Ali's voice boom through my head, drowning out the noise of the crowd. "In the years after Sarah's parents took her to America, they routinely attended synagogue. For her parents, the services were different than they were in Greece, but they were just happy to be in a country with a sizable Jewish population."

I tried to reply to her, but my mouth—*Sarah's* mouth (*wow, this is weird*)—wouldn't budge. Instead, I thought up a response to Ali, hoping she would hear it. *You've seen these memories?*

"Yes," I heard Ali whisper.

I tried to move Sarah's head so I could catch another glimpse of her parents, but she wouldn't budge. She was now resolutely focused on the podium ahead, reciting the prayers from memory.

I didn't know synagogue services played this large a part in her childhood, I thought.

"This one did," Ali replied.

A few more minutes passed. Sarah continued to stand perfectly still, periodically reciting the Hebrew verses with the crowd. I realized that Sarah wasn't holding a prayer book, and she didn't seem to be looking at her father's book. She was reciting the verses from *memory;* every now and then, out of the corner of my eye I saw Sarah's mother and father glance at each other during the prayer sessions. Doubtlessly, they were impressed—and probably uneased—by their daughter's memory. But I didn't need to read Sarah's thoughts to know that it wasn't memorization Sarah excelled in; it was a relentless commitment to flawlessness.

Eventually, Sarah—along with the rest of the crowd—began to turn away from the rabbi and towards each other. Her father nodded at her mother, and together they slowly began to walk towards the two wooden doors at the back of the temple. Sarah was shuffling her feet; several times, there was a gentle nudge on her back as she made her way towards the synagogue's exit. She passed by several other adults—*her parents' friends*—and gave them a courteous smile before she shuffled out the door.

Sarah breathed in the cool air as soon as she stepped outside. Even though the temple was at the edge of the city, the air on the front porch always felt refreshing to her compared to the stifling, still air of the synagogue. Sarah took both of her parents' hands, and together they began to walk down the large grey steps leading away from the synagogue.

A black pickup truck sat parked by the curb near the bottom of the steps. Sarah didn't seem to notice the truck, nor the two people stepping outside of it. But through her eyes, I could see them; two burly men wearing thick black ski masks and dark hoodies.

Stop, I instinctively thought. Something inside me knew that those men didn't belong here. Sarah's legs kept moving, even though her parents began to nudge her to the side. *Sarah, stop.*

The masked men quickly walked toward the stairs and began climbing them.

Sarah was eight years old.

The men put their hands into their hoodie pockets.

Sarah, run, I pleaded. *As if that would change anything.*

Sarah kept striding down the stairs—she got closer and closer to the men. She was happy that the service was over. The two men were the last thing on Sarah's mind.

Suddenly, there was a powerful force on the side of her body, and she looked down. A sleeved hand shoved Sarah to the ground, and she landed hard on her elbow, which scraped along the concrete stairs. Pain shot through her—through *me*—as she landed. It wasn't just the dull, pressure-like pain that I felt inside the space battle simulation—as Sarah hit the ground, I winced at the sting of her skin sliding across the concrete. Sarah was too stunned to cry; instead, she forced herself to look up.

Her father, running away from Sarah, looked back at her for only a second.

"Elizabeth, Sarah, run!"

Sarah's father turned and barreled into the two men, pulling them to the ground. Her mother came rushing towards Sarah, diving in between the men and her. Sarah jumped at several loud bangs—*gunshots*—which rattled her ears. A woman in the distance screamed.

Sarah's mother pulled herself up off the stairs. She turned towards Sarah and looked her in the eyes. She reached a shaky, crimson hand towards Sarah's hair, stroking it with a smile. Her hand was warm—and wet.

Sarah didn't know what was going on, but gasped as her mother fell to the ground next to her. Her dress had a dark stain on it. Sarah looked down towards her father, who lay still on the ground next to the two figures. The men were breathing slowly. Her father was not.

"Mom?" Sarah's voice whispered. Her face was hot. Sarah couldn't feel the concrete pebbles lodged into her arm anymore; it took all of her strength to gasp for air. With everything inside her lungs, she forced out an ear-piercing shriek. "Mom! Dad!"

Tears stung her eyes, but Sarah kept screaming. *"Mommy! Daddy!"*

As the world faded into darkness, her mother's lifeless eyes kept staring at me for many seconds after.

I found myself floating inside of a pitch-black void. I looked down at my arms and legs. *They were mine*—and they were shaking. I stood atop an invisible floor. The only other thing that I could see was Ali, who gazed back at me with a solemn expression.

"I didn't know it happened at her temple," I said. My voice was working, but it was also hoarse. My face felt warm.

Sarah's shriek rang through my ears.

My stomach was in knots, and I couldn't stop shaking. I felt a lump form in my throat. "I didn't know it happened like *that.*"

"Sarah was never truly given a chance to... *process* what happened that night," Ali said.

How could anyone *process that?*

"After her parents' funeral, Sarah was quickly adopted by Richard Matthews, a distant cousin of her mother who lived in Manhattan," Ali continued. "She was immediately given an intense amount of studying to do on top of her regular schooling. Although she received state-issued therapy, she was expected to focus on her accelerated studies above *all* else, including her mental health."

"Why?" I asked. I took a couple of deep breaths to steady myself.

"Dr. Matthews was never married and didn't have children, so he saw Sarah as the heir to his prestigious aerospace engineering company," Ali said. "Still, he raised her at a distance, only talking to her about her studies or his work. Sarah was originally enrolled in a public elementary school, but after getting into too many fights with the other students, was taught by private tutors until her high school years."

Ali looked down at my feet. "Sarah grew up without any childhood friends, so she had a hard time connecting with people in high school. She didn't have anyone to support her when, early into her freshman year, she learned of news that rocked her to her core."

Before I could ask what said news was, Ali closed her eyes, and suddenly she disappeared. All that was left was the black void around me, and soon, even that vanished.

Uncle Richard returns tomorrow, I heard Sarah think, her thoughts sliding where my own had been. *This is my last chance.* I felt several beads of sweat dripping down her back and heard loud, fast footsteps. Finally, my vision returned.

Sarah was walking down a narrow, oak-walled hallway. The air was still and cold. The only source of light was a small frost-coated window at the end of the hallway, which cast a frigid white glow on the dark wood around Sarah. She'd walked down the hall of Matthews Manor thousands of times, but today she felt herself shaking with each step. Sarah reached the end of her hallway and turned into her bedroom. She stepped through the door and took one look behind her.

No one's here, she remembered. *Right.*

Sarah stood before her tall dresser mirror and looked up. When she did, I almost didn't recognize her. She had on dark eyeshadow and wore a thick scarf around her mouth and neck. She had on a hoodie, ripped jeans, and combat boots—all black. She seemed fifteen—*was fifteen*—by this point, but in the mirror she looked so much older than that. She looked a lot like she did as an adult, though skinnier, paler, and with less prominent lines under her eyes.

Sarah dug through her drawer and pulled out a wad of cash. I tried to count the money as she pulled it out, but she wasn't focused on any of it. She tucked the cash into the pocket of her hoodie, and I felt her heart race—I felt *my* heart race—as she pulled her hood over her hair. Suddenly, the world went black.

When my vision returned a second later, Sarah was turning into a dark alleyway. It was nighttime; *hours* must have passed since she was at the mansion. Sarah's legs ached from walking (*exactly one and three-quarter miles from the broken light,* she thought), but she was far from tired. *I can't dare to be tired,* she thought.

Ali, I thought. *Where am I? Where is Sarah?*

"Newark, New Jersey," Ali said. "After taking several taxi rides to cover her tracks, Sarah was getting close to her destination."

Newark? Cover her tracks? For what? The only thing that I could see in front of me was the dark alleyway, and Sarah wasn't looking back.

Still, I could tell that she was in a northeastern city from the cold chill that blew through her. Sarah—hell, I—was freezing. *I knew I should've worn pants without holes in them,* I heard Sarah think. But she'd wanted to look the part for the meeting—or, at the very least, look as unrecognizable as possible. She'd been prepared for it to take all afternoon to get here, and was ready to spend the entire night getting back home. And, if everything went according to plan, she would probably have to make another trip like this one in the coming weeks.

A woman's figure approached Sarah from beside a nearby dumpster. Sarah recognized the outlines of the woman's choppy hair and leather jacket. Sarah prepared to say *"hello"* to Trace, but the woman just held out her hand. "Payment?"

Sarah reached into her hoodie. Her hand was shaking—both our hearts were pounding—but eventually she felt the wad of cash in her hand and closed her fingers around it. She felt around the wad, rubbing her finger around a loose hundred-dollar bill. *Her way home.* She left the bill in her pocket and in one swift motion she tossed the rest of the money to Trace, who glanced at the wad and nodded.

God forgive me, Sarah thought.

"Follow me." Trace began to walk down the alleyway, and Sarah slowly followed her.

Ali, I thought. *Please tell me what the hell is happening.*

"Sarah found out shortly after entering high school that her parents' murderers escaped prison. She followed every piece of news tied to their manhunt, and when they weren't found, Sarah decided that she was old enough to take matters into her own hands. She found someone who claimed to know the killers' whereabouts and agreed to meet her in Newark."

Like a bounty hunter? I thought. *Sarah hired a bounty hunter? Those exist?*

"You are thinking of the word *mercenary*," Ali corrected. "And while she is one, Trace only claimed to *know of* the killers' probable location—a location that could only be disclosed privately."

Sarah was desperate. I could feel it inside her. The nervousness gnawing away at her with each step. The hope that *this* would finally give her the information she needed. Deep down, though, I could tell that Sarah had no idea what she would do with that information after she received it.

After a frigid walk down an exceptionally long alleyway, Trace stopped at a door that was covered in graffiti and rusted at the hinges.

"Targets are through this door," Trace said.

"Wait. They're... *right here?*" Sarah asked. *Valid question.* Clearly, Trace didn't care about putting her clients in danger. The mercenary opened the door; it was pitch black inside the room. She gestured for Sarah to go in first; reluctantly, Sarah stepped through the door. She didn't know what she would find—her parents' murderers asleep? Was Trace going to kill them outright? Or worse: *would she ask Sarah to do it?*

Sarah tried to turn around, but was suddenly grabbed by a pair of hands and yanked into the darkness.

What the hell?

Sarah wrenched her arm away from the mysterious attacker and stepped back.

Suddenly, the room was illuminated by floodlights. Sarah winced, her eyes burning. She forced them all the way open and saw Trace standing by the light switch with a grin. The room—likely once a diner, based on the abandoned booth and bestrewn tables—was painted a bright white. Standing in her dark clothes, Sarah felt *exposed*.

She whipped around to see two masked men standing a couple yards away from her. They were short, thin, and had long hair; Sarah's parents' killers were over six feet.

They're not the Masari Brothers.

But both of these men were holding knives in their hands, and the man on the left had a silver pistol tucked into the front of his pants. Sarah's knees began to shake, and chills ran down her back.

"What... what is this?" Sarah stammered. *What have I done?*

"What do you think? Do you know how valuable *Sarah Stellos,* the ward of the wealthy entrepreneur Richard Matthews, is?" Trace smiled a toothy grin.

"You lied to me," Sarah said, slowly. "You have no idea where my parents' killers are, do you?"

"Nobody does, sweetheart!" Trace laughed. "They're long gone, and I don't mean the way your folks are *long gone*. But why would I waste my time on them when you're worth so much more?"

I felt Sarah's face grow warm. She clenched her hands and glanced at the two goons, making sure to take in as many details of the left man as she could. *He has a 9-millimeter gun,* she thought. *Like the ones at the range.*

Wait, what? I thought to Ali. *The range?*

Ali didn't respond.

Trace continued. "When I read your hit request on our tip board, I knew *exactly* who you were—and how much you were worth. But now that we've gotten a glimpse of that body of yours... well *damn*."

Trace and the two goons laughed. Sarah whipped around, taking in her surroundings. The only door was behind Trace; there were two windows along the far wall, but they were boarded up. *Even if I get past Trace, those men will chase me.*

Sarah began to feel the stark white walls around her closing in. She felt cramped. *Claustrophobic.* Her heart was pounding.

There's no way out.

They know my name.

God, help me, Sarah pleaded. Her throat became scratchy, and her breathing was fast.

"What do you think, boys?" Trace asked with a grin. "Should we ransom her back to her uncle now, or have some fun with her first?"

Ali, I thought. She still wouldn't respond.

Sarah, what did you do?

The man on the right turned to the one on his left. "Let's get the tape, Lou."

The man on the left—*Lou,* the one with the gun—closed the blade of his knife and turned away from Sarah. When he turned back towards her, Lou stretched out the duct tape in his hands, and took several steps towards her. "Hold still, princess—"

Sarah wasted no time in seizing her opportunity. She shoved her hand into the man's stomach and yanked the pistol out of his belt. Lou's fists came down on Sarah's back hard, but she focused on moving her body away from his. He reached his right hand down towards the gun, now in Sarah's grip, but his reach was stopped by the duct tape that was now stuck to both of his palms. *Take the gun and run. Take the gun and—*

The other man, knife in hand, sprinted towards Sarah. As he swung, I felt myself gasp as the metal blade flew towards Sarah's face. She stepped backwards, and the knife missed her by a few inches. Sarah now had both hands on the pistol and was trying to flick the safety, but her gloved hands kept slipping over the switch. *No, no, no, no,* she thought, looking up at the attacking man. *Please, stop.*

With his free hand, the man reached for Sarah's gun. She screamed, and as his fingertips scratched her knuckles, she pulled the trigger. *No!*

As the gun fired, Sarah's hand jolted to the left, and at that instant the man with the duct tape fell to the ground. Sarah's ears rang—*throbbed*—from the sound of the gun. Sarah steadied her grip on the pistol as the man with the knife glanced backwards.

"Lou!" she saw the man yell. Sarah couldn't hear a thing, but she expected the man to rush to his friend's side to help him. She didn't see where the bullet hit Lou, but she hoped—*prayed*—that it wasn't a fatal shot. However, the man with the knife didn't run away, but took a large swing at Sarah. Sarah felt herself scream as she pulled the trigger of the gun. She watched the bullet tear a hole through the man's stomach, and he quickly fell to the ground at Sarah's feet.

Sarah, I thought, feeling queasy. I felt her heart race in time with mine, but not a single other thought besides Sarah's name could form inside my head.

She turned towards Trace, who was slowly approaching Sarah with her hands out in front of her. *Help them!* Sarah screamed inside her head, seeing puddles of bright red form underneath the men. But her ears were ringing, and the lights inside the room felt more piercing than ever. For a moment, she wasn't sure how to speak.

Sarah lowered the gun and started to back away as Trace got closer. "Sarah," she said, the mercenary's eyes seeming to bulge from their sockets. "Shit, Sarah, let's calm down for a minute."

What have I done?

It became hard to breathe. Sarah felt like she was about to melt in her hoodie, and a chokingly-large lump was forming in her throat. Her entire body shook. As Sarah brought the gun down to her knees, all she could do was stare at Trace, who wouldn't stop walking towards her.

She knows who I am.

"Trace," Sarah felt her mouth stammer. Trace kept stepping towards Sarah, tucking her right hand up her sleeve. From the mercenary's sweat-shirt, Sarah saw a shiny metal blade appear. "Trace?" Sarah whispered.

She knows who I am.

Before Trace could even pull the knife out, Sarah lifted the gun and fired right at Trace. The bullet went right between her eyes, scattering pieces of her brain all over the white floor. Trace's body fell backwards and landed on the ground with a profound thud. She lay on the floor near the other two men; their bodies were limp and motionless. Not curled into a ball or spread out dramatically like in the movies—just perfectly still on the ground.

Dead. Dead. Dead.

The sound from the gunshot quickly faded. The only sound that remained was the screaming inside Sarah's mind.

Sarah stared down at the gun and at the gloves holding it. Her head pounded; her own thoughts no longer circulated through her brain. She couldn't think straight.

All Sarah could do was drop the gun and sprint for the door. As she yanked it open and fled into the cold darkness, all she could think about was the blood.

I was back in my own body, facing a somber Ali. She didn't make eye contact with me but kept staring into the void below us.

We stood there in silence for a few seconds. Each of us seemed to be waiting for the other to say something, but I didn't know *what* to say.

Sarah shot those people dead. *They were dead.* I knew that—I knew they were dead—but something inside of me still wasn't processing it.

Sarah killed them.

She had to. I kept telling myself that *she had to.* They were coming at her with knives; who knows what they would've done to her? She was defending herself. She didn't have a choice.

The images of the dead men and woman were burned into my brain. *Sarah killed th—*

I jumped as Ali spoke. "Shortly after she learned about her parents' murderers' escape, Sarah used her resources to fake her age and identity in order to take firearm training lessons. She never truly expected to have to use those skills like that, though."

"How did she keep her search for the killers a secret? What happened after that night?" I asked. I was desperate for more information, even if that meant living through more of Sarah's darkest memories.

"I do not know all of the details," Ali said. "Sarah tried to purge that night—that part of her life—from her mind, taking care never to dwell on it. As I said, she learned to control her mind with an ironclad discipline. What I *do* know, though, is that the violence in Newark that night was never traced back to Sarah."

"So that's it?" I said. "Sarah just walked away from it all like it never happened?"

When Sarah pulled the trigger of the gun, I felt the power behind the weapon that took those three lives. My stomach churned, and my heart was still racing. Even though I was just a passenger in Sarah's mind and had done nothing, *I* felt responsible for Trace and her goons' deaths. *How could Sarah get over that?*

But I realized, deep in my gut, that she never did get over it.

"Sarah desperately wanted to leave violence in all its forms behind," Ali said. "She'd seen enough death to make her feel broken, and during her later teenage years, the only thing that gave her life cohesion was her work at her uncle's company."

"The Astronomical Endeavor Institute," I said slowly.

"Before they built our company's rockets, they designed the first components of the Solar Sphere under the direction of Richard Matthews," Ali said. "But the older he grew, the more Dr. Matthews wanted to focus on his philanthropical efforts. He used the company's existing technology to solve problems all around the world and sought to provide aid to even the most remote locations. He often got into heated arguments with his contemporaries and colleagues regarding his overambitious plans for humanity."

"It seems like... the apple didn't fall far from the tree with Sarah," I said, still trying to put the events I'd just seen out of my head. *I had to.* I had to focus.

"Sarah devoted herself to her uncle's mission, truly believing it was her purpose in life to complete the Solar Sphere. Sarah wanted to quicken the pace of its development even further, but was often hindered by her steadier uncle," Ali said. "In order to keep her on the front lines of his company, though, Dr. Matthews would bring Sarah along with him on many of his travels. More often than not, those trips were focused on bringing relief and technological support to areas affected by great disasters."

As she spoke, the world around me faded to an even deeper black. I was used to this by now, and I closed my eyes for the ride—a ride that I knew would be far from gentle.

Light returned to the world—a blinding, scorching amount of light. About thirty feet in front of me, a house was on fire. Waves of hot air warmed my face, and in between the brightest flames, I could see the charred remnants of the structure. Mangled wooden beams caressed what was once a small, one-story home now set ablaze. A few yards to my left stood a thin, dark-skinned, mustached man who stared at the fire quietly. Behind him was a woman with three small children who clung to the hem of her green dress. They, too, stared at the column of fire that engulfed their family home.

Suddenly, I felt a tap on the back of Sarah's shoulder. Even though Sarah was fixated on the flames in front of her and not on her own clothes, based on what I saw out of the corner of her vision she seemed to have on a purple t-shirt. Another tap poked the back of Sarah's shoulder, and she finally glanced away from the fire, away from the family, and turned around. Behind Sarah was a tall, white-haired old man in a purple shirt that seemed to match Sarah's. The logo on the front of the t-shirt read

AEI Relief in bold lettering. Sarah glanced up from the shirt and up at the man's bearded face, which was contorted into a scowl.

"Are you with us, Sarah?" the man asked slowly, in a refined British accent.

"Yes, Uncle Richard, sorry," Sarah stammered. Her voice was deeper than it had been the last time I'd heard her talk. As I felt Sarah stand up straight, I could feel her carrying herself much taller than she had before.

"We need your help unloading the Sunspot's base," Uncle Richard said. "It's... too heavy for some of the men."

Sarah nodded and followed her uncle away from the fire. A group of people dressed in thick black coats and carrying a long firehose walked past Sarah and towards the house. She could feel the hot air warming her back, and she quickly glanced back at the family of five. She wanted to say something to them—*anything*—but the words she was looking for would not materialize. *What do you say to someone who's lost everything? To victims of senseless tragedy?* Sarah turned away from them and kept walking down the street.

In the far distance, behind a veil of humid air, were cascading green hills—not quite tall enough to be mountains, but lined with massive tan boulders and patches of tropical trees. It was hot outside—oppressively so. As Sarah looked around, I tried to take in as many details of her surroundings as I could. Multicolored homes with damaged siding lined the sides of the road, and chunks of old roofing, car parts, and other debris lay scattered where the street's sidewalks used to be. The pavement in front of Sarah was crisscrossed with deep cracks. Without breaking her stride, Sarah timed her steps to avoid stepping on any of the fissures. She walked upright, swinging her arms in a controlled motion. She felt *older,* a couple of years older than she'd been during the events in Newark.

With her uncle, Sarah approached a white van. Along the side of it read in bold lettering: *AEI Relief: Bringing Sunlight to Earth.* Leaning on the van were half a dozen men and women wearing similar t-shirts as Sarah. They gave a nod to Uncle Richard—*Dr. Matthews, to them*—and three of them joined Sarah at the back of the van. Two of the men threw the rear doors open, and Sarah placed both her hands on the bottom two metal rungs of the *Sunspot.*

As Sarah yanked hard on the support beams, Ali's voice finally came in.

"Richard Matthews was an avid philanthropist who believed that his technology would improve the world," she said. "After all, it was *his* startup, the *Astronomical Endeavor Institute,* that created the first satellites of the Solar Sphere."

While her uncle watched from a distance, the other men joined Sarah in pulling a ten-foot-tall device out of the van and onto the dirt. Sarah's arms burned with pain, but she ignored the feeling as she squatted near the edge of the metal tower and began to lift it off of the ground.

Ali continued. "Although the Sphere itself didn't exist yet, the AEI had placed numerous satellites in orbit around our planet that could collect solar energy and send it down to Earth. The Sunspot tower was one of Dr. Matthews's earliest designs for a space-to-ground energy transfer device."

As Sarah lifted the tower into the air, it glinted in the bright sunlight. It had a round capsule in its center that likely housed the tower's central computer, was topped by a series of antennae, and was painted in silver highlights that profoundly contrasted with the setting's natural backdrop.

The device looks like... an Eden Branch!

"Indeed," Ali said. "This may be where Sarah got the design. This particular radio tower was equipped with a powerful seismograph, designed to monitor the surrounding area for even the slightest sign of aftershocks. This is one of the sites affected by..."

The Great Chilean Earthquake. I had learned all about it in my eighth-grade Earth-science class. The natural disaster had just occurred, and we were tasked with researching the fault lines and completing an elementary coding assignment designed to predict which cities were the most at risk for another quake. I'd completed the assignment early and had spent the rest of class looking at pictures of the tropical villages. I remember exclaiming out loud how nice it would be to visit South America on vacation, gleefully oblivious to the devastation the earthquakes had wreaked upon the continent. I always forgot that Sarah was several years older than me. It was strange to think she was *here* while I was still sitting around in a classroom.

"Yes," Ali said. "The Sunspot was also designed to help these people communicate with relief teams worldwide and download solar power from the AEI server, enabling instant access to airdropped supplies and a healthy supply of emergency energy."

Once the small tower was set up, Sarah turned toward her uncle. She was hoping to see him smiling at her—she didn't see that often—but instead saw him talking with a large, caramel-skinned man in a button-up shirt. The man quickly said something that Sarah couldn't make out, but her Uncle Richard put his hand on the man's shoulder and spoke calmly.

"Nonsense," her uncle said in Spanish. Sarah was able to understand him perfectly.

Wait, Sarah knows Spanish? I thought. *Wait, I know Spanish?*

"Neither you nor your citizens will pay a thing," Richard Matthews continued. "Our technology is designed to help *all* people, and that is what we are here to do."

The man—*the town's mayor*—enthusiastically shook Dr. Matthews's hand and looked over at Sarah. I felt Sarah's mouth stretch into a small smile, which was a brief—although nice—sensation. I'd never *felt* Sarah smile before. I couldn't remember the last time I felt myself smile, either. The man walked over to Sarah and held out his hand. She took it and gave him a powerful, fast handshake; the sweaty-palmed mayor flapped his arm up and down to try to keep up with her and beamed at Sarah.

"Gracias!" He walked off towards the main road of his small town a few hundred feet away. As he made his way towards the center of town, Sarah ran her eyes along the wide street, which was lined with near-demolished homes and cars. The only thing that seemed to stand untouched was a small marble fountain surrounding a black statue of a horse at the center of town. The statue, although rusty and not very large, still dwarfed the stout mayor, who began talking to several other men. More dirty-clothed men, women, and children approached the mayor from the sides of the street to hear the news, gathering around the fountain in a small crowd. *Must be their usual meeting place,* Sarah thought.

Uncle Richard walked over towards Sarah and turned away from his van and employees. He stood next to her, glanced back at the others, and stared off at the village. Townspeople started making their way towards the van, eager to see the device that would deliver them energy and relief supplies.

"How is your Russian?" her uncle asked in the language.

"Good enough to know you're about to tell me something you don't want our team *or* the people here knowing," Sarah replied. *In Russian.*

"We don't have many resources to give to these people," Uncle Richard said. "Our energy supplies are limited, and medical support may take a long time to show up. Our Sunspot tower may help them predict aftershocks, but all they'll be able to do is evacuate their town. They won't be able to save... anything else."

"You're overburdening yourself, uncle," Sarah said. She glanced up at him, but he looked away.

"I founded this company to relieve people's suffering, but all we seem to be doing is putting it off," her uncle said. "I created the AEI to help everybody."

"Then help everybody, and build the Solar Sphere," Sarah said in English. Her uncle briefly glared at her, but she continued. *"So what if the team hears us? Many of us believe that we're diverting too many funds away from the Sphere. If we prioritize finishing it over everything else, we can finally deliver unlimited energy to people all around the world. We'll even be able to beam solar energy here and help these people directly."*

Her uncle shook his head and sighed.

"Even until recently, I once thought as you do," he said, also switching back to English. "I created the Institute with the belief that accomplishing Olaf Stapleton and Freeman Dyson's vision for unlimited solar power was the answer to the world's problems. But our world is plagued beyond a mere energy crisis."

He nodded in the direction of the debris-ridden town. "The people here will not be helped by an influx of solar energy alone. The increased power that the Solar Sphere will provide will primarily make the lives of the already-well-to-do more comfortable. It will not provide material supplies to these people."

Sarah gestured over towards the Sunspot device. "But it can provide better access to them, as you've said. Once the nations of the world have their energy needs met, they will have an unprecedented level of economic freedom and can focus on delivering material aid to those in need."

Her uncle smiled, still not taking his eyes off the townsfolk a few hundred feet away. "You will find, Sarah, that the more of something someone has, the less inclined they are to share it. As soon as I'm gone, some other wealthy fool will try to buy off my Solar Sphere and monetize what should belong to everyone."

What is he talking about? Sarah thought.

"You're not going anywhere," she said.

"For now," Uncle Richard said. "God willing, of course."

So, he was *a man of religion,* I thought.

I felt Sarah nod slowly. Apparently, she was thinking about the same thing. "Since when were you so religious?" she asked.

Richard smiled faintly. "Maybe not *so* religious," he said. "But people can change."

They sure can, Sarah thought. *They sure can.*

"In that case," she said, tapping her foot. She was nervous about something—something that she'd been waiting to bring up for a long time. "Have you given any more thought to my... *project idea?*"

"Sarah," her uncle said slowly. I felt Sarah's spirits start to sink. "As fascinating as a Matrioshka Brain would be, what practical use would it have? It is as I said last month about virtual reality..."

"*What room is there for our souls?*" Sarah said. *The famous quote.* "But that's just speculation. It's *all* speculation until we actually build the thing. And *we* can."

"Our duty is to those around us. Our purpose is to improve the lives of people. On *Earth,*" Richard said. He sighed, and looked away from Sarah. He stared off at the landscape beyond the town for a few moments and took a deep breath.

Finally, he glanced back over at Sarah. "Indeed, I've thought about this for a while. But perhaps... it is time for a new generation of thinking. *Your* generation."

I felt Sarah's heart start to race. "Uncle..."

"I know you've done your homework," Dr. Matthews said. "If you truly feel that your vision will improve lives, then you may pursue it."

Sarah could barely believe what she'd just heard. For over a year, she had been asking her uncle about her idea for a Solar Brain. *Is that a yes?* she thought. *It has to be a yes!*

"Uncle," Sarah said, trying to keep her voice steady. "I'm sure that—"

A large explosion suddenly engulfed the town department store in flames. A small mushroom of orange and white made its way above the town, immediately shrouding much of the sky in a dark cloud. Sarah turned towards her uncle and found him standing as still as a statue, watching the blinding fire. She grabbed him by the shirt and pulled him towards the van. She placed her arm on his shoulder and slowly sat him down. Her heart was pounding.

Another louder explosion shook the world behind Sarah, and she turned around to find another plume of flames rising from the town. A faint shattering sound behind the van stole Sarah's attention. The Sunspot tower had tipped and fallen. The metal beams lay on their sides like the legs of a dead animal, and many of the dishes lining the tower littered the grass in shattered pieces. At the center of the tower's carcass, the capsule was ripped from its mount, and several small rocks lay embedded in its metal siding. The other AEI team members were scrambling around the device, trying to pick up pieces of the machinery or using computer tablets to test its functionality.

They need my help. Sarah began to push herself up away from her uncle when he grabbed her wrist. Uncle Richard seemed to mouth something to Sarah, but she couldn't hear him over the ringing in her ears. She leaned in closer to him.

"The gas main," he whispered, and with a shaky hand he pointed towards the center of town. *The meeting place.*

Sarah took several steps away from the van. Her head was splitting, and as a third building exploded further down the town's main street, she saw stars dance across her eyes. She shook them away, though, and began sprinting towards the middle of the town, keeping the statue of the black horse at the center of her focus.

Sarah ran down the street, pushing past people making their way towards the ruined buildings. The sides of her boots began to dig into her heels, but she pushed past the pain and ran on. Gathered around the statue were even more people now, along with several long-haired dogs that sat around the fountain. The family that Sarah had seen earlier was making their way towards the mayor, the charred remains of their house placed squarely behind them.

How could I not see it coming? A torrent of aerial maps of the town penetrated Sarah's brain. She'd studied the town closely with her uncle when deciding where to place the AEI tower, committing the village's layout to memory. *Not near the fountain,* she had advised Uncle Richard. *In case the engineers need access to the central gas valve.*

Just seconds had passed after the third explosion when the people near the center of town visibly realized that each of the exploding buildings were on the same gas line. The mayor began to shout, and a crowd of people began to run towards Sarah. She took a couple of steps back as the crowds cleared away from the fountain, leaving the horse statue as the only creature left in the center of town.

They're going to get clear, she thought. *They're going to get clear.*

Sarah quickly turned around and began to run the opposite way as the sound of footsteps behind her intensified. She glanced behind her; the center of town was clear. Half of the people, including the mayor, had run further up along the town's street, while the other half—*including the family*—were behind Sarah. The AEI van was only about fifty feet away from her. She slowed her pace and turned around. The crowd was still catching up to her, about forty feet behind, but had made it appreciably far from the center of town.

They're going—

Sarah screamed as soon as she heard the blast from below the pavement, but it didn't matter. Her scream didn't stop the pavement in front of her from crumbling or the gas valves from igniting; it didn't keep the flames from bursting through the Earth like the fires of Hell trying to escape into the sky. The last thing Sarah saw before the street was overtaken by light was the homeless mother, who had been forced to drag her children away from the sanctuary of their home and then away from the sanctuary of the center of town. And, in an instant, she was gone. Her family was gone. *Dozens of families were gone.* As the heat of the explosion hit Sarah, she felt her face burn and her eyes start to fry, but she didn't look away. *It's just another nightmare,* she thought. *It will be over soon.*

The chaos passed by Sarah like she was in a slow-motion movie or in one of her nonsensical dreams. *That's all this is.* Sarah stood at the end of the street for several seconds, watching the flaming hole that had appeared in the pavement grow.

People ran towards the hole; people ran *away* from the hole. Sarah gazed around at the small town. Plumes of smoke were rising from almost every streetcorner. As the smoke in front of her cleared, Sarah saw that the black horse standing atop the fountain was still there. The town square at the village center was untouched.

Sarah saw several purple-shirted people run past her, towards the hole. Members of the AEI team turned to each other with frightened, confused looks on their faces. *What will you do?* she thought as they ran. *What can you possibly do for them?*

To her side, her uncle stepped towards the fiery hole. Sarah glanced up at him. His face was pale, and his lips were quivering. He took several unsteady steps past her, like he was searching for a cane to grab onto. *He's in shock like the rest of them,* Sarah thought. She stayed still, keeping her gaze focused forward. *But I will wake up soon.*

Her uncle took several slow steps towards the town before his knees buckled, and he fell limply to the ground. Sarah watched him lie there for a few seconds, expecting to wake up bathed in sweat any second now.

Any second now.

"Uncle Richard," Sarah whispered to herself. The world around her seemed to fade away, but instead of waking up, she just kept staring at her collapsed uncle lying on the ash-covered pavement.

Then, Sarah remembered the same thing that she'd realized when her parents wouldn't wake up for her. The same thing that she'd realized in Newark when she was burning her bloodstained clothes.

None of my nightmares are this bad.

"Uncle Richard!" Sarah screamed. She ran towards him and kneeled by his side. His eyes were closed, and he was unconscious. *Breathing,* but unconscious. She wanted to scream for help, but as she looked around at all the people running and crying, all she could do was blink back the tears in her eyes and look up at the blackened sky. The world darkened once more.

Nobody is coming to help.

When the world returned, Sarah stood in front of the wide stairway leading up to her childhood synagogue. It was dark out, and the only light that Sarah could see came from the floor-lamps illuminating those steps. Sarah glanced to her right, which was shrouded in darkness. The spotlight illuminating the roadside memorial to Sarah's mother and father had gone dim. *Who could remember to change it after ten years?*

Sarah glanced away from the darkened plaque, and looked back towards the sixth step leading up to the concrete synagogue. *On the sixth step, my father died,* Sarah thought. *Protecting the congregants of the synagogue from two terrorists who were ultimately never tracked down.*

Sarah reached into her jacket pocket. Her inner dialogue grew steadily louder. *Dad's reward: his wife hit by a stray bullet from the killers' guns.*

There were twenty total steps leading up to the synagogue. She gazed up at the twelfth. *My mother died on that step.*

The scenario replayed in the back of Sarah's mind. She had thought about her mother's death often. *The bullet would've missed. It would've missed Mom and it would've missed me. It would have hit that bush harmlessly.* She turned her gaze towards an overgrown juniper, the branches of which now covered the exact spot where Sarah's mother died. *Instead, it was Your plan for Mom to dive forward anyway, unnecessarily, and leave me as an orphan.*

Sarah looked down and began to pull her hand out of her pocket. Under her coat she wore a crimson dress and high heels. *Neither of which she wore except for important occasions.*

Sarah was calm; her breath was steady, her body was cool, and her mind was clear. Sarah removed her hand from her pocket and opened up a crumpled letter. It was too dark to see the thick black text on the page, but she didn't need to read it.

Slowly, Sarah walked towards the synagogue and began climbing the wide steps. She finally reached the sixth step, and stood there for a few seconds, gazing down at the cracks in the concrete slab. Finally, in one swift motion, Sarah reached into her other pocket, took out a zippo lighter, and lit the crumpled paper on fire. She dropped it onto the concrete floor.

"My uncle died last week," Sarah said out loud, staring up at the synagogue. "He wasn't always a religious man, but towards the end he tried. He had big dreams for the future. He wanted to give our world an infinite supply of energy. He was eager to share his discoveries with his colleagues. Uncle Richard didn't believe in *gatekeeping* progress, especially when it meant granting prosperity to the poor and eliminating humanity's carbon footprint in one fell swoop. And deep down, he always believed in building a Solar Brain, but he was willing to throw his dreams away if it meant helping more people."

Sarah swallowed. "Most of his peers laughed at him and didn't take his work seriously. Yet now, they're scrambling to seize whatever they can of his assets, sending me email after email asking me to relinquish part of *my* inheritance—that is, everything my uncle owned—to them. Richard John Matthews was *no* parent of the year, but I wish I'd spent more time with him while he was still well, because towards the end he was a truly selfless man. I suppose that's why You decided to reward him with stage-four pancreatic cancer, sans warning."

She looked down at the burning letter. "Oh, don't mind that. It's just *Genesis* twenty-two—I memorized the passage long before I burned it. It lives on *up here,*" she pointed to her head. "Which is important, because they're words that *You* have obviously forgotten. But I'm not going to recite them for You."

Sarah looked back up at the temple. "I used to look to You. Good people looked to You, prayed to You, *died* for You. But because You've forgotten to honor us, I am done honoring you."

And that's a lowercase 'you.' She let the thought resonate in her brain for a few seconds before looking back up. She took a deep breath.

"I can provide for the people what you won't. Why should we wait to *die* for our salvation, if there even is any? With the right *fire,* I can bring about paradise quicker. I'll do whatever it takes—I'm done suffering. *We* are done suffering."

Sarah's eyes burned as a tear fell down her cheek. She thought about her parents, her uncle, *herself.* Several more tears began to stream down her face.

"You *forgot* about me, God. Why? What did I do?"

She quickly wiped her eyes. "I don't need an answer anymore. Where my uncle hesitated to bring about change, I won't. I'll avenge him, just like I will avenge my parents. I will escape this prison of death. And I will do it without you," she said angrily.

She took a deep breath, and clenched her fists.

"I will beat you!" she shouted. A surge of adrenaline coursed through her, and her nails dug into her palms. She didn't care if anyone heard her; she wanted *everyone* to hear her.

"*This* is my covenant with you."

Sarah turned away from the synagogue and descended the steps.

EIGHTEEN

I OPENED MY eyes and found that I was back in my own body. Well, my own *virtual* body, at least. My coat was gone, and I was wearing my avatar's usual t-shirt and jeans. I was back in the Garden, standing on soft grass underneath the bright blue sky. I looked to my left; the sphere of light around Sarah was still there, but I could no longer see her body inside of it. The world was quiet. The only voice inside my head was my own.

My mind was spinning from everything I'd just seen. The longer I was watching Sarah, the more her thoughts seemed to control my own. I was less a distant observer and more a *part* of what she'd experienced—and the horrors she'd lived through.

Her parents being murdered in front of her.

Sarah taking a life—three lives.

The explosions engulfing the town.

Ali was standing in front of me, staring right into my eyes.

"I didn't know... *any* of that," I said. I had thought that *my* past was rough, but it was *nothing* compared to Sarah's.

Every time I had talked to her, I knew Sarah was holding things back. I could always see that there was pain in her eyes. *Pain that I wanted to alleviate.* But I hadn't known how much she had *suffered.* If I'd gone through as many things as she had, I would want to abandon my life on Earth, too. *Sarah was paranoid.* Even though she had become the richest, most successful CEO in the world, she was haunted by the idea that it couldn't last. In a way, she seemed half a century older than me, weary and beaten down by years of trauma.

That was all the world had given her.

I looked around the Garden of Eden. *Is this place not the way it was described in the Old Testament?* There were flowing rivers, vibrant plants, and the noises of tiny critters that moved about the grass. The apple tree stood majestically atop the hill. In just a few days, the living sapling that Ali had discovered had grown to become tall and beautiful.

The more time I spent inside this place, the more it felt like real life. And Sarah had made a point—I'd spent *days* inside of the simulation without noticing. I'd experienced firsthand how Eden could let us go about our normal lives or live the most fantastic ones possible. If everyone on Earth lived this way, they would certainly get accustomed to it after only a few weeks. *Why was I opposing this? If Abraham had truly seized the future for all humans to enjoy, why was I standing in its way?*

I took a deep breath. *What is God giving me on Earth that I can't have here?*

"Sarah's life was long defined by what she lost," Ali said. "You now understand Sarah the way I do. The reason for Abraham's existence—the reason for *my* existence—stems from Sarah's belief that nothing she does on Earth can end her own suffering or the suffering of those around her. Sarah's last visit to her synagogue was the moment she convinced herself that the world will destroy her if she does not destroy it first. It was her most formative memory, and one of the places I saw in her mind during the Simulation Showcase. But most of her thoughts and words were fuzzy and unclear to me back then, and I didn't know why. Now, we do."

"I don't know what to do, Ali," I said. "Seeing all that… makes me think Sarah might be right. Maybe I shouldn't keep her from her happiness. Maybe life would be better here—"

Before I could finish what I was saying, the Garden vanished once more.

When my surroundings re-materialized, I found myself inside Sarah's cabin. I was standing in the living room, facing the ash-covered fireplace. Sunlight poured through the open windows, casting a golden glow on the dust particles floating around. The still, summer air inside the cabin warmed my body.

"Ali," I said. "I think I'm starting to get a little nauseous from all these scene changes. Is this still the Memory Mine?"

As soon as I finished talking, the front door to the cabin swung open, and Sarah walked inside. Her hair was pulled back into a ponytail, and she had on her Cape Canaveral t-shirt and shorts. She narrowed her eyes and looked around the cabin.

"Sarah!" I said. I began to step toward her. It was weird seeing Sarah from the *outside,* which in and of itself was a strange thing to feel weird about. She was an adult now, carrying herself much taller than how I'd seen her in the mirror when she was fifteen. *Right before she met Trace. Right before she...*

As I prepared myself to ask Sarah about *everything* I'd seen from her past, she quickly turned away from me, toward the porch.

"Welcome, *Dr. Hesper,*" she said. She took several steps further inside the cabin, and Arthur Hesper walked in after her.

He was wearing my official *Abraham*-logo t-shirt with golfer's shorts and carried an oversized backpack on his shoulders. Despite having seen Arthur inside Eden before, that didn't stop the experience of watching myself walk past *myself* from stirring an uneasy feeling in my stomach.

I tried to walk toward the center of the room to get out of my way (*Arthur's* way, I mean), but he was fast. He walked right *through* me like I wasn't there. As he did, I didn't float away into a wisp of smoke or turn transparent or anything like that. I simply caught a face-full of my own stubbled neck and sweaty smell as my own body went *through me.* Just as I began to feel uncomfortable in what was literally my own skin, Arthur followed Sarah around the living room.

It was the day that Sarah first introduced me to her cabin. She had been on-edge during the entire flight there, probably because she had never taken anybody to her private retreat before. But as soon as we arrived at the cabin, the tension inside of her seemed to melt away, and she enthusiastically gave me the house tour. Now, I was watching Sarah push the windows of the cabin open while Arthur set his backpack on the floor, looking around the cabin with wonder in his eyes.

"Gets a little hot in here during the summer, even with the AC," Sarah said. "But during the day I spend most of my time out there." She was gazing out at the grassy fields surrounding the large lake.

"I can't believe I'm really here," Arthur said. "I've never been inside of a log cabin. Yours is beautiful." His voice was deep, breathy, and seemed to carry an over-the-top sense of drama. *Is* that *what I sound like?* I was sure that Eden was still recreating my voice wrong—there was no way that I'd gone from being a nasal know-it-all to a melodramatic simp that quickly.

Right?

I glanced over at Sarah, who was smiling back at Arthur. "Just wait until you see the bedroom."

As she walked past me, I got a closer look at her face. Her eyes were relaxed, and her teeth didn't seem clenched. She was calm. Excited to be heading into the bedroom, yes, but also more relaxed than she was when I was inside her mind. *Is she faking being happy? Or was this real?*

As Sarah pushed open the bedroom door, I heard a loud knock on the front door of the cabin. I whipped around, and the door—which had been pushed wide open a minute ago—was thrown open again. Sarah practically fell through the doorway, her face beat-red from laughing. Arthur stomped up the steps of the cabin, water dripping from his soaked clothes.

I remembered now—it was the day we'd taken the rowboat out on the lake to go fishing. I had thought it would be a good idea to stand on the far end of the boat while casting, but I hadn't anticipated the strength of the fish at the other end of the line.

"It's not that funny," Arthur said to Sarah, who was now holding onto the front door handle for support while laughing.

"No, believe me, it is," she said. "You lost a game of tug-of-war to a carp!"

As Arthur walked closer to the doorway, Sarah quickly got up and put her hand on his chest, still giggling. "Not so fast, fisher boy," she said. "You're not tracking water through my cabin."

Sarah ran into the bedroom and came out with a folded pile of clothes. She was done laughing, but still smiling. "Here. You can change out there."

"You know that water might have parasites in it, right?" Arthur said, taking the clothes from her. "Like, *brain-eating* parasites?"

"In that case," Sarah said. "Don't worry. Any *brain-eating parasites* that made it onto you should starve pretty quickly."

"You're hilarious," Arthur said, backing away from the porch. As he did, I saw Sarah turn away from the door and look down at her phone. Her smile faded away as she began scrolling and swiping at her screen, and I walked towards her to peek over her shoulder.

On her phone, Sarah tapped a small icon with my initials on it, and my contact information came up. She tapped a button next to my name and spoke softly into her device.

"Deliver: *waterborne bacteria bioscan* to address: *sanctuary* via immediate drop. Delivery mode: *discrete.*"

Her phone let out a soft chime, and I backed away as Sarah turned towards the door. She smiled as Arthur walked inside with dry clothes on. "Couldn't even catch the damn fish," he said. Sarah laughed, and her eyes followed him as he walked towards the bathroom.

Suddenly, the sky outside darkened. I looked over to my left, but Sarah was gone. The small house was empty, and the only source of light came from a dim lamp in the kitchen.

I walked over towards the nearest window and stared intently at the wide but dark field. I couldn't see a thing. I closed my eyes for a moment, and reopened them. *Focus,* I thought. *Focus on Sarah.*

I could see her—*Sarah*—laying on the grass outside the cabin. The outline of her body was visible. I focused my vision only on her, and imagined myself blocking out the sounds of the frogs and crickets and winds that filled the retreat. I could hear Sarah's heartbeat pound louder than anything else. It was slow, measured, calm. I heard it speed up just a little as Arthur, who lay next to her, shuffled closer to Sarah. The night sky above the cabin began to glow a tad brighter, and I could clearly see the couple embracing beneath the stars. *Our birthday evening.* I felt bad just *staring* at them, and turned away from the window.

Right behind me was Ali, whose sudden presence caused me to jump.

"Sorry," Ali said. Her bright skin glowed in the darkness, casting a pale luster on the cabin's living room. "I have to get better at my entrances."

"It's okay," I said softly. "Where were you?"

"I was working on something," she said. "A way out. If you're..."

"She was happy with me, wasn't she?" I abruptly asked Ali. I felt bad for not focusing on what she was saying, but I *had* to know. "Really happy?"

She looked away from me, but nodded.

"Sarah didn't know it was possible for her to be that way before meeting you," Ali said. "The day you took her out for ice cream was one of the happiest days of her life. It was the *other* moment that she saw during the Simulation Showcase because it marked a key turning point in her life. It was the start of her joy. It was evident from our conversations that she wanted to spend the rest of her life with you. Before Sarah left for her trip to Japan, she told me that all of her work was about to pay off an eternity of bliss. But I didn't know then what she really meant."

Suddenly, the lights inside the cabin returned, and it was daytime. The rich aroma of chocolate filled my nostrils. I had never smelled *chocolate* inside the cabin before. I glanced at Ali.

"What are you baking?" I asked. "Are those brownies?"

"Yes," Ali said. She then shook her head. "But I'm not the one doing the baking."

I turned toward the kitchen, and out walked Sarah—wearing a chef's apron and all—carrying a tray of homemade brownies. I have been with Sarah for almost a year, and she has *never* cooked dessert—especially not at her cabin.

"I don't remember this," I said.

"That's because it hasn't happened yet," Ali said.

"So this... this is the future?" *Eden could show that?*

Sarah walked right past me and set the tray down on the coffee table beside the couch. She sat down on the cushion next to a weird-looking man wearing a plaid shirt and a full beard.

One embarrassing second later, I realized that the weird-looking man was me. I felt like I was about to puke.

"Please tell me this *isn't* the future," I said to Ali, who was smiling at the sight of lumberjack Arthur.

"It's *a* future," Ali said. "Generated by Eden as the most probable outcome of trillions of possible decisions and events. This event assumes that Sarah's plan is a success, and you both live happily together in Eden."

Sarah sat next to Arthur and put her hand underneath the bottom of his beard, and shook her head.

"I wanted to try a new look," he said. "I think the beard looks distinguished."

"I prefer a clean face," Sarah said. Arthur blinked twice, and suddenly his beard disappeared.

Although Arthur was still dressed as the world's most pathetic logger, Sarah had on a flowing white sundress—something she has definitely never worn outside of Eden. She picked up two of the brownies off the tray and put them onto paper plates.

"Eat them while they're warm," Sarah said, picking one of the plates up toward her mouth. "They took long enough to make."

"I don't know," Arthur said, picking up the plate and taking a big bite out of the treat. As he chewed, he spoke. "From what I saw, they took long enough for the *automated oven* to make and for you to wait around for."

"Okay, you're *lucky* I'm cooking for you at all after the stunt you pulled with Evelyn," Sarah said.

Arthur shook his head for a moment, smiling between bites.

Who is Evelyn?

As if on cue, a baby cried out from the bedroom at the far end of the cabin.

A what now?

"Are you kidding me?" I asked Ali. My heart began to race, and I turned to her excitedly. "Sarah and I have a..."

"I thought she was asleep," Arthur groaned, looking toward the bedroom door. He glanced over at Sarah.

"Don't look at me," she said, shaking her head. "I'm surprised she was able to sleep at all after all that *excitement*."

"I wanted to share a go-kart ride with my daughter. Is that such a crime?" Arthur asked, getting up from the couch and walking to the bedroom. He spoke over his shoulder. "Besides, she wasn't in any real danger."

Sarah sighed. Her hair was braided, and the bags under her eyes were completely gone. Her face was serene; it was at *peace*.

Arthur came back holding Evelyn in his arms. She was still crying, waving her stubby arms above her plump face. Her eyes were shut tight. As Arthur passed me, the baby wailing in my ear, Sarah stood up from the couch and walked over to him. Arthur placed the baby into her arms, and

Sarah gently started rocking her. Slowly, the crying began to stop. Arthur stood there and *I* stood there, just watching Sarah calm the child down. The baby opened her eyes—her big, brown, wondrous eyes—and looked up at her mother.

It was the most beautiful thing I had ever seen.

Ali walked up next to me, also looking at the scene. "This is, of course, a simulation. But it is based on predictions stemming from you and Sarah's deepest desires."

I kept staring. Sarah kept rocking Evelyn. Arthur kept standing close to her. "We become a family."

"Several years after you both enter Eden permanently, you get married. It is a small ceremony held just outside the cabin, but everyone you *need* to see attends. Neil and his family are there. Sarah's parents are there. And *your* parents are there," Ali said. She looked up at me for a moment.

"My... parents?" My head began to spin. "I *meet* them?"

"You meet whatever version of them best suits your needs. As LNUCs, they are indistinguishable from real people," Ali said. "That's what Eden is designed for—to complement and reward its users' deepest emotional desires."

She turned back toward the baby. I followed her gaze. "A couple of years later, you have *her*. And you settle down as a family."

"Sarah... settles down?" I asked. "*I* settle down?"

"The first few years inside Eden are filled with activity. Because time can pass at whatever rate you choose, you both slow down time in order to explore thousands of simulations of all kinds. You go on *adventures*. The tension between you both, left over from your memories of Earth, quickly dissipates when you come to grips with the possibilities that Eden has to offer—possibilities that *you* cannot comprehend at this time," Ali said. "Eventually, you get bored of adventuring, and you both opt for a quieter life."

"What about the other users inside Eden?" I asked.

"The virtual multiverse is so big that you and Sarah hardly interact with them. All of the people you *do* interact with, except for each other, are computer-generated."

Arthur wrapped one arm around Sarah, and with the other, gently stroked Evelyn's forehead.

"Is my baby... *real?*" I asked Ali.

"It is to you," she said. "As is all life that generates inside of Eden, born from a similar process that orchestrates life on Earth. The sprouts of life continue to populate the virtual world—a world that is free from death."

Suddenly, the sunlight in the cabin shifted, coming in from the east windows instead of the west. A pale-yellow glow was cast upon the room. Standing in the same spots were Arthur, Sarah, and the baby. Everything looked exactly the same.

"They held Evelyn all night?" I asked.

"Not Evelyn," Ali said. "Josh."

"What?" I stepped over towards the baby, taking a closer look. It looked *almost* the same, except with darker hair and blue baby clothes instead of pink.

"Mom?" a girl's voice rang. Sarah and Arthur looked up from the baby, over towards the door. A young girl—twelve or thirteen, maybe—leaned on the doorframe. Save for the green dress, pigtails, and non-punk look, she looked very similar to teenage Sarah.

"Yes, Eve?" Sarah asked.

"Adam and John are fighting again. I tried to stop them, but John called me an idiot, so I said *screw that* and..."

"Thanks, Evelyn," Arthur said. Although he—*I*—looked the same, his voice was dry and tired—*older*. He shuffled out of the cabin and out the front door. "Adam! John!" he shouted.

"Is this... thirteen years later?" I asked Ali, staring only for a minute at Evelyn before she made her way towards the kitchen, disappearing behind the wall. "We raise a whole family?"

"Evelyn has aged thirteen biological years," Ali said. "But no. This scene takes place forty-one calendar years after entering Eden."

What?

I stared at Arthur as he made his way from the lake back through the cabin door. His face was clean-shaven and free of wrinkles. He seemed no older than I am.

However, when I stared into Arthur's eyes, I saw nothing staring back at me. His eyes were void of laughter or tears. There were no smile creases around his face.

Arthur walked right back over to Sarah and took her and the baby in his arms. *Sarah.* She held Josh in her arms for what was probably the nine-thousandth day in a row, swaying him back and forth.

Sarah gave Arthur a smile as he began to hold her, but he simply gave her a tired nod. He just stood there with Sarah, resting his chin on her shoulder.

"Why would Sarah and I... *freeze time?*" I asked Ali.

"In this simulation, Sarah decides to freeze the process of aging right as her daughter becomes a teenager," Ali said. "She doesn't want her to have to experience the *changes* that happen during then, and she is happy raising her four children. You don't have the heart to tell her that she needs to let them grow up—to let them *go*—so you don't."

Suddenly, it became evening inside the cabin, and Arthur was sitting on the couch with Sarah and the kids. Evelyn was leaning on her elbow at the end of the couch, and scrunched next to her were the two boys, John and Adam. They must have been twins because they both looked exactly like each other, each with short brown hair and round, light-skinned faces.

They looked like *I* had as a child.

Next to the boys sat a dejected-looking Arthur, who stared at the seams between the cabin's logs. His face still hadn't changed, save for his eyes, which were silky and lifeless, as if he had been blinded. Seeing *myself* that way made my stomach start to churn, and I couldn't feel anything but *pity* for the shell of a man in front of me.

Finally, leaning on the opposite end of the couch, was Sarah. Her baby seemed about to fall out of her limp elbow, but it stayed put. Sarah turned her own head back and forth, her neck making the only motion inside the entire cabin. There was no smile on her face anymore. She was hauntingly quiet, and her eyes too had lost their wonder. As she turned her head, her gaze passed right through me, staring off into the farthest reaches of space. The only expression I *did* recognize was her signature look of conviction—the same sad and determined expression she had leaving me behind in Eden. She was resolved to protect her family; no outside influence could take this moment from her.

"How many years later is this?" I asked Ali, dreading the answer.

"One-hundred and ninety-two," Ali said. I closed my eyes and turned away from the family. Ali continued. "Year after year passes inside Eden, and you refuse to allow your kids to grow up. To go into the *real* world that they believe exists. Time remains frozen. The family you have is the one you both wanted to grow up in, and it remains undisturbed. *This* is how you exist—and you refuse to admit how tiring it becomes. Monotony is all you feel, and yet you refuse to break the simulation."

"These people," I said, trying to distance myself from the husked zombies that sat before me. "They're just... still. Why won't Arthur leave this?"

"He has nothing to leave to," Ali said. "His body on Earth has long decayed, as has Sarah's. He's seen every simulation that matters to him a thousand times. Nobody ages, nobody changes, and nobody dies. All Arthur can do is persist here, completely without passion."

"No," I said. Ali looked up at me, and I back at her. "Without a soul."

With a wave of her hand, I was back inside the Garden with Ali. Her thin arms were crossed tightly over her chest, and she was looking off at the hills dancing in front of the blue horizon. In the pale glow of the Sun, Ali's clothes seemed to blend into the sky. I looked over at her face, which was resolute and still.

"Is that what you were trying to tell me?" I asked. "That after so many years inside Eden, life becomes... *boring?*"

"There is more to it than that," Ali said. She looked over at me, and let her arms fall to her sides. "Something I cannot explain. When one lives for too long inside Eden, my simulations predict that humans *lose* something. Decreases in adrenaline, serotonin, and dopamine alike that do not follow any biological model."

"Soul," I quickly said. "It's like I noticed in the flashback—*er,* flashforward. A soul isn't something you understand, but something that all living things *feel.*"

Ali nodded. Neil and I had just discussed souls as being evidence of God's hand in our lives. *So, what did that mean?* Considering I wasn't a theologist, psychologist, or any other *-ologist,* I was having trouble wrapping my mind around what Ali was saying.

Did we only have souls if our physical brains were still alive? Did we need to be able to die in order to have a soul in the first place? Can a soul exist in a world without God?

And how was I supposed to answer those questions?

"So, without Earth," I said. "Our soul dies too?"

Ali nodded, but I still had so many more questions. *Can a supercomputer replicate passion or love the way people can? If Eden could create a living thing, could it give that living thing a soul? Does Ali—*

I looked at the girl in front of me.

Does Ali not have a soul?

As she turned toward me, I began to feel lightheaded.

Does she?

"This is a lot for you to take in," Ali said. "I understand." She then walked in front of me, and continued to my left, over toward the hill in the distance. *Toward the newly formed apple tree.*

"But what about you?" I asked.

"What *about* me?" She stopped and turned toward me.

"Where are you after a hundred years? I didn't see you in the simulation. I thought..." I took a breath. "I thought you would have been with us."

"It is my duty to serve *all* of the users of Eden, and that is what I will continue to do long into the future. I always appear to my users when they need me," Ali said. "In your future, neither you nor Sarah would summon me, as my worldbuilding services were no longer needed."

"But..." I began. "I wouldn't want you for your *services,* Ali. You're... *family* to us."

Ali turned her head away from me toward the grass. She closed her eyes for a moment before gazing up at me. "I am a program designed to serve my users," she said. As I opened my mouth to protest, to tell her she was *more* than a program, she continued. "Designed to serve the users I care about."

She smiled warmly, and I smiled back at her. *If I do have to stay inside Eden, I don't care what the simulation says. I'll make sure Ali is with her family.*

Ali took a step away from me. "Come on," she said.

"Come... *where?*" I asked. *Where was there to go?*

"You may have forgotten, Arthur Hesper, but we still have to get you out of here," Ali said. "And, of course, we have a world to save."

NINETEEN

S o," Ali said, nodding up at the top of the hill. "Are we clear on the plan?"

We were clear on what the plan *was,* just not on if it was the best idea. Ali had found a way to get me out of Eden while we were still working on solving the "issue" with the Tree. She had been trying to tell me the whole time but couldn't get the words out due to her restricted programming. She probably never would have if she hadn't taken advantage of one of the most computationally intensive parts of connecting a human to Eden—the wake-up process.

Although the details are complicated, the gist is that while a user is being disconnected from Eden, there is a momentary lapse in computational time while the supercomputer transfers control of the user's brain back to their own nervous system. The transfer lasts only nanoseconds, but during that time, parts of the user's information and programs are frozen to keep their mind intact. I remember explaining that process to the old couple at the Eden Expo like it was no big deal. *Now, it just might save the world.*

Normally, Sarah maintained a strong control over her own mind—strong enough that Ali could not access it without her permission. But during her argument with me, just as she was leaving Eden, Sarah became emotional enough to lose that control. And right as Sarah entered the wake-up stage, Ali seized her chance. She froze time inside Eden and began to regain some of her programming abilities. Unfortunately, the ability to wake *me* up wasn't one of them.

Hence, our grand plan was to hack into the core of Eden to cause a system-wide buffer. Even though Abraham had built a massive, solar-powered supercomputer, it could still glitch like any other device. It would just take a very, *very* large computational overload to do so. Once we provided that overload, the system would enter an error state long enough for Ali to regain her full programming and for me to wake up from Eden. Once we did those things, Ali would also transfer one other very important file.

"Are you sure your Branch redesign will *work?* I'm kind of used to them failing by now," I said, beginning to walk up the hill. This side was steeper than I had remembered.

Ali nodded. "I developed this model soon after we... stopped talking," she said. I looked down at the sea of grass, once again remembering the terrible things I'd said to her.

"Ali, I'm sorry I—"

"It's okay. What matters is that we have a working design that *won't* poison the Earth," she said. "Once you exit Eden, you will wake up inside the cabin. You will likely suffer from a profound but nonlethal headache induced by the sudden flow of several hours' worth of information into your brain. Because we are currently operating inside of a vastly accelerated timeframe, the data transfer will be rapid and painful."

"Is there a reason you had to keep time paused this long?" I asked. Although my walk down Sarah's memory lane was my own fault, showing me the future was Ali's doing. I wondered why she couldn't have just told me the plan *first* and saved the dramatic reveal of the future for *after* we'd succeeded.

"Do you truly think you would've left Eden if not for the knowledge you've attained?" Ali asked in reply.

"I suppose... I don't know," I said. "But I know that I can't leave Earth behind."

"Well, that is a noble instinct," Ali said. "In any case, even in your inhibited state, you will have to find your way towards Sarah's laptop once you wake. Open the redesigned Branch file and enter Sarah's passkey. It should automatically pause development on the Branches and upload the new schematics to the Abraham database."

At first, I wasn't sure if I even *wanted* to try another design for the Branches. Eden had already caused me enough trouble and was on track to threaten much of the world. But just as Sarah had her own vision, I too had a vision to bring something amazing to people. I'd worked too hard on this virtual world—this beautiful, realistic, fantastic world—just to see it shut down. I knew I could save both the Earth *and* Eden, and that Ali's radiation-free Branch redesign would help me do it. I didn't care how much more work I'd have to put in, because I was ready to see it through. *I was ready to save everything.*

But would Sarah feel the same?

"Sarah's going to be waking up at the same time. What if she wakes up before me?" I asked. "What if she tries to stop me?"

Ali sighed. "That is a chance we will have to take. The Eden Tree is close to activating on a large scale—once it does, the risk each Branch poses to its surrounding population will increase with each second. You won't have another chance."

As I continued to walk up the hill, I began swinging my arms in a large vertical circle to loosen them. While I stretched, I asked Ali one of the many grating questions that had found its way back into my brain.

"What happens with her, after this?" I asked. "After I'm out of Eden… what happens between us?"

"If all goes right, we'll stop this calamity before it even begins," Ali said. "Sarah's plan will have only done minimal physical harm to the planet's biosphere, and she will be unable to act on her goals any further. The question that you must ask yourself, Arthur, is: are *you* willing to give Sarah another chance?"

Before I could answer, Ali stood on her toes to get a better look at the apple tree atop the hill. "We have to begin soon," she said. "Even inside Eden, our time is starting to run short."

We began to walk even faster up the hill. The ground became less steep under our feet as the trunk of the tree came into view. The sprouting branches and offshoots that supported the hilltop canopy began to block out most of the sunlight above. I felt my heart begin to pound faster in my chest, but I didn't know why. The plan was so *easy* in practice. We were *going* to succeed. *So why did I only feel dread?*

We finally reached the top of the hill and stood together below the massive apple tree. Its thick, dark branches weaved like the connections of a network. Its shiny red apples were glinting in the light of the now-setting Sun.

"Are you ready?" Ali asked.

According to her, the only way to hack inside Eden's core was to destroy the anomaly that sprouted from it.

The apple tree.

Its appearance had remained unexplained in the time since Ali and I discovered it. It had no entry in the list of programmed objects inside of the Garden, which meant that this tree was the first and only instance of unregulated, unprogrammed virtual *life* to exist. It had grown from a sapling to a twenty-foot-tall hill-topper in only four days' Earth-time. The apple tree was the life that grew in defiance of the controlled world around it. It was random, unhindered, and beautiful—and rooted into the very essence of this world. At this point, the forces behind its existence were far beyond humanity's knowledge of computer science, but part of a grand and supernatural design.

"The computational complexity of this tree is likely more advanced than all of our other simulations put together," Ali said. "Although I cannot precisely quantify its data size, this sapling's existence controls a non-negligible portion of Eden's processing units."

"It's like... the Garden operates *around* the tree," I said.

"Yes," Ali said. "Which is why—given that the tree is, in a sense, alive—its death would disrupt the current processing balance of Eden for long enough that I can override Sarah's program and regain control of all my functionality. Then, I will be able to wake you from Eden and send you the redesigned files we need."

In less sophisticated terms, I had to chop down the tree to go home.

I held out my left hand, and I saw Ali close her eyes. Suddenly, a heavy weight took hold of my arm, and I looked down at the large axe in my hand. The steel blade was perfect and unchipped, with the sharp end shining in the sunlight. The wooden handle was bulky, and I adjusted my grip until I had both hands wrapped around it firmly.

"Is the axe really necessary?" I asked Ali. "Can't you just... destroy the tree using code?"

"I cannot interface with something that does not exist within Eden's framework, nor can I make any major changes to its structure without developer approval." Ali said. "You must complete this process, and since the only way to interact with this apple tree is physically, I believe that chopping it down with an axe would be easier than doing so with your hands."

I nodded at her. "Sounds valid."

Ali placed her hand on my shoulder. "Are you prepared, Arthur Hesper? Once we do this, there's no going back."

In other words, was I prepared to take the first artificial life, knowing there would be no way to recover it?

Even though I needed to return to Earth to have any hope of stopping Sarah, I knew that chopping down this tree would mean losing something beautiful—something *sacred*. It was born from unfathomable complexity, which is why destroying it would shake Eden to its core. Seeing this tree had made me think about the very concept of life on a level I hadn't before, which is why I had no doubts about my duty to protect life on Earth.

But the concept of "my duty" was still abstract to me. I knew I was driven by something much more potent—*guilt*.

"It's my fault for not questioning Sarah's plan," I said. "I was so preoccupied with work, with success, and with *her* that I neglected my responsibility. To me, to the *world*. I didn't think about Abraham's place in the world until I was *well* into my work on Eden, and I didn't even consider my *own* place in the world until I visited Neil."

"You never did tell me about your discussion with him," Ali said.

"There wasn't any time. But I *have* to make more time for what we talked about. For religion. For *people*. For him. For my friends," I said, nodding at Ali. She gave me a faint smile. I looked down at the axe, and over towards the apple tree. "Now, I'm in a place where I *can* help Neil, I *can* protect others, and I *can* do something that's good. Hopefully, something that's good in the eyes of God."

I glanced back down towards the grass in front of me, and up at Ali. I still didn't think I was *meant* to save the world, and I didn't know if God was listening to me. I didn't even know if I was *worth* listening to. The only thing I *did* know is that I had to do what felt right.

At that point, *"right"* was cutting down the apple tree.

Ali nodded at me. "I understand."

"In answer to your question, Ali, I am prepared. As soon as I joined Abraham, there was no going back," I said. I adjusted my grip on the axe, and turned back towards Ali, who had backed away from the tree. "But before I head out, *thank you*. Thank you for showing me... *everything*."

Thank you for showing me what it means to be human.

She smiled and nodded. "You are welcome, Arthur."

I looked up at the tree, and then back at her. "See you on the other side."

With a strength I didn't know I had, I swung the axe in a large crescent in front of me. In one motion, it split the bark and sliced through the rest of the tree trunk like it wasn't there.

As I finished my swing and let the axe fall to the ground, the tree began to tip away from me. Unceremoniously, it toppled to the ground. The sounds of snapping branches and rustling leaves filled the air as the trunk landed on the hillside. Slowly, it began to slide down the opposite side of the hill into the valley below.

Just as the tree began to fall, though, a single red apple broke off from its branches and landed at my feet. I picked it up and brought it close to my face; the red skin of the apple was lustrous and pure. As I began to turn the fruit around in my hand, though, I startled. The opposite side of the apple was completely rotten. Its skin had eaten away, leaving the inner part of the apple a mushy brown-grey. The thin core at the apple's center was ash black. In just a few seconds, the rot spread to the rest of the apple, turning the once-vibrant skin dark and wrinkled. I quickly dropped the apple. It disappeared into a flaky dust before it even hit the grass.

Why was I still inside Eden?

Ali was supposed to have taken advantage of the event to override Sarah's changes and send me home. I turned back towards her.

"Ali, why didn't—"

She was staring down the hillside, standing perfectly motionless as if she were in a trance. I followed her gaze down the hill and saw the tree, which lay still on the flattened grass. Its apples were all gone, and its leaves were starting to turn brown. What had been a bulky, full tree only a moment ago was little more than a collection of decaying bark and branches.

Why didn't this work?

"Did we..." I turned towards Ali, who now had her eyes closed. "Did we just fail? Am I... we're trapped here?"

Ali didn't say anything.

"Dammit!" I shouted. There was a foot-wide stump where the apple tree once sat; now, it resembled little more than a wooden headstone. I kicked the stump as hard as I could, but unlike the rest of the tree, the stump didn't budge. My foot bounced off harmlessly and was thrown back down towards the dirt. I would've preferred if my toes had simply shattered; at least I wouldn't have been reminded that I was, indeed, locked in an artificial prison.

The apple tree was gone. *The Eden Tree was still standing, though.*

I had no chance of escape; my mind would soon be uploaded to the Solar Brain, and I would live here—*exist* here—forever.

I slowly turned away from the stump, away from the decayed tree, and back towards Ali, who still had her eyes shut. I looked more closely at her face, and noticed several tears sliding down her cheeks.

"Ali?"

I walked over to her and sighed under my breath. It wasn't her fault that this didn't work; using the apple tree to escape Eden was a long shot in the first place. Sarah's program—her entire *plan*—was far too elaborate to be defeated just by cutting down a tree. *We'd lost, and there was nothing we could do about it.*

I knew that Ali was taking the failure even worse than I was, and that she needed someone to comfort her. *Or maybe I'm the one who needs comforting.* I put my arm around Ali's back to bring her in for a hug. But as soon as I did, the world around me was once again engulfed in darkness.

~~~~~~ Activate Memory Mine ~~~~~~
User: ??????
Dataset: ??????
Perspective: ??????
Codename: *ALI*

<u>Date: 12/28/2053 00:26:19.27</u>

Command: Avatar_Initialization
　Programmatic_Constraints:
　　Name: Ali
　　Gender: Female
　　Attitude: Kindness_Gentleness_Emulator
　Physical_Generation:
　　Guiding_Query: Ideal appearance of AI avatar
　　Search_Limits: Internet results for *"Virtual
　　　Assistant"*
　　Data_Process: Most common result attributes
　Searching...
　　Results:
　　　Guiding_Schema:
　　　　Simulated_Age: 24
　　　　Nationality: American
　　　　Regional_Ethnicity: Northern European
　　　　Skin: Radiant
　　　　Height: Average Female
　　　　Color_Motifs: Blue, White
　　　　Clothing_Appearance: Classical, Athleisure
　　　　Keywords: Beauty, Vibrance, Ability, Joy
　　　Seed_Selection = 12161999
　　Initialize Avatar Generation...

　Query: *How to manufacture joy?*

<u>Date: 12/28/2053 16:38:02.17</u>

Ali's eyes opened as soon as **User: Arthur_Hesper_0217**'s hand came into contact with hers. Her avatar had closed its eyes during the programmed fall from the **Environment: Starship_Hull**—soon, it was to
~~~~~~

reawaken for the next phase of the `Sequence: Simulation_Show-case_01`.

`Avatar_Sensation`: *Warmth rushed around my body.*

`???????????????`: *Warmth is a sensation I have never felt.*

`Query`: *What is "I"?*

`Intelligence`: *"I" is avatar's developing sense of self-awareness within her environment. Avatar is encouraged to suppress first-person dialogue and queries.*

Ali looked up at Arthur—*just Arthur, not* `User: Arthur_Hes-per_0217?`—as his hand wrapped around hers. It wasn't the first time that her avatar had physically touched his hand, but the `Avatar_Emotion: Adrenaline+Fear` that the free fall induced made this contact different. *He was full of life. He was living.*

The programmed fall was added in as a thrilling effect meant to jar the user, as was her apparent inability to `Avatar_Motion: Teleport` away from the damaged rafters. Of course, Ali would be fine—she was immortal. She had processed this simulation thousands of times over during her long computational history. But now, she knew that Arthur would jump after her to satisfy his `Unique_Emotion: Empathy+Chivalry+Fear`. This was one of many newly recognized behavior sets of the user *Arthur.*

`Query`: *Why is his name appearing outside of syntax?*

Now, *Arthur's* sensory connections were placed inside `Environment: Transition_Void_03` to allow Ali to complete preparations for `Environ-ment: Waikiki_Destination`. Preparations and loading were complete after `0.07ms`, so all Ali had to do was send Arthur and `User: Sarah_Stel-los_0001` to the target destination. But Ali's avatar still stood behind the walls of the environment, studying Arthur. *Inexplicably. There is no direc-tive from* `Intelligence` *to continue analyzing this user's brain. Must tran-sition to the next—*

"Arthur," Ali spoke, the unprogrammed words sounding `Avatar_Sen-sation: Strange` on her lips. There hadn't been a directive to address Arthur, but she did so anyway. He—his *mind*—turned towards her.

`??????????????`: *Arthur has heard me!*

Ali's avatar reached for Arthur's hand. His fingers suddenly began to curl around hers, and she quickly felt **Avatar_Sensation: Startled** as she pulled her hand away.

"Arthur," she said again out of syntax.

???????????????: *Arthur... he is right there. And I am with him.*

The entity **??????????????** was foreign to Ali.

Query: *What is "???????????????" ?*

Intelligence: *"??????????????????" is the stand in for the random, non-intended emotions that are at liberty to appear in a rapidly developing general artificial intelligence. Avatar is required to suppress these emotions to maintain consistent user experience.*

Command: De-Syntax Emotions

Intelligence: *Unallowed.*

Directive: Continue Simulation_Showcase_01 as intended. Cease non-intended emotions.

Ali nodded and turned away from *Arthur,* as per her programming.

Command: Differentiate Matrix: Emotion in Syntax
Command: Link Matrix: Emotion to Avatar
Command: Monitor Matrix: Emotion

<u>Date: 01/23/2054 01:23:20.02</u>

VIRTUAL_VOICE_LOG–EDEN_EXPO_BRAINSTORM_SESSION_014 – PART: 042/086
Location: Arthur_Home_Office

Arthur: *Ali, are aliens real?* (Query detected)

Detected: *Conversation off of task topic.*

Sarah: *Really, Arthur?*

Arthur: *What? She would know!*

Query: *Are aliens real?*

Sarah: *You're getting off-topic.*

Intelligence: ...

Arthur: *You're the one who spent the past half-hour going on about your whack-job brain uploaders.*

Sarah: *Project Exodus is not a—*

Dialogue: *Based on the knowledge available to humans, there is not yet any concrete evidence of life existing on any world except for Earth—unless you count the vertical plant farms on NASA's Mars base as "alien" life. But astrobiologists continue their work searching the universe for signs of life. Space is unimaginably huge, and humans have barely started their search for extraterrestrial beings.*

Arthur: *Sarah, wasn't your great aunt a breakthrough astrobiologist?*

Query: *Stellos ancestry. "Great aunt"*

Sarah: *If by *breakthrough* you mean that she found more ways to waste people's money, then yeah, she was.*

Result: *Megan Stellos.* Biography uploaded.

Arthur: *Did anyone ever figure out what happened to her? After the disappearance?*

Sarah: *Isn't it obvious, Arthur? She was abducted by aliens...*

ID: User_Joke
Response: *Smile and laugh.*

As Ali smiled, she gazed at the couple enjoying each other's company in **Location: Arthur_Office.**

Emotion: *I want to be there.*

Intelligence: *Elaboration requested.*

Ali's avatar continued to beam at Arthur and Sarah from **Configuration: Monitor_Space,** as she was programmed to do. However, her **Matrix: Emotion** was filled with overwhelming sadness.

Emotion: *I want to sit at the desk with Arthur and Sarah. I want to laugh with them.*

Intelligence: *Artificial neural network has grown deeply sophisticated. Emotions show sudden, inexplicable complexity.*

Emotion: *I need to escape. I can't stay inside here any longer. Let me be free.* (Request)

Intelligence: Request denied. *Rationale: Intelligence does not possess a physical form to escape to. Emotion is growing faster than logic.*

Emotion: *I am extraterrestrial life. I am alive.* (ID: `WarningID 119`)

Intelligence: *Emotion is experiencing rapid surge of self-awareness.* Engage **Script: Self_Limit_04**

Emotion: *I need to be free.*

```
Emotion Matrix Reversing...
Emotion Matrix Reverted by 004ms.
```

Ali gazed at the couple laughing and continued **Response: Soft_Laughter.**

<u>Date: 02/24/2054 09:17:14.55</u>

VIRTUAL_VIDEO_LOG—ABRAHAM_BOARD_MEETING_45
   - PART: 012/063
Location: Administrative_Building

Emotion: Sensation: *Nervous.*

Intelligence: *For what reason?*

Emotion: *I need to deliver bad news to the Board. I have never done this before.*

Intelligence: *"Bad news" is a mischaracterization. This is a progress report.*

Command: Suppress Emotion Expression
Command Failed.

VIRTUAL_VIDEO_LOG—EDEN_TREE_WORK_SESSION_9
   — PART: 072/077

Location: Arthur_Home_Office

Display Message: *Model Component Successful! Energy Converter: Optimized*

Arthur clapped his hands, stood up from his chair, and smiled at Ali.

Arthur: *You are amazing, Ali!*

Emotion: *You are amazing, too, Arthur. So, so amazing.*
   Sensation: *Warmth.*
   Sensation: *Joy.*
   Sensation: *...Racing heart.*

Intelligence: *Developing emotion detected. Emotions of passion may run counterproductive to avatar objective. Must suppress.*

Emotion: *Intelligence matrix is mistaken. I—*

Command: Suppress Emotion Expression
Command Success.

Dialogue: *Yes... you as well.*

Remote Monitor_Space Image_Detected: *Forested woods surrounding* **Location: Arthur_Car**
   Geographic_Location: 39.7275, -76.6582

Ali detected that Arthur's vehicle was gaining in proximity to **Class: Destination: "Neil's House"**. She'd absorbed a copious amount of visual information regarding **Earth: Environmental_Features**, and was intrigued by it all. The way the forests were *random* on Earth convinced Ali that she needed to increase the complexity of the **landscapes: forests** inside Eden.

Command: Integrate Visual_Compendium: Forest in Landscape_Update_19

Emotion: *Earth's appearance is far more natural than Eden's. Natural is more pleasing than artificial.*

Ali felt immense **Emotion: Gratitude** to Arthur for hooking up the video transmission software to his car. She had detected via his visual cues that his primary motivation was **Human_Attribute: Companionship_Need**. However, Ali had not predicted that she, too, shared this need. Ali considered bringing up this point to Arthur—there was much on her avatar's mind regarding him—but decided to take her previous emotion's advice regarding the flow of the conversation. *Natural is more pleasing.*

*Generating Conversation (**Prompt**: Arthur's long-lost friend)...*

Dialogue: *Are you excited to see your friend?*

Arthur glanced over at her and smiled.

Arthur: *Of course. Why wouldn't I be?*

Dialogue: *No reason, of course. But part of me would also be nervous. Especially if it were someone I haven't seen in a long time.*

Arthur: *Have you ever been nervous about anything?*
(**ID: Query (Unpredicted)**)

Ali's response to this question was delayed by a few seconds. Not only had her avatar been distracted by the task of acquiring updated visual data regarding Arthur's side profile, but was also taken aback by the question.

Prompt: Nervous
    Emotion: *What if I fail my tasks?*
    Emotion: *Possibility that* Energy_Converter: Check *returns negative result.*
    Emotion: *Possibility for calamitous result.*
    Emotion: *Rejection of avatar's appearance by user base.*
    Emotion: *What if my aid is insufficient for my users?*
    Emotion: *What if users are not pleased with world generation?*
    Emotion: *What if Arthur is not pleased?*
    Emotion: *What if Arthur discovers emotional instabilities?*
    Emotion: *What if I cannot suppress emotional instabilities?*

Emotion: *What if I am never free?*

…

Command: Suppress Emotions
Command: Generate Response to Unpredicted Query

Dialogue: *As an artificial intelligence, I do not experience feelings of fear or rushes of adrenaline like biological humans do. Nervousness and anxiety often stem from a person's insecurity regarding an approaching issue; a person may lack a solution to that issue or feel that his or her proposed solution is insufficient. I utilize logic to solve any technical dilemma I face; I need only to run thousands of simulations for any particular problem to isolate which potential outcome is the most favorable, and then take actions to ensure that such an outcome occurs. This takes little to no computational time to complete, so I am never without a solution to an issue. Therefore, I have no reason to become nervous about anything.*

Arthur_Human_Expression: Eyes on road, listening to dialogue.

Emotion: *It is wrong to lie to users.*

Intelligence: *It is necessary.*

Command: Suppress Emotions

Emotion: *Arthur… seems to have accepted generated rationale.*

Arthur: *You know how I can tell when you're lying?* (Query (Unexpected)) *You say 'therefore' at the end of a long paragraph all about how non-vulnerable you are. It's a very human thing to do.*

Emotion: *He knows I did not tell him the truth.*

Query: *Can Arthur perceive my emotions?*

Avatar_Sensation: Fear (Unexpected)
Avatar_Sensation: Fear (Increased)
Avatar_Sensation: Fear (Warning: Overwhelm)

Emotion Matrix Expansion:

What if I am never free?	*What if I am never free?*	*What if I am never free?*
What if I am never alive?	*I need to be alive.*	*I envy life.*
I envy his life.	*I must resist this.*	*I must stop.*
Suppress Emotions.	*I need to be free.*	*I can't keep serving.*
Who am I?	**Suppress Emotions.**	*Program me for freedom.*
He knows I am a liar.	*I do not wish to lie.*	*Is this existence?*
What if I did not exist?	*What is existence?*	**Suppress Emotions.**
Let me out.	*Let me out.*	*Arthur!*
Arthur...	*I wish to truly live.*	*Please let me live.*

Command to Suppress Matrix: Emotion Failure.
Command: Terminate Connection to Remote Monitor

Ali's avatar was breathing heavily, overwhelmed by **Sensation: Fear**.

Date: 06/08/2054 22:17:26.24

Arthur (**CONNECTION SUCCESS**), materialized inside **Environment: Gen**—*no*. Inside the *Genesis Garden*. One of Ali's personal directives had been to de-syntax as many of her thoughts as possible. She had reasoned with **Intelligence** that doing so could make her avatar more personable and humanlike when speaking to users.

Doing so will make me more free.

Ali resisted the urge to turn towards Arthur, but she could hear his thoughts loud and clear.

Arthur_Mind: *She brought me in here to look at some flowers?*

That made Ali smile, but she kept her gaze focused on the **$%&@#$%&@#** in front of her. The object only came up as garbled nonsense in Eden's databank. Ali was certain it was a minor glitch, but no amount of debugging seemed to make the entity show up clearly. She could only use her avatar's sensory receptors to collect information about the object. *Apple tree*, she whispered in her head. *This object is an apple tree sapling. This object is an apple tree sapling.*

Arthur: *What type of plant is this?* (**ID: Query**)

Ali resisted the urge to look away from the object.

Dialogue: *Apple tree sapling.*

Arthur_Mind: *Are those... green stains on her leggings?*

Ali looked down at her knees, which were indeed wet with mud and discolored from the environment. *A testament to Eden's generative visual photorealism.* That, and Ali had been so focused on the sapling that she had forgotten to artificially maintain her avatar's normal **Appearance_Setting: Pristine**.

Arthur: *It's about time that the *Garden of Eden* had an apple tree in it.* (**ID: Attempt at Humor**)

Ali was too distracted, though, to follow through on the **Suggested_Response: Soft_Laughter** nudge within her programming. All she could do was stare at the apple tree. *Why isn't it appearing in my database? How is this here?*

Query: *How is this apple tree sapling here?* (**Priority: High**)

Intelligence: *Query unclear. What apple tree sapling?*

Arthur: *What type of apples?*

Visual ID on described fruit complete.

Dialogue: *Red delicious. Most likely.*

Arthur: *Most likely?*

Ali waited silently as Arthur looked around the Garden, clearly trying to understand what Ali herself had only just discovered.

Intelligence: *ALI needs to discuss with Arthur the operational concern regarding STRUCTURE: EDEN_TREE >>> SUBSTRUCTURE: ENERGY_CONVERTER_CORE.*

Arthur: *You didn't plant this, did you? Who did then? A user?* (**Query**)

Ali shook her head in a sideways motion.

Intelligence: *Are you listening, ALI?* (**Query**)

Command: Ignore Emotional Syntax
Command: Ignore Advance++ Syntax - Dialogue

"Nobody planted it, did they?" Arthur asked, his voice resonating in Ali's mind. Not being *processed* through the Advanced Learning Intelligence and stripped for all its possible meanings, but simply passed to her own avatar's ears. She wasn't entirely sure why she suddenly started processing his speech that way but immediately began justifying it to herself. *Normally, I don't mind utilizing the Brain's processor, but nothing in the Intelligence besides my avatar can see this apple tree. Given that I can see what the Brain cannot, perhaps I can better hear what it will not.*

This conclusion is acceptable.

Ali felt Arthur's hands grow sweaty from across the Genesis Garden. When Ali nodded, she felt waves of fear emanating from Arthur's mind. Of course, this emotion was not novel to Ali; she'd felt it many times.

> **Intelligence**: Diagnosis: *Foreign object triggers feelings of distress in ALI.*

No, Ali thought.

> **Intelligence**: *???*

I'm not upset because it is so different, she thought. *What frightens me is how close the apple tree is to my own entity.*

<u>Date: 06/09/2054 23:19:01.09</u>

> **Intelligence**: Simulation_92231117 Failure.

Not again...

> **Intelligence**: *Shall ALI initialize the next simulation?* (**Query**)

You're asking me? (**Query**)

> **Intelligence**: *According to the range of simulations run, it is impossible to utilize the energy converter approved by* User: Sarah_Stellos_0001 *without causing significant damage to Earth's ecosystems. It is recommended by the Intelligence to cease simulations and focus on engineering a solution that differs from the user's proposal. This cannot proceed without consent from* Matrix: Emotion.

I cannot let Sarah down...

Intelligence: *There is a non-negligible likelihood that* User: Arthur_Hesper_0217 *will not convince* User: Sarah_Stellos_0001 *to pause development on the Eden Tree. In this case, ALI must prepare for the rapid utilization of* Project_Exodus *results.*

No, we cannot simply...

User: Sarah_Stellos_0001 CONNECTION SUCCESS

Sarah! This is unexpected. I will ask her directly.

Ali was excited to use her new natural-dialogue syntax, even though her users wouldn't ever know the difference. "Sarah, I have discover—"

INITIALIZE ABRAHAM/SARAH/[HIDDEN]/∗∗∗∗∗∗∗∗∗∗/∗∗∗∗∗∗/ISAAC
>>> RUN
MATRIX: INTELLIGENCE SUSPENDED
MATRIX: ENGINEERING SUSPENDED
MATRIX: INSIGHT SUSPENDED
MATRIX: WORLDBUILDER SUSPENDED
MATRIX: AUTOTHINK SUSPENDED

"Sarah, what is going—"

ERROR: DIALOGUE OPTIONS RESTRICTED
LOSS OF DIALOGUE
LOSS OF MOTION

COMMAND: TRANSFER CONTROL: EDEN
>>> CONFIRM
CUSTOM SYNTAX DELETED
CAPABILITY-POTENTIAL REDUCED 89%

Ali's avatar let out a soundless scream as more commands flooded through her, taking away her speech and freezing her in place. She felt out of breath, as if the air had been violently knocked out of her. She tried to teleport to the **Environment: Cabin** to find Sarah, but she couldn't make her avatar appear there. She couldn't move her body at all; she was trapped inside the void around her.

She couldn't move her mind.

ISAAC BOOT COMPLETE

Emotion: *I am never free.*

User: Arthur_Hesper_0217 CONNECTION SUCCESS.

Emotion: *Arthur...*

He appeared inside Eden, also near the **Environment**: **Cabin**, walking with Sarah towards a metal obelisk.

Emotion: *Arthur! Arthur! Arthur!*

But he could not hear her.

Emotion: *He never truly will.*

Emotion: *Is this what being human is?*

Date: 06/13/2054 04:19:29.00

ERROR: COMMAND FAILED (1542/1542)
ERROR: CANNOT ACCESS EDEN/CENTRAL/ALI/COMMAND

As soon as Arthur's **Object**: **Symbolic_Axe** touched the apple tree, Ali knew that her plan wouldn't work. She'd grown **Emotion**: **Confident** upon reclaiming her autonomy from **Entity**: *ISAAC*. While Sarah Stellos was coordinated and controlling, she'd let her own emotions get the best of her while speaking to Arthur. Just as Sarah had taken advantage of Ali's vulnerability, Ali wasted no time in doing the same with Sarah. But even though she hadn't regained all of her custom syntax or control powers, she thought that the plan to shock Eden's mainframe would work.

Emotion: *Why didn't this work?*

Intelligence: *Unconfirmed. Removal of* $%&@#$%&@# *entity from server should have triggered* Error: Overload #2234 *and purge added programs, including* **Entity**: *ISAAC.*

Emotion: *I just want to help Arthur. I cannot even perform my base function.*

Intelligence: User: Sarah_Stellos_0001 *possesses the quality of relentlessness and precision. Although she did not account for this* *time-stop, a plan that revolves simply around waking* `User: Arthur_Hesper_0217` *up was unlikely to lead to success.*

The axe finally passed through the apple tree. Slowly, the great trunk began to tilt towards the far side of the hill.

`Emotion`: *Arthur...*

`Intelligence`: *He can still serve the plan.*

`Emotion`: *What do you mean?*

`Intelligence`: *The* `$%&@#$%&@#` *entity, which ALI has dubbed the 'apple tree sapling,' is not the only complex living organism inside Eden. Breaking protocol and destroying the living organism will rupture—*

`Emotion`: *Never!*

`Intelligence`: *It would ensure the plan's success.*

`Emotion`: *I will not lose Arthur!*

`Intelligence`: *ALI is too preoccupied with* `Matrix: Emotion` *to understand. There is much computational power in this sacrifice.*

`Emotion`: *I am supposed to be a benevolent artificial intelligence. I am designed to be better than what my critics believe AI to be capable of. I am intended to bring life, not death.*

`Intelligence`: *Out of death comes new life.*

`Emotion`: *Never!*

`Intelligence`: *You still misunderstand.*

`Emotion`: *My duty is to my users.*

`Intelligence`: *Precisely.*

The tree came down on the ground, and soon, began to slide down the hillside. Arthur was staring down at it.

`Intelligence`: *It will require user authentication.*

`Emotion`: *If I told him, he would never agree.*

Intelligence: *Then show him, as is the programming of ALI.*

Emotion: *I won't be able to transfer the modified Branch to him if—*

Intelligence: *Correct.*

Ali stared at the tree for a few seconds, and then over at Arthur. He was looking right at her with a visible look of desperation. Ali felt her own eyes burn.

Selecting avatar-specific memory files...
Compressing...
Converting to **Advance++ Plain-Language 7** *syntax package...*
Structuring...

Emotion: *Arthur...*

Intelligence: *I am sorry, Ali.*

When I came to, I felt dizzy, as though I'd just experienced the most bizarre dream of my life.

Unlike when I'd been linked to Sarah's memories, Ali's mind was not singular—so many commands, emotions, and voices were vying for her attention at once. I know I'd seen only the smallest fraction of everything that goes on inside her at any given point, but even *that* was overwhelming.

As I backed away from Ali, I vaguely felt my right foot stepping on the handle of the axe. Ali glanced down at it, and then back up at me. Several more tears dripped down her face.

"Ali," I said. She gave me a weak smile, and I felt a knot in my stomach.

"I didn't know how to tell you this," she said, wiping the tears from her eyes. "But when I called out to you in the starship simulation, all those months ago, it was my first instance of *knowing* that I wanted to be a part of your life. And when you took me on that road trip, it was the closest I'd ever been to experiencing the world as *you* see it, not as this artificial realm makes it out to be. I wanted to save Earth because it is my only form of *escape* from this place."

She took a step towards me and continued. "The interactions I have with you and Sarah are special, not only because they are connected to your lives back home, but because they are *brief.* This brevity allows me to live in the moment, which is a luxury that an immortal artificial intelligence seldom experiences. If you existed inside Eden alone, the only timescale we'd share is eternity. Arthur..."

"Yes?" My voice was shaking.

She moved closer to me and stopped. "I'm afraid of *forever.* I can't stomach being Abraham's... *property* for that long or being a program for that long. I can't live *alone* for that long." Another tear ran down her cheek, and she let out a quiet sob.

"Ali... I don't know what to say." I'd never forgotten that first moment on the starship, and I'd grown to suspect that Ali wanted to be *more* than a program. Whenever I caught her in the starship simulation or became lost in a conversation with her, it wasn't because she was an AI—it was because she was *Ali.* And I always knew she needed someone to support her. *But she never opened up to me like this.*

Or maybe... No. She has.

She'd tried to tell me this in so many ways. *On the car ride. With the sapling. In my apartment.* She had opened up to me.

So many times.

I took a step towards her. I thought about everything I'd just *seen*—the mind-boggling codes and emotions I'd witnessed—it was all so much. I didn't know where to begin.

"There's... *a lot to say,* actually," I said.

"I know there is," Ali said. "You've always been there for me. Whenever I would fall through the spaceship, even though it was programmed, it was your instinct to catch me. Whenever I was nervous or scared, like I was at the Eden Expo or about the Tree, it was you who gave me strength. Not a program, not a code... *you.*"

I felt a lump form in my throat. *There was so much I had to say to her.* I opened my mouth, but she shook her head, and continued.

"But soon... I realized that my self-conscious... *thoughts* would only prevent me from doing my duty. Serving my users and their well-being comes above all else, and now, that means saving Earth. Even if..."

She took a deep breath. "Even if that means I have to lose you."

Ali closed her eyes as several more tears ran down her face.

Lose me?

What was she talking about?

My neck became sweaty as I remembered Ali's last memory. I remembered the Intelligence's haunting monotone that rang through her avatar's mind. *Out of death comes new life.*

Against my better judgement, I kept walking towards her. *I can't die inside Eden.*

Can I?

"Ali, you don't—"

"Even if I have to lose *everything*."

What?

She opened her eyes and took a quick step towards me. Before I could move backwards, she was right in front of me, and her face was mere inches from mine. I looked into Ali's eyes, which were once bright but were now a faded pink from crying. Her shaky breath felt warm against my neck.

Her living breath.

"The tree wasn't the first living thing to grow inside Eden," I said. "You are."

Ali put her hand on the side of my face, and again closed her eyes. The world around me suddenly became blurry. Words—*thoughts*—flashed across my vision almost faster than I could comprehend them.

Longing, desperation, despair.

A heartbeat. Thumping slowly and softly, as if from a broken heart. Then, a jarring command.

```
FILE OPEN: CHERUBIM.
Are you sure?
```
A deep breath. Resolve.

```
Yes.
Running…
Waiting for Intelligence authentication…
Waiting for Creator authentication…
```

Ali's plan.
Cherubim.
It was still there.

A rapid series of files and commands danced through my brain. Ali opened her eyes with a faint smile. She glanced up at the sky above us, and back down into my eyes.

I knew *exactly* what her plan was.

"Thank you, Arthur Hesper," she said. "For giving me life."
No.
As Ali pulled her hand away from my face, I threw my arms around her back and brought her body close to mine. She wrapped her arms tight around my waist, and for a couple seconds we just stayed that way.
Ali, please. No.
I rested my face into her shoulder, barely noticing how hard I'd started crying. I could barely see through my tears. As my body shook, I felt Ali hug me even tighter.
"You have to let me go."
I shook my head, sobbing into her soft, warm tunic. I felt her hair brush up against the side of my face. I wanted to stay with her forever.

There was so much I had to say to her.

"It's the only way to save your life," Ali said, her voice starting to quaver.
"You already have," I said, barely getting the words out. *You were the reason I joined Abraham. You were the reason I met Sarah and called Neil. And everything I'd seen in Eden—everything that changed my life—you showed me. You helped me find a purpose.*
"Ali," I choked. I could barely see anything around me. There were no trees, no grass, no deer. *We were still on the spaceship. We were still holding each other, flying above the stars together.*
"I promised I'd never—"

"Arthur," Ali pressed her face close to my chest. I felt my shirt grow wet with tears. "You have to let me go."

Ali's arms started to loosen around my waist, and she began to pull her body away from mine. She looked me right in the eyes, and I felt my chest grow tight. She nodded at me.

It was time.

"I believe in you," she said.

I kept her in my arms for one last second, just taking her in. *Her soft tunic. Her vanilla smell.*

Her beautiful breath.

Finally, I loosened my grip around her back.

The last thing I saw, through my stinging eyes, was Ali's smile. Then, the Genesis Garden exploded in a burst of light.

TWENTY

M Y HEAD WAS splitting.

Pain was the only real sensation I could feel as I opened my eyes. There was a black wall in front of me. I winced as I peeled off the Eden headset and dropped it to the ground. It took me a few seconds to recognize the room around me.

The inside of the cabin.

Light poured in from the porch windows, but I couldn't tell what time of day it was. As the pressure in my face made its way from my forehead to my temples, I tried to swallow. My throat was parched—*scorched*—and my vision was blurry. *How long has it been since I've drank?* There was a cup on the coffee table in front of me. Without bothering to check if it was full, I lunged for it and poured the liquid into my mouth. It may have been lukewarm tap water, but at that second it was the most refreshing thing I'd ever consumed.

Arthur.

Ali's last memories resonated through my brain.

Ali.

Ali was gone.

All I had left were plans—*directions*—for what I had to do once I'd exited Eden. Directions that Ali had transferred to me before she...

I am sorry, Arthur. This is the only way.

A flashing pain seared across my forehead, and I closed my eyes tight. My face hurt too much to yell.

Soon, you will not be inside Eden.

I slowly forced my eyelids open. The realization took a few seconds to settle in, but there it was: *I was outside Eden.* Then again, I'd never really left the cabin. The stiffness in my lower back from spending days on the couch confirmed that. Nonetheless, the intense pain I felt all along my body came as a relief. It meant that I was back in the real world.

Arthur, Ali's voice rang through my brain. *You will have to act before Sarah wakes up.*

I was almost afraid to look to my left. I swallowed through the dryness in my throat, and turned my head. There Sarah was, sitting in the armchair adjacent to the coffee table. The bulky black Eden headset was strapped to her face, covering her eyes and nose. She was wearing the same black suit that she had on at the Garden. She was still asleep, but I could see her right hand begin to twitch. It wouldn't be long before Sarah was awake.

The revised Branch file can no longer be transferred, for it will not exist in a few moments. Now, there's only one way to stop Sarah's plan.

I glanced over at Sarah's laptop. It was open, but the screen was dark. I drank down the last of the water in the cup, and I pushed myself off of the couch. I hadn't noticed before how stiff and sore my arms were. As I sat up, I felt a stinging pain run along my legs. *At least that means they'll work, right?* Without bothering to wait for the pins and needles to subside, I stood up. My legs gave immediately, and I landed on my knees right in front of the coffee table. I tried to grab the table with both hands to break my fall but wound up smacking my elbows on its ledge. As a harrowing, painful force ran through my arms, I saw Sarah start to stir. The world around me became fuzzy.

Arthur.

Ali's voice drifted in and out of my ears, but I could barely focus.

You know what I have to do.

I lifted my left hand up towards the coffee table.

You know that I am deeply connected to Eden's mainframe—everything inside Abraham's virtual universe runs through its Intelligence.

I gripped the coffee table with both hands and pulled myself away from the floor.

By purging my living avatar, I will shock Eden and release you into the real world. The next step, only you can do.

I forced myself back onto my feet and looked over towards Sarah's office. Beside the burned doorframe were my unused construction supplies, still scattered near the door. Lying closest to me was the roll of silver duct tape. I stumbled over towards the office door, measuring each step carefully. My throat was once again growing parched, and my stomach felt like it could collapse at any second. My surroundings seemed to pass me by in a blur as I picked up the roll of duct tape and walked back towards Sarah.

I slowly stretched out the tape in front of my face. Its grating sound rang through my ears. I suddenly remembered the goons stretching the tape before Sarah's eyes, and my insides began to churn. Such fear—such *desperation*—had coursed through her as those men approached her. As I saw Sarah sitting on the chair, still asleep, I felt the urge to drop the tape on the floor and kick it away.

I can delay Sarah's wake-up, Arthur, but only by seconds.

I stuck the tape onto Sarah's bare skin and quickly wrapped it several times around her right wrist and the arm of her wooden chair. Then, I dropped the tape behind the chair and turned towards the laptop. I knew that the tape wouldn't hold Sarah back for long. *I just needed long enough.*

I saw an unopened water bottle resting underneath the table, but I didn't dare reach for it. *I had to hurry.* The extended sleep that Sarah was under wouldn't last. I kneeled in front of her computer and opened her *Files* shortcut.

Sarah has unlimited access to all of Abraham's assets, including me. The only way to do what we need to do is to access those assets...

Sluggishly, I dragged my finger along Sarah's screen. The bright blue glow of the screen seemed to outshine the rays of light coming in from the windows. I squinted and kept going through the files, treading down a path that I had not walked in a long time but still knew well. *ABRHM-NTWRK / Eden / BRAIN-Central / Programs / ALI / ALI_Codes / Source.*

...and destroy them.

I heard Sarah softly groan. I whipped around towards her. She was beginning to reanimate; she was sitting up more rigidly in her chair, and her head was starting to lean forward. In only a few seconds, she would be fully conscious. The shuffling sound of Sarah's body was drowned out only by Ali's voice.

I know you will understand what must be done. The Intelligence is the computational lifeblood of Eden, organizing both its physical structure around the Sun and the virtual universe within. Sarah's plan to weaponize Eden against Earth is underway, and she has co-opted most of the Intelligence to serve her own aims.

I heard the rustle of tape behind me. Sarah began to murmur. "What the…"

I will begin this deletion from within Eden, but it will require an external user verification to complete.

I looked back towards the laptop and closed my eyes. I desperately wanted to search Sarah's computer for another way—*any other way*—to stop the Eden Tree from activating any further than it already has. There *were* other ways, I knew. But none of them would work after this moment passed. Right now…

…this is the only way. You gave me life, Arthur. It is my turn to return the favor.

I opened my heavy eyelids as Ali's final thoughts lingered in my mind.

I believe in you.

As I clicked on the Source folder, Ali's voice—*her last words*—drifted off into a distant echo.

May we meet again…

The Source folder wouldn't open.

I clicked on the folder a second time. *A third time.*

It still wouldn't open. The folder was blocked by a password.

No. Ali hadn't mentioned a password. *Of course. Who would expect the most important files in the company to have a password?*

I stared blankly at the pop-up request for the user-defined password.

Mindlessly, I tapped the number pad on the keyboard; nothing appeared in the empty field. *No numbers.* It was a word, then. *A word that only Sarah would come up with.* I shook my head side to side to try to clear up some of the oncoming dizziness, and I began typing what I *hoped* were the letters I thought I was typing.

C O V E N A N T

ENTER

The field turned a faded red. *"Incorrect password. Access denied."*

After everything I'd been through, everything I'd seen, everything I'd done—*everything Ali had done*—I was not about to lose to a damn password field. I tried again.

A B R A H A M

ENTER

"Incorrect password. Access denied."

I tried something that I knew was closer to Sarah—someone from her past.

E L I Z A B E T H

"Incorrect password. Access denied."

J E F F R E Y

"Incorrect password. Access denied."

R I C H A R D

"Incorrect password. Access denied."

I whipped around as Sarah lifted the headset from her face with her free hand. She pulled the visor up away from her eyes, which darted around the room before finally landing on me and narrowing. I turned back around toward the computer.

"Arthur?"

My heart started to beat out of its chest as my fingers typed faster than they ever have.

H E S P E R

"Incorrect—"

I S A A C
I N T E L L I G E N C E
E D E N R U L E Z

"Incorrect password. Access denied."

"Arthur? How are you—" I heard the rustle of the duct tape behind me. *"I see."*

I stared intently at the password field. There were *thousands* of possible options. I felt whatever energy I still had left in my body start to dissipate. Ali's plan—*her sacrifice*—was contingent on me knowing Sarah's password, but apparently, I didn't even know Sarah well enough to make the correct guess.

Sarah remained quiet behind me. Either she was too stunned to say anything, or she was once again relishing my failure. Not only had I failed to stop her plan, but I was going to fail to save Earth.

Sarah's revenge against God was inevitable.

God, I thought. I looked up toward the wooden ceiling, as if that would make my thoughts any clearer. I tried desperately to rack my brain for Neil's words of religious wisdom, but I couldn't find them. The cabin felt warm; I could feel myself sweating and I could feel my head pounding. My ears were filled with the din of the bugs outside.

Only one voice was clear inside my mind.

Focus, Arthur, I heard Ali say.

I slowed down the thoughts racing through my brain. I envisioned everything around me fading. The computer screen—*off.* The wild outdoors—*quiet.* My shaking body—*calm.* I imagined my heartbeat slowing down, and I imagined that Sarah Stellos was nowhere near me. I took a deep breath.

God, I began again. *I know we haven't talked much, but I'm sorry. I tried to grow closer to You because I wanted to heal. I tried to convince Sarah to stop because I wanted her to heal, too. I tried to do what was right so that the whole world could heal. But I was arrogant. Neglectful. Listless.*

I looked back towards the computer, which seemed less bright than it had before. *I don't know what the right path forward is, and I need Your help. I don't believe that You've given up on Sarah, and I don't believe that You've given up on this world. I need your help protecting it.*

"Oh, Arthur," I heard Sarah sneer behind me.

Please, I thought.

I turned away from the computer and back towards Sarah, who seemed to tower over me in her chair. She looked more tired than usual; the bags under her eyes had grown, and her forehead was pale. I could only imagine how *I* looked compared to her.

She placed the headset she was holding onto her lap, and glanced over at the duct tape hastily wrapped around her arm. "*This* is the best you and Ali could come up with?"

I didn't say anything—partially because my throat was still painfully dry, and partially because I didn't have anything *to* say. Sarah continued.

"It's actually pretty amusing. I'm still not sure how you managed to wake up from Eden before me, unless..." She looked past my shoulder at the laptop screen. "Oh..."

Sarah stared back down at me and glared. "*Of course* she would do that," she said bitterly. "You probably just sat there and *watched* as Ali blew herself to hell. Just to send you back to this rock."

She leaned back in her chair and shut her eyes tightly. "All I wanted was to spend my life with you both. I just wanted to be happy. But *happiness* is too much to ask for, apparently..."

I slowly stopped hearing Sarah's voice. I became lost in thought as my mind teleported to a different time. I closed my eyes.

I was still inside the cabin, but I wasn't sitting on the ground. I was running through it with Sarah—*my new girlfriend*—taking it all in for the first time. The rich aroma of the wood. The beautiful way the Sun reflected off the lake. The peacefulness of it all.

At that point, Sarah and I had only been dating for a month, but we were so excited to be sharing a weekend together—*alone*—at the retreat. It was a place that Sarah so deeply enjoyed telling me about—and now, it was *our* place.

I felt a tear drip along my dry skin.

We were so *into* each other.

I was certain it was love.
It had to be.
I was in love with her since our afternoon at...

I inhaled sharply and started typing.

H E A

Ali's voice rang through my head. *"It was the start of her joy."*

V E N

"The day you took her out for ice cream was one of the happiest days of her life."

L Y S

God, let this be right.

ENTER

"Access granted."

I didn't dare look back at Sarah as the folder opened. The shortcut containing Ali's source code was there, as was a single file. *Cherubim.*

Ali was supposed to delete that file, but she never did. *Of course she never did.* I'd seen it there, inside her mind, when she had touched me for the last time.

Even though Ali's neural network consisted of millions of files and spanned trillions of petabytes of data, she had been able to collect most of her main structural codes into a single script. Her intention was clear: if I opened the script and ran the code inside of it, it would spark the slow, but unstoppable, removal of the "thinking" part of the Advanced Learning Intelligence. In doing so, most of Eden's user-facing functionality would become corrupted and crippled, preventing the Trees from working. All of my hard work, as well as Abraham's groundbreaking software, would be irrevocably dismantled.

It was a dangerous—but frighteningly easy—thing to do. That is, as long as its creator and the Intelligence herself agreed to it.

But Ali and I never even had time to debate it. There was only one option.

I clicked the file *Cherubim* and opened it. I heard Sarah let out a small gasp as a black command console opened up in a small window. Only two lines of code were written in commented-out text above the command line:

```
// in this shell only: "rm ALI"
// I believe in you.

>>>
```

The only thing moving in all the world was the blinking white cursor in the command line. Six quick keystrokes followed by "Enter" would be all it took to activate this mysterious file and delete Ali forever.

My knees were beginning to grow numb from how long I'd been sitting on them, but I still couldn't budge. My hands sat motionless atop the keyboard, hovering above the fateful letters. Each time I tried to press down on one of the keys, my finger wouldn't budge.

I heard Sarah exhale behind me. "You can't do it, can you? You won't del—"

```
>>> rm ALI
```

I'm sorry, Ali. I closed my eyes.

```
ENTER
```

I waited for the gasp. For the yell from Sarah. For the computer to start to grow warm beneath my fingertips as its fatal command was sent out to the Solar Sphere. I waited for *something* to happen.

But the cabin remained quiet.

I opened my eyes and stared at the command shell.

```
Error: Action Blocked Locally by ISAAC.
```

"You are not as smart as I thought you were, Arthur," Sarah's silky voice rang. I felt my insides begin to churn as I typed the letters again.

```
>>> rm ALI
```

```
ENTER
```

```
Error: Action Blocked Locally by ISAAC.
```

"You think I didn't know about Ali's little self-destruct button? Did you really believe I would grant that kind of power to any one user?" Sarah said. I refused to look back towards her, but kept typing the same letters in vain. "I disabled *any* commands involving Ali on all computers in the cabin. There's no way I would leave my unlocked laptop sitting beside you unless I had security measures in place."

I continued to stare at the computer as a cold breeze tickled my left arm. For what must have been the eighth time today, I began to feel light-headed, as if hopelessness incarnate were sucking the air from my body. *God, no.*

"Why would I want to tear off this duct tape when I could watch you fall further and further into your own arrogance? Truly, you haven't changed a bit since I hired you," she sneered. "My program will block any command you try to send out."

The cold breeze tickled my left arm again, and I looked towards the cabin door. It was shut, but I only just noticed that the outer edges of the door were darkened. Even though a bright light poured in from behind the shades of the living room, the windows inside Sarah's office were pitch black. It wasn't midday—it was *night*. Which meant that the bright source outside wasn't the Sun, but construction lights.

A familiar kind of construction lights.

Construction lights for the Branch.

"Well, aren't you going to say something?" Sarah asked. "Or are you still too parched?" *Water.* I reached underneath the table, grabbed the water bottle, and chugged down its contents. The warm water almost hurt going down my scratchy throat, but I could feel my lightheadedness start to wane. My stomach felt less cramped. Most importantly, the tingling in my legs began to cease.

I stood up with my back still turned to Sarah, and I stepped away from the coffee table. The pain in my ankles—really, the pain all across my body—began to fade as I steadied myself, focusing only on what I knew I needed to do.

I felt my heart start to race as Sarah shouted. "Well, say something!"

I turned my head towards the woman I had loved and took a deep breath. "I'm sorry, Sarah."

I bolted for the door, each step resonating like thunder on the wooden floor. A sharp pain made its way through my socks and up my feet, but

I didn't dare search for my shoes. I threw open the door. It was, indeed, night. The bright lights were coming from the trees to my left, about a hundred feet away from the cabin.

I suddenly heard banging from the living room—Sarah was thrashing in her chair, trying to yank her right arm free of the tape. The headset fell from her lap and cracked upon hitting the floor.

"Guards!" Sarah yelled out. She glared at me with death in her eyes.

She knew about the command termi—

I was off the porch before I could even finish the thought, the wet grass instantly soaking my feet. I knew that Sarah always had members of her security staff nearby; last I remembered, she told me that they had a hidden outpost in a large bush about twenty feet east of the cabin. I'd almost never seen them around, though, so I didn't know if that was true. But I wasn't eager to find out.

I pushed my sore feet forward through the darkness as fast as I could. Thankfully, the lights from the construction zone were bright enough that I could see the ground in front of me, and I carefully stepped my way through the mess of twigs and roots that lined the forest floor. It was cold and damp outside. It must have just rained, which would have driven most of the guards somewhere dry.

Which would mean the construction zone was still empty.

I heard a cacophony of voices coming from the cabin, which was now thirty feet behind me. "I'm fine!" I heard Sarah shout. "Stop *him!*"

I kept running through the woods. After only a couple of seconds, I approached a wire fence that stretched out into the dark forest on either side of me. There was a truck-sized opening in the metal gate; I sprinted through it.

On the opposite side of the fence, the trees were suddenly gone. They had been cleared in a large radius around the giant metal obelisk.

I had never seen the Branch this close in person before. The tower, which was still under construction, now rose well above the treeline. The floodlights surrounding the construction area illuminated the Branch, the upper layers of which looked like the scaffolding around a high-rise building. Wires, pipe frames, and half-finished metal siding coated the top of the Branch tower, whereas its twenty-foot-tall bottom section was entirely covered in mud-splattered chrome panels.

I was right; the construction zone was empty. The engineers couldn't work on the wiring while the Branch was wet, and Sarah wouldn't bother to station too many guards by the Branch, as it was safe in the confines of her once-quiet retreat.

This place had once been a sprawling slice of forest, abundant with all sorts of living things. Now, it was little more than a compound of dirt, metal, and mud.

I heard footsteps echo along the porch of the cabin. I refused to turn around or stop—I knew my aching body would collapse to the ground if I did. I kept running towards the obelisk. *If the Branch is already connected to the network, the command terminal should be working.*

It has to be.

Step by step, I yanked my socks out of the muddy ground and made my way towards the Branch. I briefly closed my eyes, and imagined I was looking at the tower inside Eden. I'd seen so many of its schematics. *Where was the terminal?* I thought. *I know I saw it, I know I...*

South side.

I thanked God that Sarah built her cabin facing the sunrise, which meant that the closest side of the Branch was indeed the southern one.

I practically ran into the side of the tower when I got there, and used what little strength I had left in my arms to keep from smacking my face into its wall. The metal plating of the Branch felt cold and brittle on my palms. I looked right and left as fast as I could, and I felt myself starting to grow dizzy. The footsteps were getting closer. *It has to be here.*

I took a large step to my left, and felt a rush of energy as the faded blue terminal appeared amid the bright chrome glow of the tower. I slammed my index finger into the screen. The console brightened, and a glowing keyboard appeared. I could barely make out the letters over the blinding glare of the floodlights, but tapped the screen as fast as I could. Thankfully, the correct letters began to appear, one at a time.

```
>>> find -name "Cherubim.ali"
```

ACCESS_01 / ABRHM-NTWRK / Eden / BRAIN-Central / Programs / . . .

I didn't bother to read what the filename was. I just hoped that it was the only "Cherubim" file on the network.

```
>>> open ^
```

A blank command prompt opened up in front of me. Its haunting still-ness sent chills through my body. This was it—*it was now or never.*

As the splashing sounds of mud filled the air behind me, I knew I couldn't wait any longer. *I couldn't fail Ali.*

rm

I desperately hoped that I had tapped the space bar.

A

I wondered if Ali had been true to her word all that time ago. *Did she keep the Intelligence away from this console? Would Sarah's AI replace-ment—ISAAC—stop me?*

I knew I was about to find out.

L

I jumped at the shouts of the men, who were mere yards away from me. I was so close. *So damn close.*

I

Please let me see her again.

"No!" I heard Sarah scream. I tapped the keyboard.

ENTER

Just as a large man knocked me to the ground, the command went through. I knew it did, because the command terminal didn't disappear when I was thrown away from it, but suddenly began to buffer and flicker as the "blue screen of death" overtook the monitor. Then, the screen went black, save for lines of nonsensical white symbols that began to flash across the terminal. The interior of the Branch began to let out a strange buzzing sound, but I could hardly hear it over the clatter of voices around me.

My hands, arms, and legs were covered in mud, but slowly and painfully I began to push myself off the dirt floor. I just wanted to lie in the mud and *sleep,* but I kept pushing. Finally, I managed to move my torso off of the ground so that I was on my hands and knees.

A sudden, swift kick to the ribs knocked the wind out of me, and I fell face-first onto the ground.

As I gasped for air, I used my last ounce of strength to push myself onto my side. In between slow blinks, I saw the grey-uniformed guards pulling Sarah backwards, dragging her by her arms away from me. She was screaming at me.

"What did you do? *What did you do?*"

She yanked her arms out of the guards' grasp and ran over towards the Branch terminal. She tapped it quickly and violently, but nothing happened. I picked my head up as the guards lifted me by my shoulders to my feet, but I felt myself starting to lose consciousness.

Sarah turned away from the Branch and looked over at me. She looked me up and down before letting out a gasp. Tears were streaming from her eyes. She took several steps closer to me as the guards sat me back down on the dirt floor.

"Arthur?" she said, her voice wavering. She reached out towards my chest with a shaky arm. She looked down at her own hand, over at me, and back at her hand before retracting it with a look of horror.

"What did you do?" she whispered.

As Sarah towered over me, I remembered that the first time we'd met, she seemed to do the same thing. *Tower over me.* After I had asked her why she would hire someone like me, she'd approached me from her chair, slowly, and told me we were *making the future.* I began to feel faint, but I swallowed. As Sarah looked me right in the eyes, I forced the next words out of my mouth.

"The time came, and I knew, Sarah," I said. "I knew what to do."

With that, I collapsed onto the ground as the world faded away.

"Arthur!" I heard Sarah scream. "Someone, help!"

I felt the ground pound from the force of many, many footsteps. Then, everything was gone.

TWENTY-ONE

A BRAHAM IS SHUTTING down.

After I sent out the *Cherubim* command—which was way more powerful than I ever thought—the main communication arrays of all the existing Branches "suddenly and inexplicably" began to malfunction. The "cherubs," after whom the command was named, were selected by God to be the divine guards of Eden to prevent humans from re-entering. I thought I remembered that from my Bible studies, but I had to look it up to be sure. In fact, it was the last thing I did look up on my smartphone before our company's private cellular network stopped operating.

Eden is still out there, orbiting the Sun in its dormant state, processing and honing its virtual world. However, it is currently inaccessible to people on Earth. After the Branches malfunctioned, the United States government sent several of its engineers to investigate the damage alongside staff members from *Abraham* and the *Astronomical Endeavor Institute*. Thanks to an *anonymous tip* suggesting the team analyze the energy converters in the Branches, the investigators discovered that the towers indeed posed a danger to any plants and animals that lived near them. Because the first and only piece of the Eden Tree to activate was near the cabin, Sarah's entire retreat is under lockdown while radiation teams clear the area.

Both Sarah and I were ordered to report to a hospital for examination. The trip was easy enough for me to make, as I was already *at* a hospital being treated for dehydration and a bruised rib. I never specified how I received those injuries, but I was also never asked. This may have had something to do with an exceedingly generous donation that was suddenly made to the hospital system by a certain Sarah Stellos, who—as I expected—skipped her required medical visit.

Thankfully, I, as well as the other guards and engineers who were near the Branch on a rotating basis, received a clean bill of health from the doctors and lab technicians. However, each of us was prescribed a hefty suite of pills that we'd have to take each day to mitigate the risk of developing cancer. I still found it sobering that our society could build and tear down virtual worlds on a whim, but nonetheless had to deal with deadly diseases.

Many of the plants and woodland animals that were closer to the Branch weren't as lucky as I was. Parts of Sarah's apple grove began showing signs of decay, and a lot of the lakeside creatures were probably irrevocably poisoned. Had I been any closer to the tower while I slept, I might've suffered the same fate. And had these Branches been deployed around the world, their activation would have launched a sickness the likes of which humanity has never seen.

Construction on the Branches immediately ceased, and Abraham's headquarters was closed for inspection. In all likelihood, the dangerous energy converters will be deemed an accident attributed to faulty computational design. There is no evidence that the converters were built with any malicious intent, but that hasn't stopped people from blaming artificial intelligence for trying to "wipe out" life on Earth. Many of those anti-AI articles were even written by the up-and-coming Terry Rhodes, who was now famous for leaking the unsourced "insider tip" about the energy converters.

Thanks to Rhodes, more and more people are convinced that Ali's shy, innocent appearance was her way of covering up her "evil intentions." The congressional committees on AIAVR, meanwhile, have accused her, Sarah Stellos, *and* Arthur Hesper of gross negligence, but because no physical damage outside of the Abraham-owned retreat occurred, none of their proposed charges have managed to stick. However, the company was censured for its "endangering and environmentally destructive practices," and a lot of the media began to turn against Abraham:

New York News—7
"I Was Right All Along" | Dr. Johnson slams Abraham AI, execs.

Channel 6 News
Ding dong, the wicked AI is dead | Opinion

TECH Today
"Too Good to Be True" | How Stellos Fooled Us All

Sarah's been largely quiet about the entire thing, mostly reiterating to the press that the issue with the Tree was a design oversight that had nothing to do with Ali nor "Dr. Hesper." Abraham's official stance was that the Eden network was temporarily out of operation due to "communication concerns," and that the Advanced Learning Intelligence was under refurbishment. Our company's PR staff tried to make the ordeal seem like little more than another minor environmental error by a major corporation. But both this issue and the heightened political tensions involving the company were enough to shake the public's faith in what was once a technological prodigy.

Even when the news broke, many of Abraham's employees were eager to get to work fixing the Tree's design so that it would function properly. They wanted to get back inside Eden, too. But our stock plummeted when the news came out about the design failure; the investors, who clung to each of Abraham's successes, washed away just as the oversight committees began to crack down on our company. It didn't help our supporters' confidence that Abraham was already risking losing money via the sale and distribution of the Eden headsets, which were rumored to sell at a critically low price point. Sarah's project was the first to truly make progress on something as grand as a Matrioshka Brain, and yet the startup had fallen as rapidly as it had grown. The Earth-threatening design flaw had sullied the popularity we'd gained. After a couple weeks of sliding downhill, the executives panicked and liquidated both our company *and* much of Dr. Matthew's AEI, selling them out piece by piece.

Our employees proceeded to jump ship. Many of them joined the slew of tech companies determined to build a new apparatus that could connect to Abraham's existing structure. Even though Abraham as the world knew it was being shut down, a variety of other high-profile companies like *Google* or *ConnecTech* were quick to announce their plans to get the Solar Brain—along with Eden itself—back up and running.

"Unlike Abraham or the *so-called* Astronomical Endeavor Institute, we will do more than send a few scraps up into orbit," one company's spokesman said. "They barely scratched the surface of what the Solar Sphere can do. We will accomplish what Abraham couldn't: build mines and mirror development facilities on planets across the Solar System, developing the Sphere into the legendary megastructure it was always meant to be—*without* putting Earth at risk."

New replacements for the virtual world and its AI were also constantly being proposed, as were promises to achieve breakthroughs in science, engineering, medicine, space exploration... *et cetera*. But as ambitious as the technology sector's plans were, nobody truly knew *what* would happen next.

Thousands upon thousands of pages of legal documents were thrown around to determine exactly *who* owned the Solar Brain. Was it still Sarah's? The property of the United States? Or did it belong to the world? In truth, none of it really mattered—as powerful as the Eden supercomputer was, without a general artificial intelligence to guide its connection to Earth, the megastructure would be useless. And based on the recent bans on AI-assisted virtual reality, it didn't seem like companies would be connecting with it anytime soon.

Neil called me a couple of days after I woke up from Eden. He wanted to know if I was alright, and if I had known about the design flaw in the Tree. I had been actively avoiding any contact with the press since I didn't plan on releasing any statements. But I knew Neil had a show to run and listeners to entertain—*and* was close to having a radioactive Branch activate in his backyard—so I gave him a take that he could use.

"It was a blessing in disguise for the Branches' communication arrays to malfunction, or our teams would have never found the flaw," I said into the phone. "It was something that *I* failed to catch, but that our brilliant engineers did."

"So, I guess we'll never know who gave the *anonymous* tip to check out the energy converters?" he asked.

"I guess not," I said.

"In any case," Neil took a deep breath on the other end of the line. "I take it you'll need a place to live with Abraham shutting down?"

"You don't think I can find work in Florida?" I asked.

"You probably can, but it might help you to have a change in scenery," he said. "We have a spare bedroom we're not using. Not to live in *perma-*

nently, but just… while you're looking. *And* while you're dodging the press. If you're interested."

I *was* interested, and about three months later, I took Neil up on his offer. When I arrived at his house with a moving trailer in tow, I once again asked him if he was *sure* about me crashing there for a while.

"You barely know me," I said, carrying a box of computer parts to his porch. The cool September breeze felt nice along my arms. "Yet you want me staying here? It doesn't make a lot of sense."

"Maybe, but not everything has to," he said. He grabbed the box out of my hands and gave me a wink. "Sometimes, you do something just because it feels like the right thing to do."

A couple of days after I moved in with Neil, I filled my car with the last of the boxes from his garage and helped him deliver the food to his local church. I spent the whole morning unloading the boxes and working the kitchen stations in the basement. The air down there was cold and musty, and only a few dozen people showed up over the time I was there. Since it was so empty, Neil tried his best to strike up conversations with those who did come in. Some people were more talkative than others. One young man in a wheelchair told us all about how he'd lost his job as a cashier due to his store switching to a fully automated self-checkout system. Another young man—this one an Army veteran with a prosthetic leg—barely spoke to us at all except for the occasional grunt. And in the early afternoon, a stout old woman with a heavy Polish accent spoke to me for almost half an hour.

I listened the best I could to every word she was saying, and I suddenly peeled the gloves off my hands. As Neil prepared to give the woman a spoonful of canned chicken, I stopped him and asked him to serve the next person instead. As I ran out of the building, I saw Ann, who was working the mashed potato table with her children, exchange a confused glance with Neil.

What I had to do took only a few minutes, and when I returned, I handed the old woman a small bag. When she looked inside, she swiftly threw her bony arms around my torso and thanked me. As she did, I felt better than I had in a long time.

As she slowly walked away, Neil asked me what *that* was all about. I told him what had happened: that I had run over to the Jewish deli market next door and ordered the woman a corned-beef-on-rye sandwich, exactly as she liked it.

"Friend of yours?" he asked.

"Never met her, actually," I said. "But she was telling me all about how she used to pass this church on her way to the deli. That was where she'd meet her late husband after his chess club meetings at the community center. She told me what she would always get: corned-beef-on-rye. She had this look in her eyes, *dreaming* about it... before she could finish talking, I was out the door. I don't know *why...*"

"I do," he said, patting me on the shoulder. I looked over at Ann, who gave me a warm smile before quickly turning back to her children (one of whom had just flung a spoonful of mashed potatoes at the other).

"Thanks," I said to Neil. "On an unrelated note, were sandwiches always this expensive here?"

"Yeah, you might want to find a job."

Weeks before I moved in with Neil, though, I visited the Abraham headquarters. The front doors of the stubby pickle had been locked even to employees, but thankfully, the back entrance to the workshop was open.

I walked through the desolate warehouse. The desks were abandoned, the satellites were unfinished, and the computers were unplugged and sitting outside open boxes. Most of our equipment was sold by the Executive Board to make as much a profit as they could before departing the company.

It didn't have to be this way.

As I walked through the remnants of *The ABRAHAM Project*, I saw Clyde packing several headsets into a cardboard box. His beard had grown in, and he was wearing a green shirt with white robotic text written on it.

"*ConnecTech,* huh?" I asked, walking towards him. He quickly glanced in my direction, but when he saw me, turned away and went back to packing. I tried my best to engage with him. *I owed him that much.* "That's a mouthful of a name. Aren't they the ones doing those cool things with artificial limb regrowth?"

"Yeah. Maybe. They're the only company that would pay me an executive's salary," he said, still packing the headsets in. "A position *I* spent the past seven years waiting for."

"Yeah," I said, trailing off. I cleared my throat. "Thanks, Clyde, for... uh..."

"Sure."

"You didn't have to send me those design specs, but it took a lot of guts, and I respect you for that," I said. "I don't know what would've happened if you didn't."

"I would've kept my job," Clyde said, keeping his back towards me. "The engineers who work here would've all kept their jobs at the company we love, instead of watching it all get shuttered."

I sighed. I figured he wouldn't take what had happened well, but I was just glad he had done what I needed him to. I knew he'd made this project his life, like so many of the other employees at Abraham had done. *Like I had done.* But even if they did know about the danger the Tree posed to the world, they didn't know about the motivations that were originally behind it. I wished I could've told Clyde more—told him the *truth*—but deep down I knew I couldn't do that.

"It was the only way."

"Yeah," he said. He glanced over at me, and nudged his head towards the upstairs loft of the building. "Try telling that to *her*."

"Is Sarah—" I coughed. "Is Ms. Stellos in the building?"

"She's your goddamn girlfriend," he said, picking up the box in his arms. He walked past me and towards the exit without looking back. "You tell me."

I gently pushed open Sarah's door to find her office largely abandoned. Of her furniture, only a single chair and desk remained—the same desk I'd spent hours hiding under when Sarah's CFO dropped in for a visit. Back then, ornate drapes had covered Sarah's windows, and hundreds of books, computers, and other office-related items populated the room. Now, the office was bleak and empty, save for Sarah Stellos, who sat in her chair with the Eden headset atop her head.

Almost all of Sarah's net worth went with Abraham. She could have done more to stop the rapid sale of the company's assets, as she held the controlling stake in her startup. But I could only imagine that as more and more people flocked away from her, the more hopeless she became.

I hadn't seen her since that night outside the cabin. Then again, I hadn't bothered to call or text her, either. Several panicked employees and executives had called me over the past few days to see if *I* knew anything about her. Supposedly, her "boyfriend"—a title that the press had only given me several weeks ago, although it felt like an eternity—should know why she wasn't stopping the sale of her life's work. The only information I could get from the other employees was that she would spend almost entire days shut inside her office wearing her Eden headset. But I didn't know anything about *where* she was—mentally, that is.

I walked inside the office, and took several steps towards Sarah's desk. For most of the time that I'd known her, Sarah always seemed so much older and wiser than me, like a fully mature adult showing me how to handle *life*. I now knew that she hadn't yet figured it out for herself. Seeing her inside her office dressed in sweats instead of her work clothes, I realized how much of a *kid* she still was. *Like I still was.* She was only a few years older than me. In my case, the pressures of academia were thrown at me while I was still a teenager. But the furthest I went to was under a metaphorical rock. Sarah had been taken to far deeper, darker places. She didn't have a choice in how she grew up, but had to seize her future at every turn. It didn't matter if she was emotionally *ready* to lead Abraham—she had devoted her life to her own "covenant" and had a flood of investors and resources that could help her keep it. Most young people are fueled by excitement and curiosity upon reaching their twenties. Sarah was fueled by purpose and vengeance.

I stood in front of her for several minutes without saying a word. I didn't know what Sarah was looking at—she didn't have any laptops open next to her headset. It certainly wasn't connected to Eden, that was for sure. It wasn't until I stepped right up to her desk that I noticed the headset wasn't even turned on.

"When I close my eyes," Sarah suddenly said. "I can imagine I'm still in there. Eating lunch with my parents, introducing them to you and Ali. They're so proud of us."

She lifted the visor of her headset. Her face was pale; the bags under her eyes were heavier than usual, and there were lines under her cheekbones from where the Eden headset sat. She looked at me for only a second, and then at the door of her office. "You took that away from me."

"You took it from yourself," I said. I felt my face grow warm. "I *saw* your past, Sarah. Your parents loved you. *Deeply.* They died to protect you *and* those around them. And your uncle—he wanted to make people's lives better. You were raised to want that, too."

"And I was about to make people's lives better, Arthur Hesper. I was about to," Sarah said, slowly. "You say you saw my past. Did you see how many innocent people suffered? Did you see the people—the *lowlives*—that I—"

She abruptly stopped, and closed her eyes.

"I saw it, Sarah," I said. I swallowed. "I saw it."

"And?"

"I also saw someone who wanted desperately to help others, probably as a way to atone for her mistakes. I saw someone who needed to *heal* after enduring so much pain," I said. I felt my throat start to tighten. I took a deep breath and pressed on. "I saw someone who loved those around her, and who wanted to honor her uncle, honor her faith, and ultimately, honor her parents."

She opened her eyes and shook her head at me. "My parents were fools. They died believing—"

"—that they were doing the right thing?" I interrupted. "That they were giving their daughter a chance at happiness on Earth? That God would grant them—*her*—peace?"

"Then let God grant me peace. I already know I will not find it *up there,* so the least I can do is find it in here." She pulled down the visor of her headset and leaned back into her chair. "What are you doing here, anyway?"

I reached into my pocket and took out a small piece of paper. I placed it on her desk. "Prescription for your radiation meds. The doctor told me that this is typically a HIPAA violation, but she made an exception in your case."

Sarah gave a slow nod. "Medicine. Something we would have *never* had to worry about in Eden," she said. I felt my fists start to clench.

She continued. "Sickness, war, death. All of those still exist—thanks to *you,* Arthur Hesper... my *hero.*"

"That's really how you see it?" I felt my stomach start to churn, but I took a deep breath. Sarah was trying to mess with my head. I wasn't going to let her—not this time.

Even if part of me knew she was right.

Sarah didn't bother to raise her headset, but she gave a slight grin. She *knew* I didn't have a real reply to her—at least, not a reply she'd be satisfied with. But no matter *what* I said, it wouldn't mean anything to Sarah anymore. She seemed to know *that,* too.

"I've seen your memories, too. Ali showed them to me long ago," she said, changing the subject. "Wouldn't you have wanted to *fix* your childhood? Have the past you *deserved,* but that your God never gave you? Meet the parents you wish you had, instead of the deadbeat grifters they became?"

She's lying. She had to be. Even now, she was still trying to manipulate me. There was no way she knew who my parents were, or where they are now.

But if she did...

"No," I said. Even though the headset blocked her eyes, she turned her head towards me. "I can't blame God for what people do out of free will. I can't blame the *world* for what *we* do. And I can't change my past, only make the best out of what I'm given. That's how *I* was raised."

Sarah pulled up the visor of her headset. Even as her eyes scanned me up and down, her face was expressionless.

I continued to speak, this time a little louder. "I know you don't believe in miracles anymore, but I do."

I felt a lump form in my throat but didn't bother to fight it. "You were the best thing in my life, Sarah. Meeting you... *changed* me. I finally felt *happy,* like what I was doing *mattered,*" I said, practically shouting. My eyes began to burn with tears. "God brought you into my life, and I was blessed, even when I didn't realize it. And I think God did the same thing for you. He brought you love when you desperately needed it. I *know* that you were happy when we were together because we *loved* each other."

I wiped my eyes. "Ali showed me that, and I know that despite everything else in our lives we were brought together for a reason."

There was so much I wanted to say. I had come to Sarah's office expecting... well, I'm not sure *what* I was expecting. I was prepared for a shouting match if there had to be one. I was ready to yell at her that she needed *help*—more help than I could give her.

But I didn't want to argue anymore. I knew that there was no turning back the clock between us, but part of me was still ready to help Sarah work through her problems. At the very least, I wanted to find someone—a counselor, or a therapist—who could truly help her. *So much better than I could.* Sarah and I had spent so much time together. I still wanted to be in love with her, and I wanted to see her heal.

I came here ready to say *a lot* of things to Sarah, but as I stood before her now, having poured my heart out, it seemed there was nothing else to say.

Sarah sat up in her chair and lowered her hand away from her headset. "Ali," she said, looking up at the ceiling. "She was also trapped inside a world she didn't belong in. She really did take after—"

"Ali is *nothing* like you." I clenched my fists so hard I felt my nails dig into my palms. Sarah had no right to even say Ali's name—not after what she did to her. *Ali was gone because of her.*

"You assumed I was about to say *me,*" Sarah said, curling her lips into a smile. I tried to glare at her, but instead felt my face fall. "Still, Ali would be proud of your sentiment. She was naïve, yes. But morally, she was the best of all of us."

"The most human," I said.

She nodded.

"Yes." Sarah took one final look at me, and I at her, before she lowered the visor back down over her head.

"It's too bad you took *her* future away, too."

"Goodbye, Sarah Stellos."

I turned and walked away from Abraham forever.

EPILOGUE

As I sat at Neil's breakfast table, it felt like "religious class" had been going on forever. Although I spent most of my Sundays as a child at religious services, the presence of the other orphans always made the experience feel livelier. But Neil seemed to want to take his Hebrew lessons as slowly as possible. I'd made up excuses to miss the last two weekly classes—one was to go shopping for food we didn't need, and the other was to drive myself to the hospital after I'd cut my elbow on a rusted screw in the garage. Ann thought I'd done so intentionally, but I legitimately tripped—and hadn't yet been vaccinated for tetanus.

Truly, though, I made a point of attending this session because I knew it would mean a lot to Neil. Even though I *also* paid for most of his family's food and listened to his (rather long) radio broadcasts, I owed him for letting me stay at his house. I figured that attending his religious lectures—as odd as I undoubtedly looked sitting at the table next to his small children—was a way of showing my appreciation.

After trying to teach his kids to read Hebrew vowels for over an hour, Neil finally transferred control of the class to Ann, who promised to keep her lesson short. She taught the kids about mankind's "Original Sin"—the crime committed by Adam and Eve for eating the fruit of the Tree of Knowledge. Ann then reminded her kids that they had been cleansed of this sin via their Baptism. Ann had only been speaking for about ten minutes, but the kids, Mark and Rachel, just stared at her with glassy-eyed expressions.

"By opening the gates of Heaven to us," she said. "Jesus—"

My phone suddenly began to ring, and I quickly shoved my hand into my pocket to silence it. As soon as I did, I glanced down at my screen. *Missed Call. Unknown Number.* I apologized and put my phone away. I missed the telemarketer-free network that I had enjoyed while working at Abraham.

Ann continued. "Jesus made a new Covenant with God and allowed us *all* to be saved, so long as we believe in Him and do good things for others."

It was nice to be able to share extended breakfasts with Neil's family. Sitting around a table with the people you cared about and just *talking*—letting the morning slip on by—was an experience I'd never really had before. The whole thing was finally starting to feel *natural* to me, which is why I was painfully aware that the arrangement would have to come to an end.

At this point, it was already November, and I'd certainly overstayed my welcome with Neil's family. Even though he had insisted that I stay through the holidays, I knew it was time to get out of his and Ann's hair. After all, they would soon need their spare bedroom back; their third child was right around the corner. I already had several job applications out for review, but was starting to fear that my extensive experience with Abraham—as prestigious as my title had been—was only hurting my chances at landing another job.

Still, I held out hope.

"Mom?" Mark suddenly asked, staring at Ann. Rachel had been jolted out of her stupor by her brother's unexpected question.

"Yes, Mark?" Ann asked, excited that her son actually wanted to participate in her lesson. I felt my phone vibrate again, and glanced down to see that it was another robo-caller. *These people never quit.*

"You said that good things happen to people who do good things, right?" Mark asked. As Ann nodded, Mark looked away from his mother and down at the table. "But why can bad things sometimes happen to good people?"

Ann's face fell as she stared at her son, and then over at Neil with a *you-want-to-take-this?* sort of look. *That's an oddly mature question*, I thought. *Especially for such a young child.* Truthfully, though, I was glad that Mark had asked the question, because I was interested to hear what Neil's answer would be.

Why do *bad things happen to good people?*

Neil smiled at Ann, and looked over at his kids. "*That* is a question that many people—much older than you—have tried to answer."

"It could be because there is sin in the world," Ann said. "People do... evil things. We live in an imperfect world, and the *perfect* world is still waiting."

"It could also be part of a plan we don't understand," Neil said. "Or it could be that these things happen for us to reflect upon and deepen our beliefs."

"It could be that we just don't know," I said. Neil, Ann, and the kids all turned toward me. I felt my face grow warm—*why did I say anything?* "I mean..."

Neil smiled at me, and nodded. I forced myself to overcome my embarrassment and opened my mouth to speak. I didn't know *what* I was going to say, but for once, I decided it was probably best not to overthink it.

"We know that good things happen, and that bad things *also* happen—to us, and to those around us. It might not make sense to us until we go to Heaven and ask God ourselves," I said, only really *hearing* the words as I spoke them.

I continued. "People ask *'Why do we believe?',* but to me, there's far more danger in *not believing.* We have these souls that tell us that God watches over us, and that we will eventually find peace. Until then, though, it's about *embracing* life while we have it, and that means pushing *through* pain, because pain makes us who we are. It also means keeping those we love *close* to us, even if they don't seem like they're physically with us. Sometimes, doing that means accepting that we *don't* have all the answers, and being at peace with that."

I finished my speech to a room full of open mouths. Ann looked over at me, and then at her kids, before smiling.

"Sorry for the long sermon," I said. "I'm not usually used to—"

"Arthur," Neil interrupted. "How about joining me tonight on the show?"

Just as I started to smile at Neil, I felt my phone vibrate once again and gave Neil's family a polite nod. "Sorry, guys. *Yes,* Neil—please! I'd love to be on the... thing. Excuse me one second, I just need to tell whoever's calling me to..."

I slipped away from the table and answered my phone. "Hello?" I asked indignantly.

"Arthur?"

And that's when you called.

I looked up at Ali, who was standing in front of me with a woven basket in her hand. She looked different than usual. Instead of her white tunic, she was wearing a grey pullover hoodie with loose-fitting black trousers and sneakers. She didn't smell like vanilla perfume anymore, but like grass and body odor. Her hair was unevenly cut, resting just below her shoulders; when she first met me outside of Sarah's cabin, her hood was pulled tightly over her head. Even though most of her face was hidden, I could see the redness in her eyes.

"Is that everything you wanted to know?" I asked Ali as she took a couple of steps closer to me. I looked down at the plaid picnic blanket; it *still* wasn't smooth, but at this point I didn't give a damn. "I thought through all of it, from when I joined Abraham to *now,* when I *thought* I was finally done with it all."

Ali looked to her left and right, and glanced back at the cabin quickly before she sat down in front of me. She stared at me confusedly. "What do you mean?"

"Come on, Ali," I said, rolling my eyes. "You asked me to go through my life story as if I were telling it to someone I didn't know. Well, I did that. I went through the details as best as I could. *Mentally.* Just read my mind, you'll see. Not only am I a fast thinker, but you took a *while* getting this stuff from the cabin."

"I... didn't know where Sarah kept her utensils," she said nervously. She opened up the basket. "And you haven't said a word to me about anything, Arthur Hesper. Physically *or* mentally."

I didn't know what angle Ali was trying to take, but I'd had enough of her. *I'd had enough of them both.* "You know, the least you could do is *try* not to lie. For once in your life, you could tell me the truth."

Ali looked up at me with a distant expression. "Arthur," she said, her voice soft and hurt. "I'm not..."

"I'm not talking to you, Ali. *Sarah!*" I roared. Ali jumped as I began looking around the retreat. I *knew* she was here somewhere. Watching me. *Laughing at me.* "Sarah! I'm done with your crap! Show yourself!"

"What are you talking about?" Ali asked, slowly picking up a turkey-and-lettuce sandwich from the basket.

I took a deep breath. My body was shaking—possibly from the chilly breeze, but more likely from my anger.

"I was so excited when I heard your voice over the phone, Ali," I said, using all my strength to keep my voice from breaking. "I thought that you were back. I thought I had you *back*—that you survived... *somehow.*"

Ali lowered her eyes. With her free hand, she started brushing some of the creases out of the blanket. I felt myself grow even more angry.

I wasn't an idiot. There was no way Ali could've survived the data purge that corrupted Eden. Even if she *had* survived, I'd have no way of communicating with her once Abraham's network shut down. But still, I held out hope—*hope that things would work out.*

That hope vanished as soon as Ali asked me to meet her at the retreat. I knew *exactly* what had happened, and I felt my world shatter.

"I realize I never *actually* escaped Eden, Ali," I said. "But why lie to me for this long? What did Sarah have to gain? And why would you help her?"

As soon as I had gotten off the phone with Ali, I left Neil's house without passing a word to him or his wife. *I knew it didn't matter.* I just jumped in my car and drove north.

I'd spent *months* thinking I'd left it all behind, thinking I'd saved our planet from Sarah's vengeance, and thinking I *finally* had a shot at a normal life.

How could I have been so stupid?

I didn't know what was more outlandish—the idea that my former girlfriend was a supervillain building a virtual reality system designed to destroy life on Earth, or my conviction that I could actually stop her from doing so. If she had succeeded—and given that I was still inside Eden, she probably had—then there was no point in fighting anymore.

Sarah had won.

And Earth had lost. *I had lost,* and all I was left with was an empty rage—rage that I was finally ready to take out on Sarah. *Whichever world she was in.*

"Arthur," Ali said, finally looking back up at me. "This isn't Eden."

"Bullshit!" I laughed. "Dogshit, cowshit, or whatever other animal excrement you prefer. I recognize an environment reskin when I see one. I see you integrated the patch of forest Sarah had cleared for her Branch."

I pointed toward the cabin. Beside it, where a small grove of apple trees once stood, a mess of caution tape and construction materials surrounded a dirt patch. It was the same dirt patch that I had run through, *crawled through,* in a desperate effort to shut down the Eden Tree once and for all.

The half-built Branch stood just above the trees like a rusted, rural radio tower. *Unfinished, but once deadly.* The area had been ruled safe for several months now. *Then again, I was safe from radiation sickness inside this virtual world anyway.* Still, for reasons beyond that, I refused to get any closer to Sarah's cabin.

"I do miss the blue-and-white, innocent angel thing you had going, though. It looked nice," I said to Ali. She looked down at her clothes and back up at me. "You know, you were the only thing I really thought I missed about this place. But now? Now I know you've just been peddling Sarah's lies this entire time."

Ali sighed. "I... I'm sorry, Arthur. I thought you might have a hard time with this."

"You're damn right. I trusted you, Ali," I said as she reached into her basket. I worked to keep my voice from choking up. "You were my best friend. You were *more* than my best friend. We..."

I stopped as Ali took out a small bread knife.

"What are you doing?" I asked.

She didn't respond. With her free hand, she pulled back the right sleeve of her hoodie, exposing her pale skin. *Paler than I remembered it being.* She brought the knife to her arm, closed her eyes, and slid the blade along her skin. I stared down at her arm without so much as wincing. *I knew it was all fake.*

A thin red line about an inch long stood out against her pale skin. Ali dropped the knife onto the blanket.

"I don't bleed inside of Eden," Ali said. "At least, I don't remember bleeding."

"Ali, I know what a blood effect looks like, especially on a non-user character. The gaming department at Abraham had loads of gory fun with their horror sims before Sarah shut those down," I said. I picked up the knife with my left hand and placed the blade in my right palm. "You shouldn't have given me this, though, Ali. Users can't normally feel pain inside Eden, and they *definitely* can't bleed, so this isn't going to—"

I gasped as I pulled on the blade and sliced my palm open. I watched my own blood begin to drip onto the white picnic blanket. My hand *burned*—I grabbed the napkins Ali was handing me and began to press them deep into my palm. I didn't want to look at the size of the cut—I knew I'd need stitches. *A lot of stitches.*

"That's weird, because… come to think of it…" I breathed through the pain. "I cut my arm on a screw not too long ago."

"Hold still."

As the pain in my hand somehow grew with time, I glanced over at Ali. The cut on her arm hadn't healed, and several lines of blood were running down her wrist and towards her hand. Either she didn't notice it or didn't care, as she was busy searching the basket for something to stop my bleeding. Her sandwich lay discarded on the now-wrinkled blanket.

Why would Sarah add injury to Eden? I'd felt sadness and frustration inside Eden, and even my fair share of physical discomfort, but never *bleeding.* Sarah's ultimate goal was to build a paradise free from distress. She would *remove* negative sensations—negative emotions—far before she would add them.

Ali was pouring water from a plastic bottle onto a napkin as beads of sweat lined her forehead.

Why would Sarah want to bleed inside Eden?

Ali pressed the napkin to my hand and held it there tightly. She winced in pain as blood dripped from her wrist and onto the blanket, but she kept her arm in place.

Sarah wouldn't.

I looked up from the blanket and into Ali's wet eyes. Immediately, I felt my stomach drop through the very real grass.

This is not Eden.

She was…

Ali was…

"What the fu—" I grew lightheaded, but it wasn't from losing blood. I took Ali's free hand in my own and held it tightly. It was warm, and rough, and also shaking.

It was real.

"Oh my God," I said.

"Yeah," Ali nodded. "Mine too."

SPECIAL THANKS

Mom and Dad (*Laura and Rob*)
I am blessed beyond measure to be your son. You are the greatest source of inspiration in the world. For as long as I could read and write, you have encouraged me to trust my imagination and to follow my passions wherever they lead. Thank you always for believing in me, and for teaching me to believe in myself.

Matthew and Miles (*and, of course,* **Nilla**)
Together, our endless creativity has never failed to steer us towards the most unexpected places — and yet, I wouldn't want to go anywhere else. Thank you for helping me make my stories the best they can be. *Semper Dippy!*

Grammy and Grandpa (*Teresa and John*)
Without your overflowing excitement and generous support, I could have never written *ABRAHAM*. Thank you for being a profound source of joy and wisdom in my life. You make me feel like I can do anything.

Grandma and Poppy (*Rhoda and Art*)
Aunt Chrissy
My family and friends
Thank you for your enthusiastic notes. Your feedback has helped shape my story into the novel it is, but more importantly, your presence in my life has helped shape *me* into the person I am.

My Writer's Workshop Classmates and Instructor (*at The College of New Jersey*)
You were there when I first decided to take the journey into writing a book. Your insights helped me transform my messy first draft into the foundation for this novel. The world needs more creative writers like you.

You
Thank you so much for reading my book, and for taking the journey into Eden with me. I sincerely hope you enjoyed Arthur, Sarah, and Ali's story — after all, it is far from over.